IN THE CRYSTAL . . .

She had seen his face, a face that promised happiness. So this was the stranger she would marry . . .

But the stranger who claimed her as his bride was an older man, a man of cold abrupt desires, a man who could never win her passion, let alone her love . . .

Then she met Ricardo—the one whose face she had seen in the crystal—and her heart was filled with rapture. And yet her destiny would be cruel.

IN THE GARDEN . . .

He saw her dancing, free and wild and alone, her hair flying loose. Was the flame in her eyes and the fire of her body saved only for guarded moments? Or were they the real Carlota, a woman he was seeing now for the first time . . . a woman he would never forget!

WILD GYPSY LOVE

Corinne Johnston

PYRAMID BOOKS NEW YORK

WILD GYPSY LOVE

A PYRAMID BOOK

Copyright © 1976 by Corinne Johnston

Pyramid edition published September 1976
Second printing, October 1976

Library of Congress Catalog Card Number: 76-19220

Printed in the United States of America

Pyramid Books are published by Pyramid Publications (Harcourt Brace Jovanovich, Inc.). Its trademarks, consisting of the word "Pyramid" and the portrayal of a pyramid, are registered in the United States Patent Office.

PYRAMID PUBLICATIONS
(Harcourt Brace Jovanovich, Inc.)
757 Third Avenue, New York, N.Y. 10017

Granada, Andalusia, Spain—1761

CHAPTER I

I was six years old when I first saw the gypsy woman. It was my mother's saint's day, a day bright with the sunshine we Andalusians so love, and my mother had invited some of our friends to a small celebration. During one of our games, I had run to a remote corner of the garden to hide. It was my favorite secret spot, and I giggled silently, knowing that I would never be found unless I chose to be.

The woman was there, seated on the large flat rock I had always considered my very own. In my indignation, I glared at her, expecting her to wilt beneath my gaze. But as the woman continued to sit there, staring at me silently, a strange feeling enveloped me. I stood, like a startled animal, unable to move or break my own returning stare. I noted that the woman was very dark of hair, and much darker of complexion than my mother. Her lips and her eyes, not feminine and soft like those of my mother, were lusty and coarse. Her abundant hair flowed in shining black waves well below her shoulders. A bright green sash belted her skirt of vivid red, and her low-necked white blouse was all but obscured by countless necklaces of gold and silver and colored beads. In her ears, she wore giant hoops of gold.

Fascinated, rooted to the spot by I knew not what force, I continued to stand unmoving, my eyes fastened to hers as we assessed each other in silence.

Beware the treacherous gypsies. I remembered my mother's and my aunt's repeated warnings. Had the woman made the slightest move toward me, I would undoubtedly have skittered away in panic. But she sat still as a statue, her eyes piercing, her face expressionless.

5

Oddly, I began to feel drawn to this strange woman, this unknown gypsy who had dared to invade my father's garden and was firmly seated on my own special rock. Most oddly of all, I was struck by a sudden desire—if that word be strong enough, for it was nearer a compulsion—to call her *"Mamá."* My lips, seemingly of their own volition, had begun to form the word.

At that instant, I heard my own name being called by my mother. The sound seemed to break the spell in which I had stood transfixed, and I called out with more sureness than I felt, "Coming, *Mamá*" seeking safety in the haven of voicing the last word loud and clear.

Mamá. It was my own dear *Mamá* who called me, and to whom I in turn called out. How could I ever have wanted, foolishly, to call anyone else by that name? Defiantly, smugly, with a feeling of returning from a confusing dream to the reassuring comfort of reality, I turned and ran.

Once, just before I darted out of sight of the gypsy woman, I paused to look back at her. She still sat on the rock, unmoving, but I caught on her face a softness that had not been there before. The look transformed her, and made me wonder how, a few seconds earlier, I could have thought her features coarse.

My mother was seated in a chair near the house, and seemed startled by the vigor with which I threw myself into her arms.

"Carlota Isabel, my love, what is the matter?" I felt her recoil ever so slightly at my exuberance. That she loved me I never doubted, but she showed her love as the gentle person she was: a sweet smile, a kiss lightly placed upon my brow, a hug that enfolded me, ever so softly, in her arms. It was not the first time the force of my emotions had surprised her, for my nature was full of strong feelings, and it made me uncomfortable if I tried to keep them confined too long within me.

Nevertheless, my mother seemed to sense my need of her reassurances that day, and she made no objection when I, a large enough child of six, climbed onto her lap, my weight crushing the soft folds of her dress. It was some minutes later, when my heart had stopped its wild thudding, that she brushed my forehead lightly with her lips and pushed me gently from her.

"Your friends are waiting for you. Why don't you join in their games?"

I smiled up at her before I untwined my arms from around her neck, grateful for her reassuring presence, for her under-

6

standing in not backing off from me in my desperate need a few minutes earlier.

"Yes, *Mamá.*" Again, I took delight in addressing her. *Mamá.* My *Mamá.* How could I have come so close, so terribly close, to calling a stranger by that precious name?

It was three years after our wordless encounter in the garden that I discovered the gypsy woman was my mother, after all. By that time, *Mamá* had left us, not suddenly and unexpectedly, but as a lovely flower which has reached the peak of its fragile beauty slowly fades and shrivels, till there is nothing left of it but the memory of what it once had been. The winter after I had first seen the gypsy woman, *Mamá's* pink and white coloring became even more vivid, her cheeks flushed with the fever of the lung sickness which had begun to possess her. Gradually at first, and then at an increasingly alarming rate, she began to slip away from us.

My father watched her as helplessly as I, and when at last he told me that *Mamá* would not be with us much longer, I only nodded sorrowfully. I had known and accepted the reality of her death months before, perhaps even before he had, for I had seen *Mamá's* funeral cortege in a dream.

Or had it been truly a dream? On the day they bore *Mamá's* wasted body away in a box on their shoulders, I followed in confusion and bewilderment. That she would die I could have surmised before *Papá* told me, from the worried frowns on his face and on that of *Tía* Juana, and their hushed whisperings always just beyond my hearing. But how could I have known that *Mamá's* cousin, a childhood playmate, a man I had never seen, would come from distant Cordova to help bear her to her grave, or that he would have a fiery red scar on one cheek? For I had seen him months before, in what had seemed a dream just before waking, wearing the same dust-covered black jacket he wore that day, with the same deep scar slashing across his otherwise handsome countenance. Then, as on the day of the funeral, he was helping to bear on his shoulders the coffin in which they had placed *Mamá.*

Puzzled, I had tried to tell *Tía* Juana about it several times, but she was never one to encourage childish confidences, and at my mention of the funeral, she would immediately burst into tears and remind me to continue to pray for my mother's soul. Thus I was left to my own confused thoughts about the vivid dream, until the memory of it had been supplanted by the more immediate matters of day to day happenings. I mourned the loss of *Mamá* deep inside me as well as in the somber black wardrobe which had replaced all my pretty colorful frocks, but in the way of children, I ac-

7

cepted her passing unquestioningly and went on to other experiences. Sadly, her life had ended, but my own was scarcely begun. Even the deep sorrow I felt at her death could not long suppress my natural vitality or curtail for long my zest for life.

That I was a constant trial to *Tía* Juana I well knew. She was my father's spinster sister, who had lived with us as long as I could remember, and though she tolerated me she did not understand me. Even before *Mamá's* death, she took over the supervision of our house, at which she excelled. She was a naturally methodical woman, and saw to it that the rooms were spotless, the bedding aired daily, and the meals served promptly and properly. That she did all this with no touch of imagination or affection cannot be held against her; some people are incapable of giving or accepting love, and for them life holds nothing but drudgery and duty, making one wonder at the drabness and purposelessness of their days.

I, for one, looked on each day as a totally different and exciting experience, and when I felt stifled by too many limitations, I merely ignored them and set forth in search of the promise I was certain life held for me. I could not begin to count the many times *Tía* confined me to my room on bread and water for my disobedience, or how many rosaries she decreed I must say in the hope of cleansing the evil from my soul. To her exasperation, her punishments did not cause me to hesitate even for a moment when I again wanted to defy her rules.

Thus it was on the day I next saw the gypsy woman. It was a glorious afternoon, and I had gone to my room to rest after our midday meal, as had the rest of the household. But such a day was not made for napping, and, restlessly, I slipped quietly out the large front door, intending to return before the house began to stir.

I wandered aimlessly through the hills, savoring the sun's warmth and the newness of spring all about me. My father had built our house on a large *finca* he owned on the edge of Granada, so we lived close to the city and yet set apart from it. *Papá* had given me a horse, on which I sometimes rode far into the hills, but this day I was on foot. I walked this way and that, pausing now and then to look at the strong walls of the Alhambra which crowned a hill that looked down on Granada. I mused about the people who had lived there centuries before, the Moors who had been driven back across the Mediterranean to Africa. It was said they were barbarians, but several times I had secretly slipped into the Alhambra's gardens and peeked into some of the buildings and courtyards, wondering at the beauty and grandeur of the place.

8

barbarians? Perhaps, I decided, they did not know about the church, but in the matter of living and comfort, it did not seem to me they could have been barbaric at all. I knew better than to voice such a heretical thought aloud, especially to *Tía* Juana, who would insist I divulge such sinful ponderings in the confessional, an act certain to result in many extra hours of penitence on my knees. So I kept these thoughts to myself, reasoning that since I hadn't mentioned them to anyone I was absolved from guilt for having permitted them to cross my mind.

That particular day, my pointless meanderings led me into the gypsy camp in a clearing in a wooded area. My thoughts were still upon the people who had once lived in the Alhambra, and I had stumbled into a welter of animals and wagons and people before I knew it. Fascinated, I pushed to the back of my mind *Tía's* repeated warnings that the gypsies often stole children as I continued deeper into their camp. The many dogs, which had set off an alarm of barking at my approach, soon became accustomed to my presence and quieted. The gypsies themselves seemed to accept my sudden appearance there with a sort of indifference. A few, sleeping in the shade of wagons, looked up as I passed, then returned to their slumber. Unconciously, my walking took on a purpose, for I felt inexplicably drawn to one wagon on the far edge of the cluster. It did not surprise me when the same gypsy I had seen three years before appeared in the doorway at the back of the wagon and waited for me to enter, apparently as certain as I was that I would go inside.

The interior of the wagon was dim, for daylight entered only through the open door and a shutter which opened from top to bottom on the opposite end. There was a neatly folded pile of bedding on top of a chest on one side, and opposite it were two chairs, as finely carved as any in my own house, with a small table separating them. Some cooking kettles were stacked in one back corner, and a few shallow cabinets lined the walls. It was neat and clean and cozy.

But it was the woman who held my interest, and my gaze soon returned to her. She motioned me to one of the chairs and, reaching into a high cupboard, withdrew two glasses and a wine jar.

"We will celebrate our reunion," she said, pouring a little wine into one glass and filling the other. She poured water into the smaller portion and handed it to me.

"You are my mother," I said as I took it from her. My words were not formed as a question, but as a statement of something I knew to be true, beyond any doubt. The odd thing was that I did not question the shattering fact I voiced. I knew. I accepted. It was so.

I looked deep into her eyes, saw them fill with tears. There was that same soft look I had surprised on her face during our previous encounter. Now I knew why she looked at me in that manner.

"*Mamá.*" I tested the word I had not dared utter three years before. Tears coursed unashamedly down my cheeks as they did down hers, as we sat there joyously acknowledging our relationship to each other, my mother, Tatiana, and I.

Until her death when I was seventeen, there followed a strange association between us, a closeness that was seldom physical and yet reached far beyond it. We rarely touched, and I cannot ever remember an embrace, but in many ways we were far closer than more conventional mothers and daughters, for we shared an awareness of each other's thoughts that at first startled and frightened me. But Tatiana soon convinced me it was a gift, though not always a welcome one, for one's thoughts to go occasionally beyond normal limitations to a place where time and distance were fused, where there was no separation between past and present and future, or one mind and another.

I told her, once, about the all-but-forgotten time I had seen the funeral cortege of the woman I had known as my mother, the sweet and unselfish woman who had reared her husband's child by another woman as her own. Tatiana had nodded and explained that it was the same thing that made me know without being told that I was her daughter.

My father was angry at first when I confronted him with my discovery. "She promised me she would never tell anyone, not even you. Especially not you!" he said agitatedly, pulling at his forelock as he did when he was upset. Then, as I finally convinced him that she had not had to tell me, that I had told her, he looked at me sharply and crossed himself.

"You, too!" he said despairingly, and I knew he was aware of Tatiana's powers.

"Don't worry, *Papá*," I said, feeling suddenly more adult than he and very wise for my nine years. "Tatiana says it is a gift, not from the devil, but from God, and it won't hurt me if I don't ever use it for evil. And I won't, I promise."

He crossed over to me and told hold of my shoulders, shaking me till my teeth rattled. "You must forget this foolishness, this so-called 'gift.' You must never mention it again, not to a living soul. Never! The Inquisition—if they ever heard—" His voice broke off in a sob.

"But it's nothing evil!" I protested, righteously indignant. "Not unless I use it wrong, and I won't!"

He stroked my hair softly. He was not a demonstrative man, and it was one of the few times he showed any outward signs of affection. "I know you wouldn't, my dear. But for your own protection, you must forget this—this witchery, if indeed it exists."

"It isn't witchery!" I insisted resentfully with a stamp of my foot. "And it does exist, or how would I have known Tatiana was my mother? How would I have picked out her wagon?"

"Hush!" His fingers closed tightly, painfully, around my arm. "Don't ever mention it again, not even to me!"

Hurt and bewildered, I turned and ran from the room. My father, ever reluctant to accept reality, never mentioned that conversation again, as though by his silence in the matter he could exorcise the devil he was certain possessed me. But his unwillingness to acknowledge the strange thing that was a part of me only turned me more strongly toward the one person who did understand and accept me: Tatiana, my mother.

During the years that followed, my father must have at least suspected that I spent time in Tatiana's camp whenever she was near, but it was typical of him that if he knew he ignored the knowledge.

As for *Tía* Juana, I took pains that she was always aware of the carefully staged movements with which I covered my visits. This would not have been possible had I always had a normal *dueña*, that person, usually a spinster or widowed relative, who accompanies a young Spanish girl of good family everywhere to make sure her behavior is above reproach, and her purity and innocence remain intact until marriage. Orginally, I am certain, *Tía* Juana had been brought into the house with the intention of fulfilling this function. But when *Mamá* became ill, *Tía* became involved with the task of running the house, so it fell to Dolores, my nursemaid, to accompany me wherever I went. Several times, I had heard *Tía* talking agitatedly to my father about one distant kin or another who might be brought in as my *dueña*, but my father was not a man of decision, and the conversations always ended with him absently promising to give the matter some thought, which he obviously never did. And so Dolores, who had been *Mamá's* nursemaid before she was mine, was elevated to the status of half-servant, half-*dueña*. This status she retained until my fifteenth birthday, and resumed from time to time afterwards, between a succession of *dueñas* whom *Tía* at last persuaded *Papá* to let her bring into the house. Fortunately for me, *Tía* never doubted Dolores's word, so when she reported that I had spent several hours in prayer at one chapel or another, *Tía* was satisfied

11

that at last I had begun to pay proper attention to my devotions and the state of my immortal soul. Dolores, the only person besides those directly involved to know the secret of my birth, had not been hard to win to my cause, and she was a willing enough accomplice to my subterfuge.

And so for eight years I led a life of duplicity that would have shocked *Tía* Juana to the core of her being, had she known. Several days each week, I was taken to a nearby convent, where I was taught to sew a careful seam and embroider a fine stitch and paint on china with a light brush stroke. On other days, a priest came to our house to teach me to read and write, and to school me in Latin and Greek. Until I was twelve, I was taught by *Padre* Andrés, a Jesuit, but one day in 1767 he stopped coming to give me my lessons, and *Papá* said it was because our king, Carlos III, had become angry with the Jesuits, and he had expelled all of them from Spain, and from the colonies as well. Until that time, no Spanish monarch had dared move so boldly against an arm of the church. Even more surprising than that, *Papá* said, King Carlos III had also begun to show signs of curtailing the virtually absolute power of the Holy Office, the Inquisition, which had held innocent and guilty alike in its grip of terror for almost three hundred years. But to me, all this meant little, and the only difference the expulsion of the Jesuits made in my life was that I exchanged one tutor for another. Shortly after *Padre* Andrés left, my lessons were resumed, this time under the tutelage of *Padre* Bartolomé, a Dominican. That brief interruption in my serious education was the only one until my father's death four years later, when *Tía* abruptly put an end to my lessons. She would have stopped them years earlier if she had had her way, for she thought it utter foolishness for a girl to have more learning than was necessary to do household accounts. My father was unusually adamant in the matter of my education, so her protests to him served her no purpose. From a penniless man of good family, I was given lessons twice a week in voice and on the harp, a concession *Papá* made to *Tía's* ideas of the proper education for a young lady of consequence.

But whenever I had an afternoon free and Tatiana was nearby, I would set out with Dolores for my devotions. We would go to church and light a candle and say a rosary for the woman who had mothered me for my first eight years. Then, as soon as we were out of the church, I would throw off my mantilla and leave it and my rosary in Dolores's care, and I would hasten to the gypsy camp, arranging to meet Dolores later at the home of one of her daughters.

The things I learned in the gypsy camp were vastly differ-

12

ent from my conventional schooling. Patiently, Tatiana would walk with me or ride with me through the hills and valleys and point out to me the various plants and tell me of their uses. Some were medicinal, some added strange new flavors to foods. Once, mischievously, I had thrown a few pinches of dried herbs into one of *Tía* Juana's unimaginative soups, and she had detected the strange flavor and thrown the whole pot away. A pity, because the soup would have been much improved by the savory herbs. This knowledge of herbs was to enrich my life throughout my adult years. Tatiana taught me well, and later I built upon and augmented the knowledge she instilled in me, so that her teachings formed the basis for my later renown for skill in curing simple ailments, as well as for my culinary talents. From some of the men of the gypsy tribe, I learned much of horses, for they enjoyed sharing their knowledge with me, and found in me an avid listener for all they had to tell.

Also from the gypsies, I learned that life was not as serious and uncompromising as *Tía* Juana would have had me believe. *Tía* considered most music sinful, but to the gypsies it was as much a part of their lives as eating and sleeping and drawing breath. Some of their songs were full of pathos, some were happy and brimming with vigor. They lived as they sang, with deep feeling, savoring life when it was good, expressing their sorrow or discontent with it when it was not. They were grateful for the simple things, and endured without question the ostracism that had been a part of the gypsy life since the day centuries before when society had first forced on them the role of outcasts. They wanted only to be allowed to survive in a hostile world, and asked for nothing more than they needed for bare existence. Their food they acquired partly by bartering—selling horses, or herbs they had gathered, or potions they had concocted, or something they had made with their skilled hands—and partly by stealing or begging. Hemmed in by too many conventions in my own life, I found their simplicity and lack of restrictions refreshing, and one day begged Tatiana to let me come live with her. We were sitting on the grass near the long afternoon shadow cast by her wagon, with the bright yellow-green of early spring bursting forth all around us.

She shook her head. "You cannot."

Hurt at her unqualified rejection, I immediately took offense. "Why not? Don't you want me?"

"You know I would like nothing better than having you near me always. But our way of life is hard, and it is not your way. Besides, I promised your father you would be raised in his world."

13

"I like your world better! And anyway, I never promised him that." When she remained silent, I scowled and threatened, "I'll run away!"

She smiled at me as she shook her head, which softened the sting of her words. "You would only force me to send you back, Carlota. I gave him my word."

She was adamant, and I knew I was beaten. Sulkily, I returned home, hating the cramped feeling of being inside, of having walls and a roof close about me. How much better the open air, the green grass, the wind blowing softly through the treetops! My young mind gave no thought to the fact that those same walls which cut me off from the outside world also protected me from the bitter chill winds of winter, or that the roof which kept me from seeing the treetops and the sky also kept the rain from my head. I could only see the easiness, the lack of confining rules of the gypsy way of life compared to my own.

When a girl reaches the age of fifteen, she passes officially from childhood to womanhood, and the event is usually marked by a special festivity, its elaborateness depending on the family's social and financial circumstances. *Papá* certainly could have afforded the most lavish affair, but it did not surprise me to be called into his book-lined study a few months before my fifteenth birthday to have him ask if I would mind very much not having any celebration to mark the occasion. He seldom attended social functions of any kind, and I had really not expected him to host one in my honor. Still, against all hope, I had been unable to keep from planning in minute detail the dress I would have had made for the occasion, and I swallowed hard to hide my disappointment before I answered that I would not mind at all.

My fifteenth birthday would, I knew, be the most important one of my life. From that day forward, I would be considered of marriageable age, and *Papá* would accept or reject potential suitors for me. The few he singled out to favor might be allowed to call, always under the watchful eye and strict chaperonage of a *dueña*. Many of my friends less than a year older than I had already passed relatively quickly through this period of courtship and were now betrothed, and a few of them had already married. I had no desire to enter the austere state of wifehood any time soon, but I was not at all opposed to the idea of being courted in the time-honored manner by handsome young men of my acquaintance. Of course, I knew it was by no means considered necessary that a girl be courted, or even consulted concerning arrangements for her marriage. Many times, these things are managed through the two families involved, and frequently

14

by the time a girl reaches maturity, she has known for years the name of the man she is to marry. But *Papá's* contacts with the outer world were few, and at any rate he always tended toward postponement and inaction in any matter, so that nothing had been arranged for me in the way of a betrothal.

Several times in the previous year, I had sensed admiring male eyes on me at mass. Once, I had happened to look up to see the Castilian cousin of one of my friends staring at me in open admiration. I blushed hotly, suddenly aware of my profile, and the way my developing bosom thrust my bodice out sharply, perhaps a little too far. I was also aware of the fact that I did not dislike being stared at so audaciously, and that I hoped it would happen again. I was not disappointed, for this happened at the beginning of Holy Week, and each day the Castilian attended mass at the same time we did and was in the same pew he had occupied the first day. And each day, I carefully nudged Dolores toward the end of the pew directly across the aisle from him. On the second day of Holy Week, as we were walking slowly up the crowded aisle after the service, I felt the brush of a hand against mine, and glanced up fleetingly to see the young man who had stared at me so boldly walking by my side. I quickly averted my eyes, but it made my heart beat faster to realize that his presence in that particular spot was no more accidental than had been the brushing of his hand against mine.

After this had been repeated several days, he grew bolder still, and let his hand linger on mine. Once, his fingers sought my own and held them briefly. Then, with a slight squeeze, he released them, but my hand remained searingly warm from his touch. I was so conscious of his nearness, of the warmth and vitality of his body next to mine, that I could scarcely continue walking straight ahead. I kept my eyes on the back of the matron directly in front of me, and, in my confusion, I forgot to pace my steps to her slower deliberate ones, and stumbled into the back of her shoe. The hand that seconds before had enclosed my fingers in a clandestine clasp reached out for my elbow to steady me. I looked up at him and nodded my thanks, hoping the encounter had appeared impersonal and circumspect to any watching eyes. But all the way home, I remained acutely aware of my flesh in the two places his hand had touched me, and I was almost surprised to see the contact had left no visible marks.

The youth returned to Castile shortly after Easter, but for many months afterward, I remembered with a strange mixture of guilt and pleasure the touch of his hand on mine, and found the recollection pleasant. I never saw him again,

15

and gradually the memory of his face grew dim and I even forgot his name, but I never forgot that it was he who made me aware of the strange new feelings developing within my changing body.

A few months after that, something else had occurred which made me realize that I was no longer thinking the simple thoughts of childhood or evoking them in others. Giorgio, a gypsy boy several years older than I, had long been friend and companion to me during my visits to Tatiana's camp. Our relationship had always been so innocent and carefree that it had led Tatiana to comment that we were like two butterflies fluttering about happily together in the sun. I had always been totally unself-conscious whenever I was with him until one day during the summer I was fourteen, when our relationship seemed to change abruptly from one moment to the next.

Giorgio had taken me to see some puppies born since my previous visit to the camp, and I exclaimed over them delightedly and picked up one to fondle. I looked up from the puppy to see Giorgio smiling down at me, and in that moment, I saw him not as my playmate and companion smiling happily at all the world, but as a tall, darkly handsome, muscular young man with flashing white teeth, smiling in an intensely personal manner at me and me alone. Or did I only hope it was so? As I returned his smile, I felt the heat rise in my cheeks, and I had to look away quickly to hide my inexplicable embarrassment. From that day on, a feeling of awkwardness always came over me when Giorgio was near. He seemed affected in a like manner by my presence, so that we both became much quieter when we were together. One day a few weeks after the sudden change in our relationship, he handed me a bunch of brilliantly colored flowers he had gathered, and he seemed almost shy as he told me he had felt compelled to pick them because they reminded him so much of me. I thanked him, and we smiled at each other, and that time it was he who looked away first.

I remembered all this as I sat in *Papá's* study, listening to him trying to justify and soften the harshness of his decision to deprive me of a celebration on the day that was to mark my advent to womanhood. He was seated at the big library table, his books spread out before him, his papers scattered everywhere. He had motioned me to a chair on the opposite side of the table before he explained why he had called me in. Even with me, he was never completely at his ease. The only people in whose presence he ever seemed wholly comfortable were his few scholarly friends, with whom he would haggle happily for hours over the translation of one Greek

16

word or another, or the intent of a certain writer to convey this thought or that.

"You can attend certain adult parties, of course, once you pass your birthday," he said, "and I plan to give you your mother's jewels on that day. You'll miss nothing but the celebration itself. You are certain you won't mind?" I had already told him I wouldn't, but he seemed to be pleading for my reassurance that I had meant it.

"No, *Papá,* I won't mind at all," I repeated dutifully, knowing that was what I must say. This time, the lie was rewarded with one of his rare smiles. *Papá,* I noted, was really quite handsome when he smiled.

"We can have a little private family dinner party, if you like." He held out the offer as a consolation. "*Tío* Umberto and *Tía* Luisa can join us—"

"That won't be necessary," I protested quickly, and again I knew I had said the right thing, for my words were met with a second smile of relief.

In this instance, I was as relieved as he to have eliminated the prospect of sharing my fifteenth birthday with his and *Tía* Juana's closest relative. *Tío* Umberto was not really my uncle at all. He was my father's first cousin, and handled financial affairs for *Papá,* who could not concern himself with such mundane matters as the administration of his considerable estate. Because of this dependence on him, *Papá* was forced to invite him and his wife to dinner on occasion, but I had heard him telling *Tía* once that it was certainly not necessary to invite them every month of the year. I could not think of anyone with whom I would care less to mark such a special occasion in my life, for I did not care for *Tío* Umberto at all. He was an overbearing man, so full of his own self-importance that he was callous to the feelings of others. Though I was practically grown, he still spoke to me with the condescension one might use in talking with a very small child. *Tía* Luisa, his wife, was tolerable though colorless, but she had been too involved with the task of rearing her own children to take time to establish a bond of affection with me.

And so my fifteenth birthday was spent much as any other day, except that *Papá* came to my room after dinner and presented me with *Mamá's* jewel casket. He said he hoped I was having a pleasant day, gave me a quick kiss on my cheek, and hurried away to shut himself in his study.

I had long outgrown my hopes for any show of affection from *Papá* besides an occasional perfunctory kiss on the cheek. Still, I knew he loved me as much as his reticent nature would permit. He showed a deep and sincere concern for my welfare in matters he considered important, as in his

17

elaborate planning to cover the truth about my birth, and his insistence that I be as properly schooled as though I had been a boy. In another matter, too, he stood firmly against *Tía* in my defense. She wanted him to promise me to the church, start me in as a novitiate. The first time I heard her broach the subject—though I did not doubt that she had spoken with him about it long before that—he said that as I would be exceedingly well-dowered, there was certainly no need for such a future, unless I preferred it. When I violently denied any desire for the cloistered life, he said firmly to *Tía*, "Then that settles the matter." Every time after that when she determinedly brought up the subject again, he reminded her that they had already concluded that I would not be going into the church.

On my birthday, after he had given me the jewel box, I carried it to my bed and unlocked it, having no idea of what I might find. Jewels had not suited *Mamá*, whose beauty was so fine that all but the simplest of gems would have overpowered her. The only jewelry I could remember her wearing besides some tiny diamond earrings was the string of pearls *Papá* had given me the year before.

As I opened the chest, I was struck by the great variety of the jewelry it contained, and also by the carelessness with which it was heaped in a massive tangle. It was obviously of great value, but I was impressed with it as a symbol of adulthood more than for its worth.

"Dolores!" I cried. "Come and look!"

Dolores glanced up from her mending and smiled indulgently at me. "I know, *querida*. I have seen them. They belonged to both your grandmothers. Your mother never wore most of them, you know. Some people are too delicate for jewelry." She bit off her thread close to the fabric and laid the dress aside.

"But I am not!" I said, throwing my head back defiantly, knowing there was nothing of fineness or delicacy in my own features, and knowing, too, that my tawny skin would show off the gems to advantage, and my dark hair and eyes would also set them off well.

"I would never call you delicate, *querida*," she agreed with a laugh as she pushed herself to her feet and walked over to me.

I jumped up and thrust the box into her hands. "Come! Let's go close to the window. I'll get a mirror, and you can help me try them on."

Each time I tried on something new, we studied the effect, like two connoisseurs judging a work of art. There was no doubt that the strong colors looked far better on me than the

18

paler ones. My own bold coloring was too intense for the subtle beauty of the diamonds; and the fragility of the lighter stones, particularly the aquamarines and the more translucent of the amethysts, was lost against my skin.

I turned from the mirror to find Dolores frowning as she studied the effect of the ruby necklace and earrings on me. "They are perfection itself!" she said. "But . . . " She left the thought unfinished.

As she hesitated, I asked teasingly, "But what, Dolores? Do they make me look too much a woman?" I turned back to the mirror to study my reflection. *At last I have grown up to my mouth*, I thought with satisfaction as I looked critically not at the gems, but at myself. My mouth had always seemed overly large during childhood, and too red as well. I remember running to Dolores once in tears because my playmates had said I always looked as though I had been eating berries, and the juice had run onto my lips. She had soothed me, and said they were merely jealous because they knew they would have need to resort to the use of berry juice to erase the pallor from their mouths when they were older. At the time, that had seemed scant consolation, but Dolores had been right, for later the same friends often deplored the lack of color in their own lips and were frankly envious of it in mine. At any rate, I realized at last that a pale mouth would have looked absurd against my tawny skin.

I found Dolores's reflection in the mirror, saw her nodding. "I think that perhaps that is exactly what the jewels do, *querida*. They make you look too much a woman. It is not that they change anything, but rather that they call attention to something that is already there, something we had not noticed before."

I laughed delightedly at her admission. "I must take some of them to show Tatiana tomorrow," I said, for I could not stare for long at my own reflection without remembering how I had come to have such vivid coloring.

We continued to occupy ourselves with the jewels until the afternoon light began to fade. Reluctantly, I removed the last of the gems. As we put them back into the box, we seemed by that action to be concealing my newly acquired identity as a woman and forcing my return to childhood. I watched her walk away with the box feeling suddenly very deprived for not having had any festivities on that special day, as though the failure to mark the occasion would, in itself, keep the world from acknowledging my changed status.

But why should I be deprived of my special day? Why couldn't I, by my own actions, make the day different, and festive as well? Suddenly, I decided that is what I would do. I

19

would create a celebration of sorts, for my own benefit if for no one else's.

I called to Dolores, told her to bring the jewel box back. When she hesitated and looked at me questioningly, I explained that I wanted to dress for supper, just as splendidly as I could, and have her pile my hair high upon my head. And I would wear my jewels.

She returned with the chest, and I rummaged through it busily, partially destroying the order so recently restored within its velvet-lined interior. "Where is the ruby necklace?" I asked impatiently.

"Don't wear any of your jewels tonight," Dolores said unexpectedly.

Irritated at her failure to share my enthusiasm for the idea, I asked crossly, "What can be wrong with a little innocent pleasure?"

"Your aunt will not like it. You know she considers adornments sinful."

"*Tía?*" I sighed exaggeratedly in exasperation. "There is nothing about me she has ever liked, as you well know, so what does it matter if there is one thing more?"

"I—I don't know," Dolores admitted, "but I just think it might not be wise—"

"A pox on wisdom!" I said flippantly. Then, when she still seemed hesitant, I begged, "Don't frown at me like that, Dolores! Please help me. My friends all have parties of one sort or another, and I am having none at all. Surely I am entitled to do something different tonight! How can there be any harm in wearing a few jewels to supper, with only *Papá* and *Tía* to see? After all, the jewelry is mine now, and *Papá* will probably be pleased to see me wear it."

Her eyes softened. "This is very important to you, isn't it?"

"Oh, yes!" I nodded, relieved that she understood my need to assert myself on that particular day.

"Then I cannot refuse you."

And so Dolores—my servant, my *dueña* and my friend— helped in making me appear as adult as possible in the next few hours. But that help was punctuated with the oft-repeated remark that she hoped we were doing the right thing, which I tossed off each time with a light reply or a flick of my fingers. She swept my hair expertly on top of my head, piling it higher and yet higher as I urged her on. Against her advice, I ripped out a lace panel in the bodice of a beige satin dress, making the neckline exceedingly low and displaying the top portion of my breasts. By the time the supper hour approached, I had gained considerably in height, and felt like a totally different person from the girl who had climbed the stairs after the midday meal. Last, we added the rubies and gold bracelet and the effect was complete. Before I left for supper, I paraded sedately about the room for Dolores's benefit, holding my head high and measuring each step carefully. Then I laughed and ran to give her a hug. "My dearest Dolores, thank you!"

"Be careful, my little love," she said as she watched me walk to the door, and I thought it an odd thing to say.

When I entered the dining room, *Papá* and *Tía* were already seated at the long table. As I walked self-consciously toward them in the sedate manner I had practiced so briefly in my room, *Papá* said, *"Dios mío!"* and stared at me in open-mouthed wonder. *Tía* gasped and crossed herself, as though she had just seen the devil himself.

I twirled around, pleased at the startling reaction my masquerade had produced. For to me, it seemed just that: a masquerade, a game in which I wore a disguise in order to conceal the youthful uncertainty I must no longer admit to feeling.

I stopped by *Papá's* chair and ended in a deep curtsy to him, smiling up at him as I finished. He stared at me wordlessly, making me wonder if I had displeased him. In the silence, I felt the smile slowly shrinking from my lips until surely no trace of it remained. "You said we could have a small family celebration for my birthday," I said timidly, feeling the need to explain my appearance. "And I thought you would be glad to see me wear *Mamá's* jewels." I looked into his eyes, silently pleading with him to accept and approve what I had done. He seemed about to speak when *Tía's* voice stopped him.

"She is no longer a child!"

For a minute, I couldn't understand why her words upset me. That, after all, was precisely the admission for which I had hoped, and I should have been delighted with her statement. But it was the way she had said it that bothered me, for she had made it sound more like an accusation than an acknowledgment.

"Take your seat, Carlota," she continued, and, with a last imploring look at *Papá*, I did as she told me.

"Don't you think I look nice?" I addressed my petulant question to *Papá* as I took my place at the table and, ill at ease, helped myself to the food the servants brought around. When he still didn't answer, I continued nervously, "I have no dress to set the rubies off to best advantage. I must have one of deep rich red—two, in fact, velvet for winter and silk for summer. I think they should both be cut quite low, and the silk one would be nice with touches of white lace."

Abruptly, I stopped, unable to keep up my foolish soliloquy any longer. Unless *Papá* or *Tía* said something kind to me in the next few minutes, I knew that what was supposed to be my triumphant evening would turn into a disaster. I, who looked so adult, was on the verge of dissolving into very childish tears.

Papá was introverted but not insensitive, and his voice was gentle as he said at last, "You look beautiful, my dear, and I'm glad the jewelry pleases you. It is only our realization that you have grown up, and into a startlingly lovely young woman at that, which has made us speechless." He looked the length of the table at *Tía*. "Isn't that so, Juana?"

Tía did not answer directly. "She certainly looks mature." She hesitated only briefly before she continued, "That is why you must listen to me, do as I have been telling you. Luisa's cousin—"

"We can talk about that some other time, Juana," *Papá* said with an unaccustomed harshness in his voice, "not now." He added in a far more gentle tone, "I suggest we drink a toast to Carlota's health, and to her future."

I looked at him gratefully. He had realized that *Tía* had been about to spoil the day completely for me, turn it into the disaster I feared, and he had stopped her. As he raised his glass to me, I acknowledged his toast with a smile. Then my own glass was filled, and for the first time in my life *Tía* was overridden and I was allowed a glass of unwatered wine. Through the rest of the meal, *Papá* tried gallantly to keep the conversation light and pleasant, which could never be an easy thing to do in *Tía's* presence. As he was not a man normally given to inconsequential talk, the atmosphere became increasingly strained. I appreciated his efforts, but it was with relief that I finished my meal and asked permission to retire to my room. And I suspected it was with an equal measure of relief that my request was promptly granted.

The next afternoon, Dolores and I managed to arrange an opportunity for me to get away to see Tatiana. I took the ruby necklace and matching earrings to show her.

"Put them on for me, Carlota," she said, and I complied. She nodded her approval. "You haven't quite grown to them, but you will. Few women could wear them as well. They are your stones, your own special ones. And red is the color of courage, my dear. Always remember that, and if you ever feel frightened or unsure of yourself, wear red, as much of it as you can. For sometimes it is necessary to show your defiance of life, to make yourself feel stronger and more certain. You can never feel truly defeated when you are wearing red."

I laughed at her words, but I never forgot them.

She also had a present of jewelry for me, and removed the gigantic gold hoops she always wore in her ears and gave them to me. When I protested that I had plenty of jewelry and she needn't give me hers, she insisted, saying, "You have no earrings like these. Take them, to remind you always of your gypsy blood. And of me."

"As if I could ever forget you!" I said, accepting them, knowing I could never wear them in conventional society, and yet pleased that she wanted me to have them.

I put them on for her and looked in the mirror she set in front of me. Amazed, I saw my own reflection as though I had never seen it before. Without thinking, I removed the combs that held my hair back off my face and shook it free around my shoulders. Tatiana slipped some colored beads over my head, and the effect was complete.

"I am a gypsy!" I said in startled wonder, for the girl who looked back at me was no gently-reared young Spanish lady. She was lusty and voluptuous, a gypsy born and bred, and there was something of abandon deep within her eyes, and a defiance in the way she held her head.

It was a trick of the earrings, it had to be! I looked away uncomfortably, quickly removing them. I had the feeling that I had just been given a glimpse of the person I really was, that I had gazed momentarily at my own soul, laid bare and naked before me. And I had been frightened by what I saw.

Later, as I was leaving the camp, I heard Giorgio call after me. Pleased, I turned and smiled at him as he ran toward me, his legs moving in long effortless strides. I never entered the camp any more without looking around for him, and I was always sadly disappointed if I failed to see him.

Tatiana told me it was your birthday yesterday," he said, "and I wanted to give you a present."

I looked up at him, noting the breadth of his shoulders, the way he towered over me. Giorgio was the first-born of six orphaned children who lived with their aging grandparents. As the oldest, he had been doing a man's work since he had been strong enough to lift an axe, and at seventeen, he had the powerful muscles and broad chest of a man.

He held out a string of bright green beads. "These were my mother's. My grandmother said it would be all right if I gave them to you." He added shyly. "I wanted you to have them."

"Oh, thank you! They're such a lovely color." I looked down at the beads and thought of the earrings Tatiana had just given me. Did Giorgio, too, see me as I had just seen myself, I wondered?

23

He shuffled his feet. "I'd better go. My grandmother needs wood for supper."

I fingered the beads nervously, said, "I must go, too. *Tía* will wonder if I stay away too long."

"Good-bye."

"Good-bye, Giorgio. And thank you."

Clutching my gypsy adornments, I turned and hurried away from the gypsy camp to the place where Dolores would be waiting for me.

On our return to the house, I realized I should not have dismissed so lightly Dolores's apprehensions about *Tía's* reaction to my masquerade the previous day. She met us at the door with the triumphant announcement that *Tía* Luisa's cousin would move in with us, and she would be my *dueña*. I heard the words with a sinking heart, and my qualms multiplied the next day when I saw the woman, who was as colorless as *Tía* Luisa and as sour and humorless as *Tía* Juana.

"What will I do?" I wailed later to Dolores, after we were alone in my room on the night of her arrival. "How will I ever manage to see Tatiana now, with that woman about, spying on my every movement and reporting it to *Tía?*"

"We will manage," Dolores said reassuringly. "I understand your new *dueña* is sickly, and I doubt if she cares for riding. Surely you are not to be deprived of your exercise just because you have become a young lady, though of course you must no longer ride off into the hills by yourself. I'm sure it can be arranged so that Hernán will go with you on your rides." The corners of her mouth turned up in a sly smile.

I laughed delightedly. Hernán was one of the older grooms, older even than Dolores, and he had worked for us ever since I could recall. Even *Tía* would not be able to find fault with having him accompany me. She had no idea of the conspiracy that had been going on for years between Dolores and me, and I doubt if she even remembered that Hernán was married to Dolores's cousin. Hernán respected Dolores, and would do anything she asked of him.

After that, my visits to Tatiana were more limited, but at least they were not halted completely. Nor was my new *dueña* as good a watchdog as *Tía* had hoped, for the woman's poor health kept her from exercising the eternal vigilance expected of her, as her thoughts were more often focused on when she could take another dose of medicine for her headache than they were on my actions.

One day about four months after her arrival, when she was chaperoning a visit by the older brother of one of my friends, she sent a serving girl to fetch one of her medicines. When the girl failed to return in a reasonable length of time, she left the room to get the medicine herself. The youth lost no time in taking advantage of such a unique opportunity. He moved quickly to my side and blurted out embarrassingly extravagant statements about my beauty and equally wild claims of his love for me. I listened with my head lowered modestly, but my heart thumped wildly, for this was the first time I had ever been left alone with a young man. My lowered head also served to hide my confusion, for I had no notion of what to say or do in answer to his declarations. There was no need, however, for me to say or do anything, for the ardent young swain swept me into his arms, and when I looked up at him to protest his impetuosity, he took advantage of my upturned face to crush his lips down on mine. I tried to say something, but my lips were imprisoned by his, and I finally gave up trying to object. Dizzily, I closed my eyes, but this only served to heighten the strange breathlessness I felt, and I wondered if this was because his arms were wrapped around me so tightly. A few girls had whispered to me of stolen kisses, but, from their accounts, these had been quick and timidly administered. None of my friends, I was certain, had ever been kissed so thoroughly. His lips left mine briefly, but before I could utter anything but the weakest of protests, they returned again to mine. My insides seemed to be churning, and gradually I felt my lips responding to his, as though they would do so with or without my conscious approval. Just as my arms started to reach up to encircle his neck, he released me with a surprising suddenness and pulled away from me. By the time I opened my eyes, he had sprung to his feet and was looking toward the doorway, which *Tía's* big-boned frame seemed to fill completely. At that moment, she looked more formidable to me than she ever had when I was a child. My suitor, no longer the suave lover of a moment before, was only a callow youth after all, I realized, for he was stuttering and stumbling ineffectually under *Tía's* accusing eye and violent tirade.

She lost no time in sending the subdued young man on his way. Regretfully, I watched him go, knowing he would never be allowed to call again. I sighed dejectedly at the thought. Such a lack of restraint was unforgivable, of course, where a girl of good family was concerned. And yet, marriage with such an ardent young man as he would surely never have been dull.

As soon as my suitor had departed so hastily, my errant *dueña* returned, and it was her turn to be berated by *Tía*, who shamed her for her laxity. The woman, as weak in will as she was in body, erupted into tears, and, saying she would not think of remaining another night in a house where anyone had spoken to her so insultingly, she ran from the room.

Since, in all this time, *Tía* had not budged from the only doorway to the room, I had been powerless to escape to the sanctuary of my own room. When the woman who was no longer my *dueña* had gone to pack her things, *Tía* turned all the fury of her frustrated spinsterhood on me.

"You!" she said, pointing her finger accusingly. "Just because you look like a strumpet doesn't give you leave to act like one! For shame, Carlota Isabel! How can you dare to even face me after such disgraceful behavior? You have sullied the name of Muñoz, sullied, too, the memory of your dearest mother. Thanks be to God she was spared seeing her only daughter behave like this, she who had the face of an angel and the soul of a saint! How she could have produced a child such as you, I cannot imagine. Your wanton appearance, your sluttish features must be your eternal cross to bear. Your face you did not choose, but your actions you could control, if you tried. But, no, you have always listened to the devil's whisperings, let him direct your thinking, tell you what to do. I have seen it, ever since you were small. This wildness, this wickedness! Now perhaps your father will listen to me, when I tell him how you have disgraced our name. You must be sent to a convent at once! Perhaps a few years in such surroundings can purge the evil from your soul!"

I had been listening in shocked silence to her cruel words, stunned by the depth of the hatred and malice they revealed. Our natures had never been compatible, but I had never suspected, until that moment, how much she detested me. When she mentioned putting me into a convent, I found my voice. It was not the presence of the sisters I would mind, or the hours which must be spent in prayer, but there was something about being forced to stay within the confines of convent walls that was abhorrent to me, and I would fight it with all the strength I could muster.

"No!" I protested. "Never! *Papá* has told you, again and again. I will not go into a convent, not even for a little while! He won't listen to you!" I stood facing her defiantly, my hands on my hips, my breath coming in angry gasps. I no longer felt subdued or contrite as my own outrage asserted itself, an outrage directed not at *Tía's* accusations, but at the unfairness and viciousness with which they had been hurled. I knew my behavior had been improper, but what, after all, had I done? I had listened to a secret declaration of love and received a few stolen kisses. Some of my friends had done the same.

26

Why, then, did the identical experience make me a strumpet?

Fired by my indignation, I wanted to hurt her in return for the irretractable hurt her words had inflicted on me. "You are only jealous," I cried, "that is all, because no man ever felt compelled to declare his love for you or wanted to steal kisses from you!" I brushed past her, angrily shaking off her hand as she grabbed at my arm to stop me, and ran up the stairs to my room and the comforting arms of Dolores.

There were other *dueñas* after that one, a succession of them. One I particularly liked was a young widow from Cordova, but she caused her own downfall when she arranged a secret meeting in our garden one night between another young suitor and me, and then retired just out of earshot. Innocent though the episode was, *Tía* sent the permissive young *dueña* away immediately when she discovered it.

Tía, exasperated at the problems I was causing her, and finally having accepted the fact that *Papá* would never accede to her demands to put me in a convent, began to press for the only other alternative she could think of to rid herself of my presence: she suggested that *Papá* arrange a marriage for me as soon as possible. But here again, my father spoke in my behalf, saying he disapproved of young ladies marrying too soon, and he would not even consider marriage for me until I was seventeen at the very least. I could not resist shooting a triumphant glance at *Tía* when he told her.

But *Tía* was not easily discouraged. "You would do well to consider the suit of *don* Guillermo," she continued undaunted.

We were seated at the dinner table a few days after my permissive *dueña* had been sent on her way, and I nearly choked in surprise at *Tía's* words.

"*Don* Guillermo!" I said, looking at *Papá* in horror. "Has he spoken to you? Surely you wouldn't consider him a likely suitor for me!" *Don* Guillermo was our closest neighbor, and ever since I could remember, I had thought of him as a withered old man. He had already outlived three wives and now, apparently, was casting about for a fourth. *Holy Virgin Mary*, I prayed in silent desperation, *don't let it be me!*

"He has asked my permission to call," *Papá* admitted.

"But you wouldn't grant it?" I asked in growing alarm.

Before he could answer, *Tía* interrupted.. "Carlota needs taming. Obviously, only the stern hand of an older husband can keep such a one as she in check. If you won't put her in a convent before she disgraces you completely, and you won't let her marry just yet, you would do well to betroth her to stop her foolish notions of romantic love. If she were promised to *don* Guillermo—"

27

"No!" I interrupted violently, unable to keep from shuddering at the thought of the horrid old man. I jumped up, ran to *Papá's* side, knelt by his chair. "Oh, please, *Papá*, don't listen to her! I won't do anything I shouldn't. I will be very proper from now on, I promise you. But you mustn't let *Tía* talk you into this!" I burst into tears at the thought.

Papá patted my shoulder clumsily, and I knew he was embarrassed by my show of emotion. "Don't concern yourself needlessly, my dear. There is no reason to upset yourself like this. I only told you *don* Guillermo had asked my permission to call on you. I did not say that I granted it to him. Come now, dry your eyes and return to your dinner before your food gets cold."

When I had returned to my place, he said to *Tía*, "I see no need for a betrothal so soon. After all, Carlota has not yet turned sixteen. You heard her promise she will give you no more trouble."

I let out my breath on a long sigh at his words. I could not have been more relieved if I had just been saved from burning at the stake.

Once the threat of betrothal to *don* Guillermo had dimmed in my mind, so also did my promise of exemplary behavior. One day as I was returning on horseback from a visit with Tatiana, I was overtaken by a man whom I recognized at once. My friends and I had dubbed him *El Guapo*, The Handsome One, and I had seen him often, for he was also of Granada. But we had never been formally introduced, nor would be, for the taint of bastardy was upon him. His parentage was wreathed in mystery, but it was commonly conjectured that he had been sired by someone of the noblest blood. This supposition was borne out by the fact that he never wanted for material things, for he maintained a large house, always rode the finest horses, and wore clothing that was expertly and fashionably tailored. In fact, he lacked nothing but a name, and was not even recognized by his sire as his bastard. He was about eight years my senior, which to my young eyes gave him an added appeal.

He bade me a good afternoon as he approached me, then drew his horse alongside me and slowed his mount to match the pace of mine. His action threw me into a state of confusion and indecision. It would have been improper for me to acknowledge his greeting, yet he was so close to me that our legs almost brushed, making it impossible to pretend I didn't see him. I finally returned his greeting with a curt nod of my head, then fastened my eyes on the terrain in front of me. Undeterred by my coolness, he continued to ride by my side, talking to me as though I were answering him, even though I had not said a word. When we approached the place where Hernán waited for me, he bade me a good day, saying he had enjoyed our delightful conversation and hoped we would meet again. His manner was so charming and the whole episode so absurd that I could not keep a smile from my lips as he removed his hat and bowed his head toward me in a sweeping cavalier gesture before he rode away.

I found myself thinking often of that encounter during the days that followed, and thought it a shame that one so amusing could not be among my official callers. When he appeared several weeks later in much the same manner as before, I was secretly pleased, even though I had to frown my disapproval at his forwardness. As I rode beside him in silence, a gust of wind blew my hat from my head, and I was forced to break my silence in order to thank him for retrieving it. Once I had spoken, it was but a short step forward to be drawn into a conversation with him.

Several other times, he appeared as I returned from Tatiana's camp and rode by my side until we approached the place Hernán always waited for me. One day, *El Guapo* and I raced, and when he suggested we rest our lathered mounts before I returned, I agreed. He reached up to help me dismount, but after I slid from the saddle, he made no move to release me. Instead, he tightened his arms about me and brought his lips down on mine in a long hard kiss that sent my blood racing and made me gasp for air. I pretended to more indignation and anger than I felt in order to conceal the fact that his kiss had stirred something inside me and left me more shaken than I cared to admit.

"Sir," I protested, trying to push him away, "you take liberties!"

He seemed totally untroubled by my rebuke, for he grinned and said, "My apologies, *Señorita*. I only assumed that one who looks to be so passionate a woman could harbor none but the warmest of hearts." He released his hold on me in a slow unhurried manner, almost mockingly. He did not touch me again that day, except to offer me his hand as I lowered myself to sit on the ground, and to help me rise again a short time later. But just sitting near him was disturbing in itself, and I could only hope that I showed no outward signs of the turbulence within me.

I never rode with him again, for that day Hernán had unexpectedly ridden out to meet me, and saw us together. Hernán promptly told Dolores, and she in turn reproached me for my folly.

"Would you so foolishly endanger your visits to Tatiana,

after we have gone to such pains to arrange them for you?" she asked quietly. "And if you won't think of yourself, what of Hernán and me? Do you suppose your aunt would let us stay through the day if she discovered we had helped you meet a man who is known to be a wastrel and a rogue?"

A deep shame overcame me, and I lowered my head contritely as I listened to her words. When she finished, I threw myself into her arms and said, "Oh, Dolores, I would die if *Tía* took you away from me!" I apologized tearfully, promising never to ride with *El Guapo* again. I was surprised at the relief the promise gave me, and was forced to admit to myself for the first time that, ever since my first meeting with him, I had had the vague feeling that I was getting into something far beyond my years and my wisdom. I puzzled over the way his kiss had stirred me, and I wondered if perhaps *Tía* was right, after all. Maybe I was a wanton, as she claimed, and had need of prayer to cleanse my soul.

Thanks to Dolores's intervention in time, *Tía* never knew of my rides with *El Guapo*, so I was spared any punishment and restrictions such discovery would have been certain to bring. Nevertheless, my behavior never satisfied *Tía*, and the conflict between us continued unceasingly. Poor *Papá*, who would have much preferred to stay out of our quarrels, seemed always to be caught between us, and had no choice but to serve as mediator. Then, three months before I was seventeen, he was thrown from a runaway horse and killed instantly. I ran to Tatiana to sob out my sorrow at my loss.

"Why didn't I know?" I asked her unhappily. "What good is what you call my 'gift' if it can't warn of something like this so I can keep it from happening?"

Tatiana looked up from her work of crushing and mixing dried herbs, her eyes berating me. It was one of the few times she ever spoke sharply to me. "You wonder you could not foresee your father's unexpected death with your gift? It is because it is just that—a gift, not something to be summoned at whim. You must learn to accept it as such, and not wonder why some things are foretold you and others are not." Her voice softened. "It is often better that way. There are some things it would cost you double sorrow to know."

"But maybe if I had known, I could have stopped him, told him not to go riding, prevented what happened."

She frowned. "I have never known it so. We can only see, at times, what is to come. We cannot change it." She put down her pestle and looked at me a long time, as though she were considering something. At length, she said, "I have something to show you." She opened a small trunk and removed from it

30

a cloth-wrapped bundle. Carefully, she unwound the cloth, revealing a rounded polished piece of crystal. It was the same size and shape as a very old multi-colored paperweight on my father's desk, but this one was clear. She motioned me to sit opposite her and, pushing the herbs to one side of the table, she set the piece of glass between us.

"Look into this," she commanded. "Stare at it. What do you see?"

I obeyed. "It's pretty," I said irrelevantly, then added, "I see the surface of the table right through it."

"Is that all?" Her voice held an edge of impatience.

"Of course. What else is there?"

"Nothing, unless you try very hard."

"Try? To do what?"

"To think. To see something more."

"There is only the table," I insisted, wondering what she wanted of me. Still, the piece of glass fascinated me.

"For some, there is more."

My fascination gave way to irritation, because I felt she was talking in riddles. "Are you trying to tell me there is some black magic connected with that piece of glass?" I asked exasperatedly. "Some witchcraft?"

She scooped up the glass with a swift angry stroke and returned it to its many-layered wrapping. Her face was marred by an angry scowl. "Don't ever accuse me of witchcraft!"

Immediately contrite, I stammered, "I—I'm sorry. I didn't mean—"

"What you don't mean, you must never say! Such careless utterances can send people to their deaths!"

Later that afternoon, I tried to return the conversation to the piece of polished crystal, but she pointedly ignored my attempts.

After the worst of my grief over *Papá's* death had passed, my distress was as much for the injustice of being left alone at the mercy of *Tía* as for the loss of a parent who had always maintained a remote distance between us. However, for the next year, our lives proceeded with an unexpected tranquility. Our state of mourning halted any sort of social life except a few discreet private calls, and it was not proper for me to receive any suitors during that time, so much of the cause of conflict between us ceased to exist. Besides, I took special care to avoid doing things which I knew were irritating to *Tía*, lest I push her into some irrevocable action against me. The two things I most feared—an early betrothal to someone of her choosing or being forced to go to live behind convent walls—did not come about. *Tía* was undoubtedly relieved at my improved behavior, but I don't think that in itself would have kept her from doing either of these things. Rather, I think the main reason she did nothing about me during that first year was because she feared people would say she was anxious to get rid of me. She made no secret to me of her desire to be shed of the responsibility of me and retire behind the walls of the Capuchina convent she visited with increasing regularity, but others did not know this, and for a time at least, I began to feel safe from any action on her part that would drastically alter my future. I did not let my thoughts dwell on what might happen after this period of enforced inaction expired.

I continued to see Tatiana whenever I could get away without arousing *Tía's* suspicion. One day almost a year after *Papá's* death, I went to visit her and was surprised to find her looking intently into the piece of polished crystal. It was the first time I had seen it since the day she had shown it to me.

As I entered her wagon, I started to speak, but she motioned me to silence, continuing to focus her attention on the glass, as though she were looking at something very small and difficult to see. At last, she looked up and smiled at me, but her smile had a weariness behind it I had never noticed before.

"Sit down. I want to talk to you."

I sat opposite her, remembering how much larger the chair had seemed to me when I had sat in it that first time, when I was nine.

"How you have grown since the first day you came to see me!"

I nodded. I had learned not to be surprised when Tatiana's thoughts paralleled mine and she spoke as though she were continuing a conversation we had been having, when in fact we had not yet spoken. I waited for her to continue, smoothing imaginary wrinkles from my skirt. I had become acutely conscious of my appearance, and was quite vain about the pleasing arrangement of my flesh: my bosom had matured to a well-rounded fullness, and my waist was so tiny it sent the seamstress into raptures of delight. The gown I wore that day was black, as were all my dresses at that time. As it was approaching a year since *Papá* had died, *Tía* occasionally yielded to my pleadings and allowed me to add touches of white. I had persuaded the dressmaker to cut this dress much lower than *Tía* intended for it to be, and when she objected, I agreed to tuck a white silk scarf into the bodice. The effect was perfect against my skin. I readjusted the scarf as Tatiana talked, plucking at it so the folds fell with a studied casualness.

"You have grown up, Carlota, and our time together is limited." She sighed, and later I remembered that even the sigh had seemed to cost her effort. I would have protested her statement, but she gave me no chance. "We mortals must recognize, above all else, that nothing goes on forever, that happiness and contentment are but fleeting things. But, by the same token, when sorrow and unhappiness are upon us, it is comforting to know that they, too, will pass.

"Tell me, my dear, have you seen anything lately that puzzles you?"

Instinctively, I knew she referred to the inward visions I sometimes had. "Nothing much. Only a green valley, with steep mountains nearby. I have seen this place several times now, and each time I feel the pleasant warmth of the sunshine, with the comforting touch of a soft breeze, as if I were there. And flowering trees and bright-plumaged birds such as I've never seen before—they're a part of it, too. There is a city, and I see it as though from a hillside, with well-ordered streets and the spires of many churches. And off to itself, standing all alone behind the city, is a cone-shaped mountain, its sloped sides rising into the deep blue sky almost to a peak at the center." I stopped, giving an embarrassed laugh at what I considered a flight of fancy. "It's such a pretty place, and yet there is something about it that frightens me, and makes me shudder." I looked at her questioningly, waiting to see her reaction to my words.

She did not laugh at my vision. She held up the flat-bottomed piece of crystal. "Do you remember when I showed you this, you asked me what there was to see in it? I told you there was nothing, unless you tried very hard."

"I remember. You got angry with me and put it away when I would have asked you more."

She nodded. "You didn't understand, and I lost my temper. But now I have seen something of your future in it, and I think I had better tell you about it."

I smiled, amused, and pointed at the crystal. "You saw my future? In there?"

Crossly, she reprimanded, "Don't anger me again. Would you deny the sight that you and I share?"

"No," I agreed quickly, remembering how, a few months before, I had seen in my mind a cart turned over in the road with the driver pinned underneath, and not long after, when I was out riding, I had come upon the same scene, no more vivid in reality than it had been in my vision. "I can't deny it. It's there."

"You asked me once, shortly after your father's death, if

33

there were some way we could summon our gift at will and use it to change the future, to keep the things we see from happening. I fear that directing the future is up to God alone, but sometimes, when it is especially important, I can use what powers I do have to bring snatches of the future into sight deliberately. Here." She tapped on the piece of crystal. "It is not without effort, and often I lack the concentration to succeed. But today, it has shown me what I would know."

"About me?" I asked, excited. "A handsome husband, perhaps?" I flushed, remembering Giorgio and all the other handsome youths I knew.

"I have been thinking often of you lately," she said, seeming not to notice my interruption. "Your childhood is over, and you are a mature and lovely woman now. I have seen an ocean voyage for you, a long one, perhaps—yes, perhaps to your green valley."

"An ocean voyage?" I protested in alarm. "But surely there are green valleys nearby." I felt suddenly panicky at the thought of going far from all that was familiar. "I wouldn't leave you—"

She shook her head, smiling sadly. "I know you would not, but I cannot change what I saw."

"A long ocean voyage? Where would I be going?" Accepting the truth of her words, awed at their import, I could only speak in a hushed whisper.

She didn't answer, and I asked another question. "Will I be happy there—wherever I'm going?"

I thought she wouldn't answer that question either, and the silence lay heavily between us for some time. But at length she said, "You will be happy." The hushed hoarseness of her voice matched my own.

Her assurance should have set me somewhat at rest, but instead it made me uneasier still. That she had seen much more than she had told me, I was certain. And why had she hesitated so long before she reluctantly promised me the happiness I demanded from life? I prodded her with questions, begged her to tell me more, but that was all she would say about the matter.

Later, she took me to the cabinet where she kept her herbs and made me tell her about each one and its use, for all the world like *Padre* Bartolomé making me recite my Latin conjugations. She gave me a generous portion of each herb, some of her own mixtures, and packets of seeds, insisting I take them. "It is time you started your own herb chest," she answered when I protested that I needn't take them all, that I could always ask her for some.

That was the last time I ever saw Tatiana. Later, I realized that she had been trying to let me know her last thoughts were of me, and to prepare me for our separation.

She had been saying good-bye.

Granada, Andalusia, Spain—
August, 1772

CHAPTER II

It was two days later that my world began to shatter. *Tía* had invited *Tío* Umberto to dine with us at midday, which in itself was nothing unusual, for, after *Papá's* death, he had continued to administer the business affairs of the estate. Except for a generous bequest to *Tía*, *Papá* left everything to me, but as I was only seventeen, it was *Tío* Umberto who made all the decisions about the estate, with the tacit approval of *Tía*, who was my guardian. That was fine with me, for I had no desire to tire myself with bothersome details and difficult tallies. Business conferences between them usually followed our meal, when they retired to the library, and I went about my own plans. This day, however, was different, for I was asked to join them, a request I could not very well refuse.

"Certainly," I agreed unenthusiastically, assuming that they had decided it was time I began to acquaint myself with business affairs. I made a comment to that effect.

Tío Umberto, always unnecessarily pompous about the simplest of matters, smiled fatuously at me and said, "Perhaps that won't be necessary. We might find someone to take that burden from you." He winked elaborately at my aunt. "Eh, Juana?"

An unaccustomed smile broke the severity of her usual dour expression, and she answered, "Perhaps."

Apprehensively, I followed them into the library. Obviously, whatever conspiracy they shared concerned me.

As the door closed behind us, I had to fight down the impulse to turn and run from the room. I forced myself to walk slowly to the chair to which *Tío* Umberto motioned me. I sat

36

down, and my mouth went dry as I waited for him to speak. When he did, my worst fears were justified, for he said the words I had long been dreading to hear.

"Well, Carlota Isabel," he said at last, "we have found a husband for you!" His tone of voice implied the task had not been an easy one.

My irritation at the condescension of his words momentarily overcame my apprehensions about their shattering import to me and I snapped, "That surely should not have been too difficult, since I am not unattractive, and I shall bring a large dowry to my husband."

Tía glowered at me and admonished darkly, "Carlota Isabel, vanity is a sin."

"It is surely no sin to know that I am not ill-favored, *Tía*," I protested.

Tío Umberto frowned his irritation at the interruption. In the way of all self-important men, he did not like to be stopped when he was talking. "You are well-favored and well-dowered, it is true, but still it has not been easy to arrange a match I deem suitable. My task would certainly have been easier had your recent lineage not been so deplorably lacking in infusions of titled blood. My own daughters were more fortunate since, on my mother's side, I claim close kinship with the Duke of—"

"I know all about him," I interrupted, knowing as I did so that I was being excessively rude. But my anxiety had set my nerves on edge, and I lacked the patience to listen to the boring recitation of his superior lineage.

If only they had let me choose for myself! I thought as I waited for him to come to the point and tell me the name of the man to whom they had decided to betroth me. Though it disappointed me to learn that a match had been arranged, it did not really surprise me, for neither of these two people who held my destiny in their hands had approved of *Papá's* leniency in letting me have a voice in the selection of would-be suitors. But in the past year, I had succeeded so well in keeping any concern about the future from my mind that my worries about *Tía* making some overt move against me had gradually diminished, and I had even grown complacent. I had not, until that moment, stopped recently to consider that she and *Tío* Umberto had surely only been waiting for the period of deepest mourning to pass before they settled my fate. Who could have asked for my hand, I wondered? Perhaps I was worrying needlessly about them choosing someone I wouldn't have chosen for myself. I began to remember, hopefully, all the young men I knew who had intimated by a brief admiring glance or a slightly raised eyebrow or a hint of a smile that they were anxiously awaiting the time when it would again be seemly to court me. Of course, I knew that an offer of marriage could have been presented with no hint to me that I was being considered. Hope rose within me, but it quickly diminished when I looked at the faces of the two people who had made the choice for me. Tensely, I leaned forward. "Who is it? Who has spoken to you?" I did not seem able to continue breathing until I knew the answer.

"A man you have known and respected all your life, a man held in the highest esteem by all who know him—"

"Who?" I demanded again, all patience with *Tío* Umberto's foolish delays exhausted.

He beamed at me. "None other than your neighbor, *don* Guillermo Ramirez Ibarra."

For a moment, I could only stare at him open-mouthed, speechless in my stunned disbelief. Finally, my revulsion at the thought of marrying the bald, arthritic old widower made me find my voice in protest. "I'll not marry him! He's a horrid old man! Why, he must be old enough to be my grandfather!"

"Don't be such an ingrate," *Tía* snapped. "Cousin Umberto has gone to much trouble to arrange this match for you. He had no easy time convincing *don* Guillermo to wait a full year after your father—"

"Then he must convince him he has wasted his time waiting!" I wailed. "You know that *Papá* would never have made me marry him!"

They both chose to ignore my objections. "Come now," *Tío* Umberto said coaxingly. "Think of what this will mean to your children. Your dower, plus *don* Guillermo's wealth—"

He could not have touched on a worse subject. For all my visits to the gypsy camp, I was still in many ways sheltered and unworldly. I knew I had begun to feel certain yearnings of the flesh, but I did not yet know what they signified. Vaguely, I knew that they were related to something I did not quite understand, something intimate that transpired between husbands and wives, and created babies. A fresh wave of revulsion swept over me at the thought of *don* Guillermo's withered knobby hands upon my body, and I shuddered. How could anyone, even these two heartless people, have chosen so poorly for me?

I glared from one to the other, my fury building. "There must be others who would speak for me, if you will curb your impatience to be rid of me a while longer!" I brushed at the tears that scalded my eyes.

"No other match as suitable as this is likely to be found,"

Tío Umberto said stuffily, scowling his disapproval at my outburst. "I have studied carefully each one that has been presented—"

"Then there have been others! Why wasn't I told? Why didn't you let me choose?"

"Young girls are not capable of choosing for themselves," *Tía* interjected tersely. "They do not know what is best for them."

"I'll not marry *don* Guillermo!"

"Then you'll go to the good sisters," *Tía* threatened.

"I won't!" I said vehemently, jumping from my chair. "I won't marry *don* Guillermo, and I won't go to a convent!"

"You mustn't be so hasty, Carlota Isabel," *Tío* Umberto said. "There's no need to give *don* Guillermo his answer just yet, though of course he is an anxious suitor. I'm sure when you've had time to think about the advantages this marriage offers, you'll agree it is an excellent match. Most young ladies would be honored to marry into such a fine family."

But *Tía* would not let the matter rest so easily. "You may choose one or the other of the alternatives," she said drily. "If you've no desire to marry, the good sisters could certainly use your wealth to good purpose."

"I do want to get married," I protested, curbing my anger in an effort to try to make them understand, "but not to *don* Guillermo. If you'll only wait, I'm sure there will be more offers, ones acceptable to me as well as you. My father would never have forced me to marry someone repulsive to me."

"Your father left the matter of your upbringing to me, and your financial affairs in our cousin's hands, to do as we see fit. And this will be a most proper marriage. Now, let's hear no more." She rose and walked to the door.

Tío Umberto paused and put a hand clumsily on my shoulder. "You must accept what we have decided. We know what is best for you."

Impatiently, I shrugged his hand away. I could not believe his show of concern for my feelings was genuine, or he could never have arranged such a match. "I know better what is best for myself," I answered sharply.

"Leave her," *Tía* commanded, her voice brittle. "A few days in her room will change her thinking. Come, cousin, let me show you to the door. You may leave Carlota Isabel to me."

They walked out together. For a moment, I stood in the middle of the room, too stunned to move. But finally my mind began to work again, and I realized the only way to save myself from *Tía* Juana's threat was to get away at once, right that instant. I dared not even delay long enough to tell

Dolores what I planned to do. If I were locked in my room with the key in *Tía's* pocket, not even my good Dolores would be able to help me. Why should I have to starve in order to prove to *Tía* and *Tío* Umberto that I would not do as they wished? There was no doubt in my mind about where I would go. I would go to Tatiana. She would save me.

As soon as I heard the front door slam, I opened the library door a crack and peered anxiously around it. I saw with relief that *Tía* was walking toward the kitchen. As soon as she was out of sight, I slipped carefully out of the library and ran to the front door, which *Tía* had already bolted in preparation for the midday rest.

My fingers trembled as I slid back the bolt and unlatched the door. The massive hinges creaked noisily as I eased the door open wide enough to slip through. But the sound, which had seemed to my ears louder than a clap of thunder, had apparently not carried as far as I thought, and in a moment I was outside, my feet racing wildly over the cobblestones that led to our gate. Breathlessly, I pulled back the heavy iron gate and, leaving it standing open behind me, ran as fast as my feet could carry me to the gypsy camp. Tatiana would protect me, she would never let them force me, her daughter, into marriage with a horrid old man, or permit them to put me behind the walls of a convent for the rest of my life. Now she would have to let me come live in her world, with her and the gypsies, for life as I had known it was no longer tolerable. Besides, with my father dead nearly a year, surely she was no longer bound by her promise to him. Then, once I came of age, I could return and claim my inheritance, and Tatiana and I could live wherever and however we chose.

These thoughts whirled through my mind as my feet sped me toward my haven, the familiar green wagon. My breath came in great gasps, but I would not slow down, would not stop to rest. Once *Tía* discovered my absence, she would send a rider out to run me down. I would rest only after I had reached the protection of the gypsy camp. There and only there would I be safe.

At last, I stumbled into the familiar clearing. I stopped, stunned by disappointment, unable to credit what I saw. My eyes scanned the opening, returned to scan it again and again. The clearing, which two days before had held countless wagons and had been busily astir with the bustle of women preparing supper and the sounds of children at play and men laughing with one another, was empty. There was no one, nothing. Only the long-dead ashes of many campfires and the much-trampled grass attested to the fact that it had been inhabited at all.

I walked on, well into the grassy opening, my head turning this way and that, not believing the complete desertion that met my eyes.

Exhausted as much by my despair as by physical exertion, I made my way, half stumbling, half walking, to the familiar spot where Tatiana's wagon had stood, feeling myself drawn to that patch of ground as though I must physically occupy it before I would believe it was empty. The gypsies had often come and gone, but Tatiana had always told me when they were leaving, and she had never left at any time when I needed her. Now, in my greatest need of all, she was gone.

I threw myself down on the ground on which her wagon had stood and sobbed out my misery and my loneliness.

My tears flowed long and hard, dampening the ground as I twisted my face from side to side, calling through my sobs for the very heavens to witness my despair. I don't know how long I lay there. It no longer mattered if *Tía* sent someone to find me and take me back home. My life was over. I had run to Tatiana for protection from my tormentors and she was gone. There was no place else to run.

When my tears of self-pity had finally spent themselves, and I lay exhausted, my breath still coming in uneven gulps, I noted that a ray of sun was striking something on the ground nearby. Curious, I raised up to see what it was. As I moved my head, the glint disappeared and reappeared. I pushed myself to my feet and walked over to the shining object, dropping on my knees.

It was the piece of polished crystal. I picked it up, holding it momentarily. Then my fingers clenched around it. I needed Tatiana, and she had deserted me, and left instead this worthless piece of glass! She had left it in place of herself. She had known, she had to have known I would need her and come looking for her, or she would not have left the polished crystal. She was my one hope, my one haven, and she had deserted me. How could she be so cruel? With a violent heave, I threw the glass from me.

The afternoon shadows began to lengthen and I felt a sudden chill. I should go home, I knew, and face *Tía* Juana's wrath. Perhaps I might even be able to reason with her. And then I remembered the hardness in her eyes whenever she looked at me, a hardness she had not troubled to hide since my father's death, and I knew there would be no hope of reasoning with her. *Tía* had never liked me. In a few weeks, a full year of mourning for my father would be fulfilled, and a marriage arranged then would not seem unduly hasty or irreverent. With me safely married, she would be free to take the sum my father had settled on her and retire behind the

41

high walls of a convent, away from people, whom she neither understood nor trusted, away from life. It was what she wanted, and only I, a girl of seventeen, stood between her and her desire. The choice she offered was bleak: an intolerable marriage or the same isolation from the world she sought for herself. To me, such isolation was abhorrent. I would not, could not shut myself away from life.

Well, I would accept neither of the choices she had given me. Resolutely, I pushed myself to my feet and brushed the grass from my skirt. A gypsy train of such size could not travel quietly. I would follow it and I would find Tatiana, if she wanted me to or not. I would find her because I must; she was my only hope. It would not be hard to figure out which way they started, for the plodding of many hoofs and the passing of many wheels must leave the ground well marked. Whenever I came to a road, I would start making inquiries.

It was late the next day before I found them. My heart should have leaped with joy at the first sight of the familiar wagons and faces, but instead I was filled with a dread I could not define. The gypsies looked up, but they did not greet me with the usual smiles and careless waves, and I was overcome with a deep sadness. In vain, my eyes searched all about me for the familiar green wagon. It was nowhere to be seen.

"Tatiana!" I called, my voice a frightened whisper. Then, panicking, I called louder, "Tatiana!" But even as I called, I did not expect an answer.

It was then that I saw Giorgio standing nearby, looking at me without the usual sparkle in his eye, without his ready smile. I ran to him, demanded, "Where is she? Where is Tatiana?" But even as I asked, I knew.

"She is dead. She had been ill for some time."

"Tatiana, ill? I—I never knew. And now she is dead?" I heard my own voice, scarcely audible, as though it belonged to someone else. Tears overflowed from my eyes, quietly, for the measure of my sorrow was too deep for a normal show of grief. Never had I felt so desolate, so benumbed.

Giorgio's arms encircled me sympathetically so that my silent tears fell on his shoulder. "We shall all miss her," he said.

Even in my profound sorrow, I knew that, at another time, I would have liked the feeling of being held close by Giorgio for reasons other than the solace it gave me. At that moment, I was grateful to him for making me feel protected, no longer alone. Tatiana was gone from me forever. A moment before, I had felt that there was no one to whom I could turn. But I did have someone. I had the gypsies, Tatiana's people. I had Giorgio. He was good and kind, and I knew he was attracted to me, as I was to him. I need not go back to *Tía*. I looked up at him, said without preamble,

"Marry me, Giorgio! By the gypsy ceremony now, and later by the priest. Oh, please! Then they can't take me away!" Hopefully, I watched him, saw his face mirror surprise at my sudden proposal. He must help me! He must! When he didn't answer, I continued desperately, "Please! Marry me and let me stay with you. I can't go back, I can't! They'll make me marry *don* Guillermo, or put me in a convent. Please, let me stay here!"

He backed off, looking at me in silence. Hope flowered within me, but quickly withered at his words, for his hesitation was only a stunned reaction to my impassioned plea. When he spoke at last, he said reproachfully with a soft-spoken finality, "You can't possibly be serious. You know what would happen if you stayed with us. Would you bring added persecution and even death to Tatiana's people?"

"Nothing would happen," I promised, but even in my selfish need, the words rang hollowly in my ears. "If you think we dare not stay with your people, we can go away. Tatiana saw a ship, a long journey for me. We could go together, just you and I, somewhere—anywhere—by sea. I can talk with one of Dolores's daughters, get her to send for my jewelry. It will buy us passage, and more. I beg you."

He shook his head slowly, and I knew it was useless to plead any more. "Come, little one," he said gently, putting a protective arm around my shoulder and leading me toward his family's wagon. "My grandparents will give you a good supper, and then you will have a night's rest. Tomorrow, I must take you home, back where you belong."

Giorgio's family treated me well, but they, like all the gypsies, refused to discuss with me Tatiana's death. "She died with dignity," Giorgio's grandfather said, and no one offered to say more. They knew, as I did now, that she had foreseen her own death and wanted to spare me the sorrow of it. That was why she had left so suddenly, without warning. That was why she had told me what she had seen of my future, and given me the herbs. That was why she had left for me the bit of polished crystal.

The bit of polished crystal! Carefully, lovingly, she had left it for me, and I had thrown it away in the anger of feeling that she had deserted me! Just before I drifted off to sleep, I remembered the crystal, and it suddenly became very important to me. I must return to the clearing and find it.

We left the next morning, Giorgio and I, and twilight was

already upon us as we approached the road that led to my home. He would have taken me there at once and left me at the gate, but I pleaded with him to take me to the clearing first. "I must look for something," I insisted. "It is something Tatiana left for me there. You know they'll never let me go once I enter the house." I shuddered, reminded of the hunger and discomfort of the days that were to come, for I knew I would not submit readily to either of *Tía's* two equally unacceptable choices. The only hope I had left was stubborn resistance.

I looked up at Giorgio pleadingly, saw him wavering. "Please," I begged, "I must have what Tatiana left for me. She wanted me to have it. It will take only an hour or two longer. Then it will be easier for you to leave me near the gate and slip away in the dark."

Giorgio smiled at me, his quick easy smile. "All right," he agreed, his face alight with the affection he felt for everyone and everything. For Giorgio had always been in love with life. He loved his grandparents and his brothers and his sisters, and the sunshine and the wind rustling through the trees. And I am certain he loved me, too, but that day I had come to realize that his feelings for me were tempered with more wisdom than I possessed. Had I been a gypsy girl, he would undoubtedly have been eager to marry me. But life forces upon the gypsies at an early age a realistic acceptance of things as they are, so that he had known long before I begged him to marry me that marriage between us was an impossibility. All that day as we traveled, he seemed at pains to avoid any unnecessary physical contact between us. Whenever I needed help, he gave it freely—taking my hand to help me across a fallen tree or steadying my arm to keep me from falling—but he always withdrew his touch the moment the need for support was gone. It was not that he had suddenly begun to treat me coldly or without compassion, for kindness and love and sympathy were as much a part of him as his flashing smile, but his was a guarded affection which reminded me that he remembered, if I did not, the unbridgeable difference in our stations.

We skirted all around any houses that evening, and night had already fallen when we reached the clearing. It was a dark and moonless night, and we searched in vain for the piece of glass.

"It's no use," I said, dropping against a tree trunk and brushing a tear from my eye. "We'll never find it in the dark."

"Poor Carlota," Giorgio said, his voice full of sympathy, as he sat down nearby. "Is it that important to you?"

44

"More important than anything else in the world," I said, and I meant it sincerely, for now I appreciated Tatiana's gift. It was not just a piece of glass, but the one in which she had seen the future, my future. It was her assurance to me that though she had gone, she lived on through me in the tie that had bound us together even more closely than our blood, the gift we had shared. I might never see in the crystal anything such as she saw, but I must have it, for it was a part of her. "I can't go back without it. Please don't take me home until we find it."

"It's too dark tonight." He hesitated, then shrugged. "You have been away from home two nights already. I don't suppose one more night will matter."

He was gone for a time and returned with a scrawny chicken, which we roasted over a small fire and ate. Then he spread his cloak on the ground.

"You sleep here."

"But what about you?"

"I'll be right over there, on the other side of the fire."

"Wouldn't you be more comfortable if we shared your cloak?"

He smiled softly. "I think not." He threw a few sticks out of the way and lay down on the grass on the opposite side of the smoldering embers. "Good-night, Carlota."

I slept soundly, and awoke next morning to find him gone. Startled into instant wakefulness at the thought that he had left me, I opened my eyes wide and pushed myself up onto one elbow. "Giorgio!" I cried out in alarm.

"I'm right here." His voice came from directly behind me.

"You didn't go!" I said on a sigh of relief as I turned to see him walking toward me, a wide smile on his face.

"Look what I found," he said triumphantly. The early rays of the sun glinted on the piece of crystal he held in his hand.

"You found it!" I said delightedly. As he leaned down to hand it to me, I reached up impulsively, throwing my arms around his neck. He lost his balance and toppled over beside me, laughing at my exuberance.

But my happiness quickly dissolved, for as I hugged him, I remembered that in just a few minutes, he would leave me, this time for good, and I would be alone and bereft and at the mercy of my enemies. The thought made me panicky, and my arms tightened convulsively around his neck. I clung to him fiercely, knowing that once he was gone, I could no longer delay returning to the house, to a future I could not bear. Two days before, I had accepted his statement that I must return to my own home, but as the very moment when I must do so approached, I couldn't bring myself to go back.

45

Giorgio was my protector. As he had guarded me for the last two days, so must he continue to stay with me, protect me from my enemies, save me from the necessity of having to return to them. If he left, I would have to go back, do as they demanded. I could resist, but that would only delay them; it would not stop them from forcing their will on me. Only he stood between me and them.

How could I possibly let him go?

I wound my arms still tighter around his neck, moving closer to him. "Giorgio, don't leave me! I can't let you go! I need you!"

He could have pushed me away, but he might have hurt me, and roughness was not in his gentle nature, so he only used his hands to try to keep our bodies apart. But even this he could not do without hurting me, for I was hanging onto him with a strength that surprised us both, a strength borne of my fear of being left alone, my determination to keep him from leaving without me. Lying there, with his face close to mine, I raised my eyes to his. "Please," I whispered imploringly.

"No, Carlota. Let me get up. You already agreed, you must go home, to your people. I have brought you back to them. Turn me loose." He tried to twist his head, turn away from me, but he could not.

"Don't make me go home!" I sobbed, pressing against him, my lips so close to his face that they brushed his cheek as I spoke.

"Carlota!" His pleadings grew more urgent. "You mustn't! Let me go. You don't know what you're doing! Please!"

I sensed from the urgency in his tone that he was weakening, and I would not stop. I felt my own tears upon his face, tasted them as I kissed his cheek, driven by the wild desperation that had taken hold of me. I couldn't return, defeated and vulnerable, to those who hated me.

I did not consciously decide to use my body to hold Giorgio, to keep him with me, but, instinctively, as I clung to him, I sensed the power it held over him. I moved one hand slowly up the back of his head and whispered his name softly.

"*Válgame a dios!*" he exclaimed, and with a sorrowful choking sob, he stopped protesting and brought his lips down on mine. By that act, he admitted his surrender, and his hands, the hands that had been trying so futilely to keep us apart, suddenly took on a new purpose, and began moving slowly and sensuously over my body. Even through my clothing, I was aware of the comforting strength of them as they traced the shape of my buttocks, then moved to circle my breasts caressingly. My own hands moved over his back, his

46

arms, reveling in the vigor of his muscular shoulders, the power in his arms. That vigor, that power would be mine, would be my protection from my enemies. The thought comforted me, and allayed all my fears. I forgot *Tía* and *Tío* Umberto, forgot *don* Guillermo, so that when his kisses fell again on my lips, my response was one of passion, not of fear. His hands continued to caress me, until I was aware only of my body and his, and I felt fevered with a warmth that was different from anything I had experienced before.

And that was how they found us, wrapped in an embrace that had started as an impulsive hug and ended by costing dear innocent Giorgio his life.

"There!" a voice barked from the other side of the clearing. "Over there!"

Startled, I let my arms slide from around Giorgio. At the same moment, he hastily released me and got to his feet, but it was too late. There were many men—fifteen or twenty of them—and they had seen us, and judged us, and were looking at us with loathing and disgust.

"No!" I cried, looking from one pair of implacable eyes to another. "You don't understand! Giorgio was bringing me home, and he found something for me, something I had lost ..." I babbled on, continuing to search for some sign of understanding, some softening of the looks with which we were being fixed. But I protested in vain.

"String him up, and throw the slut on her doorstep!" The voice that spoke so harshly was that of *don* Guillermo, the man *Tía* Juana and *Tío* Umberto would have had me marry. I looked up at him, begging him, pleading with him to let me explain. I think, in that moment, I would even have promised to marry him if he had only shown a willingness to listen to me. But his toothless gums worked incessantly as his eyes continued to stare at me, hard and unyielding. If he heard, he did not listen.

I turned to Giorgio and would have spoken, but as I looked at him, my lips trembled too much for speech.

What have I done? I thought in a wild panic. *What have I done to Giorgio?*

Giorgio must have read my thoughts. "It's not your fault," he assured me. Then he picked up the piece of crystal where it had fallen and slipped it into the pocket of my dress. "Don't forget this. Tatiana wanted you to have it." He smiled at me, and there was such resignation in his smile that I couldn't bear it.

I jumped up suddenly and lunged at *don* Guillermo, clawing and scratching, hoping to attract all attention to myself so that Giorgio could get away. "Run, Giorgio! Run!" I shouted.

He did not get ten feet from me before they cut him down with a sword.

"Giorgio!" Horrified, I tried to go to him, but *don* Guillermo's fingers clamped my wrists in an iron-hard grip, surprisingly strong.

"Puta!" he spat at me. "Bitch! You cannot help your lover now. He's dead. No matter. He has saved us the trouble of a hanging."

Through my tears, my eyes saw Giorgio's lifeless form, and I remembered how just a few minutes before his face had been alight with happiness for the joy he had given me as he handed me the polished glass. Now, his face was expressionless and his eyes stared unseeingly at the sky.

I fought to twist free. I wanted to go to him, to close, gently, those beautiful eyes, but as I struggled and strained, *don* Guillermo's unrelenting grip clasped me tighter still. "You'll not touch your lover again, you filthy little slut, not even now. To think I had asked for your hand in marriage! Half of Andalusia is out looking for you, thinking you kidnapped and held captive by the gypsies. And all the time you were cavorting with your lover, like a bitch in heat." Roughly, he turned me around and pushed me ahead of him, then spoke to the others. "Come, let's cast her on her doorstep like the whore she is!"

I gave up trying to explain. What did it matter now? Gay, loving Giorgio was dead. And it was I who had killed him.

Later, confronted with *Tía's* frenzied accusations and *Tío* Umberto's cold chastising stares, I protested that I had done nothing of which I was ashamed. *Tía* insisted that my wanton behavior set me apart from all respectable people forevermore. I had run away from home, and twenty pairs of eyes had seen me in the arms of my gypsy lover. I was a wanton. She and *Tío* Umberto were puzzled by what I had done and maddened by my refusal to explain to them why I had run away. It never occurred to me to share with them the secret of my birth. My father had gone to great lengths to conceal the truth about my origin, and he and *Mamá* had traveled elsewhere on the continent for the first two years of their marriage in order to protect me from the stigma of bastardy. Only Dolores, who had been deeply involved in the conspiracy to make my birth appear legitimate, knew I had been running not to a lover, but to my mother.

"You must not tell your aunt the truth, *querida,*" Dolores said, "for she would be certain to use it against you."

I nodded my agreement, and stubbornly refused to explain

anything to *Tía*. I protested my innocence to her, but it mattered not at all whether or not she believed my protestations, for now she offered me only the dreary prospect of a convent. There was no longer, of course, any question of marriage with *don* Guillermo.

Tía would have locked me in my room, but I assured her that would not be necessary. "I've nowhere to go," I said with a listless shrug. "I'll not run away again."

Somehow, the hopelessness and despair of my words must have touched her cold heart, for she nodded and left me free to come and go as I chose. But guilt and remorse continued to tear at me for having involved dear innocent Giorgio in my problems and having brought him to his death. That, coupled with my grief over losing Tatiana, kept me in such a state of apathy that I seldom stirred from my room.

If *Tía* assumed that my spiritlessness signaled my willingness to accept the cloistered life she proposed for me, she soon learned otherwise. "I am not suited for such a life," I said flatly when she began to pursue the subject in earnest several weeks after my return. She had come to my room and had spent the better part of the morning trying to press me into agreement.

Later, when she rose to go, she fixed me with a long hard stare and said determinedly, "Whether you consider yourself suited or not is of little consequence. You will become suited soon enough."

In answer, I only shook my head. Even in the depths of my sorrow and desolation, I could not see myself consigned forever to a quiet uneventful life behind convent walls. Girls of different temperament than mine might embrace such a life eagerly, seeking peace of the spirit as the end and the meaning of life, but I saw life differently, and knew I would never be contented to hide from the challenge it held. Although I did not fully understand what had happened between Giorgio and me just before the men came upon us that fateful morning, I realized that some inner demand had taken hold of him and overcome his careful reasoning, and an answering demand had overpowered me as well. The feelings he had stirred within me were as much a part of me as my dark hair and full red lips. Never would I forget the way my body had become so vitally alive under his touch, nor would I be able to turn my back on the memory of the strange yearnings I had felt as we embraced. My failure to fully comprehend these longings or know what specific fulfillment would appease them did not keep me from admitting their existence or realizing that I could not deny them. For me, satisfying the needs of the spirit would never be enough, for I was far too aware of the vitality of the living flesh that housed my immortal soul.

As *Tía* reached the door, she paused to turn and send me one of her looks of utter exasperation. "You can't be hoping for marriage, not now. Under the circumstances, what respectable man would have such a baggage?" She opened the door, scowling at me. "I'll not wait much longer."

"And I'll not change my mind," I countered defiantly as the door slammed shut behind her.

After *Tía* was gone, Dolores, who had been bustling in the background, nodded her gray head approvingly. "You are right to refuse, *querida*. You would never be happy with such a quiet life."

I sighed heavily. "But what kind of a life can I hope for now? *Tía* says all of Andalusia considers me wicked, and I suppose she's right. I'll never forget how those men looked at Giorgio and me when they found us!" My words brought back the all too vivid memory of that horrible morning when Giorgio's life had ended so tragically, and a sob caught at my throat.

Dolores patted my hand. "Poor innocent lamb!"

"No," I answered truthfully, "I'm not innocent, Dolores, not really. I am wicked, but not because—not for the reason everyone seems to think."

Until that moment, I had not been able to bring myself to explain fully to Dolores what had happened. In spite of this, in spite of all the terrible things she must have heard about me, she had remained steadfastly loyal to me in my disgrace, never once acting as though she questioned my actions or doubted my innocence. As painful as I knew it would be for me to recount the events of that morning, I knew I owed it to her to explain. So I told her, haltingly, how it had all happened, not sparing my own feelings as I accepted full blame for the events that led to the moment they found Giorgio and me in such a compromising situation.

"Whatever might have happened if—if they hadn't found us then," I finished, "I can't say, because I really don't know. But I do know that because I wouldn't let him go, dear Giorgio is dead!" I put my face in my hands and sobbed as my self-reproach overwhelmed me.

Dolores cried, too, not for Giorgio, but for me. "My poor Carlota," she said, sniffing loudly.

I raised my face, saw the rivulets of tears running down the deep indentations on her weathered cheeks. "After they killed him," I said, "I wanted to go to him, but *don* Guillermo wouldn't let me. He held me tight, called me a whore."

"It's not as remote as you might think," he said triumphantly. "The city is capital of the kingdom, and has over 60,000 inhabitants. It is third in importance only after Mexico and Lima in the New World. And I am told the name of Alvarado is in good standing there."

"This man, *Señor* Alvarado—he—he lives there?"

He nodded. "He had business in Granada only briefly, and it was your good fortune he chanced to worship in the Cathedral two days since. He saw you at your prayers, and made inquiries, and—well, his offer followed."

At once suspicious, I said, "If he inquired of any friends of *don* Guillermo's, surely they would have turned him away from me."

"Perhaps. I did not deem it—ah—discreet to inquire as to the extent of his knowledge of your—ah—recent escapade."

"But you think he knows, and does not mind?"

He shrugged. "As you said, he certainly would have made inquiries."

"Then why has he asked to marry me? You have said no respectable man would do so."

I could sense *Tío* Umberto's growing irritation. "Perhaps, as I suggested, he feels that the news of your folly will not reach the distant land to which he plans to take you," he answered impatiently.

Still distrustful of this offer of marriage, I persisted, "But he would know. And if he thinks me guilty of whatever *don* Guillermo thinks I have done, then why would he want me for a wife?"

"You are not uncomely. Perhaps he fell hopelessly in love with you when he saw you at your devotions." He chuckled uneasily, but when he realized his attempt at joviality didn't set my mind at ease or make me jump to accept, he again became more businesslike. "There are other considerations. You are of respectable family—"

"And I am very well-dowered," I blurted out, for that was the only explanation I could think of for the unexpected proposal.

Tío Umberto coughed nervously, and I knew that he, too, had realized all along the reason behind the proposal. "Dower is certainly a consideration in any marriage."

I sighed heavily. How much better if an offer of marriage had come from one of the young men I knew and liked, instead of from a stranger from a far-away land. But a match with anyone locally was now out of the question. Well, perhaps this *don* Tomás would be likable. He could be no worse than *don* Guillermo. "Very well," I agreed. "Let me meet this man and I will decide whether or not to consider his proposal."

"I'm afraid that won't be possible."

I looked at him in surprise. "Not possible?" I echoed.

"He is in Spain for a short time only, and has many things to see to before his return to Guatemala. He left for Madrid this morning, and will not be back in Granada before he sails."

Shocked, I looked from him to *Tía* Juana, whose attention was still focused on her sewing. "But surely you can't expect me to accept his proposal without even meeting him! And how could we possibly be married if he doesn't plan to return to Granada?"

"You will be married by proxy, here, and sail from Cadiz as man and wife in six weeks."

Panicky at the thought of being married in six weeks to a man I did not even know, I protested, "So soon? But I can't—"

Tía Juana put down her mending with a show of impatience and said sharply, "Come now, Carlota Isabel, have done with your pointless protests! Cousin Umberto is completing the arrangements for a proxy marriage as soon as possible. *Señor* Alvarado is anxious to return to his home, and must sail in six weeks or wait another six months for the next sailing. You won't go in the convent, so you don't really have any choice, do you?" She fixed me with a hard stare, and I saw the satisfaction which filled her eyes. She was to be rid of me, at last!

But I would escape, too, from the impasse that held us both. The thought of my life stretching on endlessly as it was, for months and even for years, was something I knew I could never tolerate. *Tía* was right. I had already refused to consider the only other avenue of escape open to me.

I nodded slowly. "You're right, *Tía*. I have no choice at all. I will marry this *don* Tomás and go with him to the other side of the world."

And then, dimly, I heard an echo out of the past, all but forgotten until that moment: Tatiana's voice, telling me of a voyage I must take to a far-away place.

"You will be happy," Tatiana had promised me.

In the weeks that followed, I clung desperately to that remembered promise. But I recalled, too, how reluctant she had seemed to let me wring the promise from her.

Cadiz, Andalusia, Spain—
Winter, 1772

CHAPTER III

Six weeks later, I stood on a wharf in Cadiz, awaiting the approaching longboat from the ship that would carry me to my distant destination. The ship, the Santa Teresa, lay at anchor far out in the harbor, and all my possessions but the two small trunks I had with me had been sent on ahead and were already in the hold. I was taking all of my father's books and a number of household items—even some small pieces of furniture—besides my clothing.

The ship had already taken on all her supplies except for a few last-minute items, such as fresh foodstuffs. We would be part of a flotilla headed for the New World, traveling together for safety. We would replenish our food supply and, more important, take on fresh water at the Canary Islands. Our sailing was set for the next evening's tide. All this I had learned from the agent who represented the company that owned the Santa Teresa. The man had been visibly relieved at our arrival a scant hour before, and had immediately sent word to the ship to send the longboat to fetch me aboard.

We had reached Cadiz several days behind schedule due to *Tía's* continuous demands for over-long rest stops. She had made much of her suffering during the journey, and reminded me, with each jarring turn of the coach wheel, that she was being called upon to endure physical discomfort to which a woman her age should not have been subjected; nor did she fail to point out, with annoying frequency, that I, and I alone, was the cause of her misery.

I am sure she gave no thought to my misery. As I stood by the water's edge, flanked by her and Dolores on one side, and *Tío* Umberto and the ship's agent on the other, I felt an overwhelming sorrow. Until that moment, my leaving had always been a thing to contend with in the future, something to be faced another day. True, I had taken leave of the part of Andalusia I knew and loved days before, when the last view of Granada had disappeared from our coach window. Nevertheless, I still stood on Andalusian soil, and was loath to leave it.

I looked around me at this portion of land so alien to me, so unlike my part of Andalusia with its towering mountains and sweeping plains. Cadiz, built on a flat narrow bit of sand extending far out into the ocean, scarcely seemed a part of the land at all; it seemed, instead, to be reaching anxiously seaward, eager to be done with the land behind it.

I was in no such haste to give up even this meagre bit of land, to set foot upon the swaying deck of an unsteady ship that would shortly deny the land completely and carry me far away, across the vast ocean. I fought down my panic at the thought, for I knew there was no turning back.

I turned my thoughts toward the approaching longboat. It soon drew close enough to discern two men, besides the rowing figures of the sailors who propelled it toward us. Which of the two was my husband, I wondered with increasing anxiety? Then I remembered the agent, who had surely met him these past days, and I leaned across *Tío* Umberto to inquire which of the two was my husband.

"Your husband?" he repeated, looking at me strangely. I felt my face grow warm as I remembered with embarrassment that a woman should know her own husband. I stammered something about not being able to identify him at that distance.

He accepted my explanation and studied the figures in the longboat for a minute. Then he shook his head. "That's the captain and one of his mates. Your husband is not in the longboat, *Señora*. Maybe he'll await you on deck, unless he's gone ashore."

The latter proved to be the case, for the captain, a weatherbeaten man with a friendly smile, informed us that my husband had some last-minute business in Cadiz and had been rowed ashore earlier that day; he would not be back until the following day.

I was more relieved than upset at the postponement of our first meeting, but the news seemed to upset *Tío* Umberto and *Tía* Juana greatly, for they had planned on divesting themselves of me immediately upon our arrival in Cadiz, and they had not reckoned on my husband's absence. They excused themselves and had a whispered conference a short distance away, at which they obviously concluded that they would place me in the captain's charge and leave at once.

Tío Umberto returned, and spoke not to me but to the captain.

"I'm sure, Captain, that you can explain to my niece's husband that we must forego the pleasure of seeing him. If you will be so good as to accept responsibility for our niece's welfare, we will leave her with you. Please present to her husband my regrets that the press of business demands my immediate return to Granada."

"Of course," the captain replied courteously, and I wondered if he sensed, as I did, how relieved Tío Umberto was at his agreement.

There was a little small talk to which I paid scant attention. My feet felt as if, of their own volition, they were pressing themselves down into the wood of the wharf, as though they would cling for one last moment to this final contact with Andalusia.

A few minutes later, Tía and Tío Umberto stood facing me, ill at ease, ready to take their leave of me. I had never been close to Tío Umberto, and between Tía Juana and me there had existed lately an open animosity. Still, I felt suddenly alarmed at the idea of leaving them, severing forever the link they represented to all that was familiar.

"You will go now to the convent?" I asked Tía, hoping to forestall their departure for a few minutes more.

She nodded. "As soon as I see to the closing of the house. As you well know."

"It is what you have always wanted." My words, intended to encourage her to speak of the plans that meant so much to her, seemed hollow and meaningless.

Tía had no intention of being drawn into a prolonged conversation, and made it plain she did not care to remain any longer. She only nodded, that abrupt impatient bob of dismissal I had come to know so well.

"I hope you will be happy."

"I wish the same for you." Her words were spoken without warmth.

"Good-bye, then." There seemed to be nothing more to say. I kissed the cheek she turned toward me. She made no move to kiss me in return.

I turned to Tío Umberto and extended my hand. "Thank you for looking after my affairs." My words were prompted by politeness, not by sincerity, for it was his bungling of my affairs which had made such a jumbled mess of my life.

He seemed to sense my real thoughts, for he shifted uneasily from one foot to the other. "I did all I could, as I often promised your father I would," he said righteously. He held my hand in a slack grip only briefly, then dropped it and turned to *Tía.* "Come, Juana, we must get settled in an inn before nightfall."

They turned and walked swiftly away. How anxious the two of them were to be rid of me! There was an emptiness inside me as I watched them go. They had not been much comfort, but they were all I had.

I watched them, waiting for them to turn and give me a final wave, but they disappeared around one of the low buildings with never a backward glance.

Tears misted my eyes so that I couldn't see. Not even when I had learned of Tatiana's death had I felt so desolate and alone.

"You had better put on your shawl, *querida,* against the evening chill." Dolores was at my side, solicitously covering my shoulders with the soft warmth of my shawl.

I turned and smiled at her, pressing her hand as she slipped it over my shoulders, and wondering if she knew how thankful I was at that moment for her presence. I had my dear Dolores, who had given up all her family ties to accompany me. I was not all alone after all.

I turned to the captain, and accepted the hand he offered as he and one of the seamen helped me into the waiting boat.

After we had boarded the Santa Teresa, I asked the captain what time the following day he expected my husband. Husband! The word came clumsily to my lips. How strange, to have been married for three weeks, and have yet to meet the man to whom I was wed! What was he like, I wondered? Even *Tío* Umberto had never set eyes on him, I had learned, but had dealt always through an intermediary. I knew only that he was a widower, with several children by his first wife. This bit of information did not upset me at all, for I had an easy way with children, and did not doubt my ability to win them to me.

The captain answered apologetically. "I'm afraid I can't tell you that, *Señora.* He knows when we sail, and promised he will be aboard before that time."

"And what time is supper tonight?"

He lowered his eyes a minute before returning them to meet my gaze. "Your husband has suggested that your meals be served in your cabin, for your convenience. He felt you would want to remain out of sight until his arrival to avoid the discomfort of being exposed to the seamen's stares." Obviously, he did not relish the task of having to deliver such an insulting message to me.

I felt myself flush, half with embarrassment and half with

anger. So my husband did know about what *Tío* Umberto called my "indiscretion," and, believing the worst about me, would deny me the run of the ship!

"Thank you, Captain. This has been a long day, and I will appreciate not having to dress for dining. I'll go to my cabin now." I tried to speak with dignity, and I held my head high as I turned and walked away, hoping that my bravado hid the deep humiliation I felt at having the captain share my knowledge that my husband didn't trust me.

That night, I lay awake a long time, listening to the lap of the water against the side of the ship, aware of each creak and groan as the ship strained against its anchor. I mused on how little I knew of my future. I had a husband I had never met and about whom I knew virtually nothing, and he was taking me to a home in a remote country which I had scarcely known existed until six weeks before. A vast ocean lay between us and that home. Just before I fell asleep, I saw again that green valley with the town neatly laid out in its center. It was a beautiful place, and I could feel the soft balmy breezes blowing through my hair. It was peaceful and lovely, and yet. . . and yet. . .

I fell into a state of half-sleep that did not become fully undisturbed slumber for many hours, so Dolores had to wake me when she brought my breakfast tray.

After I dressed, we busied ourselves with the limited unpacking the cramped quarters would allow. About mid-morning, Dolores complained of a headache and I sent her to her quarters to lie down. For a while, I paced restlessly back and forth in the cramped cubicle, covering in a few impatient strides the space from one wall to the other. I was bored, and I was smarting from the insult of my husband's indirect orders confining me to my cabin, like a naughty child. It brought to mind the many times *Tía* had made me stay in my room, subsisting on bread and water, for my misdeeds. Could this be a sign, I wondered, that I had married a man as unfeeling and as insensitive to the feelings of others as *Tía* Juana? I pushed the thought from my mind as being too unpleasant to dwell upon.

I stopped pacing and threw myself on the bunk with a sigh. My thoughts, as restless as my spirit, wandered from one thing to another before coming to rest on my last meeting with Tatiana. This, then, was my sea voyage, the one she had seen for me in the piece of polished crystal.

I sat up suddenly. Perhaps, since she had been able to see in the piece of polished crystal something of my future, I could do the same, right now.

I jumped up and opened my trunk, reached deep into a

59

bunch of petticoats and brought out the piece of crystal. With it before me, I lay on my bunk again, propped my chin on my elbows, and willed the glass to show me something of the new life on which I was embarking. At first, irrelevant thoughts continued to flit in and out of my brain, much as first one sea gull and then another I had watched from the wharf the day before had swooped and dived into the water in search of food.

But then, gradually, my thoughts came to bear on all the things I had wondered about my life from that day forward. My own knowledge about my future matched the blankness and emptiness of the glass. There were so many things I would know! I stared at the glass until my gaze became so fixed on it that I doubted if even by conscious effort I could have moved my eyes.

I lay there, staring, unaware of the passage of time. I am sure that at some point the ship's bells announcing the hour and half-hour must have rung, but so complete was my concentration that I was not aware of any sound at all.

When, at last, I did see something, I thought at first it was merely an illusion, a trick of my imagination. I ran my fingers over the glass, as though to clear a smudge, my gaze still unbroken. It was not a smudge, but a blur, which gradually took the shape of a man's face.

Finally, the image became clear, as clear as though the man had been in the room with me.

My husband, surely, I thought with joy! For the face I saw was that of a young man, and he was smiling. The beard and moustache he wore made it hard to guess his age, but I knew he must have been married very young in order to have two children by his first wife.

My fears of my husband dissolved. It was the first time I had admitted to myself that I had been afraid. How could I fear a man with so pleasing a countenance, and with such a warming smile? My father had a Norseman friend, one of the most agreeable of men, and this face I saw now reminded me of him. I stared harder, as though I would fix in my mind every detail of the face, memorize every feature. The eyes I liked especially, for they seemed to be looking directly at me, as though they could actually see me, and they were brimming with candor and sincerity—a foolish fancy, perhaps, as though a face in a glass could be alive any more than a man in a painting could see and think. His light hair—unusually light for a Spaniard, I noted—was well-suited to his face, for it shone and glistened with the same vitality as his lips and his eyes.

So that, then, was the man to whom I was wed, I thought

happily. Then I heard myself laugh aloud with delight at the pleasant surprise. With that sound, as though disturbed by it, the vision blurred again into nothingness and I was looking once more at a translucent piece of polished crystal and aware of the pattern of the blanket beneath it. I picked it up, clutching it contentedly in both hands and hugging it to me. Then I sprang from the bed and hummed a lively gypsy tune as I carefully replaced the glass among my petticoats, remembering the handsome face it had shown me. Surely such a man would be easy to like; I was half in love with him already.

There was a tap on my door, and Dolores entered, bearing my dinner tray. I stretched languidly and smiled at her.

"I think, Dolores, after dinner I will put on my green silk dress and venture onto the deck."

She looked shocked at my suggestion. "But your husband, *querida*—His instructions to the captain—You know he as much as forbade you—"

I watched her remove the food from the tray and arrange it on the tiny table, remembering the happy countenance of the face in the glass. I smiled to myself. "I don't think he will mind at all," I said, seating myself on the edge of the bunk and motioning for her to push the table in front of me. "In fact, it wouldn't surprise me if the captain had misunderstood his instructions completely." I turned my full attention to the food, both spirits and appetite miraculously restored.

Later, over Dolores's continued protests, we went on deck. I soon became absorbed in the feverish activity all about me, watched as the men lashed some of the deck cargo in place. A small pen containing four good saddle horses took up much of the small deck. They were lovely creatures, two of them of the fine Arab breed, and they were all obviously distraught at their strange surroundings. I went over to stroke their long sleek noses and talk softly and soothingly to them until at last they quieted somewhat. So engrossed was I that I did not hear approaching footsteps.

"I am surprised to see you on deck, my love."

The voice that had spoken was right over my shoulder, and it took a moment for the words to register on my brain. When they did indeed register, I whirled around indignantly to fix the middle-aged man who had spoken them with an icy stare. Where was Dolores, I wondered agitatedly, that she had let a man accost me so? I looked around for her, and saw her only a few paces away, looking upset and twisting her hands together helplessly. It was not like Dolores to be helpless.

I looked again at the man, and it was then the full meaning of his words took hold. *I am surprised to see you on deck, my love.* My love! Who but a lady's husband would have the right to address her so?

"Oh, no!" I gasped, covering my mouth with my hand. How could this man be my husband? He bore not the slightest resemblance to the young and happy face I had seen in the crystal earlier that day! This man was much older—over forty, at least, I judged—and, far from smiling, he was frowning his disapproval at me. He was dark, of medium height and slender build, nor would he have been ill-favored except for the scowl with which he fixed me. He was impeccably dressed, I noted, and his beard and moustache were neatly trimmed. But he was nothing like the man I had been expecting since that morning.

"You—you aren't my husband?" I asked hoarsely, hoping my denial would make it so.

He must have mistaken my shocked surprise for fear, for his scowl softened. Yes, I am your husband," he said, taking a step toward me. "You must not be afraid of me, Carlota Isabel. If you are concerned because I found you on deck, you needn't be. I am sure you had good reason for disobeying my orders."

"I needed some air," I explained feebly. "The cabin was so close I could scarcely catch my breath." As I talked, I sought to regain my composure, to swallow my bitter disappointment in the man before me who said he was my husband. Until a few short hours before, until Tatiana's glass had shown me that young and handsome face, I had entertained no fine expectations concerning my husband. Indeed, under the circumstances of my marriage, I should have accepted without rebellious thoughts anyone who was an improvement over *don* Guillermo. But now my spirits, which until that moment had been soaring at such heights, were plunged suddenly and violently into the depths of disappointment. Tatiana's glass had lied to me.

Fortunately, I had the presence of mind to try to conceal my feelings. *"Señor,"* I said, lowering my head and dropping into a deep curtsy. I remained down, my head bent, longer than would have been necessary, playing for time to hide my shock and disappointment, and to reorganize my emotions in the light of this new revelation. The face in the glass had been a vision, a dream, conjured up, perhaps, by some girlish hopes or foolish fancy. I had seen what I wanted my husband to be. But this man, this man to whom I curtsied—he was in truth my husband. And surely he was not to blame for my mistaken vision. He must never be allowed to guess my disappointment.

Slowly, I stood up and raised my head, forcing a smile to

lips that seemed not to want to respond at all, searching for some pleasantry to utter, unable to think of anything to say. What was the proper comment on meeting for the first time a man to whom one had been wed for three weeks? Did one acknowledge an introduction that had never taken place? Or inquire about the unknown husband's health? Or make some inane impersonal remark about the weather?

As it was, my husband saved me the trouble of finding something to say to him. "You must call me Tomás," he said, taking one of my hands in his and patting it.

I must be grateful to him for trying to set me at ease, I thought as I looked up at him. Our eyes met and locked, and it was then I felt the second shock of our meeting. As our eyes held, there came over me a feeling similar to that I had experienced the night before, when I had seen, in my mind, the lovely green valley. This was my husband. His countenance was not unpleasant, his manner courteous, his words intended to set me at ease. And yet. . . . and yet. . . .

I shuddered involuntarily, and quickly withdrew my hand. I hoped he had not noticed.

If he did take note of it, he gave no sign. He backed away from me and bowed. "If you will excuse me for a few minutes, I've some delicate porcelains coming aboard, and must see to them personally. I will join you in your cabin shortly for tea."

"I'll tell Dolores to serve it to us there," I answered, thankful for the promise of a few minutes' respite.

He nodded, then turned and walked away. I watched him for a minute, then motioned to Dolores. As she approached, I could see she was anxious to have me share my thoughts with her on my first encounter with Tomás. I often confided in her, but I had no desire to do so then, for my thoughts were too tumultuous to discuss or share with anyone.

"My husband and I will take tea in my cabin," I said brusquely. "Would you see to ordering it, please?"

"Of course, *querida*." She made no motion to leave. "He did seem pleasant once you got to talking, didn't he? And he is quite a handsome man, though older."

I purposely ignored her comments. "Please attend to the steeping of the tea yourself. You know how horrid it is if the water isn't boiling, or poured directly over the tea leaves."

"Yes, *Señora*, I will see to it," she answered in a hurt voice. She turned and walked away. Dolores had been with me all my life, and knew when she was being dismissed.

I craved a few minutes of solitude to sort my thoughts and compose myself. I walked to the rail, found a quiet spot away from all the activity and leaned over, watching as a small sailboat passed by. There were two men in it, and one of them was sitting far up in the prow. I realized, then, what they were about, for they were almost upon a small empty boat, which must have broken away from its moorings and was being buffeted about by the wind-whipped water. The man in the prow swung a small anchor into the loose craft, then drew it toward him with the end of the rope he had retained. The other man brought their boat about, and they returned the way they had come, with the loose boat in tow.

Hadn't I been like that small boat, I mused, until this man's proposal had put purpose back into my life? Hadn't I been caught in the current of misunderstanding, buffeted by the winds of hopelessness, until he had rescued me?

Yes, I reminded myself, Tomás had saved me when I was adrift in a situation that had no plausible end, and I must ever remember that and be grateful to him. I must try to please him, be a good wife to him, and a proper loving mother to his children. I must force from my mind the vague ill-defined feelings I had when our eyes met. I must forget that other face, the one in the glass, the eyes candid where Tomás's were guarded, the mouth ready to smile where Tomás's was creased down at the corners, the hair vibrant and unruly where Tomás's was closely confined and showing signs of graying.

I closed my eyes, to pray for the strength and wisdom to carry out my intentions, but I could not shut out from my mind the face of the blond young man, with whom I had already become enamored. The face I had seen in Tatiana's glass was not that of my husband; it was the face of the man I would have liked him to be.

Later, as Tomás and I talked over the light refreshment that had been set up on the small table in my cabin, he seemed amused when I said I wished I might have known the ages of his children so that I could have brought them some appropriate toys.

"How old are you, Carlota?"

I bristled, for I was sure he was laughing at me. "Eighteen," I answered defensively, "but I've a way with children."

"I don't doubt that you do," he said, putting his hand over mine. I resisted the impulse to draw my hand back. "But my daughter is nineteen, a year older than you. You will like her very much, I'm sure."

"Oh." I felt the blood rush to my face in embarrassment at my foolish mistake. "I had assumed—but don't you have two children?"

His lips set in a hard line. "Ricardo is twenty." The sharpness in his voice left no doubt that just the mention of

64

his son had displeased him. Obviously, he did not care to discuss Ricardo. He stood up and came around to pull my chair back for me.

As I rose, he took hold of my shoulders and turned me to face him. He stared at me, studying my face so unblinkingly and with such intense concentration that I had to look away in embarrassment. I could not keep from tensing as he pulled me toward him to plant a kiss on my forehead.

"*Dios mío*! How lovely you are!" he said as he released me. "I will be the envy of all Santiago with such a beautiful wife." He walked to the door. "I will leave you to rest. Tonight, after we have weighed anchor, we will have our wedding supper, just the two of us, in my cabin."

That night, as I was dressing for supper, Dolores protested when I chose a dress of bright crimson.

"It is far too bold a color for a bride," she insisted. "And besides, your father is not yet dead two years. If not gray or white, then a muted tone. Your pale lilac, perhaps."

"I will wear that one," I said, determinedly pointing to the one I had selected. I did not explain to her why I insisted on wearing the red dress. "*Red is the color of courage, my dear.*" I heard again Tatiana's voice as she had spoken to me three years earlier, the day I had shown her *Mamá's* earrings. "*If you ever feel frightened or unsure of yourself, wear red, as much of it as you can.*"

"And I will wear *Mamá's* rubies, the necklace and the earrings both." I wondered only briefly why I should feel such desperate need of courage and confidence to face the man who was my husband.

"If you are certain . . ." Dolores cast me a doubtful glance as she took the crimson silk out of the trunk and shook it. But by the time she had helped me bathe, she seemed to sense the bravado that had dictated my choice, and it was she who suggested arranging my hair in the most elaborate of coiffures and selected the fanciest and largest of my combs.

She fussed and clucked over my hair until at last she was pleased with the results, refusing to let me see until she had finished. Only after she had carefully slipped my dress over my head and helped me put on my jewels would she agree to hand me the mirror.

I stared at myself in surprise, remembering another day, the day I turned fifteen, when Dolores had helped me make myself appear more adult. Then, I had been a child playing at being a woman, but now, as I looked in the mirror, I saw that I was truly mature. I noticed approvingly that I looked completely self-confident and quite sophisticated. Perhaps

65

there was some special magic about red, after all. I smiled, and my eyes met those of Dolores.

She nodded her approval. "My little girl has grown up, and is a woman now," she said. Her eyes misted as she said, "You will melt his heart, *querida.*"

A loud knock on the door made us both jump. Dolores opened the door and, as my husband entered, I stood up and curtsied to him. He crossed over to me and took both my hands in his as his face mirrored his approval of my appearance.

"Come. Our supper is waiting."

He led me to his cabin, next to mine, where a small table had been set with the finest silver, and even with wine glasses of delicate crystal, which winked their reflection of the two lanterns hanging from the beams above.

He seemed to sense my surprise at the well-appointed table. "I always carry my own table settings when I travel. I dislike eating off dented pewterware." He poured two glasses of sherry from a crystal decanter and offered one to me.

"To us." He raised his glass to mine.

I drank the wine quickly, feeling need of its warmth. Nor did I lack for wine during our supper, for he never allowed my glass to get empty.

Our talk was impersonal, mostly stilted, as it might have been between any two strangers who had known each other only a few hours. It was hard to realize that, though we were scarcely acquainted, we were man and wife. There was no mistaking the possessive pride with which Tomás looked at me, his eyes alight with a strange glow as they followed my every movement. I could not hope he would wait until we had come to know each other a little better before he claimed his rights. I knew this stranger had every intention of sharing my bed before the evening was over.

"What of the city of Santiago de los Caballeros?" I asked once in an effort to end an uncomfortable silence that had grown between us. We had finished our meal, and I felt a need to prolong our conversation as long as possible in order to delay what would inevitably follow.

Before he answered, Tomás held the decanter containing the red table wine over my glass and looked at me questioningly. I nodded, and watched the level of the red liquid rise in my glass, then in his, as I heard his words. "It is very beautiful," he said, setting the decanter down. "A treasure of art, of paintings and sculptures. There are some magnificent buildings, and there are many beautiful churches. The churches possess countless treasures, some of them of immeasurable value."

66

"It's in a lovely green valley, isn't it? And there are the tops of steep mountains visible . . ." I was remembering the visions I had had of such a place.

He looked at me in surprise. "How did you know?"

"I have seen it," I answered unthinkingly, picking up my glass.

"In a painting, you mean?"

I reminded myself to guard my tongue, which the wine had loosened. I grasped at the opportunity he gave me. "In a painting," I quickly agreed.

He raised his eyebrows quizzically. "Really? I knew of none in Granada."

"I—I don't recall just where I saw it," I stammered. "It was long ago, and I scarcely remember it at all. Only the sharpness of the nearby mountain-tops remained in my memory." I did not tell him that I had seen, too, the carefully laid-out streets, neatly cobbled, and the spires of churches everywhere, and the mountain with the oddly sloping sides. Nor did I mention that each time I saw the city in my mind, I was filled with a feeling I could not explain, even to myself.

We sat at the table a while longer, and even though I knew that our supper had been leisurely and unhurried, the time had seemed to me to be racing by toward the moment when I must learn what it was that Tía Luisa had blushingly referred to as allowing my husband the privilege of my bed. "One must submit," she had said, which had sounded an easy enough thing to do, but as I watched Tomás rise from the table and walk around to pull out my chair for me, I could not help but feel apprehensive and wish the evening were just beginning. He offered me his arm and accompanied me ceremoniously the few steps from his cabin to mine. Before he opened the door for me, his arms closed tightly about me and he pressed his lips to my forehead. His lips did not brush me lightly as they had earlier in the day when he had taken leave of me. This time his kiss was hot and moist and lingering, and I welcomed the respite as his arms slackened and he withdrew from me, saying hoarsely, "I'll send your woman to you."

Both Dolores and I were unnaturally silent as I let her help me out of my clothes and into a new silk nightgown. I felt myself relax just as I always did when she took the combs from my hair and brushed it in long soothing strokes. The unaccustomed amount of wine I had drunk made everything seem unreal, enveloped my mind in a hazy glow. I seemed to watch as one in a dream as Dolores helped me into bed and left me alone.

Almost immediately, the door opened again, and Tomás, in

his dressing gown, came into the cabin, this time without knocking. Wordlessly, he stood over my bunk, his form outlined by the lone lantern that cast its flickering flame on me but not on him. I could tell from the tilt of his head, outlined against the lantern's glow, that he was assessing me. Briefly, a vision of the face I had seen in the crystal that morning flashed through my mind and was as quickly gone, and I felt a twinge of regret that it could not be that man standing over me, his eyes looking at me as warmly as they had seemed to do from the crystal. But that face, that man had been a product of my girlish dreams, woven of fantasy. This man standing by my bunk was real, and he was my husband, come to claim his rights to me. And though his eyes were clothed in shadows, I could sense that he was looking at me with no warmth save that kindled by his own desire.

I still felt as though it were all a dream as I watched him turn and extinguish the lantern, and even my apprehensions seemed unreal. I heard the soft swish of his dressing gown as it dropped to the floor, and a moment later he was crowding beside me in the narrow bunk, which was scarcely wide enough for one, and his body was hot against mine.

It was the fieriness of his flesh against mine, with only the thin layer of silk in my gown between us, and his heavy breathing so close to my ear that cut through the euphoria of the wine and returned me to reality, made me wonder if the misgivings I felt were not beyond any normal virginal apprehensions. As he leaned over me and brought his lips down on mine, I tried to suppress the sudden panicky feeling that I was suffocating. I told myself that I owed it to this man, my husband in the eyes of God and man, to force my misgivings from my mind. I knew I must try to at least accept his kisses, if I couldn't return them, try not to tense as his hands moved urgently, demandingly over my body as his lips continued to imprison mine. I waited, hoping that my body would overpower my thoughts, make me respond to him. But I waited in vain, for nothing he did evoked any of the yearnings that had arisen in me so spontaneously at Giorgio's touch. Instead, my repulsion made me stiffen anew each time he touched me, and the only desire I felt was a scarcely controllable urge to leap from the bunk and run from the cabin.

Suddenly, as though he had run out of patience with my lack of response, Tomás reached down and lifted my gown, thrusting his hand abruptly underneath it. At the same moment, I heard a choking sob, and did not realize at first that it was my own. His hands continued to probe ever higher. and I recoiled with shock and shame as his hand touched the soft flesh of my inner thighs and moved between my legs.

"No!" I cried out, trying to twist away from him.

For the first time since he had entered my cabin, he spoke, and though his words were whispered, they could not have held more anger if he had shouted them at me.

"Come, Carlota, don't play the coy and frightened virgin with me!" With an unexpected quickness, he pulled my gown out of his way and moved his body to cover mine, forcing the air from my lungs as the weight of his body came down upon me.

Shocked and indignant at the unjustness of his words, appalled at his unexpected roughness, I flinched, recoiling convulsively.

My reaction seemed to make him angrier still, and he forced his knees between my legs, hissing furiously, "Spread your legs for me as you did for your gypsy lover. I have the right to you, as he did not!"

After that, I remember crying out again at a sharp stab of pain as he forced his way into my unyielding body, and mingled with the memory of the continuing pain is the remembrance of the way his breath seemed to boom in my ears. Finally, his body relaxed heavily over mine and his breathing again became normal. I lay, unable to move, feeling trapped in my marriage to him even as my body was pinioned by his. When at last he pushed himself from the bunk, I took a deep breath, which ended on an uneven sob.

Shaken by the abruptness and unpleasantness with which I had learned what lay beyond the kisses and embraces of men and women, I was too stunned to move even after Tomás had returned to his own cabin, too weak to reach down and pull my rumpled gown down about my legs. It seemed to take tremendous effort just to raise my hand to my face, which I found was wet with tears I had not even known I was shedding. Then, benumbed by pain and shock, I fell into a deep sleep which was undisturbed until some time before morning, when I was awakened by the feeling that I was being watched. Slowly, I forced my eyes open and saw Tomás standing by my bunk, studying me intently. This time, he held a candle in his hand, illuminating his face. I wondered how long he had been standing there, watching me. When I became fully awake, I realized I had not moved during my exhausted slumber, and I was suddenly aware of my state of deshabille, and reached down to pull my gown over my thighs.

"Carlota?" When he spoke at last, there was no hint of the anger his voice had held earlier, nor was he looking at me unkindly. When I did not answer him, he continued, "I think perhaps I wronged you. This was the first time for you, wasn't it? The first time you have been with a man?"

"Of course," I answered indignantly, still shocked and physically pained by his unfeeling use of me.

"I was led to believe otherwise."

"You were led to believe wrong," I answered, hiding my shock and disillusionment behind my haughty words.

"You have no idea how much that means to me."

In the last flicker of light before he blew out the candle, I saw that his face mirrored only satisfaction, not contrition. Then he was in the bunk beside me again, and his more gentle use of me was as close as he ever came to an apology. That, and his words as he hesitated at the door of my cabin when he took leave of me shortly before morning.

"Carlota, you may take the air on deck whenever you wish."

My husband, I was to learn, was not a man who apologized for his actions.

As the door clicked shut behind him, the irony of the situation struck me. I suppressed a bitter laugh. Now I knew, at last, what it was *don* Guillermo had accused me of, and it was because of those accusations that I was leaving my homeland and was wedded to a man I scarcely knew. Only Dolores, Tomás and I knew that *don* Guillermo's accusations were false, but now it no longer mattered whether they were or not, for neither that knowledge nor I were ever apt to return to Andalusia to clear my name.

At least, I mused with a newborn cynicism, that knowledge had secured for me my husband's permission to walk freely on the deck of the ship that carried us far from Andalusia.

At Sea—December, 1772

CHAPTER IV

The sea journey was long and tedious. Until then, I had never given much thought to the enormity of the span of water that separated the New World from the Old, but I had ample time to ponder it as endless swells tossed our little ship this way and that, day after day. It seemed impossible that we could be making headway through the mountains of water that frequently surrounded us and which appeared sometimes about to swallow us, but the captain said we were steadily on course. In mid-ocean, there was a bad storm, in which two of the horses were injured so badly they had to be destroyed, and that storm separated us from the rest of the fleet. We continued on by ourselves, and a steady wind in quieter seas for several days after the storm served to push us forward again. And so we headed toward the New World alone, now slowly, now at a faster pace, sometimes scarcely seeming to move at all.

I had hoped that perhaps once the memory of the unpleasant manner in which our marriage had been consummated had faded somewhat in our minds, Tomás and I might become more comfortable in each other's presence, but no such easiness developed between us. I finally concluded that the fault lay within his very nature, which was too utterly selfish to include any real affection for another person. It was not that he was unmannerly with me. He went through all the motions of a devoted husband, especially when others watched, but when we talked, it was still as two strangers addressing each other, as though he did not come into my cabin nightly and slide into my bunk, his hands reaching impatiently, demandingly under my gown.

71

In my own mind, I had excused him for his treatment of me on our wedding night. In all fairness, I felt I must accept a portion of the blame, in that I had scarcely been what could be called receptive, or even acquiescent, toward his initial advances. Certainly under the circumstances, his anger with me had been justifiable, I realized, for he had been given to understand that he had not married an innocent virgin. I reminded myself repeatedly that I must be grateful to him for marrying me, since a marriage more to my liking had become an impossibility. I forced myself to accept his presence in my bed in a more dutiful manner, but I still could not quell my distrust of him, that distrust I had felt the first time he took my hand and which I could not logically justify. Yet it was this which seemed to stand in the way of his awakening any response in my body, which for so long had shown the promise of being easily roused. I could force myself to accept his love-making, but I could not force any answering affection. This did not seem to trouble Tomás, who gave no indication that he was concerned with my lack of response. He appeared satisfied with my dutiful acceptance of his right to fulfill his own needs upon my body. In our daytime encounters, he was courteous and polite, but his actions seemed born more of a memorized set of manners than of any special desire to please me or any sincere concern for my comfort.

Only with Dolores did I feel at ease. I would have traded discreet pleasantries with the sailors as I strolled the small deck when the seas were calm enough, but the few times I did as much as wish them good morning, Tomás frowned his disapproval, so I soon gave that up. At times, I felt that Dolores and I were alone, afloat in a hostile world, with water stretching endlessly behind us and ahead of us.

And then Dolores was taken from me. She suddenly sickened, and within two days she had died, in spite of my constant prayers and my desperate attempts to cure her with Tatiana's herb mixtures. I kept a vigil by her bedside day and night, and was there when she slipped quietly away from me late the second day of her illness, just after the priest had shriven her of her sins, which I am sure must have been venial, if indeed there were any at all.

At the sound of Dolores's shrouded body splashing into the sea, I could not hold back the tears I had denied myself for two days. Poor Dolores! For me, she had left everyone, every place she loved, and now must lie forever within the unknown depths of a cold and hostile ocean, far from any hallowed ground. How far beneath its murky surface would her body come to rest? At the thought of her body sinking end-

72

lessly down toward the center of the earth, I burst into uncontrollable sobs.

Tomás came over and put his arm around my shoulder, patting it consolingly. "There, there, my dear," he said. "You must not carry on so. I know you will be inconvenienced by the loss of your personal maid, but I'll find you another as soon as we reach Santiago."

I looked up at him sharply, aghast at the lack of feeling revealed by his callous words. We had been together for three weeks by then. Could he fail to realize that Dolores had been far more than a serving woman to me? Did he think it was the loss of her services and not her person I mourned?

He seemed not to realize my shocked surprise and went on, "There are few Spanish maids to be had, of course, but I'm sure we will be able to find a suitable *india*. Some of them have been surprisingly well trained, a few even educated. In any case, I've been intending to enlarge our house staff."

I started to protest his insensitivity, but thought better of it. After all, my relationship with Dolores had been a unique one for mistress and servant, so perhaps I should not be shocked to find that Tomás did not understand it. I continued to mourn Dolores in silence.

The ship plowed on toward the New World, sometimes through swells twice as high as itself. As we approached Guatemala, the seas calmed, and in the coastal waters the lookout spotted a sail. The captain, certain she was a pirate ship, dodged this way and that, and we all breathed more easily as twilight closed in to protect us. The next morning, no sails were in sight. The captain seemed relieved.

"They'd have been more dogged in their pursuit, I think, if we were heading away from the continent instead of toward it," he told us that day at dinner. "It is the treasure ships which interest them most, the ones headed toward Spain with the King's gold. They'll be waiting for us on our return journey."

We made landfall at the mouth of the Rio Dulce, and journeyed up the river for two full days, during which I spent much of my time on deck, enjoying the beauty and peace of the river after the often violent buffeting of the open sea. Finally, the river opened out into a large body of water known as the Golfo Dulce, and it was there, at last, that our long sea journey ended. We spent several days at the *Castillo de San Felipe*, the fortress built over a century before to protect from pirates of both land and sea the King's treasures awaiting shipment to Spain. There, Tomás argued ceaselessly with the authorities about the amount of taxes he would have to pay on our belongings being brought ashore.

"The King would bleed us poor," he complained to me. "Taxes, heaped one upon the other, and then the tithe, in gold! They tax us on what we bring here for our own homes, and they tax us as well on everything we ship to Spain! It's too much to bear!"

As Tomás haggled endlessly with the men in charge, I welcomed the period of rest from the sea journey and the few days' respite before we started on our overland trek to Santiago. Of the four horses which had started with us, the two Arab horses were the ones who had survived the journey; since they belonged to Tomás, we had good mounts for our arduous travels. Tomás arranged for well over half of our things to accompany us on the backs of donkeys and slaves, who had just carried the annual tithe, in gold, from Santiago citizens to the fort, where it would be shipped to Spain on the Santa Teresa. They would have left, with the force of about thirty soldiers who had accompanied them, to return to Santiago immediately if it hadn't been for Tomás's pleas for them to wait for us. I was certain he reinforced his pleas with an ample bribe to the officer in charge.

"It's rare good fortune to find them here," Tomás said. "The trail to Santiago can be dangerous without adequate protection. Though, as the captain mentioned, bandits and pirates alike prefer to snare a cargo heading toward Spain. In any event, we'll be safe enough with our escort."

The commander of the garrison promised to send the rest of our things as soon as the opportunity presented itself.

"That may be months!" Tomás grumbled. "Careless storage or improper handling could ruin things!"

As we moved farther inland, he seemed to resign himself to the situation for which there was no remedy, and began to look with a sort of detached interest at my awe and wonder at the strange surroundings. Everywhere I looked, I saw something I had never seen before: butterflies of fantastic beauty; brightly colored birds, some of them with raucous ear-splitting calls; and trees and plants unknown to me in such profusion that it was all I could do to refrain from dismounting at every step to investigate and gather particularly interesting specimens, some of which I was certain would merit cultivation in my herb garden. Whenever we rested, I busied myself picking leaves and hunting seeds to take to Santiago so that I could study them and learn their properties, as Tatiana had taught me to do.

There were animals, too, in the forests. Chattering monkeys swung high over our heads in the branches above us, and one night when we were camped I was nearly frightened to death when a jaguar darted across my path. There were snakes,

74

many of them mortally poisonous, and Tomás warned me to look carefully wherever I stepped. A number of times, my horse shied from something I did not see, probably, Tomás said, because he had seen or sensed a snake nearby.

There were about as many slaves as soldiers, and they carried loads of tremendous weight by means of single straps around their foreheads. Never had I seen countenances so unsmiling and enigmatic. I was concerned about the terrible strain their loads must have placed on their heads and necks, but when I mentioned my concern to Tomás, he dismissed it with a brusque wave of his hand.

"They are *indios*. They are used to it. It is the way they have always carried things, and does them no harm."

I wondered, as I studied their expressionless faces, what they were thinking. How deeply must they resent us, I thought, we who had come out of the east two hundred and fifty years before to usurp their land even as we enslaved their bodies. What did they think right now, these men who plodded silently along in a line, as they carried yet more of our burdens so that we could establish ourselves that much more firmly in their land?

One day, when I idly posed that question to Tomás, he laughed. "My dear, you attribute deep reflection to slaves? I will tell you their thoughts, if they have any. They think of food, and creature comforts, just as dogs or horses or any other lower forms of life think of them, and they are undoubtedly grateful to us, as their masters, for supplying them with enough food to sustain them. But profundities? Surely you jest!"

I sighed and was silent, and knew I would never again confide such thoughts to Tomás. But for now I could only look at the way they plodded laboriously forward, occasionally stumbling under the weight of their loads, and wonder how they could be as devoid of feeling and emotion and thought as he said they were.

The heat of the coastal lowlands gave way to a refreshing coolness, which turned to cold after sunset at the higher elevations as we made our way further into the country, into the heart of the highlands. Here were many different kinds of trees from those we had seen at lower altitudes, and hundreds of varieties of plants.

It was the last day of January, 1773, when we arrived in Santiago. Even though I had seen the city clearly in my mind, the reality of its size and the neatness of its well-ordered streets surprised me, as did the sight of people going about their business just as people did in Granada. I admired the endless rows of cobbled streets, the church spires thrust heavenward into the bluest sky I had ever seen, the façades of many sizable homes and large business establishments. I marked the preciseness of its plan and the solidity of its buildings, which contrasted so sharply with the unruliness of the land which we had just traversed. I even experienced a brief moment of regret that man had won the small battle for dominance over nature's disorder in this valley. He had not yet been able to dominate the coastal lowlands, where the land and everything on it seemed to draw its very breath and life from the waters which were so much a part of it. There, the hot humid air and thick verdant foliage were laden with the fevers and plagues that repelled man, had driven him inland, through the all but impenetrable mountains to the highlands.

And here in this valley, where man had penetrated deep into the mountains that had challenged him, he had shown his own answering defiance by using the very mountains themselves as a protective wall to enclose himself, to shut out the realization that this was only an infinitesimal portion of the whole which he had been able to overcome.

True, native villages had dotted our route, and many of them had probably stood where they were for a time longer than any man could remember. But the *indios* had been content to live off the land, make do mostly with what they could find, clearing only small plots for their simple needs, scarcely imposing their mark on the earth at all. But then our *Conquistadores* had come to Guatemala searching for gold and silver, and they had found little in comparison with the lavish wealth of Peru and the unbelievable richness of Mexico. So they had begun to extract the payment for their disappointment from the land itself. As we had neared Santiago, the villages we passed had been stamped with the unmistakable touch of Spain, for in the center of each, rising high over the simple huts of the villagers, was the spire of the Holy Catholic Church.

With increasing frequency as we drew closer to the Spanish heart of Guatemala, we passed large farms, where the descendants of the *Conquistadores* had made inroads into the wilderness, and had subdued large patches of land, ruthlessly taking what they could use and destroying that which they could not. My husband told me that he had such a farm. I knew that slowly, as endless spokes reach ever outward from the hub of a wheel, the sons of these descendants would continue to push out from Santiago, from this small bastion deep in the heart of Guatemala, until everywhere there would be evidence of such order as had been superimposed so defiantly on the Valley of Panchoy. We would struggle with the land that had tried to repel us, fighting until there was nothing further to conquer. This might take decades, or even centuries, but eventually we would emerge victorious at the edge of the sea, where the challenge had begun.

I felt all this as I entered Santiago for the first time, and I knew that from that moment forward, I was committed to be a part of it. I had been committed back in Cadiz, the moment I had stepped from the soil of Andalusia, but I had not known it then. Nor had I realized it when I first stepped ashore, or during the long and difficult journey from the coastal lowlands.

But at that moment, as I rode into Santiago behind Tomás, I knew that I was no longer an Andalusian, but a Spaniard, and whatever we Spaniards did here, good or bad, I would have to accept a share of both the credit and the blame. I abhorred the greed that had made men wrest the land so cruelly from those who had long been its caretakers, yet I could not help but admire the determination and defiance which had moved these same greedy men to design a city that bespoke permanence and declared so clearly their intention to remain. It was a surprising city to find so far from home, and I wondered at my foolishness for feeling a twinge of apprehension as the hoofs of our horses and the many donkeys resounded on the cobblestones.

We entered the city at the busy hour just before the shops closed for the long break at midday for the main meal and the rest that followed it. Tomás led us past the north side of the *Plaza Real*, the very heart of the city, calling greetings to all he saw. I had a feeling that he had planned our entrance carefully, and suspected that he had insisted we rise early that morning and ride without rest just so we could ride into Santiago at the time we would be most likely to be noticed. It did not escape my attention that those who returned Tomás's hail seemed to do so with a sort of restraint. For the first time, I began to wonder about my husband's place among the people of Santiago. Was he liked or disliked? Respected? Admired? Feared? Resented?

But such thoughts did not concern me overlong that day, for I was too busy taking in all there was to see to puzzle long over something which would be revealed to me in due time. My visions of the city had always been as though I saw it from afar, and I was truly amazed at the sophistication of its architecture. Already mingled with my curiosity and my amazement was this new-found pride in knowing that I was now a part of the accomplishment that was Santiago.

In the center of the *Plaza Real* was a large fountain into which stone mermaids spewed water from their abundant breasts. Across the plaza was a two-story building with double rows of graceful arches down its full length.

"What a beautiful building!" I commented enthusiastically, as Tomás waited for me to pull up alongside him.

"That's the Palace of the Captains General," he answered. He seemed pleased at my wonder at all I saw. "It was just completed in '64. Some of the rooms are exquisitely finished."

As I reached his side and we continued on together, he pointed to the east side of the plaza. "That's our Cathedral, and we're passing by the Palace of the *Ayuntamiento*." He nodded toward the plaza. "On market day, that will be full of natives. They come from miles around to sell whatever anyone will buy. They weave excellent fabrics."

Before we turned away from the plaza, I looked around once more to fix in my mind everything I had seen. As I did so, anxieties crowded in upon me. I pushed them to the back of my mind. Santiago was a bright city, throbbing with a life of its own. Momentarily, I thought of Granada, but the memory of it was already growing dim. Santiago was my home now, and I would certainly come to love it.

Tomás's house pleased me most of all, for it was patterned closely after those of Andalusia, and made me feel I was not so very far from home, after all. Two giant doors fronted on the street, and the house extended half a block to the corner, so that some of its windows faced on another street. It was quite obviously the house of a man of means. I felt a twinge of guilt for having misjudged Tomás, to have suspected that my dower had been of more interest to him than my person when he asked for my hand in marriage.

Tomás remained mounted as he hammered on the door imperiously with the ornate brass knocker. Then we dismounted, and he handed the reins to two slaves nearby. At length, a small door built into one of the two massive doors opened, and a native woman stood in the opening.

"*Señor*, you have come back!" Her features registered no emotion as she looked from Tomás to me. I thought again how adept the *indios* were at masking their feelings, and I wondered if she felt joy or sorrow at his return, or neither. Surely she must have wondered at my presence, but she gave no indication of curiosity.

Tomás did not bother to explain my presence, or why he had not sent a message ahead of us to advise the household of our arrival; in his mind, there was no need to apologize or explain to servants, since he credited them with no feelings and scant intelligence.

"Call my daughter," he demanded brusquely, "and tell Ricardo I have need of him at once."

78

"They are not here, *Señor*. Your daughter goes every morning to do charitable work at the hospital, and your son is at his studies at the University of San Carlos Borromeo."

"Well, then, send someone to fetch them, and at once," he insisted, obviously irritated at their absence. "And, Teresa—tell Simón to come immediately and see to the unloading of the things I have brought. I will be out shortly to direct him."

Though Tomás was upset at not finding his son and daughter on hand to greet him, my reaction was one of relief. I had been dreading the meeting and welcomed the delay. It was not only that I preferred to see my new home first. I was more than a little frightened at the prospect of my ambiguous position in the household, I the younger by far to be the *dueña* of the house. Tomás and I had lived together as man and wife for several months, and I still did not feel at ease in his presence. I had never lost the feeling that I had had the first time I raised my eyes to his, the feeling I called disquietude; I did not dare to call it by its other name of fear. What if his son and daughter also made me feel ill at ease? How could I endure living in such an atmosphere?

"Come!" Tomás said irritably. "You can't stand in the *zaguan* all day. I would think you would be anxious to see your new home."

I murmured an apology and followed behind him.

We had been standing in the entryway, the *zaguan*, which was the full width of the double entry doors, roofed but completely open on its inward side. Built into one of its side walls was a bench made of tiles of a rich deep blue and gold. Beyond this area was a grass-covered central patio, surrounded on all four sides by pillars of wood and stone, which supported the roof to a wide porch that completely surrounded it. Along the tiled walls beneath this overhang were placed various groupings of settees and chairs and tables, between the doors to the rooms, which all opened onto the patio. Giant pots containing flowering plants of every description edged the grassed area. Here and there along the inner walls were also stone and marble sculptures. As we passed them, Tomás must have noticed me looking at them with open admiration, for he smiled his approval and said, "They are the best to be found on this side of the Atlantic Ocean. Come, let me show you my real treasures. They're in the *sala*."

He took my arm and led me to the large room that occupied the front corner position of the house. He removed from his pocket a key I had noticed he always carried with him, even on shipboard, attached to the end of a gold chain. It seemed almost a ritualistic proceeding as he stood now in front of the *sala* door and hesitated. Briefly, he looked up at me, his eyes unnaturally bright. Then he inserted the key in the lock and turned it, pushing the door to the darkened room wide open.

Teresa had been behind us, and without seeming to hurry she entered the room ahead of us, and began opening the draperies and the shutters.

"I have cleaned in here only myself, *Señor*," she said as she moved from one window to the next. "Everything is just as you left it."

As the light flooded into the room, I looked around in amazement. Never had I seen such a profusion of paintings, tapestries, porcelains, carvings, and objects of handwrought gold and silver. The room was of gigantic proportions, but it was dwarfed by the clutter everywhere. I must have gasped, for Tomás said,

"It surprises you, doesn't it? You see, you married a man of considerable property."

I nodded dumbly. My father had been a wealthy man, but he had cared only for his books; the few art objects he had were of historical interest, and as a scholar he enjoyed having them in his home. Never, in our home or any other, had I seen anything to approach this concentration of such items, large and small. Richly colored oil paintings and minutely patterned tapestries crowded together on every available bit of wall space, and Persian carpets were laid end to end across the entire floor surface. The cushions on the chairs and settees were of deep crimson velvet, and the windows were hung with matching brocade. The dark wood tones of the furniture contrasted richly with what little could be seen of the white walls behind them. Individually, most of the items in the room would have been startlingly beautiful. Massed together, the opulence was so stifling I felt like running from the room.

Tomás had crossed to the inside corner of the room and was standing in front of an ornately carved triangular table. He stroked a figurine displayed on a stand centered on the table.

"A Meissen. Such a lovely thing." He seemed to be speaking more to himself than to me. "I think I shall move it into my office to make way for the other porcelains I have brought back." He walked to a smaller table. "The Abbasside miniature will look well there." It was apparent from his manner and his caressing tone of voice that he loved his treasures well.

I felt suddenly too overwhelmed by the room and its contents to remain there any longer. I slipped outside to the bright sunshine of the open patio, where I knew I would spend much of my time. I did not think I would return often to the *sala*.

After a few minutes, Tomás came out to join me, locking the door behind him and replacing the key in his pocket. "Come, I will show you to our room."

Our bedroom opened onto the main patio, as did all the major rooms of the house. Again, as I walked into the room he had indicated was ours, I was confronted with rich tapestries and brocades, and ornately designed furniture and objects of art, though not in quite such oppressive profusion as in the living room. Obviously, the more costly pieces were kept in the large locked room.

In our room, there was one dominating piece of furniture: a gigantic bed of finely carved mahogany. But even this massive item was in turn dwarfed by the immense crucifix that hung behind it. The carving reached up past the crossbeams of the high ceiling, and the bed had been moved away from the wall to make room for the bottom of the wooden cross to disappear behind it. On this cross hung the most agonizing figure of Christ I had ever seen.

Tomás stood by my side.

"Magnificent, isn't it?" Obviously, he mistook my awed silence for approval.

I started, too taken aback to answer. Such a figure would have been at home in a church, above an altar, where it belonged, where its proportions would have been in keeping with its surroundings. But here, in a bedroom—my bedroom!—the effect was hideous. A small crucifix, perhaps, such as the one I had always had at the head of my bed in Granada, but this one . . .

Clearly, Tomás did not share my opinion. "I am certain it is a Quirio Cataño. Even the experts agree, though they tell me there is no way to be positive. But I know, and that is what counts." Again, I noted the soft affectionate tone in his voice, as I had back in the *sala*. He looked at me expectantly, waiting, I knew, for an enthusiastic comment of approval. I continued to stand there, speechless, knowing I didn't dare voice my real feelings about the carving. "Is—was Cataño a well-known sculptor here?" I asked evasively.

"One of the best of our colonials." He moved closer to it, touched the nail-riddled feet of Christ. "I found this in a small village church not far from my farm. The priest and the people were reluctant to part with it, of course. But I had to have it. It took me five years, but I succeeded."

"It—I'm sure you must be very proud of it." What I did not say was that I wished fervently he had failed in his efforts or, having succeeded, had chosen some other place to hang

81

his coveted carving. It depressed me, and I knew I must see it there many times each day; it was not something which could be ignored. It depressed me just as had *Tía's* insistence that Jesus had died expressly for the sins of such as I, and as a sinner, I had caused his death. *Tía's* religion was one of suffering and eternal repentances; mine was one of hope. She would have been delighted to have such a gigantic suffering figure over her bed; I did not want it over mine.

"I bought a desk for you in Cadiz," Tomás said. "It is inlaid with ivory and silver. I'll have it put in here. Unfortunately, I had to leave it behind at the *Castillo de San Felipe,* so it may be some time before it arrives."

"Thank you. That will be nice." I tried to sound appreciative, though I would have been content with the desk I had had in my room in Granada, which I had shipped with my things. Silently, I wondered how another piece of furniture could possibly be crowded into the already over-full room.

On the other side of the arch separating the main patio from the kitchen and service patio was the dining room, which opened onto both patios. Several bathrooms and the kitchen also fronted on this second patio. The bathrooms had water piped to them, a luxury I had never had in Granada. On the side wall of this patio was a small fountain, from which water ran constantly. I commented that water must be abundant in Santiago. Tomás said it was brought down from the mountains directly into the city in three gigantic aqueducts, so that there was a never-ending supply. Most of the houses of any size had at least two fountains, he said, and some had even more.

Beyond the second patio was an area containing the stables and the servants' quarters. There were a few trees, which Tomás told me grew strange fruits. After the excessive opulence of the house, I was delighted to find such an unadorned spot, rich only with the green of nature and uncluttered with the trappings of civilization.

"Tomás, could I please have just a little corner of this area for my herbs?" I asked hopefully.

"If it pleases you. You are the lady of the house."

Pleased at his answer, contrite at having misjudged his motive in asking for my hand, I turned impulsively to him and threw my arms around his neck. "Oh, Tomás, I will try to be a good wife!"

He pulled away from me, said reprimandingly, "Come, Carlota, you must be more decorous! It would not do for the servants to witness such a demonstration."

The harshness in his voice quickly squelched my spontaneous outburst. I lowered my eyes, knowing it would not do to let him see the resentment that was bound to show in them. "I'm sorry. It will never happen again." Nor would it, I knew. Tomás's nature, distant and aloof, did not inspire such spontaneous outbursts. It was only my delight at finding that I could have my own little herb garden and my contrition at finding he had no need of my wealth that had prompted what he referred to as a "demonstration."

We were returning to the house proper when there was a flurry of sound coming from the front of the house. A young girl came running into the kitchen patio. I took in the large oval eyes, the vivid well-shaped lips, the delicately chiseled nose, the carefully coifed brown hair, the slender, softly curved figure. I would have thought her the most beautiful girl I had ever seen but for the fact that her face was cruelly pocked. It was as though nature, having created something too perfect, too lovely, had felt compelled to destroy its own handiwork, like an artist gone berserk and defacing his own masterpiece.

"Father! Why didn't you send word you were coming! I would have stayed home. Are all those things down the street yours? The line of burros stretches the whole block, and slaves—" The girl's eyes suddenly fell on me, and she stopped talking abruptly, then stammered her confusion. "Oh! I thought—well, I assumed you were alone—"

"Not quite, my dear." He pinched her cheek and kissed her, the gesture somehow out of character for him. "Now that you have greeted your old father, curtsy to your new stepmother, *doña* Carlota Isabel Muñoz de Alvarado y Paz." He turned to me. "My dear, this is my most priceless treasure of all, my Cecilia."

The girl looked at Tomás for a long minute, not troubling to hide her shock. Then she turned toward me, and the light went out of her eyes as though a veil had dropped over them. She curtsied and said coolly, "Welcome to your home, *doña* Carlota Isabel."

"Thank you, Cecilia." I tried to answer her as cordially as I could, though I was stung by her failure to hide her displeasure at my presence. I had blithely assumed that she and I would be the best of friends; it had never occurred to me that she might resent me on sight. I continued, "Please, let's have no formality between us. Will you call me Carlota, as all my friends do?"

"Certainly, Carlota." Her words complied, but there was nothing of warmth in them, and her manner remained openly disdainful.

But my concern over her obvious disapproval of me was soon pushed from my mind, for just then the heavy door at

83

the front of the house banged shut and a masculine voice boomed.

"Father! Where are you?"

When the owner of the voice appeared in the archway, filling it with his tall wide-shouldered frame, I felt as though an unseen fist had struck me a mighty blow.

I caught my breath sharply and heard myself gasp, "It's you!" before I realized I had spoken.

It was him, the young man in the glass, the one I had thought was to be my husband. I could only stare in disbelief. There was the same unruly hair, the same red-gold beard, the same face—though he was not smiling now as he had been in my vision. He had stopped talking and was staring at me open-mouthed, and it took me a moment to realize that it was my peculiar behavior that was causing his own reaction of confusion and surprise.

"I wasn't aware that we had ever met," he finally blurted out. "Who the devil are you?"

Tomás said reprovingly, "That is scarcely a proper greeting for your new stepmother, Ricardo!" As he made the formal introduction, I tried to regain something of a composed manner, and returned Ricardo's bow with a nod, my every motion feeling unreal and somehow detached from my body.

Still, everyone continued to stare at me, and I felt compelled to invent some sort of excuse for my odd behavior.

"I—I'm sorry," I stammered ineffectually, looking from one to the other. "Ricardo looks so much like someone I knew back in Granada—for a moment, I was startled. Please forgive me." I felt my mouth shape the words, heard myself say them, but it was still as if I remained apart from them and the woman who spoke them.

The explanation must have satisfied the others, for their conversation continued on around me. I was only too relieved to be momentarily ignored. In fact, I did not even hear the words that followed between the three of them, for the sound of their voices came to me dimly, as from a great distance, over the thumping of my own heart resounding in my ears.

The man in the glass was here. He existed, after all. And he was in this very house, standing not a few feet from me. But why, why had it been his face I had seen in Tatiana's crystal instead of that of my husband? Why had the crystal tricked me so cruelly, shown me not the unfeeling, arrogant, possessive man to whom I was married, but his son, young and vital and—I sought for the right words—easy to love?

It took great effort to force myself to return to the present. What the crystal had shown me had been wrong, I told myself reasonably. It was not to Ricardo that I was irrevocably wed, but to Tomás. Even as everything within me protested that I could no longer continue to accept Tomás now that I had met his son, the young man in the glass to whom I had felt so drawn, I knew that I must.

Besides, if the glass had lied to me about my husband, maybe the happy smiling young man it had shown me was a lie, too. Maybe Ricardo was not like that at all, but like his father, cold and aloof. Certainly, he showed nothing of pleasantness now as he and Tomás talked.

I was to learn that there was seldom any pleasantness between Ricardo and Tomás, for every conversation soon turned into an argument. Indeed, most started out that way. Now, as I forced my attention to what was being said, I realized that Ricardo was speaking disparagingly of the great volume of Tomás's baggage. I felt compelled to defend Tomás—perhaps because of my unwifely feelings a few minutes before—and jumped into the argument on his behalf.

"Much of what you see out in front belongs to me," I said, "My father died a year and a half ago, and since I am an only child, I brought anything from my home which I thought might be of use to us here. I also brought all of his books, and of course my clothes—"

Ricardo interrupted, "I am not referring to your things, doña Carlota, but to my father's baubles. I recognize too well his careful crating." He turned again to Tomás, said accusingly, "I thought you went to Spain to sell a few of your precious possessions, to bring back gold to pay your creditors. They've not stopped dunning us since the day you left, you know. It has been all we could do to keep them from breaking down the door! If it hadn't been for our legacies from Tía María, Cecilia and I would have starved! The bakers even refused—"

"That's quite enough, Ricardo," Tomás interjected angrily. "I want no advice from you on the handling of my financial affairs!" Then he turned to me. "The excitement of our arrival has certainly wearied you. Cecilia can tell Teresa to serve you dinner in our room. Then you can rest as long as you like."

I let him take my arm and lead me to our room, knowing I had heard more than he cared to have me hear, and knowing, too, that he was using such a show of solicitousness as an excuse to keep me from hearing more. He could not have known that I, too, was relieved to have an excuse to escape so that I could sift my thoughts in private.

Thus it was that my first meal in Santiago was a solitary one, and one for which I had little appetite. Why, why had it been Ricardo's face that I had seen that morning a lifetime

85

before on the ship? The shock of meeting him face to face was too great, my thoughts too tumultuous for any interest in food. I knew I must try to eat something, so I picked up my fork and took a few bites of beans. But I swallowed them only with effort, and soon gave up trying to force appetite where there was none.

Remembering how Dolores had always brushed my hair when I was upset, I pushed away the dinner tray and removed my combs, then started to brush, trying to imitate the soothing rhythmic strokes she had so often used. But it was no use. I found no comfort that day in brushing my hair myself.

Exhausted by the months of travel, saddened by the loss of Dolores, disenchanted with my marriage, discouraged by Cecilia's hostility, and finally, totally unnerved by finding that Ricardo was real after all, I threw the brush down and gave way to the confusion and frustration that filled my eyes with bitter tears.

Santiago—February, 1773

CHAPTER V

In the days that followed, I avoided Ricardo as much as possible, unwilling to trust my reaction to his presence. But it was impossible to evade him at mealtimes and that time, after supper, when the four of us usually went into the room adjoining the dining room. This was one of two rooms in the house which had a fireplace—our bedroom was the other—and frequently I ordered a small fire to take the chill off the cool evening air.

The furnishings of the room were, in contrast to the rest of the house, startlingly simple. It was not a room to which those outside the family were invited, which earned it Tomás's neglect. In that very neglect lay its charm, for it contained little bric-a-brac, the plainer pieces of furniture, the more mellowed carpets. I found it a delightful relief from the over-decoration of the rest of the house.

At the times the family was together, Ricardo and Tomás were usually so busy baiting each other that they scarcely took note of Cecilia or me. I found this constant bickering excessively wearing, but on the other hand I welcomed the distraction it presented. I could keep my eyes down, either upon my plate or my sewing, and was seldom called upon to speak.

And yet, despite the impersonal nature of our meetings, I felt irresistibly drawn to Ricardo. He had done nothing to make me feel this way, and I knew I must fight the feeling with all my strength, but the easier solution was to avoid him. I had learned on what days he came back from lectures early, and I generally managed to be in my room at those times. Sometimes, he returned at an unexpected hour and caught me sitting on the covered porch that surrounded the central patio, but he would greet me so brusquely at these times that I began to wonder if he were anxious as I to avoid any unnecessary encounters between us.

Friendship with Cecilia I would have welcomed, for never had I so felt the need of someone to talk with, but she remained cool and barely civil toward me. The second day after my arrival, she handed me her ring of keys and with it the responsibility of running the household, which numbered fourteen including the servants.

I had been surprised to find that Cecilia had been acting as *dueña* of the house for the previous three years, since the death of Tomás's oldest sister, who had come in to manage the affairs of the household on the death of his first wife, Pilar. It seemed odd to me that no replacement had been brought in for his sister when she died, with a young unmarried girl in the house. When I had learned there had been no older woman in the household all that time, I had unthinkingly blurted out,

"Then you have had no *dueña* for three years now, Cecilia?"

"You may be sure my behavior has been above reproach," she had replied icily.

"I didn't mean—I didn't intend to imply that it hadn't been," I had stammered, embarrassed, and she had made no effort to set me at ease.

Now, I accepted the keys from her. "I'll need your help," I said as I attached them around my waist. "There are so many things here to which I'm unaccustomed—different foods and different customs, perhaps—and I would like for you to tell me about them. Besides, I want to manage the household as it has been done in the past. Would you show me around and tell me what is expected of me?"

She shook her head and said flatly, "There's nothing I can tell you that you can't learn from Teresa. Certainly you will have your own way of doing things and won't care to copy mine. Besides, I have little time to spare. I work many hours as a volunteer at the hospital."

"Very well," I answered, trying to swallow my resentment at her abrupt rebuff. "I'll do the best I can."

She was right in saying that I did not need her help, for I soon learned that it was Teresa and not Cecilia who had controlled the household staff in the absence of a firmer hand. And without the authority of a *dueña*, the house had been run only poorly.

If Cecilia secretly hoped that I would fail to maintain order, she was disappointed. I was determined to be successful, and kept constant check on the *indios* who served us to be certain that meals were served promptly and properly, the horses kept well-groomed, the furniture polished frequently, and Tomás's treasures kept free of dust. I threw myself wholeheartedly into my responsibilities, welcoming them as something to keep from my mind my confused feelings about Ricardo, the lack of understanding in my marriage, and my inability to win Cecilia's friendship.

I only wished I had not minded Cecilia's disdain, but such was my nature that I felt compelled to win her approval, and was determined to break through the barrier of her hostility.

One morning after I had been in Santiago several weeks, I came upon her seated on one of the settees under the roofed porch of the main patio. I smiled at her, hoping, as always, that a pleasant manner might melt her icy reserve, though that would seem as impossible as trying to remove all the snow from a mountaintop in midwinter. She was reading one of my books, a volume of Cervantes I had always treasured.

"I see you're enjoying one of my favorites," I said, seating myself in a chair near her. "I have always loved Cervantes's writings. I couldn't stand the thought of leaving his works behind."

Cecilia looked at me and closed the book with a snap. "I'm sorry. I didn't realize it was one of your favorites, or I certainly would never have taken it." She offered the volume to me.

I tried to wave it away, bewildered to realize she had misunderstood my intention, and had mistaken my friendly remark as a reprimand.

"You don't understand," I protested. "I was only delighted to know that you were enjoying it, as I do." My father had been bound to his best friends by shared tastes in literature. How could I explain to her that I had only been grasping at her interest in the book as a possible wedge on which to base the friendship I sought?

She leaned over and dropped the volume in my lap, and she shook her head, refusing to take it back, when I protested and proffered it to her. I laid it on the table between us, and stood up, wishing I had never interrupted her. "I should not have disturbed you. It was thoughtless of me. I'm sorry. If you'll excuse me, I must see what vegetables Teresa found in the market."

On that flimsy excuse, I left her. When I passed by that side of the patio a few minutes later, I noticed that Cecilia was gone and the book lay where I had left it on the table.

There was a third patio in our house, which Tomás had not shown me on our first day in Santiago. It was the *patio de placer*, too small for anything but family use, and was accessible through a passageway that led from an arch of the main patio, diagonally opposite the *zaguan*. It could also be entered through a gate in the wall that separated it from the kitchen garden and stables. Only one side of that patio had a roofed area, and that was the side formed by the back wall of the house. The remaining two sides were enclosed by two high masonry walls that formed the back corner boundary of the property. On one of these walls was a small decorative *pila*, a fountain of running water. Behind it, on a niche of colorful tiles, stood a small statue of the Virgin, which, I was to learn later, was a painstakingly exact replica of Our Lady of Mercy in the Church of *La Merced*. It was a mark of Tomás's character that he could not bear for the churches to possess treasures which he could not own, so he frequently commissioned silversmiths or sculptors to copy what he could not buy.

Nevertheless, the statuette of Our Lady of Mercy was lovely in its setting, and I had been delighted to find the quiet corner, away from the comings and goings of the family and the servants. I liked to sit in one of the chairs under the roofed area and read, or, if the day started out cool, move into the open portion of the tiled patio onto one of the stone benches and bask in the warmth of the mid-morning sun. The constant murmur of the water was soothing, and drowned out the distraction of the street noises on the other side of the wall.

I had been in Santiago almost a month when I decided one morning to sort through the herbs and seeds I had brought with me, looking for similarities between some of them and any of the local plants and leaves I had gathered and pressed. I took them to the small patio and knelt on the weathered red tiles, laying out the various packets and leaves in front of me. So engrossed was I that I didn't notice that Ricardo had returned from his morning at the University. I heard the gate from the kitchen garden swing open and I looked up, startled to see him coming toward me.

"Oh! I didn't think you would be back to early!" I jumped up and brushed off my skirt guiltily, as though I had been a naughty child caught doing something I shouldn't. I had the uneasy feeling that he had been standing at the gate watching me for some time. I wanted to pick up my leaves and herbs and run from there, but I would have been at a loss to explain such an action.

In my haste to get up, my foot caught in the hem of my dress, and I stumbled. Ricardo's arm shot out to steady me.

"Steady, there!" He smiled at me, and it was as if I were

again looking into the polished crystal as I had that morning on the ship. I could no more have broken my gaze at that moment than I could have on that previous occasion, and I stood, unmoving, held by his smile, by his eyes, unable to talk, or to move, or to think of anything except his nearness and the way the flesh of my arm tingled where he was touching it.

It was he who broke the spell, for his smile turned at last to a puzzled frown he asked,

"Why do you run from me, Carlota? Do I frighten you so?"

I noticed that he had dropped the title *doña*, and I knew that it was right that he had. It was unthinkable that he could continue to use the formal title of respect.

I could not tell him that I was frightened not of him but of myself. I could not tell him that I was powerless to fight the way my heart raced at his smile and my flesh tingled at his touch. I felt my hand rise involuntarily to my throat, as though it could stop the wild beating of my heart, but it couldn't. Nothing could stop it while Ricardo was near me. Nothing could stop the way I felt I was being drawn to him in spite of my resolve.

A voice of reason inside me cried out that I could not be attracted to him, that I did not even know him, that I was married to Tomás. But my feelings at that moment were ungoverned by either reason or rationalization, for my emotions held me in their sway.

I could not blurt out to Ricardo the shamefulness of what I felt, so I told again the lie that had come to my lips the first day we met. "You remind me of someone—"

"And this—someone? Was he someone who meant a great deal to you?" His voice was understanding, sympathetic.

I groped for an answer, could only say in a whisper, "He—he might have, if things had been different."

"I'm sorry," he said. "I've sensed that my presence makes you uncomfortable, and I've been trying to give you time to get used to me. But we can't go on avoiding each other forever, Carlota, can we? After all, you are married to my father and we do live in the same house."

"Of course. I know I've been foolish, and—"

"It's nothing I've said or done, is it? I have the feeling that it isn't just that I remind you of someone, but that it has to do with me—"

"You've done nothing!" I interrupted hastily. "Nothing at all. I'm sorry—"

"It's I who am sorry for making you uncomfortable."

He moved away from me toward the arched passageway,

and as he did so, he smiled again. I am certain he intended his smile to set me at ease. How could he know it did anything but that?

Until that brief encounter, I hadn't realized how much I had hoped to find him as ill-tempered as Tomás, how much I had wanted to feel repelled by him, to have him shatter the dream conjured by me in a piece of polished crystal. Until now, I had seen him only as a hostile young man, and I had noted with relief that he had shown no tendency to be either as smiling or as agreeable as I had thought the man in the glass to be. But until then, I had never seen him except in Tomás's presence, with each of them like a piece of flint, ready to strike fire at one word from the other.

Now, with me, Ricardo had shown the side of himself that I had hoped did not exist. He had been gentle and understanding and considerate. He had sincerely tried to end the uneasiness he realized his presence caused me.

Instead, he had only increased it.

I tried to return my attention to my herbs, but I was too distraught to concentrate. My heart continued to race as I carefully returned the herb packets to their box and replaced the pressed leaves in the pages of a book.

As I emerged into the large patio, still upset, I almost collided with Tomás. I had no desire to talk with him just then, and would have walked around him, but he barred my way.

He took my shoulders in his hands and stopped me, asked suspiciously, "What's the matter? You're upset. I saw Ricardo just come from this direction. Did he say something to offend you?" It was easy to tell from his tone of voice that he hoped to be able to blame Ricardo for my agitation.

"Of course not," I insisted. "It's just that I was sorting my herbs, and I was thinking of how I missed the hills around Granada." I spoke hesitantly. Lying never came easily to my lips, and it seemed that lately I must heap lie upon lie.

To my relief, he appeared to accept my explanation. "This is your home now," he said sternly as he released my shoulders. "You must not make yourself feel badly by letting your thoughts dwell on Andalusia."

"I know," I agreed readily, anxious to be gone from his prying questions. "I'm sure I'll grow to like it here. It is so beautiful, and the climate so pleasant."

"You've been doing very well with the servants and the house. The meals have improved, and the house is much cleaner than it used to be."

"Thank you. I've tried to do my best. Teresa is a great help. I don't know what I would do without her."

"She seems to do well under your supervision."

I nodded, surprised by his unaccustomed praise, accepting the subject as an excuse to leave. "I must go speak with her about dinner. If you will excuse me?"

He stepped aside to let me pass. Relieved, I put my herbs in my room and hurried to the kitchen patio to find Teresa.

At first, Teresa had been suspicious of me. But *Tía* Juana's insistence that I learn her exacting methods of housekeeping stood me in good stead, and I won from Teresa what was first grudging respect and later became open admiration by bringing order into the loosely run household. I introduced economies, some of which were exceedingly obvious, and, by close supervision, turned slackness into efficiency. Once I had gained Teresa's acceptance, the other servants acknowledged me fully as the mistress of the house.

Teresa's acceptance began to show itself in little ways; at first, she told me only reluctantly what she had bought at the market and planned for the day's meals. Her manner was not insolent, but in a subtle way she seemed to let me know I was being tested, almost dare me to change her plans, which I knew I could not do if I expected to have her help. So I began a subtle campaign of my own, suggesting but never insisting on changes, and gradually she began to consult me before she made the menus. A little later, she began to ask my advice about what to buy at the market each day, and about what rooms I wanted cleaned on certain days. She was particularly pleased when I mixed for her a special paste *Tía* had always used to polish our silver at home.

"Why, this will save hours each week!" she exclaimed when I showed her how effectively it removed the tarnish. Her even white teeth showed in one of her rare smiles, making her look almost a girl. Her wide face, her high cheekbones, her hair drawn back severely into a knot at the nape of her neck, her mouth usually set in an expressionless neutral position, she had seemed to be well into middle age. When she smiled, I was not so sure she was more than thirty.

One day in early March when I had shown her how to make a delicious stew from left-over lamb—actually, a copy of the gypsy stew I had eaten so frequently and often helped to make—she remarked, "Oh, if only you could teach *Señorita* Cecilia to do things like this, how much better prepared she would be to manage a house of her own some day!" Then she frowned and added, "Though I doubt she'll need to know, the poor girl. It isn't likely she will ever marry."

"She has no suitors?" I asked, but I knew the answer. Not one had come calling on her in the month and more I had been in Santiago.

"Not now, not since—ah, *Señora*, it is so sad! If only you could have seen her before." She shook her head slowly from side to side. "Such a lovely girl she was, and so gay, so popular. She was like her mother, who loved a fiesta—"

I interrupted her sharply. "When I asked you last week what the first *Señora* was like, you said you didn't remember her."

Teresa shrugged. "I don't remember much about her. I only heard . . ." She left the thought incomplete and continued, "It was no wonder *Señorita* Cecilia had no time to learn to manage a house. Many suitors were trying to win her favor, and even a good many of the married men liked to crowd around her at the fiestas. Her old aunt used to tell her she must learn something of housekeeping, that there was more to marriage than fiestas and dancing. 'Time enough when I'm married, *Tía*' she would say laughingly, and the old woman would click her tongue as though she disapproved, though it was plain to see she did not.

"How those two loved each other! But it was that devotion that brought *Señorita* Cecilia her misfortune, for in the smallpox epidemic three years ago, the old woman was struck down, and nothing would do for *Señorita* Cecilia but that she must nurse her herself. If the *Señor* had been here, surely he would have prevented it, but he was at the farm. The old woman did, and *Señorita* Cecilia caught the pox—a bad case, the worst I have ever seen, and I have nursed many. But she had the strength of youth, and she recovered.

"Perhaps because *Señorita* Cecilia's skin was so clear, so smooth, that was why the sores looked so big and ugly, and festered so much. And there were many of them, too, on her beautiful face. But while the scabs held, there was always the hope that perhaps the pits might not be too deep. Then, one by one, the scabs fell off, and each one seemed to cut a little deeper into the skin that had been so creamy white a few weeks before.

"When the last scab fell off, she scrubbed her face clean and dressed bravely in one of her best gowns and sent word to her fiancé that she would see him, that the contagion was over. They were to have been married that very day, but of course when the disease struck the wedding had to be postponed. He was handsome, the son of a nobleman from Spain. A fine match, everyone said. But I was there, in the room, when he first laid eyes on her again, and I watched him, saw the look of horror that crossed his face. He soon recovered himself and said he was glad she was better at last.

"Then she dismissed me, and I left the room, but I knew that she, too, had seen that look on his face."

"Did he break their engagement?" I asked, feeling sorry for the girl who suddenly found herself without the beauty that had earned her so much adulation.

"There was no more talk of a wedding, from that day on," she said, "but later that day, after her fiancé had gone, *Señorita* Cecilia told me she could never marry him, waking up each day with the fear she would surprise him and catch again that look on his face. 'You were there, Teresa,' she told me. 'You saw it, too. I know you did.' She studied her face in the mirror in much the same manner I have seen the *Señor* study a painting he had commissioned and which displeased him.

"And I had seen it. What could I say? So I answered, 'Some day, another young man will come along, one who sees past the scars, and he will see the beauty deep inside you, the beauty of your soul that made you nurse your aunt, even knowing you might get the pox.'

"She put down the mirror and said, 'I am too ugly.' After that, she never gave any other suitors a chance. She wore the heavy veil of mourning for a full two years, and she refused all invitations, refused even to attend the fiestas in the streets, long after mourning for her aunt would have permitted her to go. Now she no longer has the excuse to wear the heavy veil, and she stays at home except to visit a few friends or to go to mass or to work at the hospital. Even before you came, she spent much of her time there, but now, as you know, she is seldom home except at mealtimes."

I nodded, knowing that it was my unexpected presence that had deprived Cecilia of a feeling of usefulness in the house. She no doubt felt resentful about Tomás's remarriage, but what could I possibly do to make amends? At least, Teresa's story had explained, in part, Cecilia's behavior toward me.

"Thank you, Teresa, for telling me this. Knowing it helps me understand. Maybe she and I can get to be friends."

"If only she would meet some nice young man!" Teresa said. "But how is that possible, when she tries so hard not to be seen?"

Poor Cecilia! I could sense what a tragedy it must have been for her, a girl whose life had revolved around her beauty and her popularity, to be transformed in so short a time into such ugliness that her own fiancé could not—or would not—hide his aversion to her! Now, her scars had mellowed, but the damage to her spirit had been permanent. It was hard to imagine that the quiet bitter girl I knew had once been the fun-loving girl Teresa had described to me.

That explained, then, why Cecilia always begged a headache or something pressing she needed to do when she was at home at the time we left on our daily carriage ride. It was the custom for those who would see their acquaintances and be seen by them to go riding in the late afternoon, making at least four or five turns around the *Plaza Real* in the heart of Santiago, then getting out and strolling around the plaza. Tomás seemed to delight in making a fetish of this ritual, which I thought totally pointless, and he insisted I be bedecked in my finest afternoon dresses. Occasionally, we were invited to some home for coffee or tea or a glass of prized sherry, or Tomás would hail someone and invite them to our house, but usually we had no place to go, and I found the custom tedious. Tomás knew any number of people, but there is a world of difference between acquaintances and friends, and it was soon apparent to me that Tomás had no real friends. However, as the fourth son of a minor nobleman, he automatically had some standing in the community, which was augmented by his apparent wealth. The only good that came of our pointless rides was that I did meet a few people, and several of the wives came calling on me afterward. I returned their calls, and was certain enough of my ability to make friends to know that eventually some of these beginnings would result in lasting friendships. But that would take time, I knew, for life was very formalized in Santiago, and even though I was a *chapetona*, recently arrived from Spain, which in itself gave me an elevated status, I must first be inspected and appraised before I was accepted. Social strata were strictly observed, with *indios* at the bottom and those of noble birth or born in Spain at the top of the scale. It was as though Santiago must enforce a code far more strict than that of the homeland to prove to itself that it was indeed a part of it. The riding of a horse was limited to those of pure Spanish blood, and a *mestizo* who dared mount a horse would soon find himself shipped to the mines for several years—a form of slavery from which few returned, for not many lasted throughout their terms.

One day as I was waiting for Tomás to send word to the coachman to bring the carriage around, Teresa was working nearby and I asked her if Tomás had taken Cecilia out in the carriage for such rides before her illness.

"Yes, *Señora*, every day, unless he was at the farm. He bought her fine clothes, and it was plain to see he was very proud of her. But afterwards, she did not want to go and he did not press her. In fact, the rides stopped almost completely then, except for the few times he went alone."

I had become accustomed to Teresa by then, and had learned to look for clues to her thoughts in a slight change in tone of her voice or a clipping of her words. Now, I caught the faint tone of disapproval in her voice, and I nodded my understanding, knowing well why the rides had stopped, why he had not insisted Cecilia go. Tomás loved perfection, in women as well as in art objects. I felt that he counted it extraordinary good fortune that I was comely as well as wealthy, and I knew that he merely wanted to display me on these foolish afternoon rides, like one of his statuettes or bits of carved jade, for all of Santiago to see. I wondered if he had felt more affection for Cecilia before her illness, when he could display her loveliness?

I tried to push the unworthy thought from my mind, but another quickly took its place. Tomás seemed to think a lot of Cecilia still. Perhaps it was because her illness had changed her from the spirited young girl Teresa had described to one whose meekness matched her subdued appearance, and now she lacked the spirit to disagree with him. Tomás liked to dominate people.

But Ricardo he could not dominate, and it may have been this which irked him constantly. The two of them never had a conversation that was not laced with barbs and undercuts, as though each must try to outdo the other. They were forever parrying and thrusting, like two skilled swordsmen, each refusing to let himself be bested by his opponent.

From a conversation between them accidentally overheard, I learned what seemed to be causing much of the friction between them. One morning, I happened to be sitting at the inlaid desk Tomás had given me—which had arrived only a few weeks behind us from the *Castillo de San Felipe* after all—when they started to bicker just outside my door. They never argued quietly, so I could not have failed to hear them.

I heard Tomás hail Ricardo as he was passing by. "I want to talk to you."

"Can't it wait?" Ricardo asked irritably. "I'm late for an important lecture."

"No, it can't." Tomás's voice reflected the answering irritability they never failed to provoke in each other.

"What is it then?" Ricardo spoke impatiently.

"I have arranged for an appointment for you this afternoon at *La Merced*."

"Why?"

"So you can talk with them."

"I've no desire to enter their order."

"You could at least hear what they have to say." Tomás's words were spoken with an attempt at persuasiveness, but he could not keep the impatience out of his voice. "What harm would it do?"

Ricardo countered, "What good would it do? I've nothing to say to them or they to me."

"It's a good life, Ricardo. You'd never have to worry about a thing. I understand they have their own private fishing area, and boats, and they say their library is the finest."

"I'm studying law, remember, Father? I intend to be a lawyer, a good one. And I have never cared for fishing."

"You like to read. They live very comfortably." Tomás's tone was almost cajoling.

"I'm not a monk."

"Is it the celibacy that bothers you? Remember, I was a widower for nineteen years. One grows accustomed—"

Ricardo's laugh was sharp and derisive. "Come now, Father, how would you know about celibacy? You've had Magdalena out at the farm all the time, even, to judge by the ages of her children, while my mother was alive. And you still use her, don't you?"

"Silence!" Tomás roared, his voice more desperate than angry, and I knew that Ricardo had spoken the truth, a truth Tomás had probably considered his own discreetly guarded secret.

Nor would Ricardo be silenced. He continued, "All the while Cecilia and I were growing up, we weren't supposed to guess about Magdalena, were we? But we knew! Her children, the whole string of them—*mestizos,* not full-blooded *indios* as you would have us believe—"

"Get out of here!" Tomás shouted. "Go to your precious lecture, since you're in no mood to listen to reason!"

After that, there was only the sound of the door at the front of the house being banged shut.

I suppose I should have been shocked to realize that my husband had fathered a string of half-breed children, though I knew that *india* mistresses were not uncommon in Guatemala. Had I felt any affection for Tomás, the matter might have bothered me. But even the gratitude I had felt toward him at the beginning of our marriage had disappeared the day of my arrival in Santiago, when Ricardo had let slip the fact that Tomás had been in desperate financial straits when he had asked for my hand.

When my original suspicions were not only confirmed, but I found out that his need for gold had been more frantic than I could have imagined, I had felt not disappointment but relief, for the burden of guilt I had carried at not being able to feel the slightest love for my husband was lifted from me. It had been a marriage of expediency for both of us—one of us desperate as the other—and any debt of gratitude I had previously felt I owed Tomás was cancelled by that knowledge.

98

Nor was I particularly grateful for the courtesy with which he treated me, for I had a feeling that his consideration for me was the same as that he showed toward his other possessions, his figurines and sculptures and paintings, knowing that good care enhances and protects. Nor would he have let the world see him behave in any but the most correct fashion toward me; that would have gained him disapproval, and above all he craved approval. But, paradoxically, though no one could have found fault with his manners, the approval for which he yearned was awarded him grudgingly, if at all. And only those who were dependent on him for business dealings pretended to friendship with him. It had not taken me long to realize that my husband was not a popular man.

I had thought it odd that Tomás had never mentioned anyone in his family to me, with the exception of his eldest sister who had died of the pox three years before. I knew he came from a large family, but sensed that he did not want me to ask about them. Shortly after our arrival in Santiago, I discovered why.

Tomás had two sisters and three brothers living in Santiago, but of the five, I learned that not one remained on speaking terms with him by that year of 1773. That, then, had been the reason Cecilia was left without a *dueña* on the death of her aunt. Her mother, I learned, had been an only child of two *chapetones*, so there were no relatives on that side of the family on whom Tomás could call. And he could scarcely call on his own family, when they refused to even acknowledge him when they passed on the street! It was certainly an unfavorable testimony to his character. It was easy to understand the estrangement, however, if he had been as ill-tempered with them as he had just been—and always was—with Ricardo.

As the house fell into silence after Ricardo left, I wondered idly if Tomás still took the native woman to his bed. He probably did, and, if so, I was not sorry about it, for it undoubtedly limited the nights he took possession of me.

And that is the way I thought of our relationship. He took possession; he never tried to awaken in me a response to the feelings I seemed to arouse in him. His caresses were for his own pleasure, never for mine, and when, his passion slaked, he lay beside me totally relaxed, I had to fight down the feeling that my body had been used. Each time, I would hope that something I wanted would come of our being together.

I desperately wanted a child, even though that child must belong to Tomás, too. He also wanted a child—in fact, he was almost obsessed with his desire for me to conceive—but I did not imagine it was for the same reason. I could not imagine him a doting father. He wanted another possession, I supposed, another son to bear his name, one perhaps more easily molded to his liking than Ricardo, and less rebellious.

I wanted a child—many children—to fill my days, to accept the love lying dormant within me, waiting for someone on whom to lavish it. I had loved *Mamá; Papá*, in his quiet undemonstrative way, had loved me, and I had loved him in return; and Tatiana, I realized even more since she was gone from me, I had loved very deeply. But they were all gone, lost to me forever. There was at that time only one person on whom I felt I could have lavished my love, and I dared not even think his name, lest it release an uncontrollable flood of passion, which I was able to keep in check only with conscious effort.

We had arrived in Guatemala during the season they call summer, which does not come at the same time of year as our Andalusian summers. There, though less pronounced than in the higher altitudes of some of the other Spanish provinces, the seasons come in rotation, easily defined by the difference in temperature. Not so in Guatemala, where, because of its closeness to the equator, there is relatively little variation from one month to the next, and the main thing that differentiates one season from another is the rainfall, or lack of it. Tomás and I had arrived in late January, just as the dry portion of the year, called summer, was getting well under way. In May, or sometimes not till June, I was told, the rains would start, beginning in the months of winter, of predictable daily thunder showers, usually in the afternoons, quickly over and followed by a resumption of the sunshine. And this, they said, was a slightly warmer time of year than the portion called summer.

In the mild climate of the Valley of Panchoy, it seemed odd to talk of the coming of winter, with all its meaning to me of chill winds and shortened days. I found the climate of Santiago a delight. It was never too hot, yet I had no need to reach for a wrap after mid-morning until the sun had set. Then, the temperature again dropped until the sun showed itself over the mountains the following day, spreading again its blanket of warmth over the valley. And these months I was experiencing, I kept reminding myself, were still the cold months of late winter back home.

Yet to some, most notably the servants, there was something wrong with the weather this year of 1773. When I heard their vague complaints, I asked them what fault they could possibly find with such an enjoyable climate. They would only shrug and say, "It is not the same this year."

Simón, the *indio* who was in charge of our stables, said to me one day as he was adjusting my stirrups when I was preparing to go riding with Tomás. "*Agua* and *Fuego* must talk with each other. They do not like this weather."

Tomás had to ride to the adjoining Valley of Almolonga on business, and I had begged him to let me accompany him. He had finally reluctantly agreed.

Puzzled at Simón's odd remark, I asked, "What do you mean?"

He pointed toward *Agua* to the south, the volcanic mountain whose gradual sloping sides came almost to a peak. "*Junaipú*— you call it *Agua*— is there and cannot get out to talk to *Fuego*." As he spoke, his finger moved along the horizon to stop at one of the trio of peaks to the southwest. "Sometimes, *Agua* and *Fuego* must talk with each other, and one must go see what the other wants. Then the ground shakes as they talk."

"Do you mean an earthquake?" I asked impatiently. I had become well aware of the history of the Valley of Panchoy. Since the capital had been moved there from the Valley of Almolonga over two hundred years before, countless tremors had shaken it. Maybe Simón was right, maybe much of it was tied in with *Agua* and *Fuego*, for I knew that, from time to time, *Fuego* had erupted violently, disgorging tongues of flaming lava on the countryside. And our valley had been shaken often by violent tremors. Hardly a building had stood intact, I had heard, after the big quake that had come on the day of San Miguel in 1717. But since the less catastrophic quake of Santa Casamiro in 1751, only minor rumblings had occasionally shaken the city a little, setting chandeliers to swaying, or tumbling a vase or water jug from a table or shelf. There had even been some faint rumblings since my arrival, but they were so fleeting and insignificant that I had not even been aware of them unless my eyes had happened to be fastened on something that swayed ever so slightly. I had become accustomed to these small tremors, and scarcely took note of them anymore.

Now, Simón looked at me long and hard. "I am talking about *Agua*. And *Fuego*. There are those who can talk to the gods that dwell in *Fuego*. They should go and talk to them, find out what they want. Maybe they can be stilled."

It was a measure of the way the servants had accepted me that he dared voice such pagan thoughts to me. Still, I knew I must admonish him. If Tomás were to overhear such talk, he would be quick to raise shouts of heresy and see that the man was publicly beaten in the *Plaza Real*.

"Hush, Simón," I hissed softly, lest my words reach Tomás, who was just emerging from the stable with the

101

groom who led his mount. "The priest has taught you there is only one God."

"Yes, *Señora*," he said obediently. "I know, and He is very powerful. Perhaps then He will talk to the gods that dwell in *Fuego* for us." A fleeting smile played around the corners of his mouth before he resumed again that look devoid of all expression.

He tugged at the lower stirrup and took hold of my booted foot to slide it into place.

I could not repress my own smile. I had heard that the natives had obediently accepted the religion of their conquerors by allowing themselves to be baptized and dutifully praying to the one God. But I wondered how many of them concealed a pagan heart behind a Christian exterior, as Simón surely did. I had not the slightest doubt that he would continue to hope that someone would discuss things properly with the gods he was certain lived in *Fuego*.

Tomás was soon ready, but it was easy to see he was not in the best of moods. "I don't see why you are so anxious to come with me," he grumbled as our horses clattered over the streets of the city. "There is nothing in the Valley of Almolonga that can possibly be of interest to you."

"It's a beautiful day for a ride," I insisted, refusing to let my own spirits be dampened by his dourness, "and I love getting out into the open countryside."

"I shouldn't have agreed to let you come. The jarring—it's no wonder you can't conceive. Be sure that when you do, there will be no foolishness about rides in the country, or anywhere else."

It was the expectation of just such a threatened limitation that had kept me from sharing with him what I had suspected for several weeks. I would keep silent a few weeks longer. Time enough to tell him when I was certain, when I could no longer put it off. And by then perhaps I would no longer feel inexplicably uneasy about my pregnancy, for it was just as much this uneasiness that kept me from telling him as my fear of the limitations he would impose upon me once he found out. But perhaps it was not too soon to try to make him change his mind about permitting me to ride, at least during the early months. Nine months of inactivity seemed unbearable to contemplate.

"My mother rode every day until two days before I was born," I boasted, immediately wishing I had not spoken the foolish words. No lady, gently born and properly reared, would have ridden a horse once her pregnancy became easily discernible, and I could never tell him I spoke of a gypsy woman called Tatiana. "She rode only in private where no

102

one could see her, of course," I added lamely when he looked at me sharply.

Once we were out of the city, we urged our horses to a gallop, and it did not take us long to reach the Valley of Almolonga. It was here that the capital of Guatemala had been established in 1527, there to remain until the rain of utter destruction visited on it by *Agua* less than twenty-four years later, which had prompted the movement of the capital to Panchoy.

Almolonga was situated directly between *Agua* and *Fuego*. No wonder, then, that it had been so thoroughly devastated when, as Simón would have claimed, *Agua* had gone to talk to *Fuego*, sending a destructive torrent of water amid the harsh tremors that leveled all but a few walls of the town, killing Spaniard and *indio*, rich and poor alike.

I looked from *Agua* to *Fuego*, and I knew, then, what it was that I had sensed when I had first seen Santiago and the Valley of Panchoy in those recesses of my mind where I was able to see things and places and people I had never laid eyes upon. Here, right here, beneath my horse's hoofs, was the force I had sensed and feared. And I knew now that one day soon, such a force would destroy the tranquility of the peaceful green valley in which Santiago lay, just as it had destroyed the other city long ago in this valley. I could see it all too clearly, in my mind: the Santiago I knew, with its walls crumbling and its roofs caving in. I saw people running, dogs scurrying, horses bolting. And I felt it, I who had never felt an earthquake, save for the few minor tremors I had experienced in Santiago, felt the ground tremble and sway beneath me. I saw the front door of our house, felt my eyes riveted on it. It was open, and swinging crazily, and I wondered irrelevantly why Teresa hadn't latched it. Someone had just gone in there, was inside, someone important to me. Who?

"Carlota! What's the matter?" Tomás's sharp voice brought me abruptly back to the present. "You look as though you have seen the devil himself."

I looked at him, hardly seeing him, overpowered with my sudden realization of the tremendousness of the power trapped within the earth, power which certainly no mortal could control.

But I could not share with Tomás what I had just seen and felt. He would think me mad, or possessed.

"I was just thinking of what it was like here, when the valley shook and the side of *Agua* broke, and water poured down on the town." I hoped the semi-truth would explain to his satisfaction the expression he had caught on my face.

103

"What foolishness! That was over two hundred years ago." He dismissed it with a wave of his hand, as though time for the earth were measured by the same dimension as for man. "Come now, let's hurry along. I must see about ordering some maize. If we don't hurry, we'll be out after dark." He signaled his horse to action.

"I'm sorry," I said, nudging my horse to follow. "I didn't mean to delay you."

He did not answer, and we rode the rest of the way in silence. Later, as we returned by the same route, I felt again the overpowering force massed beneath the earth between the two volcanos, and I shuddered.

Next time Tomás had business here, I knew I would not ask to go with him. I did not want to come to the Valley of Almolonga again.

Santiago—March, 1773

CHAPTER VI

One night several weeks after our ride to Almolonga, we were sitting in the informal room next to the dining room. I was mending one of Tomás's shirts, while he expounded at great length about the prestige enjoyed by the Franciscan order. Ricardo, who had moved close to the candelabra so that its light would fall on the pages of his book, finally snapped the book shut and looked at his father exasperatedly.

"Why, Father?"

"Why what?" I looked up from my mending to see his displeasure at the interruption.

"Why do you keep trying to push me in a direction I have no desire to go?" Before Tomás could answer, he continued, "It's not that I'm costing you one *cuartillo* by remaining at home while I attend the University. You know I've been contributing generously for my board and paying all my own expenses from *Tía's* legacy to me. So I'm taking nothing from you. Then why are you so eager to be rid of me? I have offered to move out of the house, but when I tried it last year you begged me to come back, because it had set people to talking. So that can't be what you want. Just what do you want of me?"

Tomás fixed Ricardo with a hard stare. "You know very well what would please me most. I want you to enter the oldest and most respected order in the New World. Why shouldn't I? It's certainly more commendable to work for the glory of the True Religion than to spout your foolish notions about the laws of Spain not being fitted for life here. Those are treasonable thoughts."

"They're not treasonable, Father. And it's high time some-

105

one voiced them. Many people feel as I do, but we need spokesmen. Spain must see the need for a change, to let us rule ourselves instead of being dictated to by a series of Captains General sent over here to govern a kingdom they know nothing about. If those of us who have been born here can't make our needs known, then who can?

"But you've been pressing me to enter first one order and then another ever since I can remember, since even before I had any notions about studying law, as though you would parade all the orders in front of me until I find one that is irresistible. Why? I'm not a second son, so I'm not flouting tradition. I'm your first-born son, and till now, your only one. At this point, it's still up to me to carry on your branch of the Alvarado family for you. And in due time, perhaps after I finish my studies, I'll marry and do just that."

I caught my breath sharply, then tried to cover the action with a light cough. Ricardo marry? It had not occurred to me to consider such a possibility, and I was shocked at how the thought bothered me.

Cecilia looked up from her bandage rolling and said, "You might be too late. I have it on good authority that María Elena's cousin from Spain will be here before the end of the year, and her family favors a match between them."

I glanced quickly at Ricardo. Now he would deny any interest in the girl whose name Cecilia had mentioned. But to my disappointment he did not deny it. Instead, he smiled and said, "And I have it on the authority of her little sister that María Elena will have none of him; in fact, vows to join the Clarisas if her family will not leave her free choice."

"And that choice would be you, of course," Cecilia teased.

"Of course," Ricardo agreed.

Tomás interrupted them sourly. "What sort of foolish talk is this? Any matches in this family will be arranged properly, through me."

Ricardo opened his mouth as though he were about to protest. Then he clamped it shut and shrugged indifferently. He hastily gathered together his books and papers, and with a mumbled, "Good-night," he left the room.

Cecilia and Tomás continued to talk, but I paid no attention to their conversation. I focused my eyes on my sewing, not wanting to look up, not daring to raise my eyes, lest either of them suspect how panicky I felt at the prospect of Ricardo getting married.

Woodenly, I followed Tomás to our room later when he suggested we retire, and, woodenly, I submitted to his demands upon me. Later, lying awake after he had sated his desire, I began to consider the dreary prospect of the years

106

ahead, giving myself to a man I neither loved nor who loved me, bearing his children, with no ties between us to bind us together. But that was not wholly true, for there was one tie, and that one held us fast.

It was the irreversible tie of marriage.

I tossed and turned restlessly, and it was a long time before I slept, for I could not stop thinking of Ricardo. Ricardo and a girl. A girl named María Elena. What kind of a girl was she? I wondered. Was she plain or pretty? Fair or dark? Flirtatious or shy? Coquettish or modest? Why, I realized, I was thinking of her as a rival, my rival for Ricardo's affections! How could I be so foolish? He was unencumbered, free to choose a wife. What difference did it make to me if he married or not, or whom he chose to marry? What was he to me but the son of the man I married? What else could he ever be? Just because I had seen his face once in a piece of crystal before I met him gave me no claims on him. He must live his life, and I must live mine.

And mine was with Tomás, whose child I was going to bear.

I still did not want to tell him I was certain by now that I had conceived. He was gone to the farm much of every week, so it was easy to put off telling him. My uneasiness about the pregnancy continued, and I could not understand why. I wanted a child, even if it must belong to Tomás, too. I had no fear of childbirth. So why, then, should I have misgivings about the child barely started in my womb? And these misgivings continued to keep me from telling him about it, and even from accepting the fact of it myself.

One afternoon, my uneasiness was particularly strong. It was a still day, almost oppressively so, as though the earth, becoming more parched with each passing day, had hushed the breezes that blew upon it as it awaited the start of the rains. Earlier that day, I had overheard a whispered conversation between some of the servants about the weather this year of 1773. There had certainly been no need for them to whisper, but it was almost as if they were afraid to voice their thoughts aloud.

"They say it is always like this before . . ." One maid, feather duster halted in mid-motion, left the thought unfinished. The second maid nodded, pausing, mop in hand. "True. My grandfather told me it was like this before the earthquake of San Miguel. And we have had tremors."

Then they looked up and saw me and the first maid scurried away while the second returned to her mopping.

This episode, small and insignificant though it was, contributed to my depression that day. Tomás had left early that

107

morning for the farm and expected to be gone four or five days. Ricardo was at the University, and Cecilia had gone to spend a few days at the *finca* of one of her friends. I had completed our menus for the following week, supervised the rearranging and inventorying of the linen chests, and had watered my herb garden, which was progressing nicely. I had tried earlier to read, but though my eyes had followed the print, my mind had taken no note of the words.

It was getting on toward late afternoon when I decided to try again to lose myself in a book. I sat on the settee next to the door of our room and opened my old favorite, the much-worn volume of Cervantes' short stories. But even these failed to hold my interest. The feeling of uneasiness grew stronger as I sat there trying to focus my attention on the printed words, until I realized that my restlessness was not just mental, but physical as well, for a sensation of pain had begun to gnaw persistently at my stomach. Alarmed, I closed the book.

At that moment, I became aware of the clear-sounding bells of Santa Clara, first of the many bells of Santiago to ring out the call to five o'clock mass. In rapid succession, the bells of the other churches began to ring, often more than one at a time, as though the need to remind the people of the importance of prayer were too urgent for one to wait until the other had finished. I had heard the bells often; they rang morning and night in the same fashion, and often between times as well. But now I felt their urgency was directed at me, and the desire to go at once to church to plead for the small life within me was so strong that I sprang up immediately and went to tell Teresa that I was going out for a while. I did not tell her where I was going, and refused her offer to accompany me. This was something so personal, so private, that I knew I must go alone. I stopped by my room to get my *mantilla*, taking also a light shawl from the wardrobe in case it was cool when I emerged later from church.

I went to *La Merced*, because as I walked out of the house it seemed to be its bells which were summoning me. As I hurried down the street, I felt even more strongly that the tiny life I bore was perilously close to slipping away from me. I ignored the growing physical discomfort and kept walking, almost running, toward *La Merced*. Where better to pray for the safe delivery of my child than in the church of Our Lady of Mercy, herself a mother? I covered the distance to the church quickly, pausing only briefly by one of the ornately patterned columns which flanked the main entrance to slip my *mantilla* over my head. Then I went inside and slid into one of the pews near the back.

"Holy Mary, Mother of God . . ." But even as I prayed, I

knew it was too late, that the baby I so wanted was going to be lost to me. My physical discomfort increased, and my prayers gave way to quiet tears as I accepted the fact that my first pregnancy, scarcely begun, was coming to an end.

I continued to kneel there long after the priest had gone, and those few people who had been scattered here and there throughout the pews had drifted away, one by one. Several times, I started to rise, but at each attempt, a fresh pain would stab me and I would drop to the pew, hoping the pain would subside enough so that I could manage to get home.

I lost all conception of the passage of time, but I knew it must be getting late. Pain or no pain, I could not stay there all night. Tears stung my eyes as I forced myself to my feet and, leaning heavily on the back of the pew in front of me, made my way to the center aisle.

Before I turned to leave, in spite of my discomfort, I unthinkingly made a slight gesture toward the altar, intended as a sort of genuflection. I did not lower my knee much at all, but the gesture was my undoing, for a fresh stab of pain shot through me and threw me off balance. I lost my hold on the end of the pew and slipped to the floor.

I lay there crying, unable to will myself to move, and heard a feminine voice gasp, and then the sound of scurrying footsteps.

I learned that the voice I heard belonged to a native woman who had been in the pew behind me; I had not even known she was there. She summoned one of the monks, who immediately came to my aid. I insisted there was no need to call a doctor, but I did accept the offer of a buggy to take me home.

As I was helped into the waiting buggy, I noted with surprise that it was completely dark outside, and realized it must be far later than I had thought The buggy swayed and bounced over the uneven cobbles, and I knew that I was miscarrying; knew, too, that I must guard that fact from Tomás. He would blame the riding, and forbid me the use of the stables.

As we stopped in front of our house, the lackey who had run ahead of us with a torch to light our way knocked on the great door with the lower of the two knockers.

The knocker was jerked from his hand as the door flew open almost immediately. Ricardo came out and covered the space between the door and the buggy in two long strides.

"Carlota! What—? Are you all right? I was afraid something had happened to you."

I nodded, even in my discomfort pleased to note the concern and alarm in his voice. Would he have been so concerned if I meant nothing to him? "I just—I got dizzy in church." Was my life to be nothing but a series of lies here, I wondered? "I don't feel too well. If you'll just help me into the house—"

"You should have told someone you were going!" he scolded.

Before I could answer, he swept me up in his arms as though I were as weightless as a rag doll and carried me into the house. I let my head rest against his chest, grateful for the strength of his arms, and through my pain I was acutely aware of the beating of his heart. I found comfort, too, in the warmth of his body, for I had lost my shawl and was shivering uncontrollably.

Weakly, I thanked him as he placed me gently on my bed. I dared not admit to myself how much I would have preferred to remain in his arms.

He was standing over me, looking at me solicitously. "Shall I send for the doctor?"

"No!" That was the last thing I wanted. "If you'll just send Teresa to me, I'm sure I'll be all right. And please thank the good brothers of *La Merced* for me."

"Are you certain you don't need a doctor?"

"Quite certain."

He seemed hesitant to leave, but finally he said, "I'll get Teresa," and he turned and left the room.

Long after he had gone, I could still remember how it had felt to be enfolded in his arms, so strong yet so tender, with my cheek pressed against the rough wool of his shirt. I shut my eyes, as though to blot out the pain in the pit of my stomach, and also the realization that I had liked being in Ricardo's arms too well.

When I opened my eyes, Teresa was there.

"Oh! I didn't hear you come in." It never ceased to amaze me how quietly the natives could move. "Please close the door."

She nodded and did as I said.

"Teresa, I need your help. I think—I'm certain I'm having a miscarriage, though I wasn't too far along. When I was in the Church of *La Merced*, I started cramping violently. I hoped it would stop, but it only got worse and then it was so bad I couldn't walk home. I finally tried, and I—I couldn't. That is why I returned in the buggy."

"I think we should send for the doctor, *Señora*."

I reached up to put a restraining hand on her arm. "No!" I shook my head. "There's nothing he can do. It's too late, I know. I can feel—"

I had never before so fully appreciated Teresa and her

unemotional common-sense reactions. Wordlessly, she nodded her understanding and walked to the table, where she poured some water into the bowl. This she set on the small table next to the bed. "If you can roll onto your side, I will unbutton your dress."

Feeling helpless as a babe, I gave myself gratefully into her hands, which were strong and competent as she rolled me gently from one side to the other and bathed me, then slipped my nightgown over my head. She even insisted on plaiting my hair so it would not bother me as I slept.

Before she left, I instructed her to measure a certain amount of one of the mixtures in my herb chest into a glass and fill it with hot water. It was the mixture Tatiana had made specially for the bad pains that plagued me monthly. I drank it, explaining that the pain was already subsiding, but that the potion would make me more comfortable and make me sleep more easily. I finished it, then handed Teresa the cup.

"Teresa, when I said I wanted your help, I meant more than the help you've just given me. I would like the others—and my husband particularly—to think I just became violently ill from something I ate earlier. Otherwise, my husband will blame the riding, and I know it's not the cause of this. He would be angry, too, because I hadn't told him."

Teresa's features remained impassive, and she nodded. "Of course. I understand."

With that nod of agreement, I knew that Teresa's first loyalty would always be not to Tomás, but to me.

She left a candle burning by my bed, and I was vaguely aware of her presence at various times during the night, and her hand placed upon my brow from time to time, testing for fever. I remember seeing the candle burning low and then seeing it tall again, so I knew she had been in to replace it.

Once, I sensed something different about the hand on my brow. The feeling that it was not Teresa's hand puzzled me, and it took a while to penetrate through my sleeping state. When at last it did, and I opened my eyes to see who was there, the hand was gone and the room was empty.

Another time, I thought I had half-opened my eyes and seen Ricardo standing at the side of my bed, a worried frown on his face. A few minutes later, remembering having seen him there, I forced my eyes to open, to look for him again. They opened on emptiness, and I was not sure if Ricardo had ever really been there at all, any more than I knew if it had been his hand I felt upon my brow.

Teresa's help in guarding my secret did not save me from Tomás's wrath. When he returned four days later, I casually

111

mentioned being a little upset when he was gone and having to be brought home from church. When he had looked at me hopefully, I quickly assured him it was only from something I had eaten. He accepted that, and I thought we had finished with the subject until one afternoon several days later, when he strode in angrily from the street and said he wanted to see me in our room.

I had been sitting in the main patio sewing and looked up at him questioningly.

"At once!" he said sternly, walking toward our room.

Puzzled, I put down my sewing and followed, wondering in what way I had aroused his anger. He had frequently shown minor irritation with me, but never before had he appeared so incensed.

He pushed the door shut with an angry shove and motioned me to the edge of the bed.

"Sit down!"

I did as he asked and he paced up and down in front of me as I waited in bewilderment for him to explain. I did not have to wait long.

"I have just talked with *Señora* Ramirez, who lives across the street. Why did you come home after dark one night last week? You were in a buggy. Who were you with? And what were you doing out alone at that time of night?" His words were accusing, and his voice full of innuendos.

Shocked at his implications, I said, "I told you about it! I got ill in church—"

"I assumed you had meant in morning mass. Do you expect me to believe you were in church at night? After dark?" Again, the implication, the accusing tone.

"Of course I was!" I answered in exasperation. "I had gone to matins at *La Merced*, and after mass I didn't feel well and kept sitting there, hoping to feel better in a little while. It must have been longer than I thought, and when one of the brothers saw I was not well and offered to bring me home in a buggy, I accepted gladly. I'll admit I was surprised to see how dark it was outside. Certainly, you don't think—"

"It isn't just what I think! Even if you were sick, as you say, what do you suppose the neighbors thought, seeing you come in late at night unchaperoned?"

"I wasn't thinking of the neighbors," I protested bitterly, my fingernails biting into the palms of my hands as I fought to suppress my anger and indignation. "I was very ill and I was only relieved to be home. And it was not late at night. It was dark, but you know what short twilights we have here, and I didn't realize—"

"As my wife, it is important that you do realize! Don't you

112

know something like that can set people to talking? Pilar never went out unchaperoned, not even in the daytime. I would expect you to follow her example, if you have any consideration for my position in Santiago!"

I bit back the sharp retort I would have made, knowing that he would only be appeased if he thought he had bullied me into humility. It was not without effort that I forced to my lips the words that I thought would satisfy him and end the unpleasant conversation. "I'm sorry if you think I behaved thoughtlessly. I'll try to be more careful in the future."

I did not tell him that it was to pray for his child that I had gone out so impulsively alone late in the day.

This was not the first time Tomás had mentioned his first wife and implied that I would do well to pattern myself after her behavior, which had apparently been above reproach. I wondered if Tomás, in his youth, had loved her, if he were capable of loving anyone. I had seen the mausoleum he had built for her sepulchre; it was one a man would have built for a much beloved and sorely missed wife. And he had remained a widower for nineteen years. What sort of woman, then, would she have been, to have inspired such love in so strange a man?

Curious, I asked Teresa again one day the following week what Pilar had been like.

She shrugged. "As I told you before, I was only a child at the time. I worked in the kitchen then, and she did not often come out there." She volunteered no further information.

Clearly Teresa did not mean to do more than answer my direct questions. I had sensed a hesitancy before when the subject of Tomás's first wife had come up. Was this Teresa's natural reticence, or was she trying to deliberately discourage further inquiry? We were polishing the silver in the large room I had secretly dubbed "the museum," and she seemed especially intent on a spot she was trying to remove from a silver vase.

"But you must have seen her sometimes. Was she pretty?"

Teresa nodded. "Not as pretty as you, but she was pretty."

I smiled at the compliment. "How old was she when— when she died?"

"Only eighteen. Ricardo was fifteen months old, and Cecilia three months."

"Then they never really knew their mother! What a tragedy, for her to die so young! How—how did it happen? Was she ill very long?"

"She was never sick, never a day."

"Then how did she die?" I persisted.

113

"She was thrown from a horse." She put the vase down and picked up a bowl, inspecting it for tarnish.

"Oh, how terrible! No wonder Tomás isn't pleased when I want to go riding with him. It would bring back unpleasant memories for him. He must have loved her very much."

I waited for a nod of agreement or a comment to the effect that that had indeed been so, but Teresa met my statement with silence.

When she didn't answer, I asked, "Was he with her when it happened?"

She shook her head, setting the bowl back on the table. "She was alone."

"Alone?" I echoed in surprise. But Tomás had said Pilar never went out alone! I felt prickles along the back of my neck. "Where did it happen?"

Teresa squirmed, visibly uncomfortable at my persistence. "*Cerro del Manchen*. They found her there the next day."

"The next day? Why not the day it happened? What took them so long?"

"It happened at night. It was too dark to find her." Hurriedly, she picked up her rags and dish of polishing paste. "*Señora*, if you will excuse me, I must see if the cook has set the beans to boil."

"Of course." Puzzling over what she had told me, I nodded my permission for her dismissal. After she had left the room, I continued to polish absently a silver crucifix I had taken from the wall. Why had Teresa been so uncomfortable at my questions, and made an excuse to leave the room before I could ask any more?

And why would a woman who wouldn't even go out on the streets of Santiago alone in full daylight have gone riding, unattended, on *Cerro del Manchen* in the dark? The woman who would do that did not fit into the picture of the decorous conservative wife that Tomás had been at such pains to paint for me.

Still puzzling over the enigmatic Pilar, I closed and locked the door to the room that housed Tomás's most valued treasures. As I made my way past the entry, I noticed a bundle of bandages I had helped Cecilia prepare. They were still on the bench built into the wall of the *zaguan*, where she had put them the night before. I knew she had intended to take them with her that morning to the hospital, for she had mentioned how urgently they were needed, and I had torn up two of my old petticoats for her. Now she had gone off and forgotten them. Always glad of an excuse to go for a walk, I decided there was still plenty of time that morning to take them to her. Tomás, poring over columns of figures in his

114

ledgers in the room he used as an office, nodded absently when I told him I was going.

I picked up the bundle of bandages and made my way to the Street of the Conception. Inside the hospital, a two-story building of imposing proportions, I inquired for Cecilia. I was told she could be found assisting Dr. Gonzales on his rounds of the *indio* wards, which were housed in some lesser buildings nearby. I wondered at the fact that they had set a high-born *creole* volunteer to work in those wards; surely they had plenty of native helpers for such work.

I had to look into a number of wards before I found Cecilia and Dr. Gonzales, and when I did, they were so engrossed in their work they didn't see me until I had been standing in the doorway for several minutes.

Dr. Gonzales was a stockily built man, with straight hair of a true black combed away from his forehead. His complexion was swarthy, his cheekbones high. There was no mistaking the fact that he possessed a good deal of native blood. A *mestizo*, probably, I decided.

Cecilia was helping him change a dressing on a leg wound. Her eyes, like those of the doctor, were focused on the patient's wound. But Cecilia, I soon realized, was not giving her full attention to the patient, for I saw her eyes dart repeatedly to the doctor's face, as though she were unable to keep them from doing so. Then, the dressing completed, she looked full into his face.

There was no misreading the look Cecilia gave him. It was the look of a woman in love.

And when I saw Dr. Gonzales look at her, I knew her ardor was returned. Their profiles, eyes locked on each other, were outlined against the window and the light shone on them from behind in such a manner that it seemed as though there were a glow emanating from them, reflecting their feelings for each other.

Suddenly, I felt like an intruder, knowing that I had seen something that was too private, something they intended only for each other to see. I would have left and pretended to enter again, but at that moment Cecilia looked over and saw me in the doorway.

As our eyes met, she flushed, and I heard her murmur, "Excuse me a minute," to the doctor. She hurried over to me, her eyes sparkling angrily.

"What are you doing here?" she asked ungraciously.

"I'm sorry if I intruded. You forgot the bandages we prepared last night. You said they were urgently needed, so I walked over with them."

"To spy on me?" She snatched the package of bandages from my hand.

I winced at the unfairness of her accusation. I was suddenly weary of trying to exact friendship from this hostile girl, and retorted angrily, "I did not come here to spy on you. I only meant to help." I spun around and walked away.

"Just a minute." Her words reached me when I was halfway down the hall.

I paused and turned to face her. "Yes?"

She walked over to me. "I shouldn't have gotten angry. I suppose you only meant to do me a favor."

Wordlessly, I nodded, accepting her apology as grudgingly as I felt it had been offered. I turned and left, determined that I would no longer try to force my friendship on her.

But as I walked home, I could not stop puzzling over what I had seen. Perhaps the attraction Cecilia and her doctor felt for each other was merely a passing fancy, a fleeting thing that would soon come to an end. But somehow, remembering the way they had looked at each other, I didn't think so. And, if what they felt for each other was indeed a lasting passion, what good could possibly come of it, of a love between a high-born *creole* and a *mestizo*? Tomás was not alone in his fanaticism about the superiority of pure Spanish blood; in fact, it had certainly been the desire to set aside all doubts as to the purity of my own blood that my father had gone to such pains to make it appear indisputably that I belonged to him and *Mamá*. And since station was determined by birth in Guatemala perhaps even more than in Spain, Tomás would certainly never consider a match between Cecilia and a *mestizo*. But even if, by some chance, he should permit it, Cecilia's life would not be an easy one. *Mestizos* were considered little better than *indios*, and a woman who married beneath her station must share the life of her husband.

When I returned home, I said nothing to Tomás of my visit to the hospital, but what I had seen weighed heavily on my mind. Later, I was standing in front of the mirror in my room tidying up for dinner when there was a knock on my door.

The young native maid Tomás had brought back from the farm for me was in the room mending one of my skirts. I nodded to her and she answered the knock. It was Cecilia.

"Come in," I said tersely, brushing a stray wisp of hair behind my ear.

Cecilia closed the door and continued to stand there, ill at ease. The maid returned to her sewing until I realized that whatever Cecilia had come to say must be said in private. I

116

dismissed the girl, and as the door closed behind her, Cecilia said urgently,

"Carlota, I've come to ask you a favor. I hope—I hope I'm not too late." She twisted a silk kerchief nervously around her fingers.

I put down my brush, but I did not turn to face her. Through the mirror, I looked at her expectantly, waiting for her to continue.

"It—it would be better if Father didn't know which doctor I am working with at the hospital. He always assumes I am helping one of the *chapetones* or *creoles*. If he knew—well, he might forbid me to go."

Suddenly, watching her, I was overwhelmed with compassion for her, and my anger melted. At that moment, I saw her not as the haughty disdainful girl who had so often rebuffed the friendship I had offered her, but as the bewildered and uncertain daughter of an unbending man who would surely never permit her free choice in seeking happiness in the manner she chose.

Poor Cecilia! How unfairly life had dealt with her, I thought, remembering Teresa's story of how her fiancé had been only too ready to forget his vows. She had been cheated out of happiness once; surely she was entitled to whatever she could salvage from her broken life.

I turned to face her. "If you and your doctor are serious about each other, as serious as I suspect you are, maybe I could talk to Tomás for you, make him see—"

"No!" she protested quickly, with a vehemence that surprised me. "You mustn't. He would never understand! You haven't said anything to him, have you?" Her eyes watched me desperately.

"I've said nothing."

Her shoulders relaxed in relief. "Thank God! And you mustn't! Please! All I ask is that you don't say anything."

"You're right," I agreed, knowing my suggestion for the foolish notion it had been. All Cecilia asked of me was my silence. Nothing more. It seemed so little to ask. How could I refuse it? "I won't say anything to him, I promise."

Her eyes filled with tears. "Oh, thank you!" She threw her arms around me and hugged me. Stunned by the suddenness of her action, it took me a minute to return the gesture. "Carlota, I know it can't be too pleasant for you, being married to my father. He's not an easy man to live with. It doesn't seem fair, for someone with your youth and vitality and beauty."

I smiled wryly. "Life hasn't been exactly fair to either of us, has it?" Then, I continued, certain the barrier between us

117

had been pulled down forever. "I hope you don't mind, but Teresa told me about your fiancé and how your engagement was broken."

"But I was scarred! And you——"

"I was scarred, too, in a different way. Not my face, but my reputation." I told her, then, of how I had come to marry Tomás. I told her everything except that Tatiana was my mother.

When I finished, she asked me, "Why did you tell me this? You didn't have to."

"I know, but I wanted you to know. I feel that I share your most precious secret, and I thought it only right that you should share this secret of mine." I was certain that she would never use what I had told her against me.

"I'll keep your secret, as I know you will keep mine," she said, her eyes shining. She smiled at me for the first time since we had met, and I was amazed to see what a remarkable improvement it made in her appearance. The marks on her face seemed to recede in the brilliance of her smile. What a dazzlingly beautiful girl she must once have been! And when she smiled, she was beautiful still.

I smiled, too, my smile prompted by relief, for I knew that the undeclared war Cecilia had waged against me since my arrival had, at last, come to an end. She had approached me as one would approach a friend, and I had responded as the friend I had longed to be to her.

"Shall we go in to dinner?"

Arm in arm, we walked into the dining room.

And so, purely by accident, I was drawn into Cecilia's conspiracy to keep from Tomás the knowledge that it was not only her desire to help the sick that drew her daily to the hospital. Had he ever suspected her true motive, he would have put a stop to her visits at once. And yet, though I would not have denied Cecilia and her *mestizo* doctor the help my silence gave them, I wondered how their romance could possibly end happily.

Lying awake that night, I thought again of the expressive looks exchanged by Cecilia and her doctor. Then I thought of my own loveless marriage, and I could not help but be pricked by jealousy. Fleetingly, inexplicably, another thought came to me, and I remembered the warming comfort of being enclosed in Ricardo's arms the day he carried me in from the Mercederians' buggy. With a sigh of longing and regret, I turned away from Tomás and drifted off to sleep.

Santiago—April, 1773

CHAPTER VII

Our social life in Santiago revolved far more around the church than it had back in Granada, and scarcely a week went by without one sort of religious procession or another. Some of the special church days were all somberness and solemnity, and others were excuses for celebration, usually ending with street fiestas and elaborate displays of fireworks.

During Lent, however, there had been no fiestas. There was only the solemnity, and all social life came virtually to a standstill. Anything that evoked the least bit of gaiety would have been unthinkable, so deeply rooted was the tradition, in Guatemala as in Spain. Lent was a time to remember and reflect, with deep sorrow and guilt, the progress of Jesus Christ down the melancholy road that led to His sacrifice on the cross, for our sakes.

Holy Week itself began with the blessing of the palms on Palm Sunday and the procession from the Cathedral. After matins that day, the scattering of noblemen we had living in Santiago, with white cloths thrown across their shoulders to identify them as the alms collectors, came to each house for the *demanda*, a sum to help pay the heavy expenses of the church during Holy Week. Tomás gave a big bag filled to bursting with silver *macacos*, with a great show of piousness and generosity I knew he didn't possess, and only after the men had passed on down the street did he grumble about the amount he felt his position had compelled him to give.

As all of Lent was a time for pious reflection and prayer, so Holy Week was a magnification of this piety, and a time to remember and pray for the souls of those we loved who had gone beyond their own prayers.

119

I reflected often during that time on the deaths of Tatiana and Giorgio. Certainly, neither of them had been to the confessional to be forgiven of their sins for some time before they died, if indeed they had ever gone in their lives. Tatiana's religion, like that of most of the gypsies, had not been formalized; nor, I was certain, had Giorgio's. The gypsies accepted religion in much the same manner as they accepted the harshness of their lives, with a resignation that was at once both exceedingly childish and extremely adult.

My own religious training, under *Tía's* watchful eye, had been far more exacting. According to her, we were all guilty of an overwhelming amount of sin. In my heart, I disagreed with her insistence that the simplest enjoyments of life were sinful. Still, she had forced some doubt upon me and I was too uncertain about just what did constitute sin not to go along a little with the rigidity of her beliefs, at least insofar as the necessity of prayer was concerned. And perhaps, if Tatiana and Giorgio had died with a number of unconfessed sins on their souls, they had need of as many prayers as I could say. At any rate, an excess would surely do them no harm.

I resolved to say some prayers for my father, too, and as I thought of Dolores, I was thankful that she, at least, had had a priest by her bedside just before her death and had been able to die without tarnish on her soul. *Mamá*, I was certain, had long ago earned her place in heaven.

I went daily during Holy Week to say my prayers for all of them at the stations of the cross, hoping that this would lighten a little any burden of sin they had carried with them to the next world. Tomás accompanied me every morning, but for him, I suspected, the ritual was far more social than religious, for he showed much more concern over the clothes we wore to the Cathedral than he did over the time we spent kneeling in prayer. There were long waiting lines at all the churches during this time, with the longest lines of all at the Cathedral. I suggested to Tomás that we go to one of the less crowded churches, but he brushed off my suggestion with an impatient wave of his hand. "Nonsense!" he answered. "The Cathedral is the only place to go." And so we continued to go there, often spending more time waiting than praying.

Then on Thursday night, the *animeros*, dressed all in black with flowing capes, called forth dolorously from each street corner in Santiago for everyone to say an Our Father and a Hail Mary for a soul in purgatory. We heard their funereal sing-song cries echoing from one corner to the next as they approached, till at last they were at the corner of our house with their doleful reminder of the debt owed by the living to the dead.

Good Friday was a day of religious processions. At midday, *El Nazareno*, a sculpture of Christ on the cross much renowned in Santiago, was carried slowly down the street toward the *Plaza Real* from its home in the Church of *La Merced*. Then the procession solemnly wended its way around the plaza, pausing frequently so that the priest could give the benediction. Even the convicts housed in the city jail on the ground floor of the Palace of the *Ayuntamiento* were allowed to come out and receive the blessings of the church.

Also on Good Friday was a procession starting from the Church of *Santo Domingo*. Behind the prostrate figure of *Cristo Yacente*, carried on its ornate glass-enclosed platform, marched many of the leading figures of the city, both political and religious. This was a colorful procession, for banners and family coats of arms were proudly displayed, and some of the men dressed in suits of armor. I could not help but wonder how the natives who watched in silence felt about this display. Were they perhaps recalling how so few such men similarly dressed and mounted had literally frightened them into giving them not only their land but their bodies and souls as well?

On Sunday, we attended Easter Mass in the Cathedral. All the pews were filled with those who had some special right to be there: officials of the kingdom and the province, lesser officials of the city, or those belonging to the nobility, no matter how remotely, legitimately or illegitimately. The common people crowded into the aisles. Tomás's status as the son of a minor nobleman entitled us to seats for the service, but he was indignant because we were not seated in the main nave. After all, he complained, hadn't he given generously the previous week to the men who had come to collect the *demanda*?

I noticed Cecilia's doctor standing in one of the aisles near us, and wondered if Cecilia was aware of his presence. Once, I saw him looking at her with such open devotion that it made me glance quickly at Tomás to see if he had noticed. With relief, I saw that he had not.

The Cathedral was filled to bursting with white flowers that morning, more than I would have thought existed in all of Guatemala, and there were cages hung all around in which *cenzontles*, not seeming to mind their captivity, trilled joyously all during the service. The natives called these the birds of four hundred voices, and it was difficult to imagine that such glorious singing could come from such drab-looking little creatures.

When we left the Cathedral after the service, it was with renewed faith and lightened hearts. The season for solemnity

121

and introspection and self-chastisement was over, the time to reflect overlong on death was past. It was a time for the living, and Santiago was like a city newly awakened.

In the weeks that followed Easter, fiestas were held frequently, with or without excuses, and the city, for a time, belonged to the young. Ricardo spent little time at home, and I would sometimes hear him come in during the early morning hours and wonder where he had been. How my heart ached to be included with the young and free during that period of festivity and release! They danced in the streets during the day and gathered in homes at night, but I was a matron, so the dancing and the fiestas were not for me. Tomás and I did attend a few dinner parties during that period, but they were proper and formal and, to me, stifling and boring. I was still young, and I yearned to dance and laugh and sing, to join in the gaiety of other young people. I resented being cast in the role of a spectator. I felt that it was my life I watched passing by, without being allowed to participate in it. My youth and my gypsy heart combined to make me tug against the restraints of passivity and smart at the inaction, but there seemed to be absolutely nothing I could do about it.

The Universities suspended lectures for several weeks, and the students, released from their studies, took advantage of their freedom to revel at all hours. During the day, the young single girls somehow contrived to meet the young men outdoors, and the meeting was at once an excuse for an outburst of song and dance. Meanwhile, the girls' weary *dueñas*, fatigued from the festivities they chaperoned in the evenings and not a little abashed at their inability to maintain the decorum of the rest of the year, gathered ineffectively in little clusters of their own nearby.

Sometimes, even in the early morning hours when I went with Teresa to the vegetable market, I would hear the strains of a guitar strumming one of the *algerías*, the happiest of the *flamenco* songs, and hear the sharp clapping that accompanied it. It was at times like these that the revolt within me festered dangerously close to the surface, ready to burst forth at any time. I yearned to fling away decorum, to forget that I was a matron, forget that my marriage was repugnant to me, and pretend, if only for a few minutes, that I was free of care. My feet ached to tap out the staccato beat, my fingers twitched to snap the accompanying rhythm with sharp resounding clicks, my body longed to sway and twirl in the dance I had learned in the gypsy camp.

But I was in Santiago de los Caballeros, in Guatemala, far from the gypsy camp. Even had I been allowed to join in the dance, it was not the same as I had known it. On those occasions when I stopped to watch the dancers, I realized how stilted and stylized were their movements. It was all I could do to keep from pushing my way through the cluster of young people who customarily gathered around the dancers and showing them how the *alegrías* should be done—not as they did them, with restrained steps painstakingly memorized and self-consciously executed, but with feeling and exuberance and abandon. I was sure that only I, of all the people who watched, could express the freedom that was the very essence of the *alegrías*. How could those who knew nothing of the sweet taste of freedom interpret it for others?

Tomás left for the farm in the middle of the second week following Easter. Before he left, he told me sternly that, in his absence, I was to go out on the streets only if accompanied by another woman of my station. I listened in silence to his latest demand. It would do no good to protest, I knew, and it would only fire him to add further restrictions. But even before he left, I knew I would not obey this latest edict, for this time he demanded too much. Sometimes I found the house suddenly too confining, and was overwhelmed with the need to get away from it, even though I just went walking alone in the streets nearby. At these times, it would be impractical if not impossible to find someone to accompany me on such short notice. Besides, I did not want company when this mood came upon me. It would be futile to attempt to explain all this to Tomás, so I decided not to try. Nor would I give up this simple assuagement of my restless spirit.

As he bade me good-bye, I turned my cheek for his kiss and perfunctorily wished him a pleasant journey. I felt, as I did so often lately, that I was a player upon the stage, enacting the role of a dutiful and obedient wife, while rebellious thoughts seethed inside my head. It was dishonest of me, but it was a pretense I could not afford to drop. And the longer Tomás and I were married, the more conscious effort it took to keep it up.

Did Tomás know how I felt? Was that why he was becoming increasingly fastidious about my behavior, trying to shape me into the paragon of virtue Pilar had been and he thought I ought to be? Did he hope to forge a chain of the restrictions he imposed upon me, winding it ever closer about me till it would crush the insurrection in my heart?

The afternoon after Tomás left, the house seemed unbearably quiet, perhaps because I knew that elsewhere in Santiago there was laughter and gaiety. I needed some red embroidery thread for a set of pillowcases I was stitching, so I seized that as an excuse to leave. I slipped out quietly, telling only Teresa I was going. Some day, I was certain, Tomás would return unexpectedly and discover that I had gone out alone, in defiance of his orders, but it was not likely to happen that day. At any rate, it was a chance I knew I would continue to take until I was caught. Not until then would I weigh the consequences.

On my roundabout way to the shop, at the corner of *Las Pilitas* I encountered the dancers, surrounded, as usual, by a mixed group of young people. A short distance away, the girls' *dueñas* formed a smaller circle. I watched the feet of the girl who was dancing, a rose in her hair, her skirts twirling. She was good, the best I had seen in Guatemala, but I knew I was better. If only . . . I sighed wistfully and scanned the faces of those who had formed a circle around the dancers, slapping the fingers of one hand against the palm of the other to form the sharp accompanying beat so much an integral part of the dance. One lone guitar strummed out the tune.

It was then I saw Ricardo. He was dressed in black riding clothes of fine wool, richly embroidered with threads of gold and silver. He was hatless, and the red-gold of his hair glinted in the sun, matching the sparkle of the metallic threads on his jacket and contrasting sharply with the black fabric of his clothing. As I watched him, I realized he was not watching the dancers, but talking to someone at his side. I moved around and raised up on my toes to see the object of his attention, and realized with a start that it was a petite young girl, and that she was beautiful. Her hair was of pale gold, complementing the red-gold of Ricardo's hair, and her complexion was milk-white and smooth. I noticed with envy that she and Ricardo, with their striking blond coloring at once the same and different, looked as if they had been created to belong together, a blond god and goddess set apart from lesser humans. In that moment, I hated my dark hair and my tawniness and the redness of my lips. I yearned for the delicate pale beauty of the petite girl who held Ricardo's rapt attention. With a stab of jealousy, I realized that she was flirting outrageously with him. Couldn't her *dueña* see this, put a stop to such an open breach of good behavior? I wondered indignantly. With growing irritation, I looked over to the knot of *dueñas*, was disappointed to note that, from their vantage point, only the back of the girl's head would have been visible. And Ricardo—did he have to be so intent on what she was saying, leaning close to her, as though he would not miss a word she said? Did he have to act so—so approving of her conduct? Did he have to smile at her as he answered, that disarmingly open smile he had smiled at me in the glass?

As I stood there, my eyes focused grudgingly on them, I

124

realized that the guitar had strummed its final notes, and the dance was finished. The circle began to break up, and I turned away quickly, unwilling to have Ricardo know I had seen him. I hurried home, not bothering to stop for my embroidery thread. For the rest of the afternoon, I was sunk deep in dejection and misery.

María Elena. Now, no longer only a name to me, but a presence, a real person, a living enemy. I hated her for the shallowness of character I was certain I had read in her face. I hated her for her coquetry. I hated her for her petiteness and her fairness and her beauty. But most of all, I hated her because she had held Ricardo's attention and because I feared he loved her.

That night was the first time that week that Ricardo ate supper at home. During the meal, to my intense irritation, Cecilia kept bringing up the name of María Elena. She was encouraging Ricardo, urging him to commit himself to her. Provoked by Cecilia's persistence, I ate my food in silence. I listened to them, not wanting to hear what they were saying yet knowing I must as I waited, tense with apprehension and dread, for Ricardo to say he planned to speak for María Elena soon. He didn't, but I found little relief in his failure to make such a statement, for he certainly did not try to deny an interest in her. He seemed, in fact, to enjoy extolling her virtues. I could scarcely keep from screaming at the two of them to stop their senseless talk, or from jumping up and leaving the room, for each of their remarks stung me anew with the fear that Ricardo might soon marry. I did not reason that he would be no more lost to me if he married than he already was. I only knew that I could not bear the thought of him belonging to someone else.

I was relieved when the meal at last came to an end and Ricardo left immediately afterwards. I could not have stood a whole evening of such foolish chatter.

"You're very quiet tonight, Carlota," Cecilia said as we settled with our needlework like two old *dueñas*. I had never really liked needlework, for I lacked the patience to count off carefully an exact number of tiny threads before every stab of the needle. The work was tedious, and I was clumsy in my impatience, and often pricked my finger.

But I had to fill my evenings with something, and reading was difficult in the company of others, so I tried to keep my fingers busy and my mind at least partially occupied watching the colored threads slowly fill in the white blankness of a piece of cloth with endless rows of cross-stitched flowers, about which I cared nothing at all.

"I've little cause for hilarity," I snapped ill-naturedly, my nerves taut from the strain of the mealtime conversation.

"Nor I," she agreed with a sigh, seeming not to be offended by my shortness. "I can only hope that Ricardo, at least, will be happy. He must get out of this house, away from Father, as soon as he can."

"Surely he won't be leaving any time soon!" I protested in panic. Life here in this house, so close to Ricardo and yet having to keep a remote distance from him, was a torment to me, but it would be worse torment still to have him leave, catch no glimpse of his handsome face, never hear his strong firm voice. I pushed the thought from my mind. It was unthinkable.

"I wish he would, for his sake," she continued. "He and Father never got on well, but lately it's much worse. Since Father came back, he seems obsessed with the idea of getting Ricardo to commit himself to enter one of the religious orders. If Ricardo and María Elena would announce their betrothal, then Father would have to let up."

"Why must you keep pushing Ricardo toward María Elena?" I asked peevishly. "Maybe he doesn't like her that well. Surely it's for him to decide who he'll marry, not you!" I jabbed my needle viciously through the fabric of the pillowcase I was embroidering.

I did not look up as I spoke, or afterwards, but I felt Cecilia's eyes on me and knew that she wore a look of shocked surprise at my outburst.

I felt myself flush hotly, knowing that my angry words had exposed the feelings I had, until then, taken such pains to hide. I tried to keep my voice calm and level as I added hastily, "After all, he's only twenty. He has plenty of time to meet other girls. He might find someone he likes much better."

"Perhaps," she agreed, and I was relieved by the silence that followed, and grateful that she had not pursued the suspicions that must certainly have taken root in her mind.

That they had taken root, I had no doubt. Later, we were talking about Tomás's latest acquisition, a Sung Dynasty vase that he claimed was priceless. We were discussing the special locked display case he was having built for it, so that no one could touch it or knock it over, and Cecilia said,

"No one can steal it, either, for it will be locked into place. My father is a very jealous man. He covets his possessions, and guards them well."

Cecilia's words referred ostensibly to the vase, but I read into them a deeper meaning I was certain she intended, a warning to take care lest Tomás, too, guess my feelings about Ricardo.

I gave a short sharp laugh, and was shocked to hear the bitterness in my voice as I spoke. "Too well, perhaps. He would possess things so totally, he would hardly ever let them out of his sight."

"But they belong to him."

"Yes, they do belong to him," I agreed with a deep sigh.

"I don't think Father means to be unkind. It's just that gruffness is his way. I know you must feel he's unduly harsh sometimes, but that's just the way he is."

"I often wonder if he was so harsh with your mother. I suppose he must have loved her very much." I laughed wryly. "Certainly, he considered her behavior impeccable, for he has often told me so. He has also reminded me on a number of occasions that mine falls far short of her standards." Then, as always when I thought of Pilar, I was overcome with curiosity about her. It was more than mere idle curiosity; for some reason I could not understand, I felt a pressing need to know more about her. "What do you know about your mother, Cecilia? I know you can't remember anything, since you were a tiny baby when she died. But surely Tomás has told you about her. What was she like?"

She shook her head. "I don't know. It's odd, I suppose, but I know very little about her, except that she was beautiful, and that I know from a miniature I have. It was one Father had painted not long after they were married."

"You have it?" I interrupted, looking up in surprise. "He gave it to you? Then he must have had another."

"Not that I have ever seen. And he didn't exactly give it to me. It was strange, the way it happened. It was a long time after my mother died, after Tía had come to live with us. One of the maids accidently threw it out, and Tía found it in the trash and rescued it. I was about five or six at the time, and I begged Father to let me keep it. He must have sensed how much I missed having a real mother. Tía was a second mother to me, but she was already very old when she came to us. Anyway, Father let me keep the miniature.

"But outside of being able to see that she was lovely, I really don't know much else about her, except what you said Father told you—that she took great care to behave as a lady should. He made certain to tell me that, too."

I looked up in surprise. "Did he find your behavior below her standards, too? At least that's some consolation to me, to know I'm not the only one he disapproves of. But surely you never do anything he feels is wrong!"

"Not any more, not now. But I used to love fiestas, before . . ." She left the thought unfinished and hesitated a moment. When she continued, the quality of wistfulness I had noted briefly in her voice was gone. "Perhaps I was a bit wild at times, for certainly *Tía* was a very permissive *dueña*, as though she were trying to be a companion to me as well as a substitute mother. At any rate, whenever Father would find out I had done something he thought not quite in the best of taste, he would remind me what a perfect lady my mother had been, properly shy and demure and reserved, and how I must follow in her footsteps."

As she talked, something—what was it?—that I had heard was trying to fight its way through to my conscious memory, and I strained to recall it. We sat in silence for a few minutes, the only sound the sharp click of Cecilia's scissors as she cut the wool threads into working lengths for her needlepoint on the frame in front of her.

Finally, I remembered what it was I was trying to recall. When Teresa had been telling me of Cecilia, she had inadvertently told me something about Pilar, too. I had not taken much note of it at the time, but now her words returned to me. She had been telling me of Cecilia before her disfiguring illness and had said, *"She loved a fiesta, as had her mother."*

A shy reserved woman like Pilar? Would she have loved a fiesta, with crowds of jostling talkative people about? I thought not. Shy people hate fiestas, for to them they are tortuous occasions. Again, as when I had learned of Pilar riding alone into the hills at night, it was a jarring note. It did not fit into the portrait of Pilar that Tomás had painted for Cecilia and for me.

I was overcome with a feeling of urgency. I must find out all I could about Pilar, soon, as though that were a key to something I must know, something important but just out of my reach. And perhaps finding out the details of her final fatal ride onto *Cerro del Manchen* could be even more revealing than finding out how she had lived.

"Cecilia, what do you know about your mother's death?"

"Only what Father told me, and that just once when I was very young. He never liked to talk about it."

I heard the urgency in my own voice as I asked, "What did he tell you about it, that one time?" I leaned forward, waiting.

She put down the bunch of green threads she held in her hand and, closing her eyes, said, "I don't remember, exactly. I was only about ten. Until then, I had accepted my motherless state without question. But at that time, I was particularly jealous of my friends who had mothers. We had some affair at school, and afterwards we were all standing around

128

the fountain of *Las Delicias* just outside. I remember suddenly looking around and discovering that I was the only one who lacked a young mother. *Tía* was there, of course, but she suddenly looked so old to me, standing there among the others.

"Right then, it became important to me to know why I didn't have a young mother like my friends did, to know what quirk of fate had deprived me of her. On the way home, I asked *Tía* to tell me all about it, but she said she hadn't been with us at the time, and told me to ask Father, so I did." She puckered her brow, as though she were trying hard to remember something that had all but faded from her memory. "There was something about—about her taking a horse that was far too much for her to handle, a horse everyone knew to be dangerous. I—I seem to remember that Father said she took it when he wasn't around, so he hadn't been able to stop her. I know he must have been terribly shocked and upset at the manner in which she died, because he said that right after they found her body the next day, he tracked down the stallion himself and shot him.

"I asked him about it several times after that, but it was easy to see he didn't want to speak about it, so I didn't press him. And when I became old enough to realize how painful the subject must be for him, I stopped asking questions altogether. He had told me about it once. There was really nothing more to tell."

"I suppose not," I agreed. But wasn't there? Pilar had left, unattended, to go riding in the hills at night on a stallion she could not control. And she loved a fiesta. The Pilar who was beginning to emerge as an entity in my mind was not the shy and diffident creature who had behaved so virtuously. Was Pilar an enigma, or had the woman Tomás described to Cecilia and to me existed only in his own imagination?

The fiesta spirit continued to pervade Santiago in the days that followed, and, unhampered by Tomás's restraining presence, I went frequently out on the streets, always with one errand or another in mind to use as an excuse. But once out on the streets, my errand was forgotten as often as not, and I would stop and listen for the strum of the guitar. Whenever I heard it, even from afar, it captured me and I was drawn ever closer to it, as a moth is drawn irresistibly to a candle flame. My feet turned, seemingly of their own volition, in the direction of the music, and I followed its strains, even as I knew it held nothing for me but the sorrow of knowing that it was being played not for me, but for others.

In the same manner, I yearned for a glimpse of Ricardo among the dancers or those who surrounded them, yet as my eyes searched for his face, hungering for the sight of him, I was fearful that I would see him again with María Elena, see him looking at her in that candid way he had, admiring her, caring about her.

Tomás kept a good stable, and in the early morning hours, whenever he was out of the city, I would often go out there, an offering of sweets or freshly pulled carrots taken from the vegetable garden in my hand for my favorites. I liked to go before the house was astir, preferably even before Simón and the stable hands were about, so I wouldn't feel hampered by their presence.

Even before I had begun my visits to the gypsy camp, I had ridden a horse fairly well and felt I had a good understanding of the intelligent animals. But there, some of the gypsy men had heaped centuries of gypsy knowledge of horses and horseflesh upon my natural instinctive liking of the beasts. I was an avid pupil and an apt one, and my mentors recognized and praised the talent which developed under their tutelage. It was a talent about which I had never felt modest, for I knew, as they had, that though it was in part natural, it had become exceptional only after they worked patiently with me, adding to it their vast store of knowledge. Unfortunately, horsemanship, so widely applauded in a man, was not considered an important attribute in a young lady; in fact, it was often frowned upon as unbecoming and unfeminine. Therefore, little note had ever been taken by any but the gypsies of my ability to control even the most difficult horse not with force, but with understanding, and my talent passed mostly unrecognized by the rest of the world.

On the Saturday following Tomás's departure, I went out to the stables for one of my early morning visits. Later, as I was leaving, I almost collided with Ricardo.

"Oh!" I looked up at him in surprise. "I didn't know anyone else was up so early. Are you going out riding today?" It was a foolish question, for Ricardo, like most of the men in Santiago, seldom thought of going anywhere on foot. We stood there, so close that I could feel his breath upon my forehead. I wished I were not so painfully aware of his closeness whenever he was near. It was an awareness that permeated my whole being, so that it was only with conscious effort that I could keep my breath steady and my words coherent. And when I talked, it was usually to say something senseless, as I had just done.

"I've a very important ride this morning," Ricardo answered. "This is the day of the big race."

"Oh?" I felt a twinge of self-pity because, whatever the festivities, I was not to be included. "Where will this be?"

"At the *Prado del Cortijo*, by the Magdalena River."

"And you're going to enter?" It was another stupid question, I knew. He had just told me he was.

"Yes, but I can't decide whether to take one of the two new Arab horses you and Father brought with you or my trustworthy chestnut. Which would you ride, Carlota?" He asked the question teasingly, as though he did it only in jest, and would pay little heed to my answer.

Yet I felt puffed up with pride because he had asked me at all, and it was important to me to give him the right answer. "How long is the race?" I asked.

"Very long. Several hours of hard riding at best. We must go to one of the villages to retrieve a banner from the plaza there and return."

"Then take one of the Arab horses. They are untiring."

His eyes were laughing at me, as though he still refused to take me seriously. Yet he asked, "Which one? Emir, the one Father rides much of the time?"

I did not hesitate. "The other one."

"Why? Isn't the one Father prefers the better horse?"

"Yes, but—" I did not say what was in my mind. A man's true nature is never better revealed than when he is in the saddle. Though he can keep other men from knowing what is in his heart, he cannot lie to a horse, for the animal feels what the man is in the way he mounts, the way he sits, the touch of his hand on the reins—many things. A horse, not understanding the sense of misleading words as such but merely the tone of voice which reveals the spirit in which they are spoken, is not easily fooled. But the tragedy is that each time a horse is ridden by a distrustful rider, he loses a little of his faith in all mankind, and he himself reflects this distrust. Of the two horses we brought with us, the one Tomás favored had been the best, and was still an excellent horse. But Tomás had ridden him too often, and the mount had lost spirit. Now, the other was the better of the two.

"Take El Moro," I finished. "He has better endurance for the distance."

I saw that Ricardo was no longer laughing at me. His gaze was fixed on me intently. "I do believe you know. You're a surprising girl, Carlota." Simón came into the stables just then, and Ricardo turned to him and said, "Put my saddle on the smaller Arabian, Simón."

"Yes, *Señor* Ricardo." Simón stepped around us to get the stallion and lead him from his stall.

I smiled, feeling that somehow I had won an important victory over María Elena. She would never have been able to advise Ricardo on choosing a mount for a race. He would never have asked her.

"Good luck. The horse has tremendous power in his forelegs, and a stout heart. He'll run a good race for you."

He returned my smile. "For us," he corrected. "If I win, the victory will belong to all three of us: to my advisor, my stout-hearted stallion, and me."

He turned and went into the tack room.

A short while later, he waved to me as he rode off. I forced myself to smile as I returned his wave. But I no longer smiled as I turned to go back in the house, feeling utterly deserted, and I sighed heavily as I closed the door behind me.

I felt more restless than ever, and did not want to stay inside the walls of the house. But I knew I would catch no glimpse of Ricardo by walking in the streets of Santiago that day. Dejectedly, I went into my room and threw myself onto the bed.

It was several hours later when I heard the sound of the big brass knocker on the front door. I heard the hinges squeak as Teresa opened it to the caller, and I made a note to have the hinges oiled. Then I heard voices, and Teresa's knock on the door of my room.

"*Señora,* someone to see you," she called through the door.

In the patio, I was greeted by the couple I most liked of all of Tomás's acquaintances, Carlos and Marta Ortega Batres. They were a childless couple, Tomás's age, not mine, and there was in them a genuineness and sincerity that was warming. Already, Marta and I had become good friends, in spite of the difference in our ages.

We embraced each other and Marta said, "We've come to get you, to take you with us on a picnic. Carlos just told me as we were on our way that Tomás was gone. I thought of you here all alone and insisted we stop by for you. Carlos agreed. We won't let you refuse."

I laughed, suddenly refreshed at the prospect of spending the day with them. "You needn't worry that I'll refuse. I'll be delighted to go with you. You're so thoughtful to ask me."

A few minutes later, I climbed into their carriage and settled myself next to Marta. Carlos sat opposite us, and a picnic hamper took up the remainder of his seat.

"I haven't even asked where we're going," I said as the carriage started to move.

"Not far," Carlos answered. "Only to the *Prado del Cortijo* on the edge of town. Everyone's going. Our nephew is entering the big race, and insisted we come cheer for him."

My heart lurched. The *Prado del Cortijo,* where Ricardo had said he was going! I would see him race after all, and as

Carlos and Marta cheered for their nephew, I could cheer in my heart for Ricardo!

There were crowds of people there before us, entire families as well as the young people. This was a day for everyone, and I was grateful to Carlos and Marta for enabling me to become a part of it. Even if Tomás had been in Santiago that day, he would never have considered going on such an outing.

When we arrived, Carlos and Marta and I were welcomed by a group of their friends and families. We soon joined in their talk, but I did not give my full attention to the conversation, for whenever I had the chance I allowed my eyes to stray over the crowd, searching for the one face I wanted to see.

I did not see him until the big race was about to start. We had all walked over near the starting point to watch. He was standing next to his horse, his hand resting lightly on the reins, and he was surrounded by a group of his friends.

And she was there, too. María Elena, her pale goldenness accentuated with a dress of lightest blue silk, with row upon row of creamy white lace. In her hair she wore a rose, which must have been freshly picked, for it showed not the slightest sign of wilting. Abstractedly, I answered the questions a friend of Marta's was asking about our passage from Spain, my eyes ever returning to Ricardo. I saw María Elena laughingly take the rose from her hair and tuck it carefully under one of the embroidered threads of his riding jacket. There was something so matter-of-fact and possessive in her manner that my heart almost exploded with jealousy.

And then those who were entered in the race mounted, and were lined up at the starting point. Just before the gun signaled the start of the race, Ricardo's eyes fell on me and he smiled and waved. Exultantly, I waved back. He wore María Elena's rose, but he had smiled and waved at me!

After the contestants had gone, there were many games, some for children, some contests of horsemanship for the men who had not entered the big race. It was for me a day of magic release from the tense confined life I had been leading. Even Carlos and Marta joined in the foolish game of blind man's bluff, and we laughed so hard at Carlos's antics as he sought to catch one of us that it seemed our sides would split with the strain of laughing. And through it all, riders who had stationed themselves at various points along the outward portion of the racers' route returned to tell us who was leading. At the last report we received, Ricardo and two others had pulled slightly ahead of the rest and were holding a small but steady lead. I received the news smugly.

133

Ricardo's chestnut would never have maintained such a consistently steady pace.

We knew the riders themselves would not be far behind the last report of them, and the games all ceased as we began to look anxiously toward the direction from which they would come. They burst suddenly into sight, Ricardo and another youth riding in so closely that it would seem their horses were harnessed together. With a feeling of approval, I saw Ricardo lean forward, nudging his horse to one final burst of speed. It was a movement that was scarcely discernible, but it was effective. The horse understood and Ricardo crossed the finish line a scant length ahead of the other contestant. It was with pride in his horsemanship and the part I had played in helping him select the right mount that I joined in the cheering. This was Ricardo's moment, and I was sharing it with him vicariously.

"Ricardo won!" I turned to Marta, clapping my hands together happily. "He won!"

Marta nodded and smiled. "A good victory for the house of Alvarado y Paz. I'm afraid the house of Ortega Batres did not do so well. Here come more riders, and Carlos's nephew is still not among them."

I knew Carlos was particularly disappointed at his nephew's poor showing, but this only increased my pride in Ricardo's victory. I looked again at him. He had dismounted and there, at his side, was María Elena. With a flourish, he removed from his jacket the rose she had given him, now wilted, and handed it and the banner he had retrieved at the other end of the race to her.

I turned away; his action had extinguished my enthusiasm just as suddenly as a violent downpour snuffs out a bonfire. My joy in his triumph was utterly destroyed by that one gesture. Ricardo had said that if he won, a share of his victory would belong to me. But it was María Elena, not I, with whom he was sharing his important moment.

The return of the riders was the signal for everyone to open their picnic hampers. I was grateful for the activity as I helped Marta arrange our food on a cloth she had spread on the ground, for it helped mask the change that had come over me. Several other families brought their food and put it with ours and sat down to join us. I carried on conversations without really knowing or caring what I said. I even drank more wine than I normally did in an effort to regain the enthusiasm I had felt for the day, but it was no use. It was as if a dark cloud had moved in on a day that had held only sunshine and happiness, and had obliterated both. And it was María Elena who had done it. It was she who had spoiled my day. My jealousy of her was a a live resentment inside me, searing and burning and all but consuming me.

There were more games, and later in the afternoon Ricardo entered a jumping contest on the Arab horse. Although he didn't win that one, he did well. But the pride I had felt when I watched him cross the finish line in the big race had been destroyed by that one gesture of his, when he had handed the banner to María Elena, along with the rose she had given him as a talisman.

After dark, there was a display of fireworks, and all the people, exhausted from the day's activities, were content to sit on blankets and watch quietly, emitting soft sounds of appreciation at the more elaborate and spectacular of the patterns that flashed across the darkness. I especially welcomed nightfall, for I no longer had to keep a fixed smile on my face and pretend to a happiness and gaiety I had stopped feeling hours before.

When the fireworks display was over, there was the hushed bustle of hundreds of people getting ready to leave, and the muffled air of activity was punctuated only by the occasional call of a parent to a missing child or the over-tired wail of an exhausted infant.

It was still not late when Marta and Carlos dropped me off at the house. Cecilia had left a note saying she was spending the night with a girlfriend. I wondered, idly, if she were using the visit to cover a meeting with her doctor. Since that first day I had seen her with him in the hospital, she had confided in me no further, but I could continue to sense about her the aura of subdued excitement of a girl who loved and was loved in return. I feared for her, for the hopelessness of any future for her with her doctor, and yet I envied her, too.

It was too early to go to bed, and I had no desire to sit and stitch. I knew I was too restless to enjoy reading. I dismissed my maid for the night, told Teresa I would want nothing further, and went to my room. The house seemed unnaturally silent, and I thought of the dancing and gaiety elsewhere in the city. I felt as though I had been caught up in what I had heard sailors call a *huracán*, and while all about me there was activity, I had become trapped forever away from life in the stillness of the void the sailors claimed existed in the very center of each of the tropical storms.

I removed my combs and let my hair tumble around my shoulders, then began to brush it, hoping the familiarity of the motions would still my inquietude, soothe away my discontent. Idly, as I brushed, I glanced at my reflection. My brushing stopped abruptly, for I was stunned by what I saw: the expressionlessness of the eyes, the listless droop of the

135

mouth. Was that the same girl who had considered life such a challenge, who had refused to seek the peace and quiet of a convent, who had stubbornly refused to be shut away from life? I put down the brush and picked up the candle from the table below the mirror. I lifted it high, holding it so that it shone directly on my face, and I studied my own reflection carefully, hoping it had only been the angle of the light that had made me appear so expressionless, so apathetic. But moving the light nearer did not help at all, and only confirmed what I had seen there before.

Could that girl with the spiritless eyes, the lifeless slack mouth really be me? I remembered another time I had been surprised at my reflection, the day Tatiana had given me her golden hoops. I recalled the sensual girl in the mirror, the girl who wore the gypsy hoops and stared boldly back at me with fiery eyes. On that day, I had been frightened by what I had seen in my face, but now I longed to see myself as I had been then, if only as a sign that I was not totally dead inside.

It had been a long time since I had taken Tatiana's gold hoops out of the chamois bag in which I kept them, but I felt compelled to get them at that moment. After I had put them in my ears, I slipped over my head the string of bright green beads dear Giorgio had given me. Then I looked again in the mirror to see if the gypsy adornments had imparted to my face some of the audacity, the boldness and worldliness that had been there the first time I had slipped the hoops into my ears. But this time I saw no such transformation, and my eyes only continued to stare back at me blankly, as lifeless and still as the center of a *huracán*. Perhaps there was nothing left of the girl I had been three years before. Still wearing my gypsy jewelry, I went out in the main patio and began walking aimlessly back and forth. Occasionally, I dropped into a chair, but soon was again overcome by a restlessness that would not allow me to be still, and rose again to resume my pointless pacing.

Finally, I went into the small *patio de placer*, hoping the sound of the running water in the fountain would soothe away my restlessness, dispel my gloom. I dropped heavily onto one of the chairs, wondering what happiness the future could possibly hold for me. *Tatiana,* my heart cried out in despair, *why did you promise me I would be happy here, when nothing but misery awaited me at the end of the sea voyage you foresaw?*

From the other side of the wall on the street side came the clatter of hoofs coming to a sudden stop. This sound was followed by the laughing voices of a group of young men, and

136

then soft feminine voices as a carriage clattered to a halt. There was the quiet clip-clop of horses' hoofs moving slowly from one spot to another, and I knew they were being taken to the side of the street to be tethered. Then more laughter and talking.

And then the music.

There were two guitars, well-played, and the laughing voices hushed as they began to play the strains of one of the *soleares*. The music filled the air with its very intensity, and I knew the dance that it called for had to be full of a slow and sad stateliness and dignity. It was the music that exactly mirrored my mood.

I was scarcely aware of rising from my chair. I had made no conscious decision to get up and begin to dance, and yet I found myself in the center of the small patio, arms upraised. Then my body began to move, to reflect all the pent-up frustration and disappointment of the months past. It was not a physical response, but an answering of my soul, a necessary outlet for feelings held too long in check.

Once I had begun, I could not stop. The guitarists played other songs, and each of them touched an emotion deep within me and evoked an impassioned response. I danced to all of the songs, the sad and the proud and the nostalgic. And I danced to the joyous songs, too, for deep within me they touched the truest chord of all, a longing to know happiness once more. I knew I would keep dancing as long as the music continued. It was a release for me, a release I had not known could be headier than strong wine. When I heard the occasional appreciative bursts of *"Olé!"* from the other side of the wall, I felt it was my dancing that had brought the spontaneous cries, even though I knew that no one out there could see me or was even aware of my presence.

My passion built, until my steps were coming faster, the click of my fingers sharper, and I felt my body sway sensuously, yearningly. Never had I so clearly exposed my soul as I did in those dances, free for once from the restraints placed on me by Tomás and from my own self-imposed inhibitions as well. No longer was there a need to mask my deep sorrow at a marriage that could never bring me happiness, no longer was there a need to hide my love and longing for Ricardo. There, in the confines of that small enclosure, I was free for a time, free to express everything I felt, to release emotions kept bottled tightly within me too long. And, secure in the knowledge that I could not be seen, I expressed everything: despair and hopelessness, love and desire, sensuality and abandon. Never, I knew, had I danced so expressively, for never before had I danced with such a full knowledge of life.

The music ended with a final beat, and again I heard the cries of *"Olé!"* This time the shouts seemed to be even more directed at me than they had the other times, though I knew it could not be so.

For a few seconds after the music stopped, there was a deep silence, broken only by the sound of the water in the *pila.* I lowered my head, and suddenly was aware of the fatigue of my body, which I had not even noticed before. During the dances, I had moved as if I were disembodied, unaware of fatigue or effort, above physical feeling. But now the speaking of my soul was over, and there was only the void in which I lived, as hopeless and as pointless as ever. I became aware of the tiredness of my legs, felt my arms go limp with exhaustion. I felt, too, the dampness of tears I had not even known I was shedding.

Then there was the murmur of voices from over the wall and the sound of the carriage and the horses moving on. But from the other direction, the direction of the gate leading into the patio from the stables, I heard another sound, a muted,

"Olé!"

Startled, I looked up. Ricardo was standing there, leaning on the gate, his eyes fastened on me.

"Oh!" I gasped. "How long have you been there?"

He didn't answer my question, but opened the gate and came into the patio.

"Poor Carlota! Life isn't that bad, is it?" he said, and I knew he had been watching me for some time. He took a kerchief from his pocket and walked over to me.

"Here, let me dry your eyes."

"No!" I answered vehemently, backing away from him. He felt sorry for me, I realized, and that was the last emotion I wanted to evoke in him. "I don't want your pity!"

I turned and raced from the patio, running to my room and slamming the door behind me. I threw myself on the bed and wept.

I did not want Ricardo's pity. I wanted his love.

Santiago—April, 1773

CHAPTER VIII

The next morning, a Sunday, I awakened feeling weak and listless, as though every bit of emotion I possessed had been wrung from my body by my dancing the night before. There was no longer any sensation left in me. There was only a vast emptiness, an aloneness born of the knowledge that there was no one left in the world who cared about me or to whom it mattered how I felt. In that mood, I had no desire to go to the Cathedral, where I would be certain to meet a number of the people I knew, so I decided to avoid church that morning. I would go instead to matins at one of the smaller churches that afternoon.

As I lay in bed, I heard Ricardo's steps passing my window, and then heard the slam of the gate that separated the kitchen patio from the garden and stable yard. Cecilia was gone, would not be back till late afternoon. My feeling of aloneness increased, for listening to Ricardo leave made it seem that he had deserted me afresh.

I lay there lethargically, lacking even the will to get out of bed. Occasionally I dozed, but most of the time I just lay there, awake but motionless and devoid of thought.

Tomás would be at the farm for two weeks, and since the house always ran with less effort when he was not about, there was nothing which needed doing. It was past noon when I finally sighed heavily and got out of bed. I dallied over dressing, not from fastidiousness, but merely because I lacked any reason to hurry.

Finally, I went to tell Teresa to set the table for only one. The cook had already prepared the meal, so even though I had little appetite, I did try to eat some of everything. At any rate, I welcomed going through the mechanics of sitting at the table and nibbling at the food as a way to pass the time. But even as I sat there dawdling, I was aware that the sands were still running in the hourglass of my life on such a day, and that yet another day of boredom was eating away at my youth and my life. Would it continue thus, I wondered, until I was too old to care? Would I go on like this, not welcoming each morning as the start of a new and eventful day, but facing it with dread, wanting somehow only to reach the end of it, so that the whole hopeless process could be repeated again the following day? Where was the anticipation, the eagerness with which I had lived until that hapless day when *don* Guillermo and his men had deprived Giorgio of his young life?

For wasn't that the event that had marked the change in my life—not Tatiana's death, which had saddened me but would not in itself have defeated me? Wasn't it the knowledge that my selfishness, my foolishness had killed Giorgio, just as surely as if my hand had wielded the sword that thrust the life from his body, that had filled my soul with remorse? *Tía* had always said that life is an atonement for our sins. Could that be so? And could it be that because I was guilty, I must forever live the atonement and penance for that guilt?

Hadn't my atonement begun the day Tomás had claimed me for his wife? I remembered how much delight and unbounded hope the day had held for me earlier, when I had seen Ricardo's face in the glass, and how that hope had been cruelly smashed when I found it was Tomás I had married, not Ricardo. Since that day, the depression within me had been nurtured, bit by bit, eating away at hope and destroying any small sign of happiness as soon as it appeared. My despair was like a giant sore within me, festering and enlarging itself, and soon there would be nothing else left. No, I mused as I spooned a few bites of custard into my mouth, even now there was little left in me of anticipation and eagerness for life. I was hopelessly in love with Ricardo, who scarcely seemed to realize I existed, and married to Tomás, who was arrogant and selfish and demanding. Dreary days stretched on endlessly before me, and their sameness and their boredom and frustration would be broken only occasionally by small snatches of fleeting happiness at some kindness, such as that of Carlos and Marta the day before. But then, as on the previous day, despair would close over me again, and the feeling of hopelessness would return, more overpowering than ever, as though to reprimand me for having dared to forget that I must forever atone for bringing Giorgio to his death.

Just as I was rising from the table, wondering how to wile

away the hours before matins, Ricardo burst into the dining room.

I looked at him, startled. "I didn't expect you back for dinner!" I picked up the bell to ring for another plate and hot food.

He put his hand over the bell to keep it from ringing. "I've already had dinner. I didn't come back to eat. I came to get you and take you out for a ride."

"Me?" I asked disbelievingly. His words magically dispelled the pervading gloom of a few seconds before. "Oh, I'd love to go!" I turned and left the dining room, Ricardo just behind me, munching on a piece of fried *tortilla* he had picked up from the table.

"All morning, I've been thinking about you here alone, feeling sorry for you."

He could not have said anything worse. I had started toward my room, but his words stopped me abruptly.

Here it was again. Pity. He pitied me. Pity, that most despised of all emotions! He had come back to the house, and he had asked me to go riding with him because he felt sorry for me.

I had nothing left but my pride. I could not lose that, too. I turned to face him. "I really don't think I had better go with you," I said, trying to speak firmly and to keep the disappointment from my voice. "I had forgotten for a moment, but I promised Tomás several weeks ago I would go riding only with him."

My words were true enough. At the time I had promised, I had supposed Tomás's request had to do with Pilar and the painful memories he must have had of her last and fatal ride. So, in a burst of compassion, I had agreed. But it was a promise I would willingly have broken just then, if it hadn't been for Ricardo's last words. I was too proud to accept his pity.

But I was not prepared for his reaction to my refusal. "So he's got you cowed, too." He spoke in a low tone, and there was so much quiet disdain in his voice and in the way he looked at me that I could scarcely stand it. I did not want his pity, and yet I could not tolerate his disapproval.

"It's not that," I protested, hating myself for the pride that was making me refuse the invitation I longed with all my heart to accept. "It's just that I did promise him. Besides, I didn't go to mass this morning, and I must go to matins." I looked away, unable to bear any longer the look of contempt with which he continued to fix me.

But I could not avoid hearing his words, or the disgust with which they were uttered.

"I'm sorry I asked you. All morning, I've been remembering how you looked when you were dancing last night, so alone, so—so defiant. I thought that here at last was another person who would not bow down to Father, that here was a spirit he would never be able to conquer. It was as though I saw you for the first time, not as the meek, quiet girl I thought you to be, but as someone with a fiery determination and a zest for life that even Father, with his need to bend everyone's will to his own, could not destroy.

"But I was wrong. You're afraid of him, just like everyone else around here." He turned his back on me and started to walk away.

It was that final gesture of repudiation as much as his words that made me realize I could not let him go like that.

"Wait!" I called after him desperately. He turned and looked at me, his eyebrows raised quizzically.

"You didn't come back here just because—because you felt sorry for me?" I asked. "It wasn't just out of pity that you asked me to go riding with you?"

He stared at me for a minute, then his face lit up with sudden understanding. "So that's why you refused! For the same reason you ran from me last night! Not because you're afraid of Father, but because you thought pity brought me back here?" He shook his head slowly and took a few steps back toward me. "No, Carlota, you misunderstood, or maybe it was my fault for using the wrong words. I admired the spirit that shone from you like a bright flame last night as you danced. I wasn't wrong in thinking as I watched you that Father hasn't been able to extinguish the spark of defiance that ignited that flame, was I? Just now, when you refused to go with me because of a promise Father should never have requested of you, I thought I had been wrong.

"I'm glad to find out I wasn't. It was admiration for you that brought me back here, and compassion, maybe. But not pity. Never that." He smiled softly. "No, never that, my proud little gypsy stepmother."

Incredulous, I stared at him, asked, "Why—why did you call me that?"

His smile deepened. "Because that's what you reminded me of last night. I've never seen a gypsy, but I've read of them, and I imagine they're dark, like you are. And as I watched you last night, I thought you belonged not in a small tiled patio in Santiago, but out in the country somewhere, with a gypsy campfire casting shadows across your face as you danced, catching the highlights of your hair as you twirled. I've never seen anyone dance so expressively or so beautifully, Carlota."

142

"Thank you." I lowered my eyes, pleased at his compliment, and secretly wondering if he could guess how much my longing for him had inspired the movements of my body the previous evening. I turned and went into my room to get dressed.

Later, as we rode out of town through the back alleys and out-of-the-way streets over which Ricardo led me, the years dissolved and I was again the naughty child, sneaking out against *Tía's* wishes, unmindful of consequences, my guilt overridden by a delicious sense of mischief and escape.

We talked little as we rode, but our silence contained, for me, a new quality of comfort. The discomfiture I had always felt in Ricardo's company, the feeling that made me stutter and stammer and wonder what to do with my hands, had magically vanished, and I knew with a certainty that I would never feel bothered by his closeness again. This did not mean I had lost my awareness of his presence, but only that it had miraculously changed to a comfortable feeling instead of an uneasiness. And whenever I remembered with a smug satisfaction that he had certainly deserted María Elena to go riding with me, my heart was flooded with joy. How could I have thought earlier that very day that my life was over, I wondered? Never had I felt so alive, so vital. How little Ricardo knew the accuracy of his words when he had jokingly called me a gypsy, on that day of all days! For that afternoon, I was again the daughter of Tatiana, free as only the gypsies are free, savoring the moment for itself and not concerned with the next moment or the tomorrows to follow. There was only the here and now, and I was filled with a deep peace and contentment.

I let Ricardo lead me where he would. Most of the time, I didn't know where we were, and it didn't matter. It was several hours later when we rode to the top of *Cerro de Santa Cruz* and dismounted, pleasantly tired. We left the horses to graze and walked down a little way to a knob, saw Santiago spread out before us. As the final rays of the late afternoon sun reached the city, it seemed remote and unreal, as though it had nothing to do with us.

Far below us, I recognized the walls of some of the convents, and I was suddenly deeply grateful for my freedom at that moment, for the pleasure of being up there, looking down on the closely confined courtyards where those who had given their lives to the church, as *Tía* had wanted me to give mine, spent their days in endless prayer. I did not allow myself to dwell on the knowledge that I was not really free at all, that I belonged to Tomás as surely and as irrevocably as his slave laborers belonged to him. The moment was all that mattered, and in that moment, Tomás was far away and I was there, on top of a hill looking down at Santiago with Ricardo by my side.

"I've never seen you look so contented," Ricardo said as we sat on the dried grass, looking down on the city.

"I am contented. I feel so—so free, like a bird let out of its cage. I haven't felt like this in a long time."

"Some birds are not meant to be caged."

I nodded. "You and I are like that, I think."

"I know." Ricardo picked up a piece of grass, fingered it absently. "If only Father understood that!" He pointed, and my gaze followed his finger to the high wall surrounding the Franciscan monastery. "He would have me go in there, my life confined to those walls, always inside them. And even though I might occasionally venture out into the world beyond them, it would never again be as a part of it, for my focus would be forced to stay within those walls. And there is so much I would do outside! How could I consign myself to such confinement forever?" He pointed, in rapid succession, to some of the other monasteries. "Father would have me join any of them—that one, or that one, or that one. It wouldn't matter to him which gate I went into, which walls I disappeared behind, as long as I disappeared." He laughed, a short bitter laugh. "Any one of them would serve his purpose, for he would rid himself of me, and that is what he wants to do."

"Ricardo!" I gasped, surprised not only at his words, but at the deep resentment with which he spoke them. "How can you think such a thing?"

"How can I think anything else?" he countered, throwing the piece of grass down with a brief angry gesture. "But for Tía and the small legacy she left me, I'd have had little choice in the matter. She had a modest sum, and left most of it to Cecilia. It was right that she did, because there was always a special closeness between them. But she remembered me, too, and I'll never stop being grateful to her for realizing, even when we were children, that Father would never let me study law, as I wanted to do. Knowing that, and knowing how much it meant to me, she provided for me, too, so that Father had no excuse to stop me."

"She must have been a very thoughtful person. I'm sorry I never knew her." But my thoughts did not stray long from Ricardo. "You decided long ago, then, what you wanted to do?"

He nodded. "I sometimes wonder if I was born with the need to study laws, know them, find out how to use them to help people. I can't remember when I consciously decided.

144

But it was *Tía's* legacy, which she wisely left with Carlos Ortega Batres to be doled out to me monthly, that has enabled me to study at the University."

"Your father has no conrtol over the money?"

He shook his head. "*Tía* Maria knew her brother too well, and made certain he couldn't get his hands on it. But for that, Father would have forced me into a monastery long before this. Surely you've noticed how determined he still is, haven't you?"

"I could not help but notice it." Tomás's desire to have Ricardo take his vows was so strong I doubted if he could have hidden it. Tomás was not a man for subtleties, and his motives were apparent even when he thought he was being subtle.

"And certainly you must have realized that I have made it very clear I have no desire for such a vocation," he continued.

I smiled, remembering Ricardo's stubborn resistance to Tomás's persistent attempts to get him to consider one order or another.

"You've made that quite clear," I agreed.

He shrugged, and the gesture was full of fury and confusion. "Then how can his persistence in flaunting the advantages of first this order and now that one in front of me have any other explanation, except that he wants to get rid of me?"

"I don't know," I agreed, sharing his confusion, remembering my own ceaseless struggle against *Tía* to keep her from forcing me into just such a life. She had certainly been trying to rid herself of me. Could Ricardo be right? Was Tomás trying to do the same with him?

"But why?" I asked, unable to think of any logical explanation. *Tía* had wanted me out of the way so she could be free to pursue her own postponed religious vocation. But what motive could Tomás have? "Why would he want to get rid of you?"

"I don't know." He sounded weary, as though he had posed that question to himself many times and failed to find an answer. "The only thing I can think of is that Father has never liked me. He can't stand having anyone around him he cannot dominate."

"But that's foolish of him." I did not deny that it was so. Then I said suddenly, "Ricardo, don't ever give in! Don't let him dominate you in this matter. You mustn't!" The thought of Ricardo disappearing forever behind a monastery's walls filled me with a sudden panic, and the words spilled out of my mouth in breathless succession. "You'd be unhappy, I

145

know. You couldn't stand the confinement, the closeness, any more than I could have. You would feel, as I would, like a wild bird caged.

"I know! I know how you must feel now, how you would feel if you entered one of the orders. When my father died, my aunt wanted me to give myself to the church, but I couldn't, I just couldn't! I'd die if I were cooped up, day after day, looking at the same courtyard, spending endless hours in the same small cell. And so would you! Some people are cut out for such a solitary life, and they go to it gladly, and I admire them. But not you or me! Don't let Tomás force you into it! Promise me you won't!" I did not add that the thought of him being lost to me forever behind monastery walls frightened me for my own sake as much as for his.

"You needn't worry," he assured me. "I'm determined on the course my life will take, and it's not the course Father has in mind." He frowned. "Besides, even if I were inclined toward the church, if I did feel I had a vocation, I would have to think about it very carefully. The day of church dominance here is coming to an end."

"Why?" His words shocked me. "What do you mean?"

"The churches—all of them—have been too greedy. They have taken too much from too many for too long. They must retreat or fall."

I no longer tried to hide my shock at what he was saying. "Ricardo! That's—that's heresy!" Never had I heard such thoughts voiced openly. Even though we had seen no one, except at a distance, all afternoon, I could not resist the urge to look over my shoulder to see if anyone could have heard. The church could do no wrong. That fact had been drummed into my brain day after day until to me it had become an indisputable fact, a fact backed by the unvoiced fear of the Inquisition in everyone's heart. The Office of the Inquisition reached everywhere in the Spanish empire, even to Santiago. If they heard Ricardo say such things, they might ... The thought was too horrible to complete. "You must not say such things!" I admonished. "The Inquisition—"

He laughed. "—is notoriously inactive here. In fact, I understand they have frequently been berated by the ecclesiastical authorities for their laxness in failing to ferret out heretics. And what I said is true. The harder we *Guatemaltecos* work, the more the church demands of us. And they have demanded so much, there was not even enough left to satisfy King Carlos. He's greedy, too, so he sent a commission here to see why he was collecting so little. The commission decided it was because the churches were taking so much there was not enough left to please the King. Back in '67, the King

146

issued an edict banishing the Jesuits from Guatemala. They were loaded on a ship and ordered never to return. And who is to say what other orders may follow them? Do you want to know what I think, Carlota?"

"Yes," I answered, afraid yet eager to hear what he had to say, knowing I would always want to know every thought he would share with me, on whatever subject, even though those thoughts be heretical or just plain shocking. "What do you think?" I urged.

"I think the King and the church between them are squeezing the purses of the people of Guatemala so tightly that one day the people will rebel, perhaps against both, and they will demand to hold onto more of what they have earned. And out of it all, something new will emerge, something that belongs to those of us who have been born here as well as those who come from Spain." He frowned. "Right now, we *creoles* are second class citizens, you know. We can't hold office, except for a few minor posts—"

"You're speaking of open rebellion?" I interrupted. I could not bring myself to say that other word, the word Tomás had uttered accusingly during one of their heated discussions: treason. First heresy, and now treason!

It was as though he read my thoughts. "Rebellion? Perhaps, though it needn't always be violent or open, or even very sudden. Nor need it be treasonous." He smiled at me. "Poor little stepmother, I fear I've shocked you terribly with my criticism of the King and the church. But don't you see, criticism is good! A people can't let any institution become inviolable, beyond criticism. For whenever any institution— and institutions are made of people, after all, like you and me—knows they must answer to no one, that is the day they become a danger to everyone, most of all to themselves. For in their very inviolability is sown the first seed of their own destruction."

"I don't understand," I protested. "The church is the voice of God. Would you destroy it? And the King?"

He threw back his head and laughed, then grew quickly serious again. "I would destroy nothing, Carlota. Don't look so horrified. I only said that if institutions become too powerful, they can invite destruction, or even destroy themselves. I would only use the laws to protect people from their excesses, and work to get new laws if the old ones don't give the people adequate protection. That is why I'm studying. It's only a means to an end. We need people who are familiar with the laws, so they know what needs changing. We must get our own laws here, special ones that keep the institutions

147

from exploiting us. I want to help us get those laws, all quite peacefully and properly.

"You see, I'm not really so horrid after all, am I?"

"Of course you're not!" I quickly agreed. But I was still unsure of what he was trying to tell me. "Are you saying that we here in Guatemala must separate ourselves from Spain, and from the church? How could we do either? Or why would we want to?"

"Not separate ourselves, certainly. I don't think anything that drastic will be necessary."

He wasn't planning revolution, after all! I began to breathe more easily. But my relief was short-lived, for after a brief hesitation, he continued,

"Providing the King understands we must have a measure of independence, or at least a voice in our own affairs. If he is wise, he'll give us enough self-rule to appease us, and if he and the church will stop milking the colonial empire as though it were a cow with an endless supply of cream only for their pitchers, and treating us as though we were an insignificant bunch of dairymaids, then perhaps nothing too startling will happen."

He stood up, offering me his hand and pulling me to my feet. "That's enough of serious talk for today. I'm quite a bore when I get started on that subject, I'm afraid. Will you forgive me, please, for talking too much?"

"There's nothing to forgive. I've enjoyed it." I did not add that I would enjoy anything he said, just listening to his voice, being near him. I was flattered that he had shared with me his innermost thoughts that day, even though they had left me confused and shaken. I began to realize how complex was his nature, and how unlike Tomás he was. Tomás objected, as did Ricardo, because tithes and taxes and the church donations he was obliged to give took too much of his money, but never would he be able to get impassioned about an idea, or speak from deep within himself as Ricardo had just done.

"I think the horses are well rested," Ricardo said. "We had better start home."

My hand still tingled from the remembered contact with his as we walked toward the horses. "I suppose we must," I agreed with reluctance, wishing I could hold forever onto the afternoon. But the sun was getting close to the top of the mountains and would soon disappear below them. By the time we arrived back in Santiago, I remembered guiltily, I would have missed matins. I was not truly remorseful, and I knew I must report my lack of remorse next time I went to confession. But nothing could take from me the joy of the afternoon.

Simón was back when we rode into the stable yard. He showed no surprise at seeing us ride in together.

"Simón, I think it would be better if my father didn't know that *doña* Carlota went riding with me today." Ricardo smiled conspiratorially at Simón as he helped me to dismount.

It was obvious from the easy way in which Simón returned his smile that it was not the first time they had conspired to keep something from Tomás. "Yes, *Señor* Ricardo, I understand."

I was glad that such a conspiracy existed between them. I did not fear Tomás's anger as much as I felt that the afternoon had been something special and private, something not to be sullied by having Tomás share the knowledge of it. For a few hours, there had been just the two of us, Ricardo and me. I didn't want anything to mar the remembered perfection of those hours.

I slipped unseen into my room and changed, and not even Cecilia suspected that Ricardo and I had spent the afternoon together.

Why was I so concerned about anyone finding out about our afternoon? I wondered as I brushed my hair. Surely there was nothing wrong with it; it had been an innocent outing. I put down the brush and looked at myself long and hard in the mirror. And then I had to look away, uncomfortably, as though to break someone else's piercing gaze that saw too much.

Our outing had been innocent, an afternoon of riding and talking, nothing more. But in that very innocence lay the lie of it, for there was nothing innocent about my feelings for Ricardo. I wanted him, longed for him to want me, too. The new easiness I felt in his presence did not lessen my longing for him. I yearned for the thrill of feeling his lips crush mine, the joy of thrilling to the touch of his hands as they moved slowly and caressingly over my body, the pleasure of being able to slide my arms possessively around his neck and pull his head down to mine. From Tomás, I had learned the full meaning of carnal appetite, for I saw it in his greedy possession of me, even though I had never been able to respond to him. Had he been less than totally selfish, had he shown a degree of tenderness in his advances, I still doubted if he could have elicited any response in me. But now, shamelessly, my whole being longed to belong to Ricardo, and my body ached with desire for him.

In that desire there lay nothing of innocence.

The next day, I was out weeding my garden when Simón limped by on his way from the stables to the kitchen.

"Simón, what's wrong with your leg?" I asked in alarm. I had noticed he was limping slightly the previous day, but now he seemed scarcely able to walk. "You don't look well, either. Are you feeling all right?"

He shrugged. "It is nothing, *Señora*. Only a sore place on my ankle that is slow to heal. It will heal in time. Perhaps I am a little fevered, but that, too, will be better tomorrow."

"Your leg might need attention." I stood up and brushed the dirt from my hands. "Go in the patio and sit down while I wash my hands. Then I'll look at it. I might have something to help you."

The sore on Simón's ankle was not large, but it was festering and the skin around it had grown angry red. I had made an ointment of some leaves I had found earlier in the year, ones that looked similar to some we had back in Andalusia, which effectively drew the poison from a wound. I had not had a chance to try it, but it was all I had. I only hoped it would work, for Simón's seemingly small injury had put him in more danger than he realized. I had seen people die of such foolish little sores once the poisons from them went through their bodies. I considered calling the doctor Tomás used, but discarded the idea. Bleeding was his cure for everything, from toothache to upset stomach, and I could not see that such treatment would do Simón the least bit of good.

I applied hot steamy towels over the ointment and told Simón to continue the treatment himself. "I'll send one of the maids in to see that you have enough hot towels. You must stay off your feet for several days, at least."

"But the horses, *Señora*—"

"Alberto and the others will have to take care of them," I said emphatically. "You must go to bed and stay there, Simón. If you don't, it can be very serious."

"But Alberto is lazy, and the *Señor* has given me certain things to do while he is gone. If I do not do them, he will be angry."

"And I will be more angry if you do. I want you to promise me you will do as I say." I made a mental note to talk to Tomás about it when he returned so that Simón would not get a tongue-lashing he did not deserve. In later years, I often wondered how different my life might have been had I not forgotten to do so.

After a moment's hesitation, Simón promised.

I applied a fresh poultice to his leg several times a day for the next three days, and made certain he kept damp heat on it to draw out the poisons. At last, to my relief, the swelling went down and the fevered limb began to heal.

"It is a miracle!" Simón flexed his foot to demonstrate to me that his leg no longer pained him. "You are an angel come to us, *Señora*."

I smiled, embarrassed yet oddly touched by the devotion in his eyes. "It's no miracle. The poultice did the work. And it is my mother who was an angel, for she taught me the use of such things."

"The miracle is that you have come to us, *Señora*. The *Señor* is a very hard master."

"Simón," I chided gently, "you mustn't say such things about my husband." But as I admonished him, even I knew that it was true, for Tomás was often impossible to please.

"I am sorry, *Señora*. I should not have spoken so." I noted that he did not rescind his words.

I had expected that Sunday afternoon ride to make a great change in the relationship between Ricardo and me, and was disappointed to realize during the following week that it had made none at all, except that I was no longer flustered into incoherence in his presence. To me, the ride had been significant in that it meant that Ricardo saw me as an individual, a person in my own right, not just as Tomás's wife. But it had apparently been, to him, only a pleasant but meaningless interlude, and I had been nothing more than a sympathetic listener for his ideas.

Nor did anything seem to change in his relationship with María Elena, whom he continued to court with such concentration that I feared each day he would come home and say that he had spoken for her. And I had seen the way she looked at him when she had fastened the rose onto his riding jacket on the day of the race. How could I doubt what her answer would be?

Each day, I hoped Ricardo might again burst in unexpectedly and invite me to go riding with him, and each day I was disappointed when he did not. His lectures resumed the day after our ride, and where before I had taken note of his schedule and made certain I was not around when he came home from the University at odd hours, now I made just as certain that I was clearly in evidence when he arrived, frequently managing to be either working in my herb garden or in the stables, for I knew he entered from that direction. He always greeted me with a smile and a pleasant comment, but never did he suggest during that remaining week of Tomás's absence that we go riding again.

And then it was the day Tomás was due home, and I knew that there would be no hope of a carefree afternoon of riding with Ricardo when he was there. Even before his arrival, just the knowledge that he would be home depressed me. I knew there would be oppressive restrictions on my conduct, constant criticism and reprimands, and the boring afternoon carriage rides. But most depressing of all was the knowledge that he would again be there, lying beside me in bed each night, demanding, insensitive. Nor was he one to accept excuses, for he had never considered my feelings. I was his wife and it was my duty to accept his advances. I could not very well tell him that I found those advances increasingly abhorrent. I was not even anxious to bear him children any more, for I feared that they might bear too many of his traits—his selfishness and greed, his lack of understanding—and I would not be able to love them as a mother should. I was thankful that Ricardo had not inherited these character flaws.

It was the second week of May when Tomás returned, and at once I felt the sharp curtailment of my personal freedom his presence brought as though it were a restraining rope tied around my neck. The simplest sally out onto the streets could not be accomplished unless it were done properly, and this so complicated life that it dsetroyed the small pleasures in which I had found a measure of satisfaction. I must not work in my herb garden or be in the patio when the sun was shining, because it would darken my complexion, which was already too tawny to suit him. I must not go to pray in one of the smaller churches because our position demanded that we attend the Cathedral. I must not go to the market with Teresa in the early mornings because it was unseemly for a lady to be up and about at such an hour. At times, it seemed there was nothing I was permitted to do, except sit in our carriage while it looped the *Plaza Real*, and smile and nod at the right people, but never at the wrong ones.

Yet there was seldom any open disagreement between Tomás and me. To all who saw us, we were a normal married couple, neither more nor less happy than other couples. And thus we appeared, but it was not so, for behind the façade of a normal marriage, there was a bitter struggle going on, a struggle I knew I must win. For Tomás was trying to destroy my spirit, bend my will as he would have it bent, mold me into his image of Pilar: shy, acquiescent, and proper. If he succeeded, I knew I would exist from then on in a state of lethargy and spiritlessness. Already, I had had frightening periods—hours or sometimes entire days—when I felt myself hopelessly mired in the depths of such spiritlessness, and it was only by summoning all the determination I possessed that I had been able to pull myself out of it. I fought back with renewed vigor after these periods, yet I was cautious, for open rebellion Tomás could have quickly quashed at its onset.

So as Tomás added new restrictions to my conduct or criticized my dress or belittled, in private, something I had said, I did not protest openly. Instead, I showed my defiance in small ways, ways that could well have been accidental, but I knew and he knew that they were not. Thus because I knew he preferred rubies to pearls, I did not have the clasp repaired on *Mamá's* ruby necklace, and so, at the last minute, must wear pearls. And if something amused me, I let my laughter ring out loud and clear, with a deliberate spitefulness, knowing full well that the very sound of it grated on his ears, for he had often told me so. I even began to rise exceptionally early, earlier than I ever had when he was in Santiago, remembering that he considered it unladylike. This also saved me from some of his advances, for he sometimes became aroused after he had wakened in the morning. These were petty little things, I knew, and yet they were necessary to me, symbols of my self-assertion, my own affirmation to myself that, though as his wife I must obey his commands, he had not succeeded in subjugating me to his will.

But this was all under the surface, something that would be noticed by no one but the two of us. Only once during the week and a half he stayed home that time did we openly exchange angry words. This was the morning of the second day after his return. I had slipped out of bed in the early morning hours, taking care not to waken him, and had gone out to the stables. I was there when Simón came in, and stopped midway in my greeting when I noticed a welt on his cheek and another on his forehead, with a sharp line of darker red wherever his skin had been broken on the crest of each welt.

"Simón! Your face! What happened?"

He looked away quickly, busied himself by forking hay from one corner of a stall to another, a completely useless task which made me at once suspicious. "It is nothing, *Señora*," he said back over his shoulder. "Only a few scratches where I hurt myself when I fell." He continued to work, keeping his back turned toward me.

"But they looked like welts, as if—Simón, you haven't been fighting, have you?" Even as I asked the question, I knew fighting was not in his nature. His was a gentle and simple spirit. He loved the horses, loved to be good to them, care for them; they were his children. But why, then, was he trying to brush away my questions, to hide from me?

In his eagerness to deny having fought, he momentarily

153

forgot and turned toward me. "Oh, no, *Señora!* I would never fight!"

"Then what——?" As I saw again the welts on his face, I realized such wounds could be caused only by a rope, or a whip. A whip! An angry realization swept over me. I knew who had inflicted those welts. It could be only one person.

"Tomás!"

Simón shook his head vehemently from side to side. "Oh, no, *Señora*, you are wrong. *Don* Tomás——"

"His riding whip," I said with a certainty, ignoring his denial. "He struck you with his riding whip. Why?"

"Oh, no, *Señora*——"

"Tell me why," I persisted. "Tell me why he did it." A quiet fury was welling up inside me. How could he do such a thing to so gentle a soul as Simón, whose devotion to the horses was something seldom found? And Tomás knew he did not dare defend himself, could not strike back!

Simón continued to demur a while longer, but finally realizing I did not believe him, he admitted with obvious reluctance that Tomás had slashed at him angrily the previous morning.

"But do not concern yourself, *Señora*. My face will heal."

I puzzled over his manner. He did not want me to question him further. Why?

"Why did he do it, Simón?" I moved in so close he was forced to stop pitching hay and he had to turn and look at me. "What had you done to make him so angry?"

"Please, *Señora*, you mustn't worry." He fidgeted with the pitchfork, his eyes downcast.

"Oh!" I gasped, remembering suddenly Simón's hesitation to promise me he would stay off his leg because Tomás had given him a number of tasks to do. "Simón, it's my fault, isn't it? That's why you didn't want to tell me! I meant to say something to Tomás as soon as he arrived from the country, tell him I had made you promise to stay in bed. But he arrived so late, and there was such confusion connected with his arrival, that it slipped my mind." Remorse and shame at the thoughtlessness of my oversight mingled with my anger at Tomás, and tears overflowed out of my eyes and ran down my cheeks. "It's my fault he was angry with you, my fault for forgetting to tell him. I am responsible. Can you forgive me?"

Simón was looking full at me by then, and he said in an astounded hush, "You mustn't cry on my account, *Señora*. It isn't right. You mustn't feel you were the cause of this."

"But I was. Didn't you tell the *Señor* about your leg?"

"I tried to, but he is wicked, and when a madness comes upon him, he will not listen."

"Simón!" His words shocked me, and I knew I should protest what he said. It was unjust of Tomás to beat him, and it was cruel, but he was within his rights as a master. I knew, as mistress of the house, I should not allow him to be called wicked. Yet no words in his defense sprung to my lips.

Nor was Simón likely to have heeded such words had I uttered them, for a look of black hatred had come over his face, and he kept on, as though he could not stop. "He will beat a man and not listen to his defense! He is evil! He has his workers on the farm beaten for the smallest offenses. I know. I hear. He even sent a man to the mines once. That I know for certain." His breath came in uneven spurts, and his nostrils were distended.

"Simón!" I cried again. The look on his face had so transformed his whole being that he was frightening to look upon. Here was not the gentle creature who always looked at me with eyes openly devoted and called me an angel. This was a man who hated, who despised Tomás to the depths of his being. And though I deplored what Tomás had done to him, I could not let Simón, in his hatred, spread malicious lies about him.

"You know that isn't true," I said, trying to make my voice severe. "About the mines. He could not have done such a thing!" Surely Tomás could not have sent anyone, slave or servant, to the mines, for that meant almost certain death. He was not a compassionate man, that I knew, but that! No, I could not believe he would have done such a thing.

"It is true, *Señora*," he insisted. "It happened many years ago."

"That's enough!" I said sharply, and he looked at me with hurt in his eyes and was silent.

My vigorous denial of what he said was as much for my own benefit as for his. The beating Tomás had given him was horrid, a gross injustice. However, as Simón himself had said, his face would heal. But the mines! I shuddered. I knew a master could condemn a man there on the slightest excuse, but surely Tomás could not have been guilty of such a monstrous thing. "He could not have done such a thing!" I repeated.

The look of blackset fury I had seen a moment earlier on Simón's face had disappeared. He wore again the inscrutable look that had become so familiar to me. It was as if all the *indios* in Guatemala had the same mask, emotionless and unreadable, with which to cover their faces whenever they chose. Only occasionally, as a few minutes before, did one of them allow the mask to slip off in the presence of their masters or mistresses.

But when Simón had permitted me a fleeting glimpse of his deep hatred for Tomás, it was not only his face that I saw unmasked, but also that of my husband, revealing a side of his nature that I had suspected was there but I did not want to look upon. If my denial of Tomás's guilt in sending a man to the mines had fooled Simón, it had not fooled me. An icy chill enveloped me, as though a wintry blast had suddenly invaded the quiet stables.

"I'm sorry about what happened to you, Simón. I'll speak to my husband about it."

"But you mustn't anger him, *Señora!*" He reached out a restraining arm, then quickly withdrew it as he realized his place.

I said determinedly, "I can't keep from happening what has already been done, but I can certainly tell him how unfair he has been and keep any such thing from happening again."

I walked resolutely into the house, my anger building at each step. How could Tomás have been so terribly unfair? I opened the door of our room and slammed it shut noisily in a deliberate attempt to waken him. Simón could not speak for himself, but nothing prevented me from speaking for him, voicing my righteous indignation and anger in place of his. Such injustice must never happen again!

As Tomás opened his eyes and blinked dazedly at me, I demanded angrily, "Tell me why you struck Simón!"

Tomás was always slow to waken in the mornings. Normally, this fact did not bother me, but at that moment, I found his failure to be fully awake to hear me excessively irritating, and it added fuel to the fire of my anger.

"You struck Simón across the face! You wouldn't even let him explain about his leg!" I accused, raising my voice, as though the sheer volume of it would force him to wake up, to listen to my words.

He raised himself up on one elbow and looked at me exasperatedly. "Will you please calm yourself a little?"

His own calmness in the face of my anger infuriated me. My voice rose higher. "How could you be so unjust, so cruel? You wouldn't let him explain. And Simón is such a gentle person! How could you do such a thing?"

Tomás swung his feet onto the floor and yawned and stretched. 'Lower your voice! You sound like a fishwife!"

His failure to even acknowledge my words fired my indignation still more, and the last thread of my control broke. My voice rose to a new shrillness. "Simón had to take such treatment from you in silence, but, by heaven, I don't have to be silent! It was so uncalled for! I told him to stay off his leg. And Simón is so industrious, so good!" I kept on. It didn't matter any more what I said, as long as I vented my anger on him.

Still silent, Tomás pushed himself to his feet and walked over to me, looking down at me. If he thought to intimidate me by standing over me like that, he was wrong. I said, "You are a beast!" and opened my mouth to continue my tirade. It was then that he struck me sharply across the face.

I recoiled in stunned silence and put my hand to my cheek, staring at him in disbelief.

He had struck me across the face. Never in my whole life had anyone done that.

For a moment, he stood unmoving, his eyes staring at me coldly. "I believe that is what one is supposed to do when confronted with a hysterical woman."

He turned away and with maddening composure put on his dressing gown and walked to the door. "Now, if you please, I will ask you to leave the disciplining of the servants to me. They are like small children, and respond only to physical punishment, for that is all they understand. And I will punish them when and as I see fit." He paused as he started out the door. "I think it will be best if I tell the servants you are not feeling well today. I will have your dinner brought to you here in your room. That will be some hours from now. You will have ample time to compose yourself."

As he closed the door, I sank down onto the side of the bed, and a feeling of futility descended on me, enveloped me. I knew I had been justified in my defense of Simón and my righteous indignation at Tomás, but what, after all, had I accomplished? I certainly had not helped Simón.

Nor would anything I had said alter Tomás's character. He was as he was, and I could not change him. I pushed myself to my feet slowly and opened the shutters to let the light in. Then I walked to the table over which the mirror hung, and leaned over to look at my face. There, on my cheek, were the bright red imprints made by Tomás's fingers and the palm of his hand.

I remembered, ironically, how I had been quick to spring to his defense when Simón had said he was a hard master. Even that very day, I had defended him from Simón's accusation that he had sent a man to the mines.

I would never, I knew, defend his name again.

I turned away from the mirror, feeling as though I had aged immeasurably in the past few minutes.

But I had not aged, I was not yet nineteen, and endless years stretched out before me. Years, God help me, of living with a man I had never liked and now was beginning to despise.

Santiago—May, 1773

CHAPTER IX

Tomás left again for the farm at the end of the third week in May, and the whole house seemed to fall into a much easier pattern as soon as he had gone. Had I failed to notice the difference before, I wondered, or was it just that I found his presence increasingly hard to bear, so that my own relief at his departure made me think I saw a similar peace of mind descend on everyone else? Certainly I had not imagined Ricardo's relief, which was readily apparent. The belligerence and tension that were a part of him whenever Tomás was near disappeared, and he relaxed visibly.

The day Tomás left, Cecilia was again spending the night with one of her friends, and Ricardo and I were alone for supper. Afterward, we went into the small room adjoining the dining room, as was our custom. This night, however, I did not get out my hated needlework, but picked up a volume of poems. Ricardo noticed the difference as soon as he returned from his room with his notes and papers.

"You're not embroidering tonight, I see."

I smiled at him. I was always inordinately pleased when he said anything that indicated he had taken note of me. "I much prefer reading, but when Tomás is home, it's impossible to get any reading done in the evenings." Always aware of the false façade that must hide the ugly truth of my marriage, even within the family, I put my hand to my lips. "I didn't mean—"

Ricardo threw back his head and laughed. "I think you did mean, and I'll agree with you. I can never get anything accomplished when he's around, either. He doesn't seem contented unless he is either baiting me or reprimanding me for something. And I'm sure that is just as disturbing to you and Cecilia as it is to me." His smile turned to a look of concern. "By the way, where is Cecilia tonight?"

"She's at Luisa's. They're working on a project for *La Concepción*. Some altar cloths, I think." I did not really believe Cecilia was spending as much time as she claimed with Luisa lately, though I did not doubt she would spend the night there. Surely, the increased amount of time she was away from home had something to do with her doctor, and she was probably using the confusion of timing between the two houses to cover meetings with him. I hoped Tomás would not suspect anything. She had not spent a night away at Luisa's for the two weeks he had been home. Now, the first night he was gone, she had left again, too. That in itself confirmed my own suspicions.

And now Ricardo had apparently begun to wonder about his sister's actions. "I don't like it, Carlota. There's something strange in the way she's behaving lately, something I can't quite put my finger on."

"Perhaps you're imagining it. She seems the same to me," I said, determined to allay his suspicions. Surely he could be trusted not to say anything to Tomás, but it was for Cecilia to confide her secret to him if she so chose, not me.

"But don't you notice she acts—well, happier, but in a strange way? You didn't know her before she was sick, you didn't know what she was like then and how she changed." He gave a sharp little laugh. "You might find it hard to imagine, but she stood up to Father then even more firmly than I did. He opposed her whenever she dared argue with him, of course, but he never seemed to resent her taking a stand on anything as he did with me. But after her illness, she changed completely. She had lost *Tía* to back her up, and maybe it was that as much as her—her disfigurement. Maybe much of the strength I thought she had was really *Tía's* strength." He hesitated, seemed to be considering his own words. "You know, I think that is the explanation, to a large extent. Anyway, she seemed to have lost the desire to be a part of the world as well, and I'm sure her scars were the cause of that."

"But when she smiles, the scars seem to fade," I interrupted. "If she would only smile more!"

"That's what I mean. Until just these past few months, she hasn't seemed to want to smile. She's very devout, and always has been, but after her illness, her devotion became almost a fixation. In fact, she would have entered a convent, but for Father. She wanted to, but in that, too, she lacked the will to oppose his wishes."

I nodded my understanding. It did not surprise me to learn

that Cecilia had wanted to join one of the religious orders. She went to mass every day, often two or three times, and her temperament was suited to the life of a nun as mine would never be. How strange, I mused, that Tomás had kept Cecilia from going into a convent and yet was trying to push Ricardo into a religious life he didn't want. "Was it the Clarisas?" I asked.

He looked at me in surprise. "How did you know that?"

"I just guessed. For a girl who would literally turn her face from the world, it would seem the most natural choice."

"You have amazing insight, Carlota."

"It was just an obvious bit of reasoning." I felt myself flush under the compliment. "They are the ones who most shun the world, with their church not opening onto the street, but onto their own convent, as though they would keep the world at bay. And I understand their confessionals are especially designed so that even then they are hidden from view. The order would be the logical choice of a girl who would repudiate the world."

"You're right," he agreed. "Yet most people would not have reasoned so well."

I accepted his comment in silence, basking in his praise.

"But Cecilia has changed lately," he continued. "She started working at the hospital just before you came, and you know now she spends most of her time there."

I nodded. I also knew why. "It does her good to get out of the house," I said.

"I know. And it keeps her occupied, where she was just sort of drifting along aimlessly before. But that's not what worries me. It's the way she acts lately, I'd say she acted happier, more alive, if it weren't that there is a sort of desperation about her. She seems so taut, so strained, like—like a guitar string that's pulled too tight. The music from it may be sweet, but it's false, and sooner or later the string breaks. Do you understand what I mean?"

"In a way," I agreed evasively. "Perhaps she's just overtired from working so much at the hospital."

"I don't think that's it. Has she said anything to you?"

"Nothing." I did not want to lie to him, but I could not do otherwise under his direct questioning.

"And she's going to Luisa's so much. I don't understand that, either. She and Luisa have known each other for years, but they were never that close."

I kept my silence and pretended to be reading, hoping he would let the subject lapse. I was relieved when, with a shake of his head and a muttered, "I just don't understand it," he turned to his studies.

161

We sat there mostly in silence the rest of the evening. After an hour or so, I got up and went into the deserted kitchen to poke up the banked embers of the fire and prepare two cups of the sweet hot chocolate I had noticed Ricardo especially liked.

He looked up when I returned bearing the tray with our chocolate and some slices of cake.

"How thoughtful you are!" he exclaimed with a big smile.

"Studying is hard work," I said, again pleased by his compliment. When I had served us, he returned to his studies and I to my reading. Occasionally, I looked over at him to reassure myself that he was still near me. And as we sat in silence, I continued to play a little game of make-believe with myself, a game I had been playing all evening. I pretended, just for those few hours, that it was Ricardo, not Tomás, to whom I was married, and we were enjoying a quiet evening at home together.

We sat there until it was quite late, Ricardo lost in his studies and I loath to leave and dispel the illusion I had created for myself. Finally, he stood up and stretched and yawned. "That's all my poor brain can hold in one day." He gathered up his papers. "But you needn't have stayed up so late, Carlota."

"I've been reading," I said, "and I wasn't really very tired."

Then we busied ourselves blowing out the candles.

"Good-night, little stepmother," Ricardo said as we walked out of the room.

"Good-night, Ricardo. Sleep well."

The illusion of domestic bliss, of a quiet evening of contentment shared by two happily married people vanished as he turned to go to his room and I faced the opposite direction to go to mine.

On the following Sunday, Ricardo, Cecilia and I ate breakfast together and then went to mass. Ricardo escorted us into the Cathedral, one on each arm, and sat between us. Again, the enchanting illusion as he sat next to me. What if, instead of being married to Tomás, I were wed to Ricardo, had the right always to go to mass with him, to sit beside him? My mind, taken with the same fantasy as it had been the night before, gave little attention to the service itself, though I uttered all the responses automatically at the proper times from long-standing habit.

Since Tomás was not present to protest the lack of gentility of arriving at the Cathedral on foot, we had chosen to walk. Our return home was unhurried, made perhaps more so by my own deliberately slow steps as I tried to prolong the time I was with Ricardo. He usually spent Sunday afternoon at

María Elena's house, frequently going there with her and her family directly after church. Today, I had been relieved to see that she was nowhere in evidence. Perhaps she had gone to an earlier service. At least, I thought with satisfaction, we would probably have his company for dinner that day.

We sat in the main patio and talked till dinner-time. I watched Cecilia more closely in the light of Ricardo's description of her. She was, on the surface, more lighthearted and gay than I had ever known her to be, but it was a forced sort of gaiety, and seemed as though at any moment it could dissolve into tears. Was that because it covered a frenzied desperation, I wondered, a desperation caused by her knowledge that her love affair had been doomed to hopelessness and failure from the day of its inception?

Later, as we were finishing the usual caramel custard we had for dessert every Sunday, Ricardo suddenly suggested that Cecilia and I go riding with him.

"Aren't you going to María Elena's?" Cecilia asked. "I imagine she's expecting you. Don't stay away on our account."

Why must she keep pushing Ricardo toward María Elena? I wondered in annoyance. And how could she presume to speak for both of us? "I would love to go riding," I said quickly, before Ricardo could consider Cecilia's suggestion.

He turned to Cecilia. "Won't you come, too, Cecilia? María Elena has gone to the country with her family, so I have no obligation to her today."

Obligation! My mind snatched fearfully at the word. How much of an obligation did he feel toward María Elena? But she was gone, so I needn't concern myself about her just then.

"I didn't know they'd left," Cecilia said. "Will they be gone long?"

"A week or two, maybe more. Her father was very vague about it. I think he's concerned about these small tremors we've been having. He mentioned to me several times that he's afraid they presage a big quake. It wouldn't surprise me if they stayed more than a few weeks.

"But Carlota has already accepted my invitation. How about you? It will do you good to get out in the fresh air for a while, after all the hours you spend in that stuffy hospital."

"You'll have to excuse me if I refuse. You know I never did care a lot for riding, and I've a headache. Besides, I was planning to go over to Luisa's later this afternoon, and I wouldn't want you to hurry back because of me." She turned to me. "But you go, Carlota."

I will, I will! I wanted to shout. But instead I said quietly,

163

"If you think it will be all right." I knew it would not be all right with Tomás, but Cecilia didn't know of my promise to him.

"Of course it will be all right," she said emphatically. "After all, Ricardo is your stepson."

Had she forgotten about her warning to me, I wondered, concerning what she had guessed about my feelings for Ricardo? Or was it just that she was so anxious to be rid of us for the purpose of pursuing her own private plans that she was willing to agree to anything that put us out of her way for the balance of the afternoon? Whatever her plans, I was certain they involved more than a visit with Luisa.

I quickly pushed my concern for Cecilia from my mind, and asked Ricardo when he would like to leave. I was delighted with his answer.

"Why not right now?" he asked, flashing me a smile.

"Why not?" I agreed lightheartedly as we rose from the table. Why not, indeed? Tomás was at the farm, and María Elena was away for an extended visit in the country. I hummed to myself as I dressed carefully in a riding outfit of a rich dark green with a matching silk blouse on which were touches of ecru at the throat and wrists. I decided not to take the jacket of lightweight wool, for there was a certain mugginess in the air in anticipation of the rains that had not yet begun. It was not hot; it was never hot in Santiago. But it was vaguely uncomfortable.

I had a jaunty hat that matched my skirt, with feathers of the same color as the trim on my blouse, and I set it firmly on my head. I looked in the mirror, saw with satisfaction that the colors became me well. I also noted the unaccustomed flush of my cheeks, a flush I was certain had nothing to do with the weather.

Ricardo was waiting in the patio, "Well!" he said appreciatively as he took my hand and spun me around. "I don't know if I'm dressed well enough to accompany such an elegant companion."

I laughed happily at his obvious approval, and as we turned to go, Cecilia bid us have a pleasant ride. She was sitting on the settee by the door of her room, and I hadn't even noticed her. In fact, I was so intent on Ricardo's reaction to my appearance that I had forgotten she was still at home. At the sound of her voice, I turned to look at her.

"We will," I said. I could not bring myself to tell her I was sorry she was not going with us, for I was decidedly pleased that she was not. I only hoped that, whatever course she and her doctor had set upon, it would not hurt her, for I had grown genuinely fond of her.

"And you have a pleasant afternoon," I said, silently adding, *Be careful, be careful!* I suppose my concern for her must have shown on my face. It was a surprise to me that when her eyes met mine, I saw a similar concern for me mirrored clearly in them. It was as though she had heard my unspoken admonition and was repeating it back to me. Perhaps she was right. Perhaps we both had need to take care.

But I did not think long about admonitions. I was too contented to be spending the whole afternoon alone with Ricardo. We did not go to *Cerro de Santa Cruz* this time, but another direction, away from the city. Then Ricardo turned off the little used cart track we had followed and we started to climb.

"I want to show you something on top of this mountain," he said. "Do you think you can make it? It's a long climb."

"It's El Moro who must do the work, not I," I answered lightly, and I followed him up the path.

The trail on which we climbed was in reality more of a footpath than one intended for riders, and we were too busy ducking low-hanging branches to have a chance for much conversation. At last we reached a small clearing near the top, and Ricardo dismounted and turned to me. "This is where El Moro gets to rest and you take over. We must go on foot the rest of the way."

We left the horses there and continued up until at last we emerged at another clearing, larger than the first one, on the crest of the mountain. Much-weathered tree-stumps remained to show that the clearing had been man-made long before; fresh-cut saplings attested to the fact that it was currently maintained. Ricardo led me to one end of the cleared area, where there was an odd stone formation. On the ground all around three sides of it were signs of small fires.

"Is this a favorite spot for campfires?" I asked curiously. "It would seem terribly inaccessible for that."

"Those ashes aren't from campfires. This is an altar. The natives have been coming here for hundreds of years with their burnt offerings."

I looked at him in surprise. "But they are all converted now! They don't worship their old gods any more. They believe in the One True God. They have all been baptized."

Ricardo's head went back as he laughed, in the gesture that was so exclusively his that it made my heart turn over every time he did it. Still, I frowned, because I had not intended to say anything funny. "What did I say?"

"It's just that you're so unpredictable. Sometimes you seem so—so old and wise, and at other times, as naive as a small child. You don't think the *indios* threw out all their gods to accept ours, do you?"

"They would have to, wouldn't they?" I asked. But then I remembered Simón's all-but-forgotten remark the day I went with Tomás to Almolonga, about the gods that live in *Fuego*. "You mean they keep both, theirs and ours, too? But that's not possible."

"It's not only possible," he said, smiling at me as he talked. "They've been doing it successfully for two hundred and fifty years. I came upon Simón up here once when I was a little boy, and I don't know which of us was more surprised. He had some incense and was reciting some sort of an incantation. I just turned around and walked away, as though I hadn't seen anything. Maybe that's why he has helped me so many times to hide my misdeeds. I don't tell Father on him, and he doesn't tell him on me."

I smiled at the thought of the conspiracy. So that was why they were so easy together. "Did you have much to hide?"

"Enough," he said. "The usual boyish escapades. I got punished for some, but thanks to Simón, there were many Father didn't know about."

"I—I'm glad you showed me this," I said as we turned to leave. "I want to know more about this hidden side of the natives. Maybe we haven't taken them over as completely as we think we have." Then I realized that I should not give any sort of approval to a deliberate disregarding of one of the prime tenets of the church. "But they should give up their heathen gods, of course."

"Of course," Ricardo agreed. We were returning down the narrow path to our horses, and he was walking ahead of me, leading me by the hand. I could not see his face, but I had the feeling he was laughing at me, not with derision, but with amusement.

It was almost dark when we returned from our ride. I changed my clothes and then went to tell Teresa there would be three of us that evening for supper.

"*Señorita* Cecilia has come in, then?" she asked.

"I assumed she was already here."

Teresa shrugged. "Not unless she came in from the back, and that's not likely. The front door is bolted, and she was not here when I returned an hour ago."

"She went to a friend's house," I said, trying to disguise my concern. "Perhaps they invited her to stay for supper. If so, I'm sure she'll send a message soon."

I delayed supper for almost an hour waiting for her, but Cecilia still hadn't returned or sent a message. Finally, I told Teresa to have the meal served.

Ricardo frowned as he entered the dining room. "Where's Cecilia?" He pulled out my chair for me.

"Delayed at Luisa's, I imagine. You know how it can be, when girls are working on a project. They get so engrossed they forget the time." I settled myself at the table and passed the plate of cold sliced veal to Ricardo.

"Did she send word?"

"Well, no, but I'm sure we'll hear soon." I shrugged and changed the subject.

We were drinking a final cup of tea when Cecilia entered. Ricardo looked up at her in surprise.

"When did you come in? I heard no carriage, and I've been keeping my eyes on the front door constantly."

Cecilia slid into her chair, ignoring his question. "I'm sorry. I hope you weren't worried. We were working on the altar cloth and the priest's vestments, and didn't realize how late it was getting."

"But I didn't hear a carriage pull up," Ricardo continued, not ready to let the subject drop. "How did you get home?"

"I walked."

I rang the bell for the serving maid and told her to bring more hot tea and to refill the meat platter. It didn't need refilling, but I thought that perhaps the confusion of having the maid come and go might discourage Ricardo from continuing with his questioning, which I could see was making Cecilia uncomfortable.

"You walked? How did you get in the house?" he persisted as soon as the maid had left.

"Through the stable yard," Cecilia answered impatiently. "Carlota, I wonder if I could have the butter, please?"

"You came on foot, through the stable yard? Why didn't they send you in a carriage? The Parras would surely not have let you set out on foot alone in the dark. There are footpads about."

Cecilia looked at Ricardo exasperatedly as the maid returned with the meat platter. As soon as the young girl had gone, Cecilia exploded. "I insisted they not bother. They sent a lackey to walk with me. It was only a few hundred *varas*, after all. Really, Ricardo, I see no reason for all this questioning! I am twenty years old and quite able to look after myself!" Cecilia applied some butter to a tortilla in a brisk angry gesture, then turned her full attention to her food as if to indicate that the conversation was over.

Ricardo and I exchanged quick looks of alarm. I had been there over four months, and I had never seen Cecilia lose her temper before. I remembered Ricardo's comparision with the guitar string, and I wondered if she was nearing the breaking point. I was certain that it had not been a lackey from the Parras household who had left her to slip unseen into the darkened entrance to the stable yard.

During the next week, there were several evenings when Cecilia was working at Luisa's house, so again Ricardo and I were left alone after supper. Most of the time, we shared a comfortable silence as he studied and I read, but occasionally we talked, usually of impersonal matters. Several times, he got incensed about the King's treatment of his colonials. At those times, I wished we were once more high on a hill with a clear view all around, so that we could see there was no one near enough to hear him. What appalled me was that Ricardo seemed to have no feelings that what he said was seditious, and I was afraid for him, afraid that one day his openness and lack of caution would place him in danger. Following the thought still further, even now he could get thrown in jail for speaking too freely. And if Tomás were trying to get rid of him as he seemed to think, might not a jail suit him almost as well as a monastery? A preposterous thought, surely, but it did cross my mind.

One evening when he was telling me in his loud clear voice of the injustice of the King's demand for payment of taxes and tithes only in gold or silver, I was particularly concerned, for the window was open behind him. Even though it opened on an alleyway that led only to our stable yard, I had a feeling that someone could be listening.

"We've no natural wealth with which to fill His Majesty's coffers," he was saying. "We've neither the gold of Peru nor the silver of Mexico, yet we must pay only in these metals. The few mines we have aren't rich ones at all. Our existence is based on what we can make the land produce for us—cacao, tobacco, indigo, cotton, a few barks and resins from the forests. But it takes much of these things to trade for one *peso*, Carlota. And since we deal only with Spain, we don't always get the best price for our goods. It isn't fair to us."

"You mustn't speak so!" I said as he paused. "What if someone heard you say such things?" I glanced anxiously at the open window.

His eyes followed my glance and he laughed. "So you're concerned for my safety! Don't worry. King Carlos has not set spies upon us, not yet." He smiled teasingly and said with pseudo-seriousness, "You won't report what I said to the Captain General when you go the ball next week, will you?"

I could not share his lightness about the subject. "Of course not, but—"

He sat back in his chair and pretended to be relieved. "In

that case, I'm safe, at least for now." He lapsed into silence and returned to his notes.

His remark about the Captain General's ball reminded me that Tomás would be home in another week. It was something I did not want to think about. For the next week, at least, I would not be faced with the constant reminder of my distasteful marriage. My large dowry had served some purpose for me after all, I thought wryly, for it was the extensive repairs and improvements Tomás was making on the farm that kept him away so much lately. But for the gold and silver I had brought him, I would probably not have had such frequent and welcome respite from his presence.

On Saturday, a messenger arrived with a letter for Ricardo. The femininity of the handwriting was unmistakable, and it was easy to guess who had sent it. I was wishing for an excuse to misplace it, but I feared it would take more than a misplaced letter to dispose of María Elena.

I did not see Ricardo until dinner-time that day. I handed him the letter as we were sitting down at the table.

"Excuse me," he said as soon as we were seated, and I noted glumly the eagerness with which he broke the seal. I busied myself passing food to Cecilia. I did not want to watch his face as he read her words.

"Well!" He refolded the message. "They'll be staying in the country for a few more weeks, at least. They've invited me to come stay with them."

"Will you go?" I tried to ask the question casually, but I waited, heart pounding, for his answer. Who knew what magic spell María Elena could work on him in the solitude of the country?

"Not just now. Maybe in a few weeks, if they're still there." He helped himself to some beans. "That leaves me free tomorrow. Would you like to go riding again, Carlota?"

"Yes, I would." I tried not to sound as eager as I felt. It seemed I would have to be satisfied with what crumbs of his attention María Elena left for me.

"Cecilia?" He looked at her questioningly. "Will you come with us this time?"

She shook her head. "The altar cloth is almost finished. They would like it for next Sunday's service."

I heard her words with relief. I did not want to share Ricardo with anyone, not even with her. Yet wouldn't it be better for her if she would come with us, I wondered?

"Are the priest's vestments almost finished, too?" I asked.

She nodded. "We should finish both this week."

And what then, I wondered? What new excuse would she have to invent to slip out and meet her doctor?

169

At Ricardo's suggestion, we attended early mass the next morning and left immediately afterwards to ride to the volcano *Agua*, carrying with us a picnic lunch. I was delighted with the plan, for it meant an all-day outing. It was my good fortune that María Elena's family had elected to stay longer in the country.

We rode high onto the slopes of *Agua*, stopping at the Palace of the Archbishop to admire from there the magnificent view of Santiago below. The Palace had been built as a personal retreat by Bishop Marroquin, the first Archbishop of Guatemala.

Ricardo suggested we not picnic near there, but go higher up where it was more private. I nodded my agreement. The less we were seen, the less chance of Tomás knowing about our rides.

Later, we spread out our lunch on a quiet spot on the slope, with the horses grazing nearby. I had filled a bag with some of Tomás's best wine and put it in our basket. Ricardo grinned as he tasted it.

"You chose well. That's Father's favorite."

"I know. He'll never miss it," I laughed guiltily. "I found another cask of it in the storeroom yesterday. It is well hidden, so I'm sure he doesn't know it's there."

The cook had prepared an excellent lunch, and we attacked it with appetite. There were tortillas and olives, cold roast chicken, little fruit tartlets, several kinds of cheeses and a new fruit I had never tried. Ricardo said they were mangos.

"Here, let me peel one for you." He took it from me and used the knife he wore at his belt to remove the skin. "These trees were originally brought over from India. This is the first fruit of the season. It will be sweeter in a week or two." He handed the peeled fruit back to me.

I took it from him, and both of us laughed as I fumbled its slippery surface for a moment and then caught it in both hands. I bit into it. In spite of a slight green taste, the stringy pulp was sweet and juicy, and had a delicious flavor. Ricardo laughed as the juiciness of it surprised me and I had to lean over the grass quickly to keep it from soiling my skirt.

"I should have warned you how messy they are," he said, taking another mango from the basket and deftly peeling it for himself. We laughed as another bite into the mango made juice dribble down my chin.

I suddenly imagined how different Tomás would have reacted if he had been there. For some reason, the thought amused me, and I laughed afresh. When Ricardo looked at me questioningly, I looked down my nose and said in imitation of Tomás voice,

"Carlota Isabel, a lady would not let fruit juice dribble down her chin!"

My imitation must have been a good one, for it sent Ricardo into paroxysms of laughter, and his laughter in turn made me laugh harder, till we both had to wipe tears of mirth from our eyes.

Later, as our laughter died down, Ricardo looked at me seriously. "Do you know, that's the first time I've heard you really laugh hard at anything since you came here? I suppose you haven't had much to laugh about, have you?"

"No," I agreed, "I haven't."

"Carlota, I wish you hadn't married my father!" he said unexpectedly.

"Why?" My heart thumped wildly as I waited for his answer. *Say it, say it,* I begged silently. *Say you love me as much as I love you!*

His next words said nothing of love, and I realized how foolish had been my tenuous hopes. "For your sake. It must be difficult to be married to such a man. He expects everyone to be perfect, though he's far from perfect himself. And you're so young, so full of life to be tied to someone so—so proper and correct."

I masked my disappointment with haughtiness, said stiffly, "I can manage. You needn't concern yourself about me." How stilted my words sounded, even to me! And they were not even truthful, for I did want his concern, but not by itself. I wanted more, much more—a far deeper feeling, a commitment.

My rebuff angered him. "I won't, if that's how you feel." He threw away his mango seed with an abrupt angry motion and pushed himself to his feet. "It's a long ride. We had better be starting back."

The magic moment of foolish laughter shared was gone. He had offfered me sympathy, and I had turned away from him. Why had I bristled so at his remark? There had been more to it than disappointment. What was it? But I knew. It was my pride again, of course. My foolish pride, which I had been nurturing lest I lose it, too. But this time I was truly sorry I had let it dominate me, for I knew that where Ricardo was concerned, I could not afford the luxury of it.

The pleasant giddiness we had shared briefly was gone, and I knew there was no recapturing it. We rode back down toward the Archbishop's Palace in a heavy silence that had nothing of comfort in it.

"Do you come here often?" I asked as we were walking the horses side by side. It was a pointless question, but I felt compelled to break the uncomfortable silence between us.

171

"Not lately," he said. "The only day there's enough time is Sunday, and María Elena doesn't like to ride. Besides, her *dueña* is a large woman who can scarcely get into a carriage. I don't think she would care to accompany us here."

"Oh." The mention of María Elena made me lapse again into silence. He spoke her name so naturally, I noted with disappointment, as though she were already an integral part of his life. Even up on the slopes of *Agua*, with María Elena far away, I could not escape her. I was reminded again that his Sundays belonged irrevocably to her, and it was only because she was gone that he was here with me.

But she was gone, and Tomás was gone, and I was here. And I would not waste another minute of the day worrying about either of them or about my senseless pride. I flicked my reins and El Moro broke into a gallop.

"I'll race you to the Palace," I called back over my shoulder laughingly. I hoped Tomás and María Elena both stayed away forever!

Breathlessly, we dismounted a few minutes later at the Archbishop's Palace and paused as though by unspoken agreement for one last look at the peaceful city below.

But as I stood there, holding lightly onto the reins, the peaceful city of Santiago dissolved before my eyes, and in its place I saw a horror of tumbled walls and fallen roofs. I closed my eyes, and I felt the trembling, the quivering and swaying of the earth beneath my feet. The feeling was so real that I felt beads of perspiration bursting out on my forehead and trickling down my face.

I realized vaguely that Ricardo, standing beside me, had started to say something to me. Then, apparently alarmed at the look on my face, he stopped abruptly. I opened my eyes, still only partly aware of his presence as he took hold of my shoulders and shook me gently. The ruined city was still there, and I stood staring at it in horrified fascination, unable to force my eyes to release it.

"Carlota!" He spoke my name softly, so different from the harsh strident manner in which Tomás said it.

Ricardo moved in front of me so that his body blocked out the sight of the city below, and with the movement, the frightening glimpse I had had into the future was dissolved. I grasped desperately at the hope that it might have been not the future, but the past that I had seen. But the hope was frail, and it shattered against the hard rock of simple reasoning; nothing I had ever seen before had failed to happen at some future date.

I returned to the reality of the present, the reality of Ricardo standing in front of me, his hands gripping my arms.

Slowly, I raised my eyes to his. My arms would have slid around his neck and clung to him had I not expended conscious effort to keep them motionless at my sides. I wanted him to hold me, press me to him in safety and comfort, only because I loved him, but because at that moment he alone seemed to offer a haven from the terrible thing I had just seen. He stood there, strong and unshakable, unmoving, his feet planted firmly on the ground that I knew had never moved that day for all my feelings that it had shaken me much as I had seen a dog shake a mouse in its teeth. I wanted to tell him what I had just seen and felt, share it with him as I would share with him all my thoughts.

But I dared not. What would he think? Would he shrink from me in alarm as my father had done, unwilling to accept what I had seen? Or ignore what I told him, as had *Tía* when I had tried to tell her about *Mamá's* funeral cortege? No, I could not chance making him turn from me, not when every moment we spent together was more precious to me than gold.

I shrugged, trying to seem nonchalant. "It's nothing. I felt a little warm for a minute. I'm quite all right now." I backed away and turned, twisting free of his hands, knowing that if I didn't, I could no longer resist the impulse to fling my arms around his neck. For the touch of his hands on my arms through the thin silk of my blouse was too unnerving, the stirrings within me too unpredictable, no less dangerous than those I sensed within the earth.

We remounted and continued our descent. As we rode into the city later, I became acutely aware of the stillness of the air in the Valley of Panchoy. On the slopes of *Agua*, we had caught at least the hint of a breeze, but in the city, not a leaf stirred on the bougainvillea that hung over so many of the high garden walls we passed. The quietness, the utter breathlessness, lay hot and heavy over the city.

"It's so still," I remarked as we rode. "As if we were in an airless room."

"The natives call this earthquake weather."

"I know. I've heard them." I shuddered. "Ricardo, have you ever experienced an earthquake?"

He shrugged. "Not really. Only small tremors, such as we've had these past few months. And you know how those are. You're not even aware of them, unless you see a candle sputter or curtains move. The last big quake here was on the day of San Casimiro in '51, and I wasn't born yet. But I agree with the *indios*. There is something almost weird about this weather, as though it is waiting, too, waiting for something to happen."

"Shouldn't the rains start any day now? Wouldn't that account for the change in the weather?"

"I suppose it could, but—well, all I can keep saying is that it's different this year. If you had been here other years, you'd know what I mean. Look, we're riding without our jackets, and with the sun no longer on us, we should feel cool, but we don't."

"But surely one year always differs from another. Every year can't be expected to be the same as the last." It was as though I felt obliged to protest what I knew to be so. I, who had never known a violent earthquake, knew that it was earthquake weather, and that the ground over which we rode would one day soon create pandemonium here in the peaceful streets of Santiago.

This I knew as surely as I breathed.

But there were many who lacked my gift, if gift it was, who certainly suspected what I knew for certain. A few families, like that of María Elena, had fled the city, and there were others who lacked a place in the country to which they could retreat, but who took what precautions they could.

I did not realize how many people actively feared a severe quake until several days after Tomás's return to Santiago. We had attended the ball at the Palace of the Captains General, and it was early morning when we left. The building fronted on the south side of the *Plaza Real*, and we had to circle two sides of the plaza to return to our house.

"Well, my dear," Tomás said as we settled ourselves in the seats and he tapped his signal to Alberto to start, "a successful evening, I think. I managed to get Roberto Fuentes y Diaz to sell me a fine stallion, even though a number of other men were determined to have him. But I outbid them all. And I noticed some of the men present were casting admiring glances at you, though I don't care for that absurdly plain coiffure of yours. Nor did you have on enough jewels. Those pearls have no fire to them. I thought I asked you to wear your rubies."

I absently fingered one of my pearl earrings. "I couldn't. They need repairing."

"Repairing? I just had the clasp fixed on your necklace last time I was home. I took it to the goldsmith and picked it up myself."

"I know. But a large stone in one of the earrings is loose. I was afraid I might lose it if I wore them tonight."

"I would think you would have discovered that at the same time you noticed the broken clasp."

"I just noticed it today. Besides, pearls look much better with this satin. The rubies would have been too much."

174

"That is scarcely the point," he said petulantly, "I asked you to wear the rubies."

And that is precisely why I did not, I thought, remembering with a feeling of inward satisfaction that one of the stones in an earring had been loose in its setting ever since I could remember. The petty triumph did not raise my spirits any. Tomás had been home only two days, and already I felt stifled by his presence and irritated by the constant stream of criticism he directed at me.

I had been looking out the coach window as we made our way along one side of the plaza, idly at first, and then, as my eyes grew accustomed to the darkness, I strained to see if I had seen right.

"Tomás, the plaza! Look! It's full of people lying on the ground, sleeping. Do some of the natives come in the night before market day?" I pointed to the many humped forms of poeple asleep on a variety of mats and blankets. "But there are so many of them!"

Tomás pushed my finger down. "Don't point!" he scolded in the manner of an adult berating a child for bad manners. Then he leaned over to look. "Those aren't just *indios.* Many of the people of Santiago are refusing to sleep in their houses, they're so afraid of an earthquake. Most of them are just moving their beds into their own patios every night, but some of them move into the plazas. I've heard that a few people even take their carriages to the edge of town and sleep in them there."

I nodded. "María Elena's family went to their house in the country weeks ago."

He scoffed. "Hysterical! How can anyone know? Still, I suppose it would do no harm to crate a few of my treasures. The Sung Dynasty vase, of course, and the rest of the Chinese porcelains. Perhaps, too, the Meissens—"

"Yes, Tomás," I answered, wondering how so many people could suspect what was to come. "I think perhaps you had better. These people may well be right."

He gave a short derisive laugh. "Come now, Carlota Isabel! Do you, who had never experienced even the slightest tremor until you arrived here, set yourself up as an expert on earthquakes?"

"No, it's only—"

"Only what?" He waited, and I knew he was anxious to have me say something else he could deride.

"Perhaps—perhaps these people are not so foolish as they seem."

"Perhaps." He shrugged. "In any event, it certainly won't hurt to crate a few of the porcelains."

175

It was typical of Tomás that he thought only of his treasures. I think it was because he could possess them wholly, as he could never possess another person, that he loved them so. True selfless love is giving of oneself, and of this he was incapable, except perhaps with Pilar. But his possessions, his treasures, required no understanding and made no demands upon him, nor did they defy him. That might have been why he lavished on them the only kind of affection he knew.

Santiago—June, 1773

CHAPTER X

The next morning, the new stallion Tomás had bought from Roberto Fuentes y Diaz was brought to our stables. I watched from my garden as the spirited animal was delivered. As soon as the high bars were removed from the wagon in which they had brought him, he leaped off it onto the ground in a graceful flowing bound, landing with perfect balance far from the wagon.

I learned, then, why he had been delivered in that manner instead of having been brought on a lead rein. As Tomás and the others sought to catch him, the animal pawed and pranced, and with a nymph-like agility, continued to evade his would-be captors. I watched him in delight, admiring the grace and intelligence that kept him free. After close to an hour of this, Tomás left, barking orders for Simón to install him in the stables in a large locked stall away from the other horses. Then he stamped past me and went into the house. He did not even notice I was there, or he would have berated me for being out in the sun. His obvious irritation struck me funny, and I had to stifle a giggle. He was retiring from the battlefield, utterly defeated by a high-strung horse. Here was one spirit he wouldn't easily dominate!

When I was certain he was out of sight, I put down my trowel and walked over toward the stables. The horse was standing, quietly enough when no one was near, watching Simón and several of the others warily.

"What a beauty he is!" I said, admiring his sleek black coat and the graceful proportions of his legs, strongly built for all their appearance of delicacy and grace. He stood several hands higher than the Arab horses we had brought from Spain. He was a horse built for great bursts of speed more than for endurance, I decided. And for jumping, too, for there was power in his hind legs, I thought, remembering the apparent ease with which he had sprung from the wagon.

"He is so, *Señora,*" Simón agreed, his eyes never leaving the horse. "But I think already the master regrets having bought him."

Again, I stifled a giggle, remembering Tomás's irritation. It would not do to let Simón know that I was laughing at my husband. "What shall we call him, Simón?"

"I think the *Señor* has already named him. Several times, I heard him call him El Diablo."

"But he is not a devil! He's only frightened!" Still, I knew the name would hold.

"And wild, *Señora.* He has not been broken much to the saddle, I think." As we talked, Simón kept sidling a step or two closer to the great black stallion. The horse's ears, laid back in suspicion, finally relaxed as he sensed a friend in Simón and let him approach. Simón reached into his pocket and drew out some grain, proffering it with outstretched hand. After sniffing distrustfully, the horse began to nibble at it.

A while later, Simón lured him into the stables, and I finally heard the bolt click into place when he had been safely enticed into the large stall.

Simón came out, looking satisfied. "Now he can rest, away from people, for a few hours. He will be calmer then."

"He's lucky to have you to care for him, Simón. Some people might not be so patient, and would try to beat him into submission."

He nodded. "He did not like the *Señor* at all."

"I didn't mean—" I stopped, admitting to myself that Tomás was exactly the one I had in mind when I made that statement. Simón, in his simple honesty, had recognized that at once. I would have to guard my tongue.

That day at dinner, Tomás was particularly sullen. In contrast, Ricardo was unusually bright and cheerful.

"I heard you bought a new horse, Father," he said as soon as we were seated and the confusion of serving the various dishes had stopped. "I understand he's quite an animal."

Tomás muttered something in reply. The only words I could understand were "not properly broken." Then he applied himself glumly to his food.

"I heard you outbid a number of other gentlemen for him last night. Did you say he's not broken? But surely you saw him before you agreed to buy him, didn't you? You wouldn't buy a horse without seeing him first, would you?"

It was becoming increasingly obvious that Ricardo was baiting his father, and enjoying himself immensely.

"That's scarcely any concern of yours!" Tomás snapped angrily, and I shot a warning glance at Ricardo, knowing he was pushing Tomás too far.

Cecilia also sensed the tension that was building in Tomás, and I was grateful when she started making inconsequential conversation about the hospital. I urged her on with questions and Ricardo, well aware of what we were doing, watched us in amusement while Tomás finished his meal in glowering silence.

After dinner, Tomás shut himself in his office. Cecilia went to her room to rest, and I settled in a shaded spot in the *patio de placer* to read. A short time later, Ricardo came into the small patio.

"I hope you don't mind if I join you," he said. "The water in the fountain always has such a peaceful sound to it." He put his books on a table under the overhang. "Have you seen the new horse?"

"Yes," I answered enthusiastically. "He's lovely!"

He chuckled. "Father doesn't think so."

"What was that all about at the table? You certainly angered him."

"I couldn't resist needling him a little." He drew another chair into the shade near me and sat down. "I heard the whole story from a couple of my friends this morning. One of them is the son of Roberto Fuentes."

"What story?" I asked disapprovingly. "Did Tomás pay too much? Diablo is a good horse, and worth almost any price."

"Diablo? Is that what Father named him?" He seemed amused at the thought. "No matter how good an animal he is, he's not worth what Father paid. He gave Roberto an absurd sum for him, and in gold. The horse is a rebel. Father will never be able to ride him." He laughed again.

"I still don't see what's so funny," I scowled. I had already decided I wanted the stallion for my own, and I bristled defensively at the thought of him being made the butt of any jokes. "There is nothing wrong with that horse! He'll be a fine jumper, and I'm sure he's fast as well. He has spirit, but what's wrong with that?"

"Whoa, Carlota! You don't have to defend the horse. Nobody said anything against him, except that he's still half-wild. The joke of it is that it was all preplanned by Roberto and some of the other men. They were all talking about this wonderful horse last night and offering Roberto outrageous sums for him. Well, you know Father. If he thinks something is worth possessing, he has to have it for himself. He decided

179

this horse must really be exceptional, and did just what the men knew he would do. He jumped in and offered Roberto more than anyone else. Roberto pretended not to be interested, told him it wasn't right to sell him a horse he hadn't even seen. But Father insisted, since he was positive one of the others would agree right then and there to buy the horse if he didn't. One of the men topped Father's offer and then—well, you can guess the rest. Father let himself be bid up higher still, and finally, with a great show of reluctance, Roberto let himself be persuaded to sell Father the stallion. They shook hands and closed the deal right there."

"But they shouldn't have made Tomás the butt of their joke like that."

"Why not? They were only having a little harmless fun. He'll never be able to ride that horse."

We dropped the subject there, but I could not get it out of my mind. I had seen the anger on Tomás's face when he had stamped past me from the stable yard. I remembered that I had been amused at the time, but I was beginning to have an uneasy feeling that it could yet turn out to be more than harmless fun. I sighed. Even at best, it would make Tomás harder to live with.

The whole episode might have come to nothing if the jokesters had been content to have their laugh and let the matter drop there. But several times in the next few days, when Tomás and I were out together, men would stop him and ask him baitingly how he was getting along with his new horse. If that question didn't seem to irritate him enough, then they pressed still further and asked him when he was going out for a ride on his new stallion. And always, there were suppressed grins on the faces of other men nearby.

I did not know at the time what made Tomás decide on the day he chose, but he began to say that he would ride the stallion on the morning of the *Convite*, the Invitation.

"The *Convite?*" I repeated the first time I heard him give that answer. "When is that?" We had just come out of the Cathedral after mass on the day after the stallion had been delivered, and several men had stopped him to ask when he was going out for a ride on Diablo.

He had his hand under my elbow, supporting my arm as we walked down the steps and away from the men, and I had felt his fingers tighten as he answered them. "It's the day before Corpus Christi day," he explained, "the day of the invitation to the fiesta."

"But, let's see—this is Whitsunday, and—why, that's less than two weeks from now! You know you'll never be able to
180

ride Diablo that soon!" We had reached the bottom of the steps, and I turned to look at him in surprise.

Never had I seen him look so grimly determined as he answered, "I will ride him on the day of the *Convite*. That is what I have said I would do, and that is what I intend to do!"

At that moment, another man, one I didn't know, stopped Tomás and began talking about the horse. "Let me know when you ride him. I want to be there!"

"You can be," Tomás answered. His voice was light, his words sounded casual, but his hand still gripped my elbow yet more tensely. "I'll ride him on the morning of the *Convite*."

"Where?"

Tomás thought for a minute. "To the Matasano Bridge and back from my house."

"I'll be there. Let me know the time."

Tomás nodded and motioned to Alberto to draw our carriage nearer.

Inside the carriage, Tomás sighed heavily. "I'll show them," he said through gritted teeth. "I'll show them all!"

As the carriage moved away from the Cathedral toward our house, I wondered if it were only coincidental that Tomás had chosen the Matasano Bridge, renowned as a dueling site, as the destination for his ride.

Poor Tomás! Aware at last of the fact that he had been the victim of a practical joke, he knew the only way he could save face was to rise to the challenge of his tormentors and ride the new stallion. Only then could he know peace in Santiago. I felt sorry for him until I remembered that it was his own greed that had embroiled him in such a situation.

The training of the horse began in earnest that day. Tomás tried at first to supervise Simón as he worked with the stallion, but when Simón at last suggested that it might be best if Tomás were not there for the first day or two, he apparently realized the wisdom of that suggestion, and he backed off to watch from behind the gate into the kitchen patio, occasionally shouting instructions from there. But basically, he left the training to Simón, who carefully put increasingly heavy loads on Diablo's back, until the weight of them was almost as heavy as a man's body. Then Simón slipped the bit into his mouth, leaving it there for only a few seconds at first, and gradually increasing the length of time. I helped, and for once Tomás did not object to my actions, for Simón and I were the only two people around whom the horse behaved, and Tomás was desperate enough to accept help from any quarter, even from me. We all knew we did not have enough time.

In the early morning hours, too, I would slip into Diablo's stall, a bunch of freshly picked carrots in my hand. I began to realize I had to have him for my own. Never had I grown so attached to a horse I had not even ridden.

Finally, I was able to mount him astride. I had slit one of my old skirts in order to mount him in that manner, hoping to accustom him to the shifting weight of a human body. By that time, Tomás was able to approach Diablo without having him skitter away. That, at least, was something.

It was the bit, not the saddle, that Simón and I knew would be the real problem between Diablo and Tomás. "The *Señor* rides with such a tight rein," Simón said with a shake of his head. "Diablo will not like this. He will fight it for certain."

"And his mouth is so tender—" I broke off, not wanting to think of what must happen.

Simón looked at me, and I saw the pain in his eyes. We knew we were not discussing only Tomás's riding habits, but his very nature, the nature that demanded submission. And he knew, as I did, that Diablo was a horse that needed and demanded a measure of freedom Tomás would never be willing to allow.

"If only we had more time!" I wished aloud. But time would not eliminate the clash between horse and man; it would only delay it. For no matter how much we worked with Diablo, he would never be ready for Tomás to ride.

Even at his own table, Tomás still could not escape further conversation on the subject of the new horse. Ricardo did not hide his enjoyment of the whole affair.

"Everyone at the University is placing bets, Father, on whether or not you'll make it to the Matasano Bridge without being thrown."

"I'll make it, all right," Tomás boasted with a note of sullen obstinacy in his voice. "And I'll cover all bets. You tell that to your friends at the University!"

On the Saturday before the *Convite*, I approached Tomás with a suggestion that had been in the back of my mind for days. I knew it had to be broached carefully, however, and that the truth might even have to be twisted a bit to keep him from rejecting the idea out of hand.

He was at work in his office that afternoon, and I went into him there.

"Tomás," I began tentatively, "you know Simón has been putting various weights on Diablo's back, to get him used to the weight of a rider."

182

He acknowledged my statement with a curt nod, not bothering to look up from his account books. "That was supposed to have been done before I ever bought the animal," he grumbled.

I frowned at his irritability. Already, I could guess that the conversation would not go as I hoped. Still, I had to try.

"But that wasn't your fault," I said soothingly. "You thought he had been. What I'm trying to say is that the lighter loads bother him less."

He looked up in annoyance. "As they obviously would. That's scarcely a profound observation, Carlota."

I ignored his sarcastic jibe. I could not afford to make him angry. "Well, I was wondering—since I weigh far less than you do, I don't think Diablo would mind my weight as much as yours." I avoided mention of Diablo's tender mouth.

He frowned at me. "Why are you bothering me with all this? What are you trying to say?"

"Well—" I stammered under his cold hard stare, "I—I was just wondering—I was thinking what a good joke it would be on everyone if—if I rode Diablo instead of you."

He said nothing, and just sat there staring at me for a minute. At least he did not refuse immediately, I thought, and, as my hopes sparked briefly, I plunged into a justification of my suggestion. "I could do it, I know. He'd hardly notice my weight on his back! And you could laugh at Roberto Fuentes, because the horse was so tame that even I could ride him! The joke would be on him. Oh, please, Tomás! Let me do it! I know I could!"

"The joke?" he said at last, and there was no mistaking the incredulity in his voice. "You think this is all nothing but a joke?"

"I didn't mean that!" Why had I used that stupid word? Things were going far worse than I had thought possible.

"It's what you said! And I promise you there is nothing funny about the matter."

"I didn't mean to imply that there was," I said desperately, trying to hold onto my own temper. Could it be, I wondered, that Tomás had closed his mind completely to the knowledge that everyone—even his own son—was laughing at him? But surely he knew, he had to know! There were the snickers, the sly little darting glances, the jibes! How could he not know? But there is a difference in knowing and admitting. "It's only that everyone thinks the horse isn't properly saddle broken," I continued with increasing desperation, "and it would make them look ridiculous if even I could ride him with no trouble. Don't you see?" I half-smiled at him, trying to get him to envision his own amusement if he followed my plan.

But Tomás was a man without humor. He opened his mouth to speak, then clamped it shut without saying anything. I waited, watching him, afraid to say more, knowing that the matter hung in such a precarious state of balance that anything I might add could tip the balance heavily in the wrong direction. I kept my eyes on him, daring to hope he might possibly agree to my suggestion.

At his words, my hopes crumbled. He asked, "Are you presuming to say you think you could control a horse better than I do?"

I shook my head in vehement denial. "Oh, no! It's just that I'm so much lighter—"

"Which would make it that much easier for Diablo to throw you."

"But he wouldn't! I mean, I can sit the saddle well."

"Carlota Isabel," he said with an exasperated sigh, "I will thank you to tend to matters in the house, and refrain from meddling in outside affairs which are no concern of yours. I have accepted a challenge, and backed it with my own money as well. In my lifetime, there has been only one horse I could not ride. I do not expect there will be another."

I listened to his words with bitter disappointment. I had failed. There was nothing else I could do. I must admit defeat. As I turned to go, his last words repeated themselves in my brain. Before I reached the door, I turned. My feelings of uneasiness about the challenge I knew I could not stop made me ask, "What happened to that horse? The only one you couldn't ride?"

He said nothing for a long time, and I thought he was not going to answer me, but at last he did.

"I had to shoot him."

"You shot him?" Repelled by his words, I drew back from him in horror. "Because you couldn't ride him?" I asked incredulously.

He looked at me with disdain. "Scarcely that. I shot him," he said grimly, "because he killed Pilar."

I was immediately remorseful at the unfairness of my accusation. I remembered, then, that Cecilia had told me he had shot the horse that Pilar rode on her fatal ride. I should certainly have realized that would be the horse of which he had been speaking. Instead, I had jumped to the wrong conclusion. I walked over to him, put my hand on his shoulder. "Oh, Tomás, I'm sorry! Forgive me, please?"

"Yes, yes." he shrugged off my hand impatiently. "Now, will you please concern yourself more about matters in the house and less about things you don't understand?"

As I reached the door, he said, "And will you give more of

your attention to the food we're being served? Really, Carlota, I've been meaning to talk to you about that. The quality of our meals has gone down terribly. I think you've been too preoccupied with that horse, and have forgotten to supervise the kitchen."

I paused in the open doorway. "It isn't that. Teresa tells me there is not much to choose from in the market lately. Many of the natives are afraid to come to the Valley of Panchoy now, so there are less fresh vegetables. And those from our own garden are about gone. Even eggs are getting scarce. She found a few last week, but none since. Without eggs, the cook can do no baking."

"The *indios* are afraid to come here? What nonsense! What are they afraid of?"

"An earthquake."

"Oh, that!" he scoffed. "Well, whatever the cause, see if you can't do something about improving our meals. I'm getting weary of *tortillas* and dried beans."

"It might help if I went to the market with Teresa, saw what there was—"

"Well, why don't you, then?" he asked ill-naturedly.

"You've forbidden me to go," I reminded him. "You said it is unladylike to be about so early in the morning."

"Then go later."

"By six-thirty, there's nothing left to buy."

He emitted a small sound of dissatisfaction that I knew was all the answer I'd receive, so I pulled the door shut behind me. Here it was again, the constant contest between us. As usual, our exchange had accomplished nothing. Tomás would never admit error and let me go to the market in the early morning hours, and unless he did, there was nothing I could do to improve our meals. I shrugged. It probably would not have helped for me to go to the market with Teresa anyway.

I leaned against the closed door and sighed. I had failed in the purpose that had sent me to Tomás study. There was no way I could prevent him from riding Diablo unless—I turned another idea over in my mind—unless I could possibly get everyone to call off the bets.

I was waiting by the gate that led from the stables to the small patio when Ricardo came home early that evening. I stopped him before he could go into the house.

He drew back, startled. "Carlota! What are you doing out here, jumping out of the shadows like a footpad?"

"Please! I must talk to you. It's important!"

I was thankful that he seemed to sense the urgency in my voice and made no attempt to tease me further. He opened the gate and we went into the small patio. Then he turned and looked at me questioningly.

"Ricardo, could you possibly get everyone to call off their bets?"

"Call off their bets?" he repeated, as though he hadn't heard right. "You mean about Father riding Diablo from here to the bridge and back without getting thrown? Why, it would be easier to stop the sun in the middle of the sky! Half the men in Santiago have bet on this ride, most of them on Diablo. Even with the odds—"

"Can you postpone it, then?" I interrupted, watching his face anxiously, straining through the darkness to see some sign of hope for what I asked on his features. There was none.

"Father chose that date deliberately."

"But why? It's so soon!" I wailed in helpless frustration.

"Because of the *Convite*."

He was talking in riddles. "I know it's on the day of the *Convite,* but what does that have to do with it? Couldn't he make some excuse, put it off a week or two? That would help a little."

"He wouldn't. Don't you know about the *Convite* in Santiago?" He didn't wait for my answer. "I guess you wouldn't. Maybe it's different here than in Granada." He took my hand and led me to one of the chairs. As always happened during the slightest physical contact between us, a spark seemed to pass from one to the other, a spark that must some day erupt into a flame. As he released my hand, I wondered if he had felt it, too. "Sit down and I'll tell you about it, and maybe you'll understand why Father felt he had to ride Diablo so soon."

Puzzled, I sat down and watched as he settled himself in the chair nearest to me. "We celebrated Corpus Christi Day in Granada, of course, but there's nothing the day before."

"Well, here it's sort of a tradition for masked men to go around inviting people to the procession and the fiesta."

"But what does that have to do with Tomás and Diablo?"

"I'm coming to that. Together with the invitation, these men also recite little verses about some of the men of Santiago."

"Verses?" I shook my head. "What kind of verses?"

"Any kind. Satire, mostly. They make fun of some of the people here. Usually, it's all in good fun, but sometimes the humor of it can get very cutting."

"Oh!" I said slowly, beginning to realize what he was trying to tell me. "And Tomás knew if he couldn't find some

186

way to stop them by then, he'd be ridiculed all over Santiago for his purchase of Diablo."

"Exactly. That's why he's set his ride for the morning, so he could silence them before they do any damage."

"But will that silence them?"

"Only if he makes good his boast and completes the ride successfully."

"But we can't let him ride that horse!" I protested. "Diablo has such a tender mouth."

A hint of amusement crept into Ricardo's voice. "I know. That's why Father will never be able to ride him to the Matasano Bridge and back."

"And that's the very reason we can't let him try," I cried. "Don't you see?"

Now it was Ricardo's turn to be puzzled. "See what? That Father can't possibly win?"

I shook my head. "That neither he nor Diablo can possibly win! Oh, how can everyone be so stupid?"

"I assume you include me in that, but I don't see how—"

I jumped up from my chair in a burst of impatience and started pacing. "Whatever Tomás is, he's not a quitter! He won't give up, no matter how many times he's thrown!"

"And you're worried about him? I hadn't thought of that. I'd always assumed Father could take care of himself."

I was taken aback by his words, by his obvious misunderstanding of my motives, and I was overcome with a feeling of guilt because my thoughts had not once touched on what might happen to Tomás. But I said nothing to correct him. It didn't matter why Ricardo thought I wanted the coming contest stopped, if he could just manage to stop it, or at least postpone it.

He shook his head sadly, and looked up at me. "I'm sorry, Carlota. I'd do something if I could, but this has gone too far. Men are going to be lined up solid from here to the Matasano Bridge on the day of the *Convite*. Everyone's talking about. There's no way in the world to stop it now, and Father would never forgive me if I tried to interfere and suggested postponing it. But you mustn't worry about him. He'll be all right. I can't remember him ever being thrown. He'll hold his own with Diablo."

So there was no hope of stopping the ride, or even delaying it. I turned to go, feeling the dampness of the tears that overflowed from my eyes and ran down my cheeks.

Ricardo jumped up and caught my arm. "Will it help if I tell you I'm sorry? I hadn't really thought about Father, or what might happen to him. You've made me ashamed. If I hadn't needled him so, he might not have felt he had to ride Diablo so soon. I'd undo it if I could, but I can't."

I tried to smile. "Don't blame yourself," I said, remembering the looks on the faces of the men who had stopped Tomás on the church steps, and all the others. "It wasn't just you."

I turned and walked away, brushing the tears from my eyes. I did not tell Ricardo my tears were not for Tomás, but for the high-strung stallion I longed to ride myself.

Late that afternoon, Tomás heard of a statue of San Tomás he could buy, and he amazed me by announcing at supper that he was leaving the next morning for the village in which it was located.

"But what about your ride?" I asked. "I thought tomorrow you were going to try to mount Diablo. You can't afford the loss of a day! There is so little time!"

But thoughts of his ride were pushed far to the back of his mind by his impatience to obtain the figure.

"I must go tomorrow," he said with the enthusiasm he withheld from people and bestowed on things. "And I'm heartily sick of all the nonsense about that horse. A day away from him will do me good. Besides, Simón can continue working with him." He gave me one of his rare smiles. "I've been wanting a statue of San Tomás for years. I saw this one once in a small village church, but at the time there was no hope of acquiring it. It's very fine, with good features and richly colored robes. I heard today that the new young priest of that church wants his roof repaired so badly, he'd sell anything to get it done." He rubbed his palms together in anticipation of owning the coveted statue. "I will be gone all day. Don't wait supper for me. Alberto is leaving with the wagon tonight."

Tomás left before sunrise the next morning, and I went out to the stables after an early breakfast. Simón was busy carrying hay to the stalls.

"What can we do?" I asked despairingly. "Tomás won't call off the bet, or even postpone it."

"The master is a stubborn man, *Señora*."

A glimmer of a new idea was borne of my desperation. "What if I were to ride Diablo today? I mean a long ride, not just a few minutes on his back here in the stable yard. Do you think it might help?"

Simón hesitated. "I don't know. It might."

I jumped at his hesitant statement as approval. "I'll ask Ricardo if he'll go out with me after dinner."

But Ricardo dismissed my idea immediately. He and Cecilia and I were at the dinner table when I told him about it.

188

"It wouldn't do anything but harm," he said emphatically. "What if you were seen? Have you any idea what that would do? If you succeeded in riding Diablo, that would make Father look more foolish still if he fails. And if he does manage to make good his boast, the knowledge that you had ridden Diablo first would rob him of his triumph. You see, either way, you would only make matters worse."

Cecilia concurred. "Father would be terribly angry."

I knew that my idea, exposed to the revealing light of sound reasoning, was a poor one, but perhaps it was better than nothing. I made one last attempt. "If we could get out of Santiago without anyone seeing us, no one would ever know I had ridden him. Ricardo, you know the back streets, you can get us away."

He shook his head. "This has gotten too big for that. There aren't many people in Santiago who wouldn't recognize that big black stallion." He excused himself and stood up. "But even if you did ride him, what would you accomplish? Father, being as he is, will still choke up on the reins. And Diablo, having a tender mouth, will still fight him." He pulled Cecilia's and my chairs out for us. "But it's a good idea to go for a ride this afternoon, if you'll settle for taking El Moro. María Elena is still in the country. How about you two girls going up to one of the springs with me?"

Cecilia demurred, as I had known she would. And I accepted, without a moment's hesitation. Not even for Diablo would I turn down Ricardo's invitation.

We rode that day to a quiet spot just below a spring, where the water gurgled pleasantly in a pretty little creek.

"Another lovely spot!" I commented as we dismounted. "Is there no end to beautiful places to ride near Santiago?"

"There are many. I enjoy coming to places like this. I'm glad you do, too." Was that a slightly disapproving statement about María Elena, I wondered smugly? He had told me she didn't like to ride. I was glad that I did, and that I was in that peaceful quiet spot with Ricardo, and she was not. We sat on the banks of the creek and I dipped my hand idly in and out of the cool water, let it run through my fingers. I found myself relaxing for the first time in days as we sat there and talked quietly.

"Have you no water cress in Guatemala?" I asked at one point, my eyes scanning the places it would most likely be found. "I suppose I'll just have to bring some up here and start it myself."

"You're quite a gardener, aren't you?" Ricardo said. "I know our plants in the patios have never looked so good, and I detect your hand in that."

189

I laughed. "I sneaked a few of my herbs into some of the bigger pots when the gardener wasn't looking. Some of them have pretty blooms."

"You're surprising, Carlota, so different from most other girls. Tell me a little about yourself. Did you always live in Granada till you married Father?"

I nodded. "Sort of on the edges, actually. My father had a *finca* there, though he never took his farming seriously, as Tomás does. He was a scholar, and just liked the quietness and seclusion of it, so that's where we lived."

"And your mother? What was she like?"

I told him not about Tatiana, but about *Mamá*. "She was very sweet and loving and good, almost saintly. She died of consumption when I was eight. My aunt lived with us, but she and I didn't get on well." I smiled at him. "Just about like you and Tomás."

He nodded understandingly and the corners of his eyes crinkled in amusement as he asked, "Were you a rebel, too?"

"I'm afraid I was. *Papá* was always absorbed in his books, and *Tía* Juana had been brought into the household to be my *dueña,* but after *Mamá* died, she was too busy with the housekeeping to pay much attention to me. My father would have hired a housekeeper, but *Tía* could never find one who pleased her, so she continued to see to everything herself." I laughed. "Everything except me. I spent a lot of time in the hills, wandering around as no prim and proper child should have done. But when I was fifteen, *Tía* at last convinced *Papá* I must have a *dueña,* so my freedom was sharply curtailed. My dear nursemaid, Dolores, still helped me to get away sometimes." I hesitated, then went on. "I visited often with a band of gypsies who spent most of their time on some of my father's land in the hills nearby." I watched Ricardo to see how he was reacting to my revelation. I wanted him to know the experiences that had shaped me, but I knew that Tatiana and her relationship to me would always remain my own private secret.

He did not seem even a little shocked by what I had told him, I noted with satisfaction. "Is that where you learned so much about herbs? Did you know the natives call you 'the healer'? They say you have magical powers, like their witch doctors."

I blushed. "They exaggerate. It's just a case of knowing the qualities of some plants. I understand their witch doctors know of many medicinal herbs, too. From what I've seen of our doctors, they could learn from them."

"And from you. But I believe you really do have magical

powers. We've stayed here far longer than I thought. Look how close the sun lies to the top of the mountains. You've bewitched me into forgetting how late it grows." He offered me his hand. "We'll have to hurry to make it back before dark."

As he pulled me toward him, my feet slipped on the wet ground and I lost my balance. His free arm caught around my waist and pulled me toward him in an instinctive gesture to keep me from falling. Equally instinctively, my free hand grabbed his arm as I leaned against him. He released my other hand as he caught me, and our freed arms slid around each other. It was all a natural reaction to the situation, and yet when I was steadied and no longer in any danger of falling, our grips on each other tightened, and what had started as a series of movements to prevent my fall became an embrace. We had been laughing, but our laughter stopped suddenly as we were caught in the throes of a deeper emotion, wrapped in an embrace that was no less of one because it had happened accidentally. Briefly, I felt his arms crush me toward him even closer as my own arms twined tighter about him. The spark which seemed to pass between us at our slightest touch was magnified a thousandfold, and my whole body felt afire with love, with desire. I closed my eyes, gave myself over to the joy of being in Ricardo's arms. I did not question being there. This was where I belonged. This was where I had been heading since the day I had taken leave of my beloved Andalusia. The months between miraculously fell away, and nothing that had happened to me since then mattered. Somewhere far away in another world, there was someone called Tomás, but he had ceased to matter. I was here, and I was in Ricardo's arms, where I had always belonged.

My joy was short-lived. It could have lasted only a few seconds before Ricardo brought me abruptly back to reality. He pushed me from him with a surprising suddenness, with a force that was so violent it almost sent me reeling.

"Ah, Carlota, why did you marry my father so soon? Why didn't you wait and marry me?"

He didn't wait for an answer, but turned and went to get the horses.

Stunned, I watched him walk away, too benumbed by the power of my feelings to speak or move. His words repeated themselves in my brain. His question had been the sort any gallant might have asked in jest, but there had been no smile on his face, and his voice had been heavy with anguish.

The months since I had left Andalusia, which had seemed to fall away moments before, returned with a shattering impact. I was married to Tomás, irrevocably bound to him.

Ricardo's anguished words, which had returned me to the reality from which my mind had escaped so briefly, touched an answering anguish in my own heart.

If only I had known he existed, I would have waited.

Santiago—June, 1773

CHAPTER XI

Tomás returned late that night, his eyes unnaturally bright with pleasure over his latest acquisition. There was something almost pathetically childish in his delight that made me pity him. He could not go to bed until he had unloaded the wooden figure from the bed of straw on which it had traveled. First thing next morning, even before he would eat breakfast, he had it taken into the *sala,* and was trying to decide on a favored spot for it among his treasures. Only two days remained before he must make good his boast to ride Diablo, but he seemed totally unconcerned about it as he fussed for several hours over the statue of the saint after whom he was named.

But it was Ricardo, not Tomás, who occupied my thoughts that day. I was anxious to see him, to talk with him, for I felt I must know the full meaning of the words he had spoken the previous afternoon. He had maintained a silence all the way home, and had left the house with some of his friends while I was still changing from my riding clothes. Then, during the commotion connected with Tomás's arrival with the coveted statue, he had slipped into the house and into his room without me seeing him. Nor had I seen him since, for he was gone by the time I awoke that day, and at midday a dinner invitation took Tomás and me to the house of Carlos and Marta. But I could not forget Ricardo's words, and all day long they kept going through my brain. Dared I hope they meant as much as I wanted them to mean? Or was he purposely avoiding me because he had already regretted uttering them? Perhaps that evening, we would have a chance to talk.

That afternoon, Tomás mounted Diablo. He immediately took up all the slack in the reins, and Diablo objected with a series of head tosses. Tomás remained stubbornly in the saddle as Diablo made several turns around the stable yard, and I could see Tomás's expression of smug satisfaction. But Diablo was not finished with him, and stopped abruptly from a full gallop, digging his hoofs into the dirt and tossing his head down between his legs so violently that Tomás was jerked from the saddle and went flying into the dust.

Tomás's face was livid with rage as he picked himself up, brushing the dirt from his clothing. "Bring him back to me!" he called determinedly to Simón, who had caught Diablo and was standing quietly by him.

It was then that Simón spoke up, tentatively at first, obviously amazed by his own audacity for daring to incur Tomás's wrath. But devotion to Diablo made him bold, for it was readily apparent that Tomás intended to take out his anger on the horse.

"*Señor*, if I may tell you what I think," he began.

"Well, tell me," Tomás said gruffly.

Encouraged, Simón's voice grew a little stronger. "Diablo, he doesn't like a tight rein. I think perhaps if you would give him his head a little more, he would not try so hard to throw you."

It surprised me that Tomás did not berate Simón for his insolence. Such was the measure of his desperation that he actually listened, and said, "Very well, I'll try that."

He remounted, and with a somewhat slack rein had more success. Still, Diablo had an instinctive dislike for Tomás, and did not want him on his back. He champed uncomfortably at the bit, for what Tomás considered a slack rein was certainly far from the measure of freedom Diablo would have liked. Tomás was thrown a few more times, but for the first time I dared to hope that man and horse might compromise with each other, at least long enough to get to the Matasano Bridge and back.

Ricardo was not at supper that night. Puzzled, I asked why he was late.

"Oh, didn't you know?" Cecilia asked. "He's gone to spend some time in the country with the Estradas."

"He's gone?" I caught my breath, tried to keep my voice steady. "The Estradas? That's María Elena's family, isn't it?"

Cecilia nodded. "They've been wanting him to come down. I know they've invited him several times. But he did seem to make up his mind quite suddenly to go. Right in the middle of dinner, he jumped up and said he was leaving immediately."

"How long will he be gone? Did he say?" Did my inquiry sound casual enough, I wondered?

"No. I asked him if he'd be gone all week, but he didn't even stop to answer me. Maybe he got a letter this morning. Maybe that's what made him decide so suddenly to leave."

"Irresponsible!" Tomás said. "If he's as enthusiastic about learning as he claims, you wouldn't think he'd go running off right in the middle of his lectures like that, chasing after that Estrada girl."

I remember joining in some of the conversation at the table after that, but my mind, plagued with doubts, was busy puzzling over why Ricardo had run off so unexpectedly. Did it have anything to do with what happened up at the spring the day before? Or had that been a passing incident, out of his mind as soon as it was over? Had it really been anguish I had heard in his voice, or was it just that I had chosen to identify it as such? Perhaps it had been mockery, after all. Or a cavalier phrase, with no meaning. I had grasped eagerly at his words, as a starving dog snaps at a proffered morsel of food. Even as I sat there, had Ricardo forgotten his words to me? Was he already whispering endearments to María Elena behind her *dueña*'s back?

The next day, Tomás again mounted Diablo. By then he was wary of Diablo's tricks, and watchful for them, so he did not let himself be thrown easily. Only when Diablo reared up on his hind legs so high that I thought horse and rider must surely both topple over backwards did Tomás slide from the saddle, and then with an ease that made it seem he had just chosen to dismount in that unorthodox manner. He would have remounted, but again he surprised me by listening to Simón.

"*Señor*, his mouth will stand no more today," Simón protested. "If you mount him again, we will never get the bit into his mouth in the morning."

"You're sure of that?"

Simón nodded. "I know it is so, *Señor*."

"Then I have no choice, have I?" he said resignedly. He turned and went into the house.

At first light the next morning, I was out in the stables. It was not surprising to find Simón there, too.

I sighed heavily. "This is the day," I said unnecessarily.

He patted my arm. "It will be all right, *Señora*. I'm sure it will be all right." But his eyes were sad, and he gave me no reassuring smile.

"Things have gone better than I expected the last few days," I said in an effort to cheer us both. But I still had a strong feeling that the ride would not go well. The distance to

195

the bridge and back would allow too much time for the clash of wills between Tomás and Diablo to manifest itself. If the least little thing went wrong . . . I did not want to finish the thought.

I searched the kitchen garden, found one small carrot that had been overlooked, and took it into Diablo's stall. He seemed to sense my dejection, for he failed to greet me with his usual exuberance. I fed him the carrot and tried to pretend my visit that day was like any other. Just before I left, I leaned my cheek against his nose and whispered urgently, "Don't fight him, Diablo! Don't fight him!"

But I knew that he would.

Our breakfast that morning was a somber one. Cecilia and I came into the dining room first, and she must have seen the look of concern on my face, for she reached over and put her hand sympathetically over mine.

"What's the matter, Carlota?"

"This is the day Tomás is going to ride Diablo."

"Oh." She seemed to have forgotten it. I wondered if she were even aware of what was going on in the house. She occupied a room in it, she came to the table three times a day, but she was silent and withdrawn and was becoming a stranger to all of us. "I'm sure it will be all right."

I knew she was only trying to say something to soothe me, but her bland assurance of something she did not understand irritated me that morning. "But it won't!" I protested. "Tomás and Diablo—" I stopped. It would do no good to tell her. She knew nothing of horses, and would not understand if I tried to explain to her about the clash of wills that I knew with a dread certainty was coming. She would just think me foolish for crediting a horse with a strong will, so I said only, "If I could just stop Tomás, get him to back down on this ride!"

She gave my hand a final sympathetic squeeze before she withdrew hers. "I'm afraid I can't help you. No one can stop Father when he has his mind set on something."

The resignation in her voice coupled with the truth of her words filled me with hopelessness. She was right: she couldn't stop Tomás. And I had tried and failed. Maybe, if Ricardo were home, he would have been able to think of something, come up with some last-minute reason to stall Tomás, postpone his ride. But Ricardo was gone; he had deserted not only me but Diablo as well.

At that moment, Tomás came in and took his place at the table, so our insignificant and pointless conversation about the ride came to an end. I rang for the food and we ate our breakfast in almost total silence, all of us engrossed in our own private thoughts. Tomás was so preoccupied he didn't even complain about having only one egg.

We had scarcely finished our meal when Teresa answered the door and let Roberto Fuentes and a group of his friends into the patio.

"Good morning, Tomás," Roberto said in his harsh grating voice. He nodded and bowed perfunctorily toward me. *"Señora,"* he acknowledged. Then he turned again to Tomás. "A nice day for a ride, I see," he said with a forced joviality.

Tomás nodded curtly. "Good enough."

Roberto Fuentes was a grossly fat man, and I looked at him in distaste. I had never liked him, even before his cruel practical joke on Tomás. Now, I liked him even less.

His eyes sparkled with malicious pleasure as he said, "Some of my friends heard you were willing to wager anyone on this ride, and they'd like to be in on it. Will you cover their bets?"

Tomás nodded. "As much as they'd like. My wife will hold the bets. In silver or gold only."

I could hardly keep from gasping. No one could have guessed that Tomás didn't have the utmost confidence in his ability to win his wager. I had to admire his composure and his audacity.

"Agreed, gentlemen?" Roberto looked at the four men who had come with him, and they all signified their agreement.

"One try only, I believe was the wager," one of the men said. "From your door to the Matasano Bridge and back, without being thrown."

"Agreed."

The men came to me with their bets, which I recorded. I had to ask their names, for none of them were men I knew. Nor cared to. *Vultures, all!* I thought, not troubling to hide my disdain.

After Tomás had fetched silver and gold to match their bets, we went into the stable yard. To my despair, Roberto and his noisy friends followed us. Simón had Diablo saddled and ready to go, and the men, obviously in a party mood, circled the great stallion, making comments, laughing and joking. In the openness of the stable yard, Roberto seemed to feel he had to talk twice as loud as he usually did, and his harsh voice and raucous laughter made me wince, for I could see that all this was making Diablo nervous. I moved closer to him, tried to calm him, to act as a buffer between him and the commotion and confusion created by the presence of those hateful men.

"Carlota, get back!" Tomás snapped impatiently at me,

197

and I knew his temper was closer to erupting than the men could have supposed.

Reluctantly, I backed up, wondering if I might get the men to leave with me if I left. I turned to Roberto, said coolly, "Perhaps you men would like to come with me to the front of the house? After all, that is the agreed starting and finishing point for the bet."

To my relief, the men agreed. Simón shot me a look of gratitude as I led the noisy bunch out of the stable yard and back through the house.

As we went out onto the street, my heart sank. People, carriages, horses were everywhere. Ricardo had not exaggerated when he had said that half the men in Santiago had wagered on Tomás's ride. And obviously, all of them wanted to be on hand for the excitement.

Tomás had the good sense to let Simón walk Diablo around to the front of the house. Then Tomás walked to the side of the stallion and mounted. His face was expressionless. I watched carefully as he settled himself in the saddle and had Simón adjust the stirrups. I noted he was allowing far more slack in the reins than he ever had before. Maybe there was hope after all. But Diablo was exceedingly nervous, and even with Simón still by his side, he pawed the cobblestones excitedly.

Then Tomás said quietly, "All right," and Simón stepped aside.

Diablo started forward with a suddenness that startled Tomás, but he was ready for such action and recovered quickly, giving Diablo his head as he started to gallop down the street.

I moved close to Simón. "It's going to be all right," I said, not stopping to think how much I just hoped it would. "Did you see? He's allowing plenty of slack. He's giving Diablo his head. I think it's going to be all right."

But I had spoken too soon. When they reached the corner, a rider darted out of the cross street. Diablo, startled, shied away from the other horse. Tomás, caught completely by surprise, jerked his elbows back to tighten the reins.

"No! No!" I did not know if I protested silently or if I said the words aloud. The battle between Tomás and Diablo was joined as Diablo threw his head back violently in answer to Tomás's sudden tug on the reins, and Tomás reacted by pulling them even tighter.

To Diablo, the shortened rein was intolerable, so he responded in the way I knew he must, by ridding himself of his unwanted rider. I saw him stop with a violent shudder and lower his head with a force that sent Tomás catapulting over his head.

All of us who had been standing in front of our door watching ran immediately to the corner. Tomás stood up, not hurt but shaken, his eyes glued onto Diablo, who had trotted meekly enough back to Simón once he had thrown Tomás.

Roberto Fuentes made no attempt to hide his amusement. "I told you he'd never make it to the bridge on that horse!" he gloated.

My eyes returned quickly to Tomás, and what I saw there filled me with a dread such as I had never known. For there was upon his face a fury so intense that it seemed to obliterate his features, leaving only the raw emotion, stark and naked, upon his face.

The street was full of men. Not only Roberto and his friends, but other men had thronged out onto the street from the sidelines, and in a matter of seconds we were in the center of a closed circle. When Tomás had fallen, there had been a few seconds of stunned silence, but once he had picked himself up, obviously uninjured, the joking and laughing had begun, and there was a viciousness and a cruelty in it that would have evoked in me a deep sympathy for Tomás if I had not seen that look on his face. The others saw it, too, for the laughter died down, and even Roberto, who had been keeping up a constant barrage of boastful gloating words, stopped suddenly. I looked around. All eyes were on Tomás, and his eyes were on Diablo.

"You've won your wager, gentlemen," Tomás said grimly. "But I promise you I will ride that horse to the Matasano Bridge and back before the sun sets." He motioned for Simón to bring Diablo forward.

"Please, Tomás, don't!" I protested, not even realizing I had spoken till I heard my own voice. I rushed to him and grabbed his arm. "The wager is over. You couldn't help that horse darting out! There's not a rider in all of Guatemala who could have stayed on Diablo just then!"

"I appreciate your solicitude, my dear," he said, still not taking his eyes from Diablo. His free hand grasped my restraining fingers firmly and removed them from his arm. "Now if you will please return to the house and pay these gentlemen what I owe them, I will ride my new stallion to the Matasano Bridge and back."

"Please, no——!"

He turned his blazing anger on me. "Get in the house!" he commanded roughly.

Then he walked over to Diablo and remounted.

I couldn't bear to watch any more. I knew what would

199

happen. No matter how many times Tomás was thrown, he would remount Diablo again and again. I turned to go back in the house.

"Señora!" One of the men who had come with Roberto called after me. "Our wagers, if you please. I believe your husband said you would pay them." ·

I looked at him over my shoulder, making no effort to hide my disgust with him and his kind. "You needn't concern yourself. Your wager will be paid."

"I didn't mean I was worried. . . ." he said, his words dropping off in uncertainty.

As the men followed me into the house, Roberto gave a nervous little laugh and said, "Didn't I tell you Alvarado could never ride a horse with such a sensitive mouth?" When no one answered him, he continued, "But I never thought . . ." He stopped in mid-sentence as had his friend a moment before.

As we reached the door, I paused and looked back. The spectators, having had their satisfaction, were dispersing. Everybody had come to watch Tomás's downfall; no one cared any more if he succeeded in his substitute boast. There was no longer any joking or laughing; the crowd was quiet and subdued. An embarrassed hush had fallen over them, as though they had at last realized that their laughter tasted strongly of blood.

I paid off the men immediately, all but flinging their coins at them. They, too, were subdued, and picked up their gold and silver in silence. I did not even wait to summon Teresa to show them out, but opened the door for them myself. I did not want to have to look at them for even one moment longer than necessary.

When the last of them had stepped over the solid bottom portion of the entrance doorway cut in one of the large oak double doors, I closed the door behind them and leaned against it and sobbed. I put my hand to my lip and bit down till the taste of blood mingled with the salt of my tears. Still sobbing, I gathered together some unguents and took them to Diablo's stall, where I lay down on the straw and waited.

I don't know how much time elapsed before I heard Simón returning with Diablo. Simón entered the stall first, and I saw tears streaming down his face in unashamed sorrow. Then my gaze went to Diablo as he came into the stall. I saw blood dripping from his mouth, saw the bright red gashes where Tomás's whip had bitten deeply into his flesh. And I saw his eyes, and that was the saddest thing of all, for they seemed to be looking at me reproachfully, as though he could not understand why I, who was his friend, had permitted such a thing to be done to him.

"I suppose Tomás made it to the bridge and back?" I asked dully.

"Yes, *Señora*. But not until Diablo had thrown him five more times."

I nodded, moving to Diablo's side and gently stroking one of the places Tomás's fury had not marked him.

Simón left, returned with a basin and started bathing the horse's wounds. When he touched a particularly sensitive spot at the corner of Diablo's mouth, the horse backed violently from him with a shiver of pain.

Simón turned to me and his mouth twitched in impotent anger. "Your husband is an evil, evil man," he said through clenched teeth.

"Yes," I agreed. "He was goaded into this by other evil men, but that does not make what he did forgivable."

As I set about helping dress Diablo's injuries, I remembered my first meeting with Tomás on board the Santa Teresa. Then, I had looked into his eyes when he took my hand, and I had been forced to look away, sensing something frightening and terrible beneath the surface of his polished manners. I had been married to him for six months, and I hadn't known until that day what it was I had sensed was hidden within him.

Now I knew. It was evil incarnate.

But I still did not know the full measure of his unleashed rage, for there was more yet to come. That night at supper, he complained bitterly that the streets had been all but deserted when he had at last made it to the bridge and back successfully.

I looked at him with distaste. "It no longer mattered. You had no wager." If he had admitted defeat after he was thrown, tolerated the jeers and derision that followed with some show of good grace, I could have felt sorry for him, could even have felt a sort of grudging respect for him. But he had not; he had gone on to salve his own wounded pride, and he had all but killed Diablo to do it.

I didn't say all this. There was no need to put it into words. He had to know the terrible selfish arrogance and pride that dwelt in his own heart.

Cecilia seemed oblivious to the undercurrent of tension between Tomás and me. "I'm sorry you lost your wager, Father. I heard about it at the hospital."

"That news probably traveled fast enough," Tomás said bitterly. "But I'll bet no one bothered to tell anyone that I did make the ride later."

I looked at him. "It no longer mattered," I repeated quietly.

But he was encased in his own self-centered world and had no idea of what I was trying to tell him. He looked at me uncomprehendingly.

After supper, Tomás went into the *sala* to console himself among his treasures. I felt I could not stay in the house another second, and I unbolted the front door and went out onto the street. I didn't care if Tomás knew I had gone out or not; somehow that day I had moved beyond his disapproval. I walked by the *sala*, through the open window saw him holding a silver bowl, turning it over fondly in his hands. I turned away in disgust.

I walked far from the house, unconcerned about dangers or gossip, benumbed by what had happened that day, unable to think. I must have been gone some time when I realized I was overcome with a deep fatigue, more emotional than physical. I turned back toward the house, and was just approaching the corner onto which our *sala* windows opened when the masked men appeared.

I shrank back into the shadows of the house across the street. I would have thought they were footpads if they had not all been mounted. They dismounted and formed a semicircle near our window, and one of them began to talk in a loud clear voice. I remembered what Ricardo had told me about the *Convite,* and I realized with a sudden dread what they were about.

First the spokesman said something about the next day's festivities. Then he launched into the verse which mocked Tomás. In the stillness of the night air, his words seemed to reverberate off the walls of the building in the shadow of which I stood.

"A man twice taken, the story's told
Bought the devil and paid in gold.
He boasted loud, and fell too soon;
The devil won many a silver dubloon."

I stayed in the shadows until they had gone. As I was crossing the street, I heard a crash and the clatter of something breaking coming from the direction of our house. I ran and looked in the open window of the *sala*. Tomás was stamping out of the room. His back was toward me, so I couldn't see his face. But I didn't have to, for I could see the long angry strides with which he headed toward the door. And on the floor, directly below one of the small areas where the bare wall was visible between the hangings, were the remains of one of his Meissen figurines where he had thrown it in his choleric rage.

I picked up my skirts and ran into the house.

"Tomás!"

He was just crossing the patio toward our room when I entered. He looked at me with unseeing eyes, did not even seem to grasp the fact that I had just come in from the street.

"What are you going to do to Diablo?" I asked, afraid of the answer, knowing his fury would focus on the horse.

He eyed me coldly. "What I should have done at the start." His words were all the more chilling because they were uttered with cold deliberation.

"You can't do any more to him!" I protested. "You've about killed him now!"

"I can do with him whatever I choose."

"No! It's not right! Please, Tomás, don't take your anger out on him! That's cowardly! It's the men who have angered you, not Diablo! He can't help it! Don't make him suffer just because you hate those men!"

I hadn't realized it, but I had grabbed his arm, and was clutching it with a surprising strength. But his wrath had given him added strength, too, and he flung me aside with a ferocity borne of his rage.

"Get out of my way!"

"What are you going to do?" I sobbed.

"I'm leaving for the farm, now. Right now. And I'm taking Diablo with me. Maybe he'll learn some manners there, at the front of a plow."

"You ... can't ... be ... serious!" My words came slowly and only in a forced whisper, for I seemed to lack the breath to utter them. I was breathless with the knowledge of the supreme cruelty it had taken to devise such a punishment for Diablo. For the spirited horse, it would be a living death. Like the mines.

It was then I knew that I had to know the answer to a question that had been bothering me for some time.

"Did you ever send a man to the mines?"

If he thought it a strange time and place for me to ask that question, he gave no sign of it.

"Yes, once."

"Why?"

"For letting Pilar ride a horse just like Diablo."

"The one you couldn't ride?" It was not really a question at all, but a statement. For in that moment, I knew I had not been wrong when I had jumped quickly to the conclusion that Tomás had shot that other horse because he had not been able to ride him. The fact that the same horse had caused the death of Pilar had merely given him a convenient excuse.

Santiago—Mid-June, 1773

CHAPTER XII

It must have been hours later when I fell at last, utterly exhausted, onto my bed. I did not trouble to undress, for defeat had combined with exhaustion to overwhelm me with such a potent force that I threw myself sideways across the bed, fully clothed, and was at once enveloped by the welcome blackness of a deep and dreamless sleep.

I awoke in exactly the same position, every bone and muscle in my body aching from having slept so unmovingly. I raised my head and looked around, blinking. The shutters were open and daylight was streaming in.

I turned onto my back, staring blankly at the ceiling, trying to remember the painful events from the previous day. I didn't really want to think about them, but they had become fogged and jumbled in my mind into a welter of confused and unrelated episodes, and I felt compelled to at least sort them into their proper sequence.

First, there had been Tomás's foolish boast, and I was struck anew with a feeling of my own helplessness as I remembered Simón's sorrowful return after Diablo had been brutalized so. I recalled Tomás's stubborn insistence to Cecilia and me that he had been successful, after all. Apparently he was unable to realize or unwilling to admit that by remounting Diablo after his original spill he had nullified even the small measure of success which might have been attributed to him for his courage in accepting the original challenge. In my mind, I could see again the group of men who had hidden their identity behind the double blind of darkness and masks in order to speak their clever and cruelly taunting verse so deliberately close to our windows. I remembered running into the patio when I realized their words had snapped the last taut thread of Tomás's self-control, and accosting him there, only to be horrified at the malevolence of his intentions for the once-proud young stallion. Only vaguely did I remember running after him as he strode angrily out to the stables. With a renewed feeling of inadequacy, I recalled how Simón, who had been sleeping in the corner of Diablo's stall, had looked at me, mutely pleading with me to do something to stop Tomás from taking Diablo. I had tried, but Tomás had shoved me aside impatiently, and my efforts were as futile as though I had tried to wrest a storm cloud from the sky.

When Simón had realized I was as helpless as he to stop Tomás by any save physical means, he had even dared to fight his master in his efforts to save Diablo. But the frail *indio* was no match for Tomás, whose enraged resolve to make the horse suffer for his own folly and badly wounded pride had given him the strength of ten men.

After that, even Diablo had seemed past coping with the situation, and he submitted without a struggle when Tomás tied him to the back of the wagon. I would never be able to blot from my mind my last glimpse of Diablo, trotting off with heartbreaking docility behind the wagon. The memory of that was the saddest of all.

Simón and I had stood, utterly defeated, and listened to the rumble of the wagon moving through the city, which had seemed suddenly to have grown unnaturally hushed. It was not yet midnight. Where was the normal night sounds? I wondered. The clatter of the horses' hoofs on the cobbles, the creak of the wagon had seemed to my ears to be a deafening roar. Finally, the noise grew faint, then fainter still, until it had faded to nothing in the still night air. Simón and I continued to stand there unmovingly, as stiff as though we were carved of stone, our ears straining lest we miss the most minute final sound. Only after the silence remained unbroken for some time did we move. Then, wordlessly, with no more than a sigh of resignation exchanged between us, we turned toward the house, I to go to my room and Simón to his bed in the servants' quarters. What, after all, was there to say? We had done all we could, but at last we had been forced to admit our powerlessness to change what had happened. It had, we both knew, been inevitable from the beginning.

As I lay on my bed that morning, I did not want to dwell overlong on the painful memories of poor Diablo and my inability to help him. I could not push the thoughts from my mind, but I could, by conscious effort, keep myself from brooding about them. There was no going back, no reliving

205

of the past; yesterday was done, finished. Just as my marriage to Tomás was finished.

That much, at least, stood out with a crystal clarity in my mind. It was the one fact of which I was sure, the one thing that had sorted itself out from the confusion in my brain and emerged as a certainty. As unquestioningly as I accepted the fact that day follows night, I knew that I would no longer suffer the injustices and degradations of a marriage that should never have been. Beyond that fact, I was not yet prepared to go. There was no danger of Tomás returning soon, for he would surely stay at the farm for some time—weeks, maybe even months—until he thought the memory of his defeat was no longer so sharply imprinted on the minds of Santiago residents. Only then would he venture a return to the city. Before then, there would be plenty of time for me to consider rationally what course my actions must take.

I drifted through the day as one in a hazy dream. Everything around me was cloaked in a filament of unreality, as though if I touched even the most solid of objects they would dissolve into a cloud of dust, just as the people I saw might at any moment drift away into a dense foggy mist.

There was no one left in the house but Cecilia and me, and the servants. If Cecilia noted the oddity of her father's sudden unexplained departure or sensed any change in me, she did not comment on it at our midday meal.

"Will you be going to watch the procession?" she asked.

I shook my head. "I think not." Only after I had answered did I remember it was the Corpus Christi procession to which she referred. Yesterday had been the *Convite*, so today was the day of Corpus Christi, I reminded myself. It seemed surprising that in the midst of the turmoil that had so shaken our household, outside events were continuing as usual. "Are you going?"

She nodded, and I notcied she kept her eyes down as she said, "Yes, Luisa and I thought we might go."

I forced myself to emerge from my benumbed state to focus my attention on Cecilia. Poor girl! She did have problems, and in my preoccupation with my desire for Ricardo and the events that centered around Tomás and Diablo, I had scarcely taken note of her during the past few weeks. As she looked up at me, I noted the dark circles under her eyes, and I felt a great surge of compassion for her. What a house of unhappiness was ours! It occurred to me that it might set her mind at ease at least a little bit to know that there was scant danger of Tomás returning soon.

"Your father has gone down to the farm," I said. "I think he'll be staying there for some time."

206

"Oh."

I sensed her relaxation as she absorbed the information I offered. As we finished our meal in silence with only an occasional interlude of small talk, I studied her, realized that the slenderness I had noted on my arrival in Santiago four and a half months earlier had become an excessive thinness, smoothing and erasing the fullness of the curves that had given her such a magnificent figure. Her thin shape seemed lost inside her dress, which hung on her as limply as though it had been hanging on a peg in her wardrobe.

"Cecilia, you must eat. Please have another helping of meat and beans," I urged gently. "Teresa was lucky and found this lovely leg of lamb in the market this morning."

"I—I couldn't," she said, holding up her hand in a demurring gesture as I held out the meat platter. "I honestly tried, but I just couldn't swallow more than a few bites." Her despondency seemed to come through her words as strongly as though she had voiced a desperate plea for help.

I nodded understandingly and set the platter down. Then I said impulsively, "If there's ever anything at all I can do to help you, you will let me know, won't you?"

But Cecilia was by nature aloof, and now that aloofness kept her from confiding to me the reason for her obviously desperate unhappiness. "I wish there were something you could do," she said, shaking her head slowly in a gesture of hopelessness. "I only wish there were!"

That evening the house was deserted. Cecilia had returned in the late afternoon to collect her things, and said she would spend the night with Luisa. I had told Teresa to have a cold supper left for me on the dining room table so that she and the other servants could watch the procession and take part in the fiesta. "Tell the men in the stables they may go, too," I said. Normally, I would have gone to tell them, but I could not bring myself to go out to the stables again, not yet. The heartbreaking sight of poor Diablo being led back to his stall after Tomás had beaten and bullied him into submission was still too fresh in my mind.

It was a rare treat for the servants to be allowed an extra night out, and by five o'clock they had all left. I didn't mind being left alone, for I found the absence of the usual household bustle restful after the strain of the previous day's events. Later, when darkness had fallen with its accustomed swiftness in these latitudes, the silence seemed to close in even more completely, as outside the house there was a gradual fading of the normal street noises. The religious activities had drawn many people away from our part of the city, so

207

the stillness was broken only occasionally by the passing of a carriage or an occasional lone rider.

I lit the candles in the small family sitting room and took down a volume of poems, taking comfort in the familiarity of the motions: removing the book from the shelf, settling myself in a chair, placing it on my lap, feeling the smooth leather binding on my fingertips as I opened it. But as my eyes began to move over the pages, I found that the groupings of letters remained little more than meaningless jumbles, as though the volume were written in a foreign language with which I was not familiar. After a while, I closed the book and laid it aside, then went into the next room to the light supper of cheese and tortillas and wine which had been set out for me. Without appetite, I nibbled on the food and sipped the wine. I knew the wine to be good, but that night, to my deadened senses, it seemed flat and tasteless, just as the tortillas seemed too dry to swallow and the cheese lacking its usual mellowness.

I wrapped the stillness of the night around me like a much-needed balm, moving from one place to another in a sort of waking sleep, unwilling to apply my mind to the process of thought. I remember Tatiana once told me that time was the greatest healer of all, and that herbs and potions merely helped the body utilize time to cure itself. That is why, she had said, people who are very ill will sleep long hours, their bodies forcing a drowsiness upon them so that time can effect the healing process from within. I wonder if perhaps the same cannot also be said of the soul. My wounds were terrible and deep: Ricardo, who had possibly been just on the point of committing himself to me, had repudiated me, deserted me, run instead to María Elena; I had discovered such depths of malevolence in the man to whom I was married as I had not suspected could exist in the heart of man, and I knew that I could never again live as his wife; and I had been forced to stand helplessly by and watch this evil destroy a beautiful spirited animal.

I can remember that evening clearly still, and the odd thing about it was that, though there was much to make me despair, I had arrived at a sort of peace within myself, not unlike the deep restorative sleep Tatiana had mentioned. When events would demand that I emerge from this state of suspension between past and future, I knew there would again be retrospection, and self-blame and worries about what I must do, and with this would return feeling and pain, but for the time being, there was only a blessed numbness.

It was still early when I went to my room and prepared for bed, putting on the nightgown and robe my maid had laid out for me. I did not braid my hair that night, but let it hang loose, wanting the free unhampered feeling of it, just as I welcomed the looseness and soft weightlessness of the light silk of my gown and robe upon my body.

I walked out into the patio for a moment, as I often did before retiring, for I liked to fill my lungs with the sweet night air, fragrant with the perfume of the many flowering plants. But that night I could smell nothing, for I was as insensitive to the aroma of the blossoms as I was to everything else.

As I started to return to my room and seek the further haven of sleep, I became aware of the sound of hoofbeats on the cobbles, and realized they were approaching rapidly. The sharp sound changed to a soft thud as horse and rider turned behind our *patio de placer* to make their way to our stables.

Drawn by the sound, I made my way to the small patio. I was alone in the house, and I suppose I should have been frightened by the arrival of an unknown rider, but so beyond any deep feelings was I that I felt nothing beyond an idle curiosity as I looked over the top of the gate toward the garden, waiting for whoever had arrived in such apparent haste to emerge from the darkness of the barn. When at last a tall form separated itself from the blackness of the night, he was not far from me.

"Ricardo!"

As I said his name, saw him striding toward me, emotion, thought, memory—all the things my mind had blocked out—returned to me in a jumbled confusion. Gone was the trance-like daze in which I had languished for the past few hours. Feeling returned in a rush, and my sorrow for Diablo, my hatred of Tomás, my love for Ricardo all poured in on me. I burst through the gate, too impatient to wait for Ricardo to cover the few remaining steps that separated us.

Repeating his name on a sob, I threw myself into his open arms and leaned against his broad chest as the wall of my self-control collapsed and loosed a flood of tears.

I felt the comfort of his arms closing protectively around me, felt his lips brush across the top of my head.

"Hush, my love! You mustn't cry." He scooped me up into his arms and carried me into the *patio de placer*. Still holding me, he sat down on one of the stone benches and began to rock back and forth, as one might do with a small child who has awakened crying from the terror of a nightmare. He settled me on his lap and cradled my head against his chest, and when my tears had spent themselves and my sobbing had subsided, he said simply, "Now tell me what has made you cry."

I poured out to him the story of Tomás's ride and my helpless fury at what he had done to Diablo. When I had finished, he turned my face up toward his and dried my eyes tenderly.

"You did all you could for Diablo, Carlota, you and Simón. No one could have done more, and there is nothing anyone can do now. The damage is done. You must let the weight of Father's sins fall upon his own back. They are his to carry, not yours."

I strained, trying to see his face through the darkness as he lightly brushed away a stray tear he had felt on my cheek, and I was struck anew with the marvel of him being there, holding me, comforting me. The misery and frustration of the past days seemed to have purged themselves in the telling. Or perhaps it was just that my unhappiness could not long survive in the wonder of his presence. I felt a release, felt transfused with a new kind of serenity, so unlike the benumbed calm with which I had moved through the earlier portion of the evening. I had been existing then in an absence of feeling, a withdrawal from the world. Now, I felt vitally alive and expectant, knowing I was on the edge of a great happiness. As Ricardo's fingers moved gently over my face, searching for any remaining tears, I caught his hand in both of mine, held it tightly.

"You came back!" I said, struck by the full meaning of his return.

"Yes. But can you ever forgive me for leaving you?" The contrition in his voice filled me with tenderness and love, and confirmed what I had known from the instant I had recognized his beloved figure coming toward me, that his return had been no ordinary home-coming. He had left María Elena, repudiated her and the comfortable future he might have had with her, turned away from her to face uncertainty with me. His return had been not to a place, to a house, but to me, because he knew I would be waiting here.

"There is nothing to forgive," I answered contentedly. "It doesn't matter that you left. You came back."

"Yes." His lips brushed my temple.

"To me," I added, solely for the pleasure it gave me to say it.

"To you. I was powerless to stay away. You make everyone else in the world seem colorless and drab by comparison. There is a bright flame burning within you, Carlota, did you know that? And sometimes, when you're happy or angry, flashes of this flame shine out from your dark eyes like sparks shooting out from burning wood. And your mouth—" His fingers traced my lips lightly. "Never have I seen such a lovely red mouth, so full and soft and inviting. Or hair so dark and shining." His fingers moved to my hair, stroked it.

I reveled in the touch of his hand moving so lightly across my face, my hair, in the sound of his words, which caressed me no less than his fingers. And I was glad he did not mention María Elena by name, even though I knew he had been telling me he had been comparing me with her these past few days, and that he had left her for me. Poor María Elena! I felt a sudden burst of compassion for her, for I did not doubt that she loved Ricardo, too, and she had lost him. Well could I afford the magnanimity of compassion, for I need never again consider her a rival, need never bristle at the sound of her name or fear that he might leave me for her. Her rout was complete, as my victory was final.

But it was not the time to concern myself with others. I sighed happily, twined my arms around Ricardo's neck. "I have loved you for such a long time, longer than you can guess." How far in the past it seemed now, that first morning on board the Santa Teresa, when I had stared into Tatiana's crystal and seen the face that was to become so dear to me. Hadn't my love for him really begun to shape itself that very day, that very instant? And the miracle of it all was that at some point in time between that day and this, he had come to love me, too.

I smiled, wondered how I could ever have doubted the depth of his feelings for me when he had uttered the anguished cry, *"Why did you marry my father so soon? Why didn't you wait and marry me?"*

There was no longer any need to ask him what he had meant by those words; his return had told me. Instead, I felt compelled to give him the answer to his question, as I had not done that day near the spring. "I would have waited for you forever, if only I had known."

He nodded, his head leaning against mine, as though he knew I had been awaiting his return to answer, as though no time had elapsed between the asking and the answering.

In those first hours we were together, I can speak not only of my feelings, but of those we shared, for we seemed on that night not like two people, but one. From the moment we embraced in the darkness of the garden, we began to exist only in each other, our minds and bodies no longer separate entities. Thus he did not ask about Cecilia, or inquire if any of the servants were about; he did not have to question me about them, for it was enough that I knew. And it was together, of one accord, that we stood and locked our arms about each other and made our way toward Ricardo's room. We had no need to voice aloud our intention to lie in one another's arms that night, nor did we need words to reject the idea of going into the room I had unwillingly shared with Tomás. Even as I waited at Ricardo's door while he left me momentarily to close the shutters in my room and pull the door closed so that the servants would assume I slept there, I seemed to know where he was going and why. And when he again left my side as we entered his room, I knew even before I saw the sparking of the flint and then the growing flame of the candle that he was longing for the sight of me as I longed to see him.

He closed the shutters and removed the counterpane from the bed, then brought the candle closer, setting it on a table near the place I stood, and came to stand near me, close enough to touch me but still not doing so.

I could not say how long we stood there, motionless, just looking at each other. It could have been minutes, or it might have been only a few seconds, but to us the passage of time didn't matter, for it had just then the unhurried measure of infinity.

It might seem strange that our lips had still not touched, but neither of us felt the need to hurry. Time washed over us without touching us, and nothing and no one outside that room mattered. I often wonder if it would have been possible for anyone to break our concentration on each other just then. I believe we would have been just as isolated had we stood in the center of a crowd.

It was Ricardo who first broke the spell that held us, for he suddenly moved toward me and pulled me into his arms, burying his lips in my hair and saying my name over and over. With that, our moment in infinity was gone, and we moved forward together, carried willingly on the torrent of our shared passion, our need to belong completely to each other.

When at last we kissed, our lips pressed together and clung with all the force of desperation, of desire too long denied. We drew apart, breathlessly, only to return again as we had been before, so that each of our kisses ended in the beginning of another.

Ricardo drew back from me momentarily and his fingers pulled at the ribbons on my robe and the gown beneath it, then he slipped them together over my shoulders and let them drop to the floor. I smiled at him, feeling no embarrassment at standing naked before him. So close were we that night, so in accord, that I felt I actually shared his delight at the sight of my body, and I was glad for the pleasure it gave him. And when he picked me up and carried me to his bed, I was almost as much aware of the soft feel of my smooth flesh under his hands as I was of the strength of the arms that carried me so effortlessly and placed me so easily on the bed. I watched unashamedly as he took off his clothes, taking pleasure in the sight of his hard muscular body as he had in the soft femininity of mine. I held out my arms to him and caught my breath for the joy of it as he moved into their circle. He leaned over me, kissing my temples, my lips, my throat, my breasts, as my fingers traced the breadth of his powerful shoulders, then moved through the red-gold of his hair, which was shining gloriously in the candle's glow.

His hands moved down the length of my body and back again, slowly, lightly at first, then with increasing fervor, and wherever he touched, my flesh felt warm and warmer still, until it seemed that his hands, his kisses were red-hot brands, setting us both afire with desire. And when he moved over me, driven by the urgency that by then possessed us, I arched my back to meet him even as he thrust forward, so that it was not an action solely by him or by me, but a simultaneous joining of our flesh. As one body, we moved together toward fulfillment, and it was with one voice that we uttered a cry of ecstasy, and neither of us wondered at the perfect harmony of it, so attuned were we to the needs and feelings of the other. For a few minutes, we continued to cling together, for neither of us could speak, or move, so transported had we been by the intensity of our emotions.

Never again were we to experience anything quite like the perfection of that first time we lay together. It was not that we found less joy in our love-making, or that our feelings for each other in any way diminished, but on that night, that first time, we reached such a rare accord that there seemed no separation between us. It could not have continued in just that way any more than mere mortals can long survive in the thin air of the highest mountain peaks.

When we awoke later that night from a drowsy awareness of each other that cannot really be called sleep, we both smiled in the last fluttering light of the candle, and we found a new kind of quiet contentment in coming together more slowly, without the driving urgency that had moved us earlier. And then we dozed lightly, wrapped in each other's arms, and when we heard a rooster's crow and knew we must soon part, again our bodies moved together, as though they could never be sated. And this time our love-making took on yet another quality. For my part, I knew that whatever I had lost in no longer being totally aware of Ricardo's feelings— as totally as though his body and mind had been my own—I had gained in a heightening of awareness of my own feelings, in being yet more conscious of the delightfully sensuous yearnings he awakened in me so easily and appeased so pleasurably.

When the first faint glow of morning light became visible around the cracks of the door and the shutters, and the moment when I must return to my own room could be postponed no longer, I raised myself on one elbow and called softly, "Ricardo."

"Ricardo, my love." I repeated his name, knowing he was not asleep, but I could not forego the pleasure it gave to say it aloud again.

In answer, he reached out and pulled me toward him lazily, so that my head rested on his chest.

I settled into his embrace, wishing I could remain there. "It's getting light. I had better go to my room. The servants will soon be up." I moved my fingers idly across his chest as I spoke.

"Don't go."

"You know I don't want to, but I must. Do you see, where the shutters don't quite meet? There's a crack of light."

I could feel him move as he turned his head to look. He settled back onto the pillow, tightening his arms around me. "Maybe it's moonlight."

I laughed, pleased that he was as unwilling to part as I. "What little sliver of moon there was has set long ago," I reminded him. Reluctantly, I pushed myself from his arms, feeling his answering reluctance to let me go. Then I walked to the window and cracked the shutters a little to let a small amount of light into the room. I felt nothing of what *Tía* would have called proper maidenly modesty as Ricardo's eyes moved over my body in the half-light, just as his hands had done so lovingly during the night.

"You're lovely," he said as I picked my gown from the floor and lifted it over my head. After I had slipped into my robe, I smoothed my hair with my hands and swept it back behind my shoulders.

"With your hair loose like that, you look like a gypsy." He held out his arms toward me. "Come here, my gypsy love, and let me taste once more your fiery kiss."

I smiled to myself, wondering what he would say if I told him how close to the truth he was. But that was my secret, and would remain so. I made my way to the door, and it was all I could do to resist the pull of his outstretched arms. "There is no time," I said regretfully. If I went to him, it would not be for one kiss, but many. If I failed to return to my room now, while there was still a chance to do so unseen, there would be whispers among the servants, and the whispers would spread. There must be no scandal, I resolved, not yet. Some time soon, Ricardo and I would decide what we were to do. We must go away together, and when we did, there would be scandal enough. But for the time being, we had need of discretion.

I grasped the bolt of the door, clenching it firmly in my hand lest I weaken in my resolve. I didn't want the night to end, but end it must. There would be other nights, many of them. This was not an ending for us, but a beginning, the start of a new life.

"Ricardo—" I said his name hesitantly. I wanted him to know what this night had meant to me, and yet I was not quite certain how to tell him, for there was no way I could make him understand without mentioning Tomás. "There is something I want to tell you about—about Tomás and me."

He had been smiling at me, but the smile was quickly gone at the mention of his father's name, and as quickly replaced by a scowl. "I've no desire to talk about him."

"Nor have I. But I feel I must, just this once, my love, so that you can know what you mean to me. I was married to Tomás for six months." I noted how naturally the past tense had fallen from my lips. *I was married.* I was, but am no longer. "As his wife, my body belonged to him."

"For the love of God, don't you think I have been aware of that? Do you think you must remind me?" He propped himself on one elbow and continued angrily, "Why do you think I left here in such a hurry? It was because I couldn't go through the torture of seeing the closed door of your room another night, the room you shared with him! Knowing you were in there with him, so close to me, yet belonging to him. I couldn't stand it! I decided the only thing to do was to leave you, forget you. I even intended to ask María Elena to marry me, immediately, but I couldn't do it. You were there, between us, and every time I tried to concentrate on her face, I could see only yours, and your bewildered hurt look as we rode back from the spring. And so I came back to you, and when I found you alone, I thought you were as eager as I to forget you still belong to him. And now you must remind me!"

"Please don't get angry with me. I want you to hear what I have to say. I will mention what happened between Tomás and me only this once, and then I promise you never to mention it again." I plunged on, determined to make him listen. "You are wrong when you say I still belong to Tomás. I used to be his—his property, but that is in the past. Still, I think it is important to both of us that you know that never once did anything in me respond to him. With him, it was always as though my body was detached from me. Afterward, I felt it

215

had been—" I paused, searching for the right word—"defiled.

"But last night, with you, my whole body and soul were alight with love for you. I felt—you may think it foolish, but I felt as though I were coming to you as pure and untouched as a virgin. I do not feel that what happened between us makes me an adulteress. It was too good and beautiful to be anything but right. It is to you, not Tomás, that I belong now, you to whom I consider myself wed. And I feel that last night was my true wedding night."

"Ours," he amended in a choked whisper, and I noted that the anger had all faded from his face.

"Ours," I agreed. "I never knew anything so wonderful could happen between two people. I feel no shame for what we did, only a sort of glory." My voice, too, was choked with emotion.

"I'm sorry I was angry just now, Carlota, and I'm glad you told me." He started to get out of bed.

"No!" I said, quickly sliding the bolt back and starting to open the door. "You know I'd never leave if I so much as felt your touch again."

He lay back down and grinned, locking his hands behind his head. "Very well. I'll let you go for now, if you promise you won't stay in your room more than a few hours."

"You know I couldn't stand to be away from you for any longer." I blew him a kiss. It took all my will power to keep from running back to him. I went to my room, but I didn't sleep; I lay awake, begrudging every minute that kept us apart.

Later, we entered the dining room at the same time, careful to keep our eyes away from each other as we took our places and the maid brought in the gruel and a few mangos. When she had gone, Ricardo smiled and winked at me as though to say, *You see? This wonderful secret is ours alone, and the world doesn't suspect a thing.* His hand sought mine under the table, and gave it a reassuring squeeze.

When we had eaten, I asked him if he were going to his lectures that day. I had been reluctant to ask, assuming he would go. How jealous I was of anything that threatened to take him from me, even for a little while!

"Not today. I've missed four days of lectures already, so I believe I'll just make it a full week. Monday, I'll return to the University. But for the next three days, I'd much rather go riding with you, if you're free."

"If I'm free," I repeated, smiling happily at his answer. I turned to make certain no one was coming before I answered in a whisper, "For you, I will ever be free!" Marta was ex-

216

pecting me for tea the next afternoon, but I would write a note making some excuse for my absence.

"Can we leave soon?"

His anxiety to be gone pleased me, and I almost knocked over my chair in my eagerness to tell the cook to prepare us a lunch. "I'll see what food there is for us to take," I said as I walked from the room. "I won't be long."

I was detained in the kitchen longer than I had expected, for Teresa had just returned from the market with very little in her basket. "Just look, *Señora*," she said as she saw me. "See how little I found, and the price for what there is is so high you would not believe! I would have bought some chickens, but there were none to be found, nor eggs, either. And unless I get to the market very early, there are not even any vegetables for our soup."

I frowned, but could say nothing in answer besides, "Just do the best you can. We will manage somehow. Perhaps after the rains begin, there will be more vegetables."

"The rains will not make those who are afraid enter the Valley of Panchoy, *Señora*," She seemed hurt by my distracted dismissal of the problem. But I had no desire that day to concern myself with such mundane matters.

"*Señor* Ricardo has returned," I said, anxious to change the subject. "I must replenish some of my plants, and he knows of places they grow wild in the mountains. He will be free the next few days and has kindly offered to take me to these places. They are quite distant, so we will need to take a lunch each day. Would you have the cook prepare a hamper for us? Be sure to put in a skin of wine, the same I had last night."

"I will myself see that it is prepared at once, *Señora*," she said, and I wondered if she guessed my eagerness to be gone.

I thanked her and hurried to my room to dress. I chose a riding habit I had never worn, a finely woven wool of bright vibrant green. There would be no drab matronly colors for me on such a happy day as this!

The matching hat was high-crowned to allow room for the height of my hair, and as I was about to set it on my head, I stopped. There was something far too staid and formal about it to suit my present mood. Impulsively, I flung it on the bed, and quickly rummaged through my things to find Tatiana's golden hoops and the green glass beads that had belonged to Giorgio's mother. As I slipped the jewelry into my pocket, I noted with satisfaction that the green of the beads exactly matched that of the fabric. I removed the combs from my hair, then brushed it down and coiled it loosely at the nape of

217

my neck, knowing I would free it of even that restriction as soon as we were away from Santiago.

"My gypsy love," Ricardo had called me unknowingly that morning. I remembered the day I was fifteen, when I had been looking in Tatiana's mirror and had glimpsed so fleetingly the lusty gypsy who dwelt within the molded exterior of a young Andalusian girl of good breeding. I had been frightened by what I saw then, and had quickly looked away. But now I would be frightened no more, for it was the girl I had seen so briefly that day who had dared to set me free from Tomás. And it was she who had shown me what sensuous pleasure could be brought to me by the body of the man I loved.

When I walked into the stable yard, I saw that Teresa had already sent the food hamper out there, and that Simón and Ricardo had the horses saddled and waiting. I was glad there was no need for me to enter the stables and walk by Diablo's empty stall. I wanted no sad reminders to mar my contentment that day.

I mounted quickly, wanting to be gone, away from even Simón's friendly eyes, knowing that the happiness which was too great for me to hide might speak far too eloquently of our precious secret. I rode silently by Ricardo's side as he led us out of Santiago by the shortest route. When we had left the last of the city behind us, we urged our horses forward faster, and soon we turned off onto a path that led to another of the many retreats known to Ricardo.

"We'll stop here," Ricardo said. "The path narrows ahead." He dismounted, then came around to help me. But I, anxious to feel again his arms close around me, was too impatient to wait, so I jumped sooner than he expected, and as my toe caught briefly in my stirrup before it came free, I fell into his arms, and we both laughed for the joy and the foolishness of it, and for the happiness of being together.

Still laughing, he kissed me lightly, then, with a final hug, he released me. "We'll go on foot from here. I'll see about securing the horses."

I remembered the things I had put in my pocket, and while he busied himself, I slipped the green beads around my neck and fastened Tatiana's gold hoops in my ears. Then I freed my hair from its coil.

When Ricardo finished his task, he stood up, smiling as he noticed the jewelry.

"What manner of adornments are these?" he asked teasingly, fingering the green beads and then the hoops.

"Things my gypsy friends gave me," I laughed, shaking my head from side to side to make the hoops swing in my ears, and holding the beads up so a patch of sunlight shone on them. "This morning you called me your gypsy love, and that is what I would be."

He cupped my chin in his hands. "I think your friends also gave you some magic potion, which you've used to hold me captive to your charms."

"Then you must surely know it is useless to try to escape me." I slipped my arms around his neck and stood on my toes to bring my face closer to his.

"Nor would I try," he murmured just before our lips came together in a long hard kiss that left us both gasping for breath. He pushed me from him teasingly. "Before you kiss me like that again, we had better find a large enough clearing to spread our blanket."

He picked up the food hamper, threw the blanket over his arm, then extended his free hand to me.

I put my hand in his and, feeling lighthearted and carefree, let him lead me up the mountain-side, with Tatiana's golden hoops swaying in my ears as I walked.

Later that day, Ricardo would have spoken of making our plans to leave Santiago, but I put my fingers lightly over his mouth to stop him, for I was suddenly overcome with an unreasoning fear of what might lay ahead of us.

"Let's not talk of this yet," I pleaded.

"Why not?" he asked, turning his head to look at me in surprise. We had finished our lunch and were lying idly on our blanket, watching the changing cloud patterns in the sky, and pointing out to each other the imaginary animals we found there.

"I don't know. I'm just afraid."

"You mustn't be afraid, my love."

"But there will be so many problems, it frightens me to think of them."

"You can't make problems vanish just by refusing to think of them," he admonished gently.

"I know, and I know I'm being foolish, but I can't help it. Please, can't we try to forget about them for a little while? Can't we have just a few days to ourselves—these three days together—and not think of anything or anyone but you and me and how much we love each other?"

"But we must make plans—"

I leaned over him, stopped his protest with my lips. "Please, Ricardo," I begged. "Just these three days. Surely Tomás will be in no rush to return from the farm, after what happened. He'll want to wait, give people time to forget. We'll surely have ample time to make our plans and be gone long before he comes back. Let's pretend, just for now, that we have no worries and no cares, and that there is nobody in the whole world but us."

"I agree there's little chance of Father returning soon." He enclosed me in the curve of his arm. "We'll not talk of our problems these three days, then, if that's what you want." He wrapped his other arm around me. "How can I not do as you ask, when it's what I want, too?"

"Thank you." I relaxed, settling myself in his embrace lazily, contentedly, my head pressed against his chest so I could hear the beating of his heart, and I thought, *I am here, with Ricardo,* and, wondering at the miracle of it, I closed my eyes.

When I opened them again, I noticed the sun was low in the sky. I blinked, looked at Ricardo, saw him watching me tenderly. A smile lit his face as my gaze met his, and my heart seemed to give a happy leap, as it always did when his disarming smile was directed especially at me.

"I didn't want to wake you, you were sleeping so soundly."

"And so happily, held in your arms."

"We should leave soon."

I sighed. "I suppose we must." I stretched langorously, and my hand touched the leaves of a plant just beyond the edge of our blanket.

"Oh!" I jumped up quickly, remembering what I had told Teresa. "The plants! I almost forgot, we must bring some back. Hurry, get out your knife and help me dig. I told Teresa you were taking me into the mountains these three days to help me find some plants I would have." I found a knife in the food hamper, started to loosen the dirt around the plant nearest me.

Ricardo had sprung to his feet. "Which plants do you want?" he asked, a puzzled look on his face.

"Any of them."

"Any of them? But I don't know one from another. What if the ones I choose are poisonous?"

I giggled. "What matter? We won't be in Santiago long enough to care!" And Ricardo joined in my laughter.

We scrambled about merrily, gathering meaningless plants until I said we had enough. Then, still laughing, we started down the mountain, hand in hand. A deep contentment settled over me. Before we reached Santiago, I would remove my gypsy jewelry and tie up my hair, and for the rest of the day, I must pretend that nothing had changed. But soon it would be nighttime, and when all was quiet, I would go to Ricardo's room to spend the middle hours of the night in his arms. Then, for the next two days, we would be as giddy and exhilarated as we had been that day. We had consigned our

220

worries to another day. The future was unknown, as unknown as the properties of some of the plants we had gathered so hastily. Who could guess what problems or dangers might lie ahead? But for the present, and for two more days, we would keep them at bay, and live only for ourselves.

The next two days were as idyllic as the first had been, and our happiness in each other was complete. Ricardo knew the surrounding mountains well, and each day he took us to a new place, remote and secluded, where he knew we would be alone. Though we carried with us some of Tomás's best wine, we drank little of it, for we were already drunk with the headiness of love. Removing our clothes and putting them aside, we lay together beside a spring, or near a mountain stream, or under a sheltering tree. And always, at the first touch of his bare skin against mine as I moved into his arms, I could not suppress a gasp of joy. My hands, my eyes moved as hungrily over his body as his did over mine, as though we must know intimately every contour of the other's flesh. And every time his body covered mine to claim it, the beauty and serenity of our surroundings seemed a vast cathedral built around the altar of our love, and our pleasure in each other was as limitless as the sky over our heads.

At the end of our third day, our problems could be ignored no longer, and when Ricardo started to discuss them, I did not try to stop him. We had folded our blanket and returned our remaining food to the hamper and gathered the plants to take with us. Our three-day idyll was over. It was time to return to reality.

Ricardo had sat down and motioned for me to sit beside him. He was silent for a moment, and I dropped to the grass beside him, waiting for him to speak. As I waited, I removed my gypsy jewelry and returned it reluctantly to my pocket, then gathered my hair into a coil and fastened it at the nape of my neck. Ricardo said suddenly, "You could never get an annulment."

"No," I agreed. "Even if I could, such things take months, or even years."

"We will leave Santiago as soon as we can."

"Yes. We must be gone before Tomás returns."

We both knew we were saying things which were pointless in themselves, but there seemed to be no place to begin except with the most basic facts. I was married. I planned to break my vows. We would run away together.

"Father won't be likely to come back soon."

"No." I had told him about the masked men, the final episode which had sent Tomás into such a choleric rage. "Surely he won't come back for a month or more, will he?"

221

Ricardo agreed. "Not likely. He couldn't stand it if anyone mentioned it to him, or if he thought anyone was snickering behind his back. He'll want to give the people time to forget. But even without all of that, he usually spends most of the rainy season at the farm. He likes to be there to supervise things then. It makes travel harder, too."

"There's scarcely been enough rain for that!"

"There's been more away from the valley than here, I noticed, though not much more. Still, with the planting and the extra land he's bought to be prepared—"

"Let's hope he stays away until we can leave here. Why not soon? A few days, a week at the most."

He puckered his forehead in a puzzled frown. "There's one problem. I don't see how we can leave before we collect the bulk of *Tía* Maria's legacy. It won't be mine till my twenty-first birthday, and that's not till the twenty-sixth of July. It's not a lot, but I don't see how we can manage without it."

"Wouldn't Carlos give it to you a little early?" I knew something of the legacy, knew that Carlos Ortega Batres controlled the money left to both Cecilia and Ricardo by their aunt. Small sums were doled out to them quarterly, but the bulk of the legacies was to be withheld until their twenty-first birthdays.

"*Tía* was very specific about that," he said. "Carlos showed me her written instructions. I think she was afraid Father would take it from us if we got it any sooner."

I nodded. She had been a wise woman. But the twenty-sixth of July was still over a month away! What if Tomás came back unexpectedly before then? "Tomás?"

"We'll have to take that chance. But he's not likely to return before the first part of August, unless something brings him back."

I shuddered, not as reassured as I should have been by his words. It bothered me to realize that we would have to face the risk of delaying for something as practical as money. I had been thinking only in terms of leaving hastily before Tomás could return, of shedding our worries and going away to some vague destination where we would be together always. Never before in my life had I had to concern myself with money. It had always been there, for my use, whenever I had needed it. If only *Tío* Umberto had held back some, given it to me for my own use! If I had not been so naive, I would have requested—insisted—that he do so. But it was too late for such thoughts now. I sighed.

"It's too bad my father's cousin didn't have your aunt's wisdom. He turned over everything to Tomás. I suppose much of it is still rightfully mine, but I've no idea where he keeps it."

"Safely hidden, you can be sure. There's a chair in his office with a hidden compartment in the back, but I don't think he keeps much there."

"Nothing but the housekeeping money," I said, "and only a month's worth at a time. I've often seen him open it. In fact, he showed me how."

"I wish I knew where he got the gold and silver pieces to pay his wagers, or if there are more."

I sighed. "You said he was heavily in debt when we were married. My father left me a sizable fortune, but the way he's been spending—I suppose there must be a good deal of it left, but I doubt if we'd ever find it."

"I wouldn't know where to begin to look," he agreed. "It's probably buried, if he hasn't spent it all on his baubles. From what *Tía* said, it didn't take him long to go through my mother's fortune." He shrugged. "Maybe it's just as well that we manage without it. He might be able to convince the authorities that we had robbed him, and theft is a very serious crime."

Another time, I might have reminded him teasingly that running off with his father's wife was surely also an extraordinary and scarcely a lawful thing to do, but neither of us was in a mood for levity. The world and its problems were closing in on us. "I could sell my jewelry," I offered. "It would have to be done quietly."

"You'd get only a fraction of its worth. Anyway, I couldn't consider letting you do that. It's my concern from now on to look after you and care for you. We have no choice. We'll stay until my birthday."

Over a month! But what alternatives did we have? "We'll have to continue just as though nothing is changed. We can't afford to make anyone suspicious."

"I wish we could leave sooner, right now! But I can't subject you to poverty. We must have that legacy to start our lives somewhere else."

"Where?"

He thought a minute. "I think Mexico will be best. Northern Mexico."

"Mexico?" I was startled at the thought.

He looked at me sharply. "You didn't think we could stay in Guatemala, did you?"

"I don't know," I answered truthfully. "I guess I just hadn't really stopped to think." It hadn't occurred to me that we would have to leave Guatemala. Santiago, of course, but Ricardo's beloved Guatemala? "But you are a *Guatemalteco*," I protested at the thought, "and you love Guatemala so!" He did love it, or he would not have felt so strongly concerned about its problems, nor been so determined to help solve them. I felt the first twinge of uncertainty about the future.

"I love you far more." He smiled at me.

I searched his face anxiously, to see if there were some sign of regret at what he said. But there was no such indication. There was only his warming smile. Still, it did not leave me as reassured as it should have.

"Are you sure you love me enough to leave Guatemala behind, with no regrets?" I persisted.

"Enough and more. Surely you know that."

"It seems too much to ask of you. I wish it weren't necessary."

"But it is," he said with finality, "absolutely necessary. So let's talk no more about it." After a pause, he said, "My legacy isn't large, but I think it's enough to buy us a small farm."

"A small farm?" I repeated with growing alarm. "But you know nothing of farming. You must finish your studies and be a lawyer! It's what you've always wanted!"

He shook his head vigorously in denial. "That's out of the question now. To start with, there are only three places I could finish my studies and take my exams. Besides Santiago, the only other universities which have the authority to confer degrees are in Lima and Mexico City. Father would find us easily in either of those places, especially if I continued with my studies or if I worked in any manner connected with the profession of law."

His words reminded me of something I had not yet permitted to enter my mind. Tomás would pursue us, of course. He would not take the loss of one of his possessions lightly. I began to realize it would be more difficult than I had imagined to shed one life and begin another. How long, for how many years must we live perpetually in fear of one day opening the door to find Tomás standing there, threatening, bitter, vindictively bent on destroying our happiness? I remembered the rage in which he had left Santiago, a rage that knew no reason. In such a fury, wasn't it even possible he might be capable of inflicting physical harm? I suppressed a shudder at the thought and returned my attention to what Ricardo was saying.

"We must lose ourselves in some small out-of-the-way place," he continued. "A farm in Mexico. Or somewhere south of here, if you prefer. We could even consider the English colonies far to the north."

I did not think I had ever before realized fully the sacrifices he was making for love of me, and I burst into tears.

"How can I let you give up everything you've ever dreamed of?" I protested. "Your Guatemala, which you love so? And the career on which you've had your heart set most of your life? It's too much to ask of you!"

He brushed away my tears. "Other dreams are past, gone. Now I dream only of you."

I thrilled to his words, and yet a tiny frail voice of wisdom called out within me, asking how long it would be before he began to remember, nostalgically, those other dreams, then to long for their renewal? How long before he became embittered because for love of me he had relinquished a burning lifelong ambition? Could the flame of such ambition as his ever be really extinguished?

But I did not want to listen to such questions. I threw myself forcefully into his arms. He must never grow to hate me! "Oh, Ricardo, don't ever stop loving me!"

His arms tightened about me. "Foolish girl! As if I ever could!"

I shivered, though the afternoon was warm and Ricardo's arms were wrapped tightly about me.

I was no longer quite so certain the future held for us only the boundless joy of being together.

Santiago—June, 1773

CHAPTER XIII

The following weeks passed in a paradoxical combination of incredible swiftness and agonizing slowness. The stolen minutes and hours Ricardo and I spent together flew by too quickly, and were soon ended. But when I was involved in the performance of my routine duties as the *dueña* of the house, the actions meaningless to me now except to keep up the pretense that nothing had changed, time dragged by with a maddening slowness. How many more menus must I prepare? How many more times must I unlock the *sala* so Teresa could keep Tomás's playthings in perfect order? How many trips must I make to the kitchen to give tacit approval to the thickness of the soup or the seasoning of the beans?

And always, every day, I awakened with the fear that on that very day, Tomás might return unannounced. This fear had begun the morning following our three-day idyll, as though our return to reality had suddenly made me aware of everything that could go wrong. I did not confide this fear to Ricardo, for I knew he would tell me it was unlikely to happen, and that I was being foolish to worry about it. But even though I knew that was so, I could not fight down a feeling of panic at any unexpected sound.

I knew that, if Tomás should come before we were able to leave, I must find some way to avoid sharing his bed. The thought of any intimacy with him was intolerable to me now. If feigned illness or other excuses would not thwart him, then I would think of something else. I would stop at nothing, not even physically fighting him off, to avoid his advances. I only hoped such extreme measures would not be necessary. My lips moved frequently in a silent prayer. *Blessed Jesus, don't let him come back!*

But even if he did return, we would still have to wait for Ricardo's legacy. It was a chance we had to take. In my desk, I kept a hand-lettered calendar made by one of the religious orders to benefit the poor souls in the leper hospital outside Santiago, and sold in order to buy foodstuffs for them. Each night, I took out my calendar and marked off one more day. One more day. One day closer to the twenty-sixth of July, the magic date on which Ricardo would be twenty-one and collect his legacy from Carlos Ortega Batres. We often talked about it, for it seemed to sustain Ricardo as it did me. He would go early in the morning, we decided, at about eight-thirty. We had arrived at that hour after I had casually questioned Marta one day about their rising habits. She had told me that Carlos never left the house before a quarter till nine, so we knew that at eight-thirty Ricardo would be certain to catch him before he got away. He would remind Carlos a few days earlier that he would want to collect every *peso* that remained of his legacy that morning, so that Carlos could have it out of the hiding place in which he had kept it for the past three and a half years. It was probably buried somewhere inside the perimeter of the walls of his house and garden, as virtually all the money in Santiago was buried or hidden within private homes. False backs in furniture, such as that in the chair in Tomás's office, were common enough, but such obvious places normally held only enough for current use. Sizable sums were usually hidden with far more care, deeply buried in stone jars or secreted in hidden hollows within the thick-walled houses.

As soon as Ricardo collected his money, he would bring it to me and I would hastily stitch most of it into prepared pockets on the clothing we planned to wear when we left. Then later that day, in the quiet hours after the midday meal when Santiago rested, we would leave. Would that day, that moment never arrive, I wondered?

We made our tentative time schedule for the important day and decided what we would put in the bundles we would carry out of the city a few days earlier, to be hidden inside our picnic hamper and left in a protected spot chosen by Ricardo. Beyond that, our plans were simple and perhaps inadequate, but there was no help for it. Ricardo dared not make inquiries about Mexico lest word eventually get back to Tomás, so all we could do was start riding north. We would travel light and fast, and not until we were well into Mexico and had skirted far around the main route to Mexico City would we start to look around for a likely place to make our home.

And as we waited, again the nagging doubt within me began, stronger this time than it had been before.

It was the second Sunday in July, and we attended the final mass of the morning in the Cathedral. Immediately afterward, another ceremony began. Ricardo leaned toward me and whispered, "Investiture. Seven students are to be awarded the insignias of their new titles today." He could not hide the excitement in his voice.

Silently, I nodded and watched the ceremony. This, then, was what for love of me, Ricardo would never experience. From time to time, I stole a glance at him. He seemed to have forgotten me, forgotten Cecilia seated on the other side of him. His attention was fixed on the students who had successfully completed their grueling oral examinations, prepared and defended their two theses and not been found wanting in knowledge of their chosen field.

At the altar now, the men solemnly accepted the insignias of their degrees. I noted that the linings of the hoods on their long black garments and the tassels on their caps were of different colors. Two men wore green, three white, and one each blue and yellow. I leaned toward Ricardo and asked him the significance of the colors, but he didn't even seem to hear me, so engrossed was he in the proceedings. Was he envisioning his own investiture, I wondered? Had he forgotten that he was putting all that behind him when we ran away together? I tried to blot out the scene before my eyes, envision instead a picture of Ricardo and me, living contentedly together, with Ricardo returning eagerly to me at our farm house after a day's work. *I will make him happy,* I thought with a fierce determination. *He won't ever regret giving this up!* But when I glanced again at his rapt expression, I was not so sure.

As the men returned down the aisle, several of them wore serious expressions on their faces, but the rest could not conceal their pride and happiness, and their lips seemed to burst into smiles in spite of the solemnity of the occasion.

One of the men, wearing a green-tasseled cap and a hood of the same bright green, looked at Ricardo as he passed. Until that moment he had looked exceedingly solemn, but when his eyes met Ricardo's his face exploded into a smile. Ricardo smiled back and added a nod of approval.

The rest of the people in the Cathedral filed out after the graduates, and Ricardo, his face alight with excitement, swept Cecilia and me out the door and past other people on the Cathedral steps to the place where his friend stood.

"Come!" he said as he steered us through the crowd with a firm hand on each of our elbows. "I want to congratulate Antonio. You must meet him, Carlota."

I could scarcely do otherwise as he pushed me into the knot of people surrounding Antonio. Ricardo introduced us, and Antonio accepted everyone's congratulations amid statements like, "I thought I'd never make it through the *noche fúnebre!*" and, "My mind stopped functioning when they started refuting my second thesis!" In spite of his protestations about barely having made it through his oral examinations and defense of his theses successfully, he could not hide his pride in what he had accomplished.

"Soon it will be you!" he said ebulliently to Ricardo. He turned to Cecilia and me and said, "Ricardo is the brightest hope of us all. No one has more of a vocation for law. It is he who knows enough to ask the most searching questions in the lectures. Another few years, and he will be wearing one of these." He held out his hand, displaying the ring which had just been awarded to him to signify his new status as a doctor.

I looked at Ricardo, and in the space of an instant, saw his expression change completely. It was as though a candle which had been shining on his face had suddenly been extinguished. *He has just remembered,* I thought. *All during the ceremony, he has been imagining himself in Antonio's place, living his old dream, his enthusiasm blotting out for a short time the knowledge that now he will never follow in his friend's footsteps. But now, Antonio's words have reminded him. He will never wear such a ring.*

"Antonio, come along! We're waiting!" The other man in the green-tasseled cap called out to him impatiently.

"I must go," he said with a wave of his hand. "This is the ride I've been looking forward to for a long, long time." With a nod of his head, he turned and ran to the horse someone was holding for him. In the crowd that surrounded his horse, I recognized several of Ricardo's fellow students I had seen at the house once or twice.

Ricardo didn't move, had his attention fixed on Antonio as he mounted amid the cheers and jokes of his friends. Then the graduates lined up their horses behind a row of trumpeters and another row of drummers. Out in front of the procession, a mace bearer took his place, his heavy staff topped with the royal emblem signifying the King's sanction to the awarding of these degrees.

When everyone was in place, the trumpets blared and the drums rolled and the triumphant procession began to move.

229

The groups of students cheered enthusiastically as the graduates passed.

All but one. Ricardo stood, silent and thoughtful, as the riders went by. How many times had he envisioned for himself this crowning triumph to a successful completion of his studies? And now, because of me, he would never take part in a similar procession.

As the three of us walked back to the house, Ricardo made a gallant effort at light-heartedness, but his gaiety was forced and unreal. Since neither Cecilia nor I responded to his attempts at good humor, he soon gave up the pretense, and we continued home in silence.

My mind worked busily as we walked. Ricardo's heart was breaking at the thought of relinquishing a lifelong dream, a dream which had become so much a part of him that he would be less than a complete person without it. And if I would destroy that dream, would I not then also be destroying Ricardo?

But I love him! I protested at the thought. *My love for him is not destructive. It is a foundation, strong and sure, on which to base a lifetime of happiness!* . . . An answering voice, that same voice I had heard before, asked, *How can a lifetime of farming in Mexico be happy for a man whose only interest is the law?.* . . . Again I protested, *We will have each other. That is all we need!* . . . And the voice of truth spoke again: *That may be enough for you. But what of Ricardo? You speak of love. What sort of selfish love is this, that would let a man destroy himself?*

And that question, I did not choose to answer. Uncomfortably, I pushed it from my mind.

There was to be no ride in the hills for us on that Sunday, for Ricardo had said his friends would think it odd if he didn't attend the fiesta held in honor of Antonio and the other graduate who had worn the green tassel and hood that signified, I had discovered, a doctor of law. We had agreed that he must go to the celebration, but later that afternoon as we met, by unspoken agreement, in the *patio de placer* and he took leave of me, I wished I had not agreed so readily that he should go. I reasoned that my reluctance to have him leave was only for his sake, that it would do nothing but deepen his misery, remind him again of what he would be missing.

"Don't go!" I suggested. "You could send word, make some excuse."

He raised his eyebrows quizzically. "But why would I do that? These are my friends. I must go." He hesitated, then added, "I want to go."

"You'll come home early, won't you?" I asked hopefully.

Again, the hesitation before he answered. "I'll try. These fiestas usually last most of the night. It would seem strange if I left too early."

"Oh." I tried to hide my disappointment. "Well, as early as you can, then." I noted that there was about him a sense of animation, of anticipation. He had thrown off the dejection I had noted earlier. *He has forgotten again,* I thought in alarm, *and is once more about to share Antonio's triumph vicariously.* In that, I sensed a danger, a threat to our future. Yet I could not mold my fears into a coherent reason for not wanting him to go.

Our hands touched briefly in the swift silent signal with which we always left each other. There were no stolen hugs or quick kisses exchanged between us any place in the house except behind the closed doors of Ricardo's room. Every night, I waited in my room, listening for the last sounds of activity to fade within the house. Then I made my way silently to Ricardo's room, impatient with the extra seconds it took me to push the door open quietly and close it noiselessly behind me. As I threw myself into his waiting arms, all the passion we had to be so careful to deny in the presence of others would at last have its way. During the precious hours that followed, if it happened that in our sleep we had moved apart, I would waken with a start, filled with an unreasoning fear that he might have gone from me. Then I had to reach out and touch him, reassure myself that he was still there.

Sometimes I would go back to sleep, content in the knowledge that Ricardo still lay beside me. But other times, if the touch of my hand awakened him, he might reach out with an unexpected urgency and pull me toward him, as though he, too, had shared my desperation at the thought that we might have been separated. At those times, our desire flamed instantaneously, and we made love with an abandon that was almost primitive in its savage need.

With the first faint morning light, I always rose reluctantly from Ricardo's bed and returned to my own room, there to sleep or lie awake restlessly until it was time to begin another day, another endless day of disguising the love we had affirmed so unrestrainedly during the night. Grudgingly, I acknowledged to myself the need to keep our emotions hidden. There was far too much at stake to risk any careless show of affection, no matter how we longed to show our love; one never knew who might come unexpectedly around a corner or walk unannounced into a room.

Our partings had always been reluctant, but on that Sunday afternoon, I could not suppress a pang of jealousy when

231

I noted that Ricardo could not hide his impatience to be gone from me. I knew it was foolish to be hurt by his show of eagerness, that I should be pleased that he was going to enjoy himself at the fiesta in honor of his friends. Wasn't it after all a good sign that his earlier dejection had passed, a sign that he had accepted the drastic change in his plans which his love of me had forced upon him?

Thus rationalizing, I soon convinced myself that it was so.

Too restless to sit quietly, I rose and went to tap on Cecilia's door. Perhaps she would like to go walking with me, I thought.

I rapped on her door and called, "Cecilia, it's me, Carlota." There was the sound of scurrying about within her room, and I heard the unmistakable sound of something metallic hitting the floor. It was not till I had rapped and called a second time that she opened the door.

"Come in." She seemed flustered and breathless.

I smiled at her. "Would you like to come for a walk with me? I'm feeling restless."

My simple invitation seemed to make her ill at ease. Or was it simply my presence that affected her so?

"Thank you for asking me, but I really don't think I'd care to go. I was just resting."

My eyes moved automatically to her bed, and I noted that the spread was pulled smoothly over the mattress, the pillows were undisturbed. Whatever she had been doing, she certainly had not been resting. I saw her eyes follow mine.

"I fell asleep in my chair while I was mending," she amended quickly. "When I heard your knock, I was half-asleep. I woke up, not quite sure if I had dreamed you were at the door, or if you were really there. It wasn't till you called and knocked again that I knew I hadn't just dreamed it. That's why it took me so long to answer you." She blinked her eyes, as though to indicate they were still heavy with sleep.

Her explanation was far too elaborate. Still, it would account for her delay in answering the door. But what about the sound of something hitting the floor? Something metallic, it had been. A thimble, perhaps? But it had sounded too heavy for that. Nor had it sounded like a scissors dropping.

My eyes left the chair to which she had motioned, her open sewing basket by its side, and returned to Cecilia. She was staring at something on the floor by the foot of her bed. I followed her gaze to the object, partially hidden in the fringe on the bottom of the bedspread.

"Oh!" She gave a short cry of alarm as she realized I had also seen it.

It was a gold *peso*.

She recovered quickly. "So that's where it went!" She hurried over and picked it up. "I dropped it this morning before we went to mass, and I didn't have time to look for it."

Until recently, her hastily contrived explanations would have satisfied me. I certainly would never have suspected what she had been doing when my knock had startled her. Now I knew better, and my mind quickly found the holes in her story. If she had fallen asleep over her mending as she claimed, where was the garment on which she had been stitching? The logical thing would have been for her to lay her sewing on the chair as she rose to answer the door—or, if not there, then on top of her sewing basket. But it was nowhere in sight. She had taken pains to hide it, because she didn't want me to know what she was doing. In her haste, she had dropped the gold *peso* and, when she had been unable to find it in her hurried search, she had assumed it had rolled safely out of sight under her bed.

Who but one who planned to do the same thing less than two weeks later would ever have suspected that she had been stitching the *peso* into her clothing when my knock had startled her?

I smiled. "Let me help you," I said without preamble. "My stitches aren't pretty, but they're strong. It's the servants' afternoon off, so we can move into the patio where the light is better."

She gasped, "You know? You've guessed what I'm doing?"

I nodded. "I know. And I want to help you."

"You won't tell Father?" she asked anxiously.

"Of course not."

"But we can't go into the patio. Ricardo—"

"He just left. But you can certainly trust him. He'd never—"

"No!" she protested quickly. "I don't want him to know. He has met Manuel, and he doesn't like him. He might try to stop us."

Her reaction surprised and shocked me. She and Ricardo had seemed so close, I could not imagine her wanting to keep this from him.

"He wouldn't stop you," I said. "Not if you told him this is what you want."

"But what if he did? I just can't take the chance! Promise me you won't tell him!" Her eyes pleaded with me.

Reluctantly, I promised, As I had reasoned before, the matter of her doctor was her secret, to be shared or withheld as she chose. But I did think she was being foolish. Ricardo would be hurt when he found out.

The odd thing was that Cecilia didn't seem the least bit upset after her initial shock on realizing that I had guessed her secret. In fact, if anything, she seemed relieved. Later, as we sat in the patio stitching as rapidly as we could, she lost all the reticence of the past months, and seemed almost garrulous in her eagerness to share her excitement with me. But now it was my turn for reticence, and I did not share with her my own secret.

"We'll go south," she said as we sat with our heads bent over our work. "Manuel has friends everywhere—some in San José, some in Lima, and lost of other places, too. One of them will help him find some place we can live. Manuel is a very good doctor."

"I'm sure he is," I agreed, thinking how fortunate for Manuel that he, at least, could continue to do elsewhere what he was best suited to do. Sick people needed attention no matter where they lived. There were no geographic limitations on caring for them. But someone who had dreams of improving the laws of Guatemala to benefit its people could scarcely do so from a remote farm in Mexico.

"Except for what I spent for food when Father was gone," she continued, "I've saved most of *Tía* Maria's money that Carlos has doled out to me four times a year. It will keep us until Manuel gets started again. *Tía* had said she was leaving it to me to buy pretty clothes, but I didn't need them after— after I was sick. I've been saving it, thinking that if I took my vows before my twenty-first birthday, I would have a portion to bring the sisters until I get the rest of my money."

I looked at her and said in surprise, "You've never given up the idea of entering one of the orders?"

She bit off the end of a thread. "Not until—until I met Manuel. After Rafael and I—after we called off our marriage, I wanted to become a novitiate, but Father wouldn't permit it. I still had it in the back of my mind that I might convince him. But when I met Manuel, everything changed."

"This is a far happier use for your money," I said, smoothing the patch I had just cut and folding under the edges.

"We will be happy! I know we will! Manuel says I won't like being the wife of a *mestizo*. He says I don't know, I have no idea how different life will be from what I've known. He refused to run away with me, until—until now." She finished abruptly, and I had the feeling that she had been about to say more and had checked herself.

"You do love him very much, don't you?"

"Oh, yes! And he loves me!"

"Then that is all that matters," I said emphatically. She

234

could not know my words were intended to reassure myself as well as her.

"We're leaving the sixteenth, the day of *Nuestra Señora de Carmen*. We thought that with all the celebrating and the masks, it would be easy to break away from Santiago unnoticed. Even if anyone should see us leave, we will be masked, so no one will know who we are." She leaned toward me, said earnestly, "Carlota, if you would do something for me, I'd be so grateful! Father will surely follow us, so the more time we have before he finds out we're gone, the better. Do you suppose you could pretend that I was sick? You could bring trays to my room. Then if our servants should talk to the maids across the street and *Señora* Ramirez overhears them, she'll think I'm ill. If she thought I had run away, she's such a busybody, you know she'd send word to Father immediately, as soon as she even suspected anything. If you could do that for me, it might keep the news from reaching Father for another day, or even two. And that would be such a help, because of course he'll rush right into Santiago when he hears, and start out after us."

"I'll help you all I can," I answered distractedly, scarcely aware of what I was saying, for my mind had absorbed the import of her words: Tomás would come rushing in from the farm as soon as he found out she was gone.

A cold chill passed through me. It was one thing to suppose it was possible but unlikely that Tomás would return to Santiago before Ricardo and I left. It was quite another to know positively of something that was going to take place which would be certain to bring him rushing from the farm.

My mind had been so busy pursuing my own thoughts that I hadn't noticed Cecilia putting her sewing aside and jumping up to give me an impulsive hug. Her unexpected action startled me back to the present.

"Oh, thank you, Carlota dear! That will give us a good head start. We'll always be grateful to you."

"But—but I'm not sure I can do—not sure I can help you," I stammered weakly, embarrassed by her gratitude. How could I do as she asked, when it would mean having Tomás swoop down on Ricardo and me before we were able to get away? With this new development, we couldn't wait until Ricardo's birthday. We must leave on the same day Cecilia fled with Manuel.

I was glad that Cecilia was in a chattering mood, for it kept me from having to say much, leaving my mind free to consider the problem of my own escape from Tomás. What manner of man was he, I mused, that both his wife and daughter had need to run from him, perhaps both of us even

235

on the same day? If Cecilia ever found out later that I had not stayed to help cover up her flight from Santiago as she had assumed I would, I only hoped she would understand and forgive me.

That night, alone in my room, I set the candelabra near the trunk that contained the extra petticoats and fabrics I had brought with me from Andalusia, and started to rummage through them, looking for the sturdiest fabrics from which to make hidden patches inside Ricardo's and my clothing to hold my jewels and any money we could find in the next four days. Four days! My heart gave a joyful leap at the thought of being gone so soon, even if we should be lacking in funds! Briefly, I envied Cecilia. For the past three years, she had been able to save her quarterly dole from her legacy. Ricardo's smaller quarterly sums had all been spent on his studies. But, no matter. We would manage.

Among my petticoats, I found the piece of polished crystal Tatiana had given me. I took it out and held it in my hand, looking at it. I had all but forgotten its existence. Not since the day I had been so angered at the thought that it had disillusioned me by showing me Ricardo's face instead of that of Tomás had I even looked at it. But it had been right, after all, for wasn't Ricardo truly my husband now in all but name? So when it had shown me his dear face, it had been telling me the truth. I ran my fingers idly over the crystal, noting the reflection of the candle flames which seemed to come from deep within it. And I thought again of Tatiana, and our last day together. She had not lied to me either, I mused. She had promised me happiness here, and these past weeks had contained moments of bliss I would not have guessed possible.

The flames within the crystal began to move and take shape, and I stared in fascination. They were not candle flames any more at all, but a part of a wall, a roofless building. With a sense of profound shock, I realized it was a portion of our house, for I recognized the entrance to the *sala*. The door was closed, a dark rectangle unbroken except for the handle and the keyhole below it. I stared intently at the door, because it seemed so incongruous to see it shut tightly against intruders while the roof was open to the sky and the walls were crumbled all about it. I continued to stare, shocked at the scene of desolation. There was something else, something I was at a loss to understand. What was it, why did I feel there was something amiss about that door? I stared hard at it, concentrated on it, hoping to find the answer, when I was interrupted by a tapping on my door.

I tried to shut out the sound, tried to continue to puzzle

about why I should feel there was anything significant about that locked door. After all, it was kept locked virtually all of the time, with one key in Tomás's possession and the other on the ring at my belt. So what made me feel there was anything odd about it?

The tap sounded again, louder this time.

"Just a minute," I called in irritation, feeling that I had been close to finding the answer that eluded me, knowing that now the moment had passed. I slid the crystal back into the trunk and stuffed the petticoats and fabrics on top of it. Then I brought the lid silently down and, with the candelabra in my hand, I opened the door.

It was Teresa, come to ask some questions about our meals for the coming week.

"Pardon, Señora," she said. "I don't like to bother you at this hour, but I had to see you before I go to the market in the morning. I must leave early to find anything at all. Could I talk with you now about our food?"

I nodded and motioned for her to enter. When she had closed the door, she continued, "First of all, I know you want the cook to bake wheat bread every Monday and Friday, but we have no more wheat flour."

"None?" I asked, still irritated at the interruption. "Why didn't you tell me sooner?"

"I did, Señora. I told you last week our supply was getting low. You said you would see what you could do about it."

"I did? Well, then, it must have slipped my mind. I'll send Alberto for a barrel in the morning."

"No, Señora, that is what I want to tell you. No one has any. There is none anywhere."

"None at all? In all of Santiago? Then I suppose we must make do with ground corn. Tortillas—"

She held out her hands, palms upward, in a gesture of helplessness. "We have no more corn to grind, either."

"And there's not any of that to buy?"

She shook her head. "No, Señora, not unless a few of the villagers bring some to the market in the morning. It is because of the shortage of corn that the flour is all gone. Those who could afford it have bought all the flour."

The defeat in her voice as much as the words she spoke made me realize how serious the food shortage in Santiago had become. What had been merely an annoyance and an inconvenience was becoming a problem which could no longer be ignored. I had known it was getting worse, of course, but had been too preoccupied with my own affairs to pay much attention to it or to become much concerned over it. I fought down my vexation. I did not want to cope with such a problem now.

"If I may suggest it, *Señora*," Teresa continued, "you could send word to the *Señor*, and he could send us a cart from the farm. Surely they have plenty of everything there." I caught a faint tone of disapproval in her voice. I know she had wondered why I hadn't done that sooner, since it was the obvious solution to our problems. She could not know that I had long before considered and discarded the idea; I did not want to give Tomás any possible excuse to come to Santiago.

"I doubt if that will be necessary," I said quickly. "I'm sure we can manage without bothering him. He is very busy at the farm this time of year."

"I'm not sure we can manage, *Señora*. It is very bad. Only a very few of the villagers come now to bring food to the market." She did not have to tell me why most of them stayed away, for the earthquake fear was building among them as it was among the residents of Santiago. The minor tremors continued, barely perceptible and yet wearing on everyone's nerves. Each time a candle flame wavered or a curtain moved ever so slightly, conversation stopped until the candle again burned with a quiet unbroken flame or the curtains hung still and straight. There was a feeling that if the rains would come down in earnest, all would be well, but big dark clouds scudded threateningly through the sky without disgorging more than a few isolated drops on the Valley of Panchoy. The tension had been building daily, and what had started as a vague and seldom voiced fear had now progressed to the point of near-panic. And in addition to that, Santiago was now running out of food.

"At least we do have plenty of beans, don't we?" I was glad I had suggested she buy large quantities of them several weeks ago when meat had become scarce.

"Yes, but—"

"Then we must eat them. Do as well as you can in the market in the morning. You certainly needn't feel bound by the menus I have made. Just buy anything you can find."

"Pardon, *Señora,* but the prices have doubled, and doubled again. I will need much more than you gave me last week."

"Oh, no! How much more?" I asked grudgingly. Ricardo and I would need every *cuartillo* we could find. I certainly didn't relish spending any extra for food. "Tomás left in a hurry, and didn't leave me very much money." That was true enough, for the money in the chair back was almost exhausted.

"I will need at least twenty *pesos*."

"Twenty *pesos!*" I gasped. But I couldn't part with that much!

She nodded. "I would not try to cheat you, *Señora*."

I said quickly, "You know such a thought never entered my head. It's just that it seems like so much."

"Everyone is talking about the price of food, and they say tomorrow is sure to be worse. The people are getting hungry. The poor are starving, for they cannot afford such prices. And those who can are bidding the prices higher and higher."

I sighed resignedly. "Just get what you can in the market. Get anything that will keep us from being hungry, anything priced within reason. Then after you go to the market, I want you to make the rounds of the shops where they sell any foodstuffs and see what you can find there. On credit, if possible. Don't pay out any more cash than you must." I opened my desk and drew out my money box, counted the coins inside. Nineteen *pesos*. Grudgingly, I handed all of them to Teresa, scarcely able to resist the impulse to snatch them back again.

She accepted the coins, nodding. "I will do my best."

"I know you will."

Money. Long after I dismissed Teresa, I sat thinking, puzzling over my new concern for money. We needed every *peso* we could lay our hands on in the next four days. In the morning, I would see what remained in the false chair back in Tomás's office. But I knew there was not much there. Maybe he had some hidden in the *sala*. I would search tomorrow for any hiding places. I even pondered the possibility of selling some of Tomás's treasures. Perhaps I could easily dispose of a few silver pieces. I discarded the idea as being far too risky. But how could we manage to get any significant amount of money in the next four days?

Four days. Only four more days, and we would be gone from here, gone from Santiago and its food problems, its threat of a destructive earthquake. Gone, too, from Tomás, out of his reach. I could not suppress my excitement at the thought that the waiting was almost over at last, and we would soon be on our way.

But how to convince Ricardo that we must leave early? I couldn't tell him the real reason, because I had bound myself to secrecy by my promise to Cecilia. But I would persuade him somehow.

I closed the shutters and chose several of the strongest petticoats from my trunk, humming to myself as I cut them into squares. All my doubts were pushed from my mind in the knowledge that we would soon be free.

Santiago—Mid-July, 1773

CHAPTER XIV

"But we can't wait that long!" I insisted. For the first time since we had met, I was exasperated with Ricardo, though even I had to admit that my irritation was unreasonable. How could I expect him to guess that I had good cause for being anxious to be gone from Santiago, when I couldn't even hint to him at what that cause was? Still, I was disappointed that he would not agree to do as I had been begging him to do for the last half-hour or more: to leave ten days earlier than we had planned. Again, he countered with the questions I couldn't answer:

"Why? What has made you decide suddenly we must leave so soon? What has happened to make you think we can't wait for my legacy?"

We were in the *patio de placer*. He was seated in one of the chairs under the overhang, a sheaf of papers in his lap, and I had packets of herbs spread out on the end of the stone bench on which I sat within the patio myself. We were separated, yet close enough so that we could keep our voices low. If anyone should have happened to enter the patio, it would have appeared that we had just chanced to choose the same spot for our tasks.

To answer Ricardo, I leaned on the same argument I had chosen before. Cecilia's reasoning had sounded solid, and again I borrowed it: "I told you, I've been thinking that if we wait till the twenty-sixth and someone sees us leave here, it may make them suspicious if they notice we don't return."

He dismissed my argument with a wave of his hand. "Who would go to all that bother, to watch so carefully?"

"*Señora* Ramirez across the street might. You know she

240

sits at her front window by the hour, peering out. She would delight in sending word to Tomás if she suspected anything were wrong. You remember she told him about the Mercedarians bringing me home after dark."

He frowned thoughtfully. "She could do such a thing, I suppose, but it's hardly likely. She didn't tell Father about that until after he had come home. To send word to him when he's at the farm—"

"But you do agree it's possible," I said quickly, not wanting him to subject my reasoning to closer scrutiny. "We have to think of everything that might conceivably go wrong. That's why it would be best to leave Friday, during the fiesta of *Nuestra Señora de Carmen.* We can even wear masks, and no one will know who is behind them. On that day, if we don't return before the servants go to bed, they'll think nothing of it. They'll just assume we're out with the revelers. In fact, I'll dismiss them as I did on the day of Corpus Christi. If they're out at the fiesta themselves, they won't even know when we come in, or miss us if we don't. That would give us a full night's start. Don't you see?' How could he possibly fail to see the logic in that? I wondered. I watched anxiously for some sign of agreement.

For a moment, he seemed to be considering the idea. Then he shook his head emphatically, and I knew he had again rejected it. "Your thinking is sound, I can't disagree with that. But we must have money. How can we go with empty pockets?"

I took a deep breath, wishing Cecilia had not extracted from me that binding promise, so that I could tell him the real reason behind my stubborn insistence on leaving early. In desperation, I sought some other means of convincing him, and decided to broach a subject that was distasteful to us both. I only hoped it would be distasteful enough to spur him to action.

"If Tomás comes back," I said with deliberate bluntness, "I will have to share his bed."

Ricardo jumped from his chair, scattering his papers all over the tiles. "That would be unthinkable!" He leaned over and began to gather his papers with a series of sharp agitated movements.

"Then let's leave on Friday," I said, hiding my satisfaction at the effect of my words.

He looked up, scowling, and I didn't know whether he was angered because Tomás still had the indisputable right to make demands upon me, or because I had just reminded him of that unpleasant thought. Whatever the cause of his agitation, I hoped it would bear results. But he hesitated before he

241

answered, and I knew he was turning the thought over in his mind, subjecting it to a cooler appraisal than he had in the first few seconds of his angry reaction. The anger was still in his voice as he asked gruffly, "What makes you think he'll return before the twenty-sixth?"

Here the weakness of my argument became most apparent. "It—it just seems likely. Next Friday, it will have been a month since he left, and if he is not too busy at the farm, he might decide to come into Santiago for a few days, see if people have forgotten about Diablo." Even to my own ears, such reasoning sounded senseless.

Ricardo immediately found the weakness in my vague foolish argument. "Why a month? Why not six weeks? Or two months? God knows, I would certainly rather leave sooner—tomorrow, if possible—today, even. But we simply cannot leave, my love, without money. Besides, as I told you, Father usually stays at the farm at least until early in August." He added the last of the papers to the pile in his hand and stood up, glancing at the sundial. He seemed to feel his words had resolved our discussion. "It's late. I must go. There's a man from Lima lecturing today, a Doctor de la Cueva. He's a real scholar, I'd imagine easily the most learned man in the New World. I don't want to miss a word of any of his lectures."

I did not remind him that soon it would not matter if he had heard the man or not. With a hasty brushing of his fingertips against mine, he was gone.

I sighed heavily, realized that again I had accomplished nothing. I remembered how anxiously I had been waiting for him the night before. I had been in my room stitching for hours, and the third set of candles I had placed in the holders had already burned to stubs before I heard the long-awaited sounds of his arrival: the squeak of the gate between the garden and the small patio, his footsteps as he entered the main patio, and then the closing of his bedroom door.

As soon as his door closed, I blew out my candles and went to him, certain of his love for me and confident of my own ability to persuade him to move up our date of departure. I had intended to talk to him as we lay together in intimate closeness, but I soon realized with a pang of disappointment that there was no hope of communication during what little remained of that night. When I entered his room, Ricardo was already lying on his bed. As soon as my eyes had become accustomed to the darkness, I could see that he had not even troubled to remove his boots.

I leaned over, kissed his cheek. "Turn over on your back and I'll take off your boots," I whispered.

He muttered my name sleepily, his speech heavy with the effects of too much wine, and turned over.

I smiled indulgently to myself and tugged at his boots. It was only with difficulty that I removed them, for he was little help. But when I lay down beside him and he roused himself only enough to mutter my name once more and fling one arm heavily around me, then fell into a deep sleep from which his heavy breathing told me there would be no waking him for many hours, my feelings changed from indulgence to hurt bewilderment. He had spent himself in revelry with his friends from the University, and there was nothing left for me—not a word, nor a smile, nor even a sleepy embrace. I knew it was foolish to feel hurt, that he could not have known that I had waited up for him half the night, listening carefully for the sound of his arrival, my mind bursting with the need to talk about our plans, make him understand they must be changed. Still, resentment welled up within me, a resentment not against him, but against this other life of his in which I had no part. Now, because of the interference of that other life, he was unable to respond to my need to discuss our plans with him, or give me the comforting reassurance I so vitally needed.

He did not even stir when I slipped out from under his arm, which lay heavy and totally relaxed and meaninglessly across me. Disappointed, and bewildered at my own resentment, I padded quietly back to my room. Overhead, I saw the stars were beginning to fade in the pre-dawn light.

I lay for a long time on my bed, wide awake, my mind puzzling over my feelings. It was like a mistress, this rival, this passion of his for learning, his eagerness to acquire knowledge, the enjoyment he derived from associating with everyone and everything connected with his studies. Was it jealousy I felt? Was I so envious of this other mistress of his that I could not enjoy seeing him bid her such a fond farewell? Had I not vanquished her? Hadn't he chosen to leave her, to go with me instead?

Off in the distance, I heard a cock crow. But just before sleep claimed me at last, there flashed through my mind a moment of truth: María Elena had been a rival composed of flesh and blood as I was, one I could readily combat; that she was defeated now and would remain so, I had not the slightest doubt. But this other foe, this mistress of whom my beloved Ricardo was so excessively fond, was no mortal. She was invisible, intangible, without the form of a living opponent, without the substance of reality.

How often I had read Cervantes's tale of the lovable befuddled knight, *don* Quixote, had laughed at the ludicrous picture of the man who tilted with a windmill and thought he had vanquished a formidable foe! But when I had complacently congratulated myself on vanquishing my ephemeral rival for Ricardo's affections, hadn't I also been tilting at windmills? Just before I dropped off to sleep, I remembered Ricardo's face that morning as he shared Antonio's triumph, remembered his eagerness to be gone from me that afternoon and the late hour at which he had returned. How reluctant he was to part from this other world, this mistress who claimed so much of his affection still! In that brief moment, probably no longer than the flicker of an eyelash, I was not really certain I had vanquished her at all.

The sleep that claimed me just as the shocking thought crept into my brain served to make it seem, when I awoke hours later, no more than an unpleasant dream. I had successfully kept the thought at bay until now, when Ricardo had again so eagerly left me as this phantom mistress beckoned him once more.

With renewed determination, I left the small patio and set out to search the house for the one thing that I was certain would make Ricardo heed my pleas to be gone from Santiago by the end of the week: money. Now, it was not only the knowledge that Tomás would be brought into our lives again by the disappearance of his daughter later that week that spurred me to action. My desire to leave Santiago as soon as possible had an added urgency, the need to be quickly gone from all the temptations that might lure Ricardo into a reluctance to leave the things that had been important to him since long before he had met me. Only when we looked on Santiago from afar for the very last time would I breathe easily once again.

That morning, the maids had been cleaning the rooms off the main patio, so there had been no opportunity for me to slip into the *sala* unseen. Now, I could hear them chattering around the *pila* in the service patio, and I knew they would be occupied with doing the laundry there for the rest of the afternoon. Hastily, I left my herb packets in my room, then walked to the *sala* and unlocked the door, closing it behind me and locking it from the inside.

It was the first time I had gone in there since Tomás had left, and I half-expected to see the shattered remains of the piece of porcelain I had heard him throw in his fury. But every Monday morning since then, I had unlocked the door for Teresa, and she had gone in to clean Tomás's treasures, and of course she had immediately removed any sign of the broken figurine. Since the room was so overcrowded, it did not even seem that an object was missing.

I looked around, wondering where to begin my search. It seemed reasonable to assume that if a sizable sum were hidden anywhere at all within the house itself, it would probably be in that room. But where?

I began with the furniture, searching for false bottoms in tables and chairs, looking for hidden compartments, feeling the red plush cushions for any irregularities. Then I ran my fingers behind the tapestries and paintings, and searched for places the wall might be uneven or have an unusual seam which could be a sign of a hidden compartment within the walls themselves. Wherever it was possible to lift the Persian carpets without moving the heavy furniture that sat upon them, I did so, feeling for loose tiles underneath. But my search yielded nothing at all. Tomás was not one to hide money carelessly, especially any great sums.

It was two hours later when I at last had to admit defeat. If there was anything of value in that room besides the treasures Tomás displayed so ostentatiously, then I certainly could not find it.

As I stood at the door ready to leave, I paused to glance across the room at the Sung Dynasty vase, Tomás's most cherished possession, and I wondered bitterly how much of my money he had used to purchase it. It rested in the special display case he had painstakingly designed for it, the sides and top made of glass in order to display its beauty from all angles. Skillfully painted so that it blended with the rich green of the vase it encircled was an iron ring elevated by a single iron bar, similarly painted and attached to a crosspiece of iron he had had imbedded in the floor below the display case. The whole thing was ingeniously planned and cunningly executed, so that no one could steal the vase without first tearing up the house and destroying the vase itself in the process, making the theft of it pointless and futile; it was certainly an effective way to discourage any such intentions. There was only one key that would open the ring and release the vase, and that one Tomás carried always on his person. That key he did not carry openly on the gold chain which held his key to the *sala*. The one that opened the ring around his precious vase was hidden in secret pockets he had had specially tailored into all his clothing, so he was never separated from it except when he slept. To such lengths will a covetous man go to guard his most prized possession.

And then, for the first time since I had entered the room, I remembered it as I had seen it the night before, reflected in Tatiana's crystal: the ceiling gone, the walls crumbled. I remembered that Tomás had vaguely mentioned on the night of the ball at the Palace of the Captains General that he might go ahead and crate his valuable vase to protect it against the earthquake he did not believe was coming. But in his fixation about riding Diablo, he had apparently forgotten his statement. Now, I noted wryly that the vase was directly under a heavy beam, which must certainly shatter the vase when it fell.

Near the vase, the statue of San Tomás was turned partially sideways, his eyes seemingly straining to direct themselves toward the vase. The figure was a ridiculously ineffective guard, mute and immobile, for his namesake's treasure.

I turned away and quickly left the room, feeling suddenly that if I remained another moment, I would become immobilized as were Tomás's other possessions, unable to move, locked into place as firmly as though I, too, were bolted solidly to the floor of the *sala*. It was an absurd thought, a fantasy, but I could not help but be frightened by it. I must escape, from that room and from Tomás.

I told myself I would return to the *sala* the following day to look once more for hidden coins, but as I turned the key in the lock and walked away, I felt such a profound sense of relief that I knew I could not bring myself to go back in there again.

The room Tomás used as an office yielded only a few coins, certainly not enough to take the place of Ricardo's legacy. I pried open the drawer of his desk, feeling that the outrageous cost of feeding our household now gave me ample excuse for my action should I be called upon to defend it. Inside, I found a money box, and that, too, I broke open. My efforts were rewarded with twenty-five *pesos*, three doubloons, and several *ocho escudo* pieces, besides some smaller change. I put a few of the larger coins into the pocket of my skirt and hid the others in the chair back, where there still remained several more doubloons. I would return for all of them later. Altogether, I had not found much, but it would help. I was far from satisfied with my afternoon's work, but I had done everything possible. I returned to my room to rest; nocturnal creatures have need of daytimes naps.

That night, as I stole into Ricardo's room and slipped off my gown and lay down beside him, my foolish fancies of not having wooed him fully away from that other mistress began to dissolve.

"I thought you would never get here!" he said as he pulled me toward him eagerly and pressed his hard body against mine. "What took you so long?" He did not wait for me to answer before he brought his lips down hungrily on mine.

Our passion built quickly that night, and we came together impatiently, as though we were less than whole when we were

246

apart. As I listened to his whisperings of his love for me, heard his moans of pleasure as his body claimed mine, I wondered how I could have doubted the completeness with which he gave himself to me, belonged to me. And when we had finished, and he continued to hold me closely, possessively, I knew he was as loath to part as I.

Later, as I lay with my head on his shoulder, feeling his body relax against mine, the deep serenity that enveloped us brought with it a quiet sort of pleasure, so different from the passionate expression of our love a few minutes earlier, but no less fulfilling.

It was as we lay thus that I again suggested we leave on the sixteenth. I broached the subject reluctantly, for I did not want to spoil the perfect peace we shared or disturb the bond we felt at having given each other such exquisite pleasure. Yet I knew that, in such a mood, Ricardo might be more amenable to suggestion.

He listened, as he always did. I told him of my search, and heard the disappointment in his voice when I told him how little it had yielded.

"Still, it will be enough to get us where we're going," I said.

"Getting there is only the beginning. We've a whole lifetime ahead of us." And he stubbornly insisted on following our original plans.

I still had never told Ricardo of my visions, always afraid that such a disclosure might make him draw away from me, whether he did so in disbelief or in fear or awe of something which even I could not explain. I had known that one day soon I must tell him, for it was a side of me he would have to acknowledge if we were to spend the rest of our lives together. I had not planned to say anything until we had left Santiago far behind, but now I saw it as the only possible way left open to me which might convince him we must leave. I would pretend to have had a vision of Tomás returning the following Sunday. I didn't want to lie to Ricardo, but since my promise to Cecilia kept me bound to silence on the true reason for urgency, lying seemed a justifiable and necessary expedient. Later, when we were well away from Santiago, I would tell him what I had done, but since by then I could also disclose the real reason for a hasty departure, I felt sure he would forgive the deception.

And so, as we lay there together, I told him first of some of my other visions. I mentioned several things that had happened since my arrival in Santiago, things I had foreseen. He was incredulous at first, but when I told him of having seen his face before we ever met, of my joy at thinking it was he who was my husband, my disappointment on learning it was instead Tomás to whom I was wed, and my shock and confusion at our meeting when I arrived in Santiago, then he accepted the fact that I did, unwillingly, sometimes know things that had not yet happened.

"Why, that's why you behaved so strangely that day!" he said at last. "At the time, I thought you were a little addled." His voice grew puzzled. "But I don't understand how such a thing can be. How?"

"I have never understood it. I no longer try. I only ask that you accept it, as a part of me."

"Every part of you is precious to me." His hands caressed my body as though to affirm his words.

I laughed lightly and caught his hand in mine, asked earnestly, "You do believe me, then, don't you? You don't question?"

"I'll never question anything you tell me," he said firmly.

Perhaps it was the trusting way he said that which made me hesitate to tell him the lie I had concocted. I tried to convince myself that it was not really a lie, that by Sunday Tomás would surely have heard of Cecilia's absence—and, if I could convince Ricardo, our own absence as well—and have come running into Santiago.

I must not have told him the story convincingly. Possibly, he sensed something in my voice—a wavering, an uncertainty that communicated itself to him—for as soon as I had finished, he began to question, and rightly so, the credence of that particular vision, the one I had never truly had.

"From what you've said, it doesn't sound as though this time you're as certain of what you saw as you always were before. When you were telling me about that runaway team a few minutes ago, you said you never knew when these things you see will happen, but only that they will. How can you be so sure Father will come back next Sunday, then?"

"I just know that we must leave before then," I answered evasively, feeling guilty at having tried to deceive him. And now even that hadn't helped! I burst into tears of frustration. "Believe me, my love, we must! I can't stand the thought of being here when Tomás returns. It's not just sharing his bed."

His arm tightened around my shoulder. "I would never let that happen!" he said fiercely.

"It's more than that. I'm afraid! I saw a side of Tomás that was so full of evil, it frightens me just to remember." I shuddered. About that, I did not have to lie.

"Then you mustn't remember. I'm here, and I would never let anything happen to you. Have faith in me. Oh, Carlota, my dearest, I wish we didn't have to be so practical, but I'm

248

afraid we must! This is a very practical world. But don't worry. Just let me take care of you. Everything will work out all right. You'll see."

In spite of myself, in spite of what I knew, Ricardo's words soothed me, made my fears seem unreasonable, unfounded. Tomás would certainly not tarry in passing through Santiago. When he came in from the farm, he would have only one thing in mind: pursuit of Cecilia and Manuel. Nor would he be apt to give up his search for them easily. Surely with a good head start, they would be far ahead of him and he would be unlikely to overtake them before they could be hidden by Manuel's friends to the south. Tomás was a stubborn man, and it might easily be weeks or even months before he gave up his pursuit. This stubbornness might serve us well, for by the time he returned to Santiago, we could be far away. Perhaps having Tomás's attention diverted by Cecilia's departure was the best thing that could happen to us, after all.

Ricardo kissed away the tears that were already drying on my cheeks. "Don't worry. I'll keep you safe." He spoke as though he were soothing a distraught child. "Go to sleep, and try to see a different vision, one of us riding happily to Mexico, with *Tía's pesos* jingling merrily in our pockets. I'll wake you before dawn."

I tried to do as he said, but when I closed my eyes, all I could see was the unwelcome memory of Tomás, his face distorted with rage, as I had seen him on the night he left. I still could not completely give up the hope of leaving the following Friday. The sooner we were away from him, the better. And as long as we remained in Santiago, that other life, that other mistress from whom Ricardo seemed so loath to part would continue to tug relentlessly at his sleeve. I did not know which I feared most, Tomás or her.

The next day, Tuesday, I searched Tomás's office again, more thoroughly this time, to no avail. And with the excuse of retiring early for a long siesta, I went carefully over our room, but found nothing at all except a hollow bedpost, which was empty.

On Wednesday, without mentioning my intentions to Ricardo, I took my ruby necklace to the best of the jewelers along the Street of the Goldsmiths, and inquired about having a smaller and less ornate necklace made of part of the stones. I asked him to design something for me. "Something with fewer rubies," I said. "I feel there are far too many of them for one necklace."

The jeweler responded enthusiastically, his eyes alight at the thought of the large fee such an order would command.

He left all the other customers who entered to his apprentice while he patiently sketched various designs for me. When at last he drew one that used relatively few stones, I came to the real purpose of my ruse.

"I like this design very much," I said after I had studied his latest sketch a moment, "but as you can see, it won't use half of my stones. I wonder if you might be interested in buying the rest?" I tried to ask the question casually, as though it had just occurred to me, when in fact it had been the whole purpose of my visit.

I was taken aback by his reaction to my query. He laughed.

Puzzled, I drew back, looking at him. "Of course," I said hesitantly, "I don't imagine you could pay me anywhere near their true worth—"

"Forgive me, *Señora*," he said, curbing his mirth. "It is just that already this month, I have had to turn down the offer of three—no, four—ruby necklaces, one even finer than yours. Two of the ladies wanted me to remove the gems and melt the gold down to give to one of the churches, and the others just wanted to be paid outright. Still others—"

I did not have to wait for him to finish. My hopes had already dissolved. "Then you're not interested in offering me anything for the unused stones?" Disappointed, I picked up my necklace and returned it to the soft bag in which I had brought it.

His tone became less cordial as soon as he saw me put it away. "I am sorry, *Señora*. It isn't possible. With taxes so high, and the tithe, too many of the women of Santiago are willing to part with family jewels. In any case, I hope you will permit me to make the necklace you had decided upon. It will be very lovely, I assure you."

"I'll think it over," I said as I rose, "but I wouldn't know what to do with the rest of the stones, and I would hate to waste them."

He tried one last time. "Perhaps then you would like to give the unused gems to one of the churches. They welcome such donations. Or I could make a beautiful golden bird in which to embed them, much like the emerald lizard I am sure you have seen. I will save these sketches in case you change your mind about the necklace." He knew as well as I did that I would not. He bowed to me stiffly from his office at the back of his shop, and, greeting another prospective customer, he left me to find my own way out.

My dejection slowed my footsteps as I made my way back to the house. There was no sizable sum of money hidden in the house any place where I could find it, and my jewels, which I knew to be extremely valuable, would not even provide one *cuartillo* toward helping us get away before Ricardo's birthday. With supplies becoming scarcer all the time, I wondered ironically if soon my rubies could even buy a week's supply of food!

It was the next afternoon, Thursday, when Cecilia came to my room to ask a favor of me. This time it was I who hastily stuffed my sewing out of sight under the bed before I opened the door.

She stepped inside and smiled at me, then said excitedly,

"Carlota, you said to let you know if you could do anything to help me. Well, tonight at supper, I'm going to mention the fiesta tomorrow and tell Ricardo I'd like to go in the afternoon. Luisa and her *dueña* are busy, so I thought I'd ask him if he'd take me. If you'll go with us, you can help distract him when I slip away and get myself lost in the crowd. You can pretend I told you I saw some friends and was going with them. Then after you're sure we're well away, you can tell him the truth. Will you do that for me?"

"Of course I will. Are all your things ready?" It was impossible to be with her and not share some of the excitement she felt. If only Ricardo and I were leaving the next day, too!

"Yes, I've taken them to the hospital one at a time, with bundles of bandages. Manuel has everything of mine except what I'll be wearing."

"I'll let the servants go after dinner so they won't realize that you don't return to the house with us."

"That's a wonderful idea!" she said enthusiastically. "Then next morning when I don't come out of my room, you can go in and pretend I'm sick, too sick to come out."

"Or contagious," I suggested. "Have you ever had measles?"

She shook her head and giggled. "No, I haven't. That's better still." She turned to leave. "I must get back to the hospital. Oh, Carlota! You can't imagine how hard it is to act normal, as though nothing were changed, when I'm just about to explode with excitement!"

I stifled a secret smile. *I know*, I agreed silently, *for I've been playing the same game myself for the last month.* Under normal circumstances, if she had not been so totally absorbed in her own affairs, she would most certainly have guessed the whole truth about Ricardo and me by then. "I'm certain no one suspects a thing," I assured her. "You've laid your plans carefully. You seem to have thought of everything."

With a wide smile, which I don't think she could have wiped from her face if she had tried, she left the room. Never had I seen her look so radiant. I remembered what

251

Teresa had told me of the fiancé who had been unable to tolerate her changed appearance three years earlier, and I said a fervent prayer that this time, life would deal more kindly with her, and let her find happiness with her Manuel.

Some people seem to be forever doomed to disappointment and suffering. Perhaps Cecilia was one of them, for the next morning I found out to my horror that she was about to be brutally mauled by life once again.

Her plans had appeared to be working well. At the supper table Thursday evening, Ricardo had seemed pleased that she wanted to go to the fiesta, and had readily agreed to take us. On Friday morning, the three of us ate breakfast together. Ricardo left first, and a few minutes later Cecilia excused herself from the table and said, "I must go to the hospital, and I want to go to mass on my way." When she reached the door of the dining room and had looked around outside to satisfy herself that there were no servants within earshot, she leaned back into the room and added lightly, "This is the day!"

I smiled at her obvious joy. "Dinner is at twelve-thirty," I reminded her. "I moved it up so the servants can go to the celebration."

"I'll be here," she said gaily.

I rose from the table, watched her walk out the front door and close it behind her.

As soon as she had left, I stepped into the patio and raised my eyes to look at the sky. It was an odd day, I noted, and the heavy black clouds overhead bore no resemblance to the usual morning wisps that hugged the mountaintops and gradually increased in size as the day progressed. The clouds seemed to be racing hectically through the sky, some going one way, some another, as frantic and directionless as so many runaway teams. There was something sinister about them, and about the frenzied haste with which they seemed to be traveling.

As I lowered my eyes, something compelled me to turn toward the archway that led to the kitchen patio. I strained my eyes in the darkness. How had it suddenly become so dark, like night-time, I wondered? Cecilia was standing there, her dress torn and mudstained, her hair disheveled. With a start, I saw that Tomás was with her, looking grim, and that he had a tight unrelenting grip on her arm.

Cecilia! Puzzled, I stared at her and then at Tomás. She had left only a moment before, by the front door. How could she have circled around the side of the house and through the stable yard so quickly? And Tomás was at the farm. How?

It was then that I noticed Cecilia's eyes. She was looking at me, and never in my life had I seen such sorrowful resignation, such total and heart-rending defeat.

"Manuel?" Did I say his name aloud, or just imagine that I did?

If I spoke, Cecilia seemed not to hear. But I knew from her expression that something terrible had happened to him.

Only when I started to run toward her did the vision dissolve and daylight return. What I had seen had not really happened, not yet. But, just as certainly as the black and sinister clouds overhead were racing toward their own destruction, so we were speeding toward the time when that tableau would again appear as I had just seen it. And next time, it would be painfully real.

I spent the rest of the morning in a torment. What could I do? How could I stop Cecilia? Would it do any good to try? I yearned to confide in Ricardo, ask him what to do, but I couldn't without divulging Cecilia's secret. And that was not mine to divulge.

I wrestled with my indicision. Was it fair to tell Cecilia what I had seen? Was it fair not to? Would she believe me if I did? How could I? How could I possibly destroy her hopes, tell her that her flight with Manuel was doomed to failure even before it started?

Maybe this time I am wrong, I thought, snatching wildly at the hope. *It has never happened before, but there is always the chance that some day what I have foreseen won't happen. Maybe this is the time. Perhaps if I persuaded her to wait, not run away with Manuel today, things might not happen as I saw them. If she doesn't run away, Tomás could scarcely bring her back, could he?* That was what I would do. I would try to stop her without telling her why. I must.

The minute she came home from the hospital, I called her into my room. "Cecilia, don't try to leave with Manuel today, please!" I said as soon as she had closed the door behind her.

Her eyes opened wide in surprise. "Why ever not?" she asked.

"Because—" I paused, groping for some plausible excuse. "The sky! Did you see it? It will most certainly storm. I'm afraid the rivers will be swollen and you might not be able to cross them." I didn't know then that the excuse at which I grasped so hastily and unthinkingly would be so close to the truth.

I motioned for her to come to the window and pointed up at the sky. "Look!" I said. "Look at those storm clouds."

She looked, then turned away from the window. "I know. They're odd, aren't they? I hope the weather doesn't ruin the fiesta."

253

I shot her a look of exasperation. "The devil take the fiesta!" I said impatiently. "It's you I'm worried about."

She put her hand on my arm. "It's sweet of you to worry, but you mustn't." She laughed and said, "It's funny, but you're the one who is nervous, and I—I've never felt so calm and sure of myself, so certain of what I was doing. It's as if—as if all my life has finally been laid out for me, neatly, in a pattern. And now all I must do is follow that pattern. I've never been so happy."

"But perhaps if you told Tomás how you and Manuel feel about each other, he'd understand, and would let you marry."

"He wouldn't. You know he wouldn't. If he so much as suspected that I cared for Manuel, he would force me to marry someone he chose that very day."

"Maybe if you waited a little while—"

"No!" she said emphatically as she shook her head in a firm gesture of denial. "Please, Carlota, don't be nervous on my account. Nothing you can say can possibly make me change my mind. Let me tell you something, something very private. I have been praying for so long, praying for God to let me know somehow what I should do. And then one day Manuel and I couldn't break apart when we should have, and we—we stayed together all night. I expected to feel—well, guilty, and wicked, but I didn't. Manuel felt terrible afterward about what we had done, and he blamed himself for letting it happen, but I told him it was what I wanted, too. Before that, he wouldn't talk about us running away together, because he thought I would be unhappy as the wife of a *mestizo*, that I wouldn't be able to stand the degradation. But I knew that if he thought I was pregnant, he wouldn't let me bear his child in shame. So last week I told him I was."

"And you weren't?"

She smiled. "I really didn't know then, but now I think I am, so it wasn't really a lie after all, was it?"

"Cecilia!" I gasped in surprise. I would have laughed at the way she so blandly admitted her deception, but the memory of the dreadful tableau I had witnessed earlier quickly smothered any amusement I might have felt.

"I'm telling you this for one reason," she continued. "I just want you to know that since I've decided what to do, a blessed peace has descended on me, as if everything is finally going to be all right now. That's what makes me so sure my prayers have been answered. I do think God will forgive me for what I did, don't you?"

I hugged her. "Oh, Cecilia, I'm sure He will!" My whole body tensed with the effort of stemming the tears that filled my eyes. Not until after she left did I permit them to burst forth: tears of frustration because she had not listened to my veiled plea; tears of sorrow and futility because I knew it would not have changed anything if she had. All I could do was watch in helpless horror as Cecilia flung herself headlong down the path that would soon send her hurtling into the dark and hopeless abyss of despair.

In the back of my mind, I still had not given up the hope that perhaps when Ricardo realized Cecilia had left with Manuel, he might decide impulsively that we should also go that very day, with or without money. But I knew that now I must give up that frail hope, for I had no choice but to stay and do as Cecilia had asked me to do, to give her and Manuel a chance to put as much distance as possible between themselves and Santiago before Tomás found out they had gone. I knew it would do no good, that all my efforts would be as futile as my pleading had just been. But that made it all the more necessary to stay and try. I would never forgive myself if I didn't.

From that moment until the time late that afternoon when Cecilia slipped away from us, I could not look at her glowing face without being struck by a feeling of foreboding, remembering that time was running out on her brief spate of happiness. How many minutes or hours or days of laughter remained for her before Tomás would cause that dazzling smile to disappear forever from her face?

Tomás! I clenched my fists at the very thought of him. My hatred of him deepened as I recalled how I had seen him standing in the archway, grasping Cecilia's arm, his face grim and unsmiling, the very embodiment of callousness and cruelty.

Under ordinary conditions, I would have enjoyed the fiesta of *Nuestra Señora de Carmen*. It was held in the square formed by the church and the convent that flanked it, and every bit of space was filled with milling crowds of people. Some clustered around the usual vendors, others watched groups of native dancers or musicians, and a crowd composed more of adults than children surrounded a small monkey dressed like a gentleman, and they laughed delightedly as he doffed his hat to them and then stamped on it. Many of the people of Santiago were hungry, some of them were frightened half out of their wits by their fear of an impending earthquake, yet not once that day did I hear mention of either hunger or fears. Perhaps it was these very worries that added to the gaiety, as the people grasped eagerly at a chance to forget their troubles and banish their cares.

I was surprised to see one vendor selling sugary confections intricately done in the form of *Nuestra Señora de Carmen*.

Obviously, these had been made before Santiago began to feel the pinch of the food shortage, and the vendor took advantage of the situation to put an outrageously high price on them. Ricardo bought two of the fragile confections, one for Cecilia and one for me, before I could stop him from such a foolish extravagance. Once it was done, there was nothing to do but act pleased and thank him, especially since Cecilia seemed so delighted with hers.

In several places, crude home-made cages held *cenzontles* that some of the villagers had brought to sell. Ricardo would have bought one, but I told him it pained me to see them confined. I could not help thinking how much more suitable it would have been if the few natives who were willing to come into Santiago had brought foodstuffs instead of songbirds.

One man had a trained *cenzontle*. Whenever someone handed the man a coin for a fortune paper, he would signal the bird, who would select a tiny roll of paper from a container on the far side of his cage, then return to drop it in the waiting hand of his master and claim his reward of a seed. Then the fortune was given to the person for whom it had been bought.

Cecilia seemed to be enjoying the fiesta. That day, for the first time, I had a glimpse of the girl she must once have been—carefree, laughing, lighthearted.

But my own heart was heavy, and I could only pretend, for her sake, to share in her enjoyment. Occasionally, a man with a beast's or a man's head of papier-mâché would grab a pretty young girl and dance around with her before he released her, as the crowd applauded its approval. Other men, wearing cloth masks, went around collecting donations for the convent.

We were watching a group of native musicians, one of whom was playing a marimba. We stared in rapt fascination as the sticks in the man's hands literally flew through the air as he beat out the sweet bell-like notes on the large instrument. There was a Spanish guitar, and the rest of the musicians played small wind instruments made of reeds or beat out the rhythm with pairs of seed-filled gourds. It struck me as odd that the guitar neither sounded nor looked out of place in that grouping.

It was then that Cecilia said suddenly, "There's Isabel! I must go talk to her." Ricardo, watching the marimba player, didn't even seem to notice when she slipped her arm from his. As she passed behind me, she gave my arm a quick squeeze. "I'm going," she whispered, her voice fluttering with subdued excitement.

It was not until a few minutes later, when the musicians had finished their song and were passing their hats, that Ricardo missed her.

He looked around. "Where has Cecilia gone?"

"She saw some of her friends," I said, trying to keep my voice casual. "I imagine she'll stay with them until after mass."

He frowned. "She shouldn't have run off without saying something."

"She didn't. She told us she was leaving. You were too busy watching the marimba player to notice." I looked around for some distraction. "Oh, look, Ricardo! Over there. There's another man with a *cenzontle* that fetches fortunes. Give him a *cuartillo* and let's see what he says of my future! Please?"

He laughed at my apparent eagerness. "How can I refuse?" Then he added in my ear, "I can tell you for certain, your future holds a tall blond man."

We made our way through the crowd to the fortune-teller and his trained bird. Ricardo gave the man a coin, and he in turn coaxed the bird to hand him one of the rolls, which he gave to me.

I unrolled it and read it aloud. "The owl cries over your roof-top, but not for you." Puzzled, I held it toward Ricardo. "I don't understand it."

Ricardo took it from my hand with a sudden anger that startled me. Then he turned to the *mestizo* who was the bird's master and released a torrent of words, berating him for having given me such a fortune. The vehemence of his outburst puzzled me.

"It isn't important," I said in an effort to calm him. "What does it mean?"

Ricardo ignored both my protest and my question, and demanded that the man give me another fortune paper in place of that one.

The *mestizo*, who had been disclaiming responsibility for the fortune, repeated that it was the *cenzontle*, not he, who had chosen it. But he apparently realized that further argument was useless, and finally shrugged his shoulders resignedly. "Well, then, perhaps the bird did make a mistake. If the *Señor* will return the paper to me, we will let my little friend try again."

He took the paper from Ricardo and shaped it again into a roll, then urged the bird to repeat his performance. This time the message was certainly innocuous enough:

Joy returns to those who give it.

I handed it to Ricardo. "Surely you can't object to that one!"

"That's better," he muttered grudgingly after he had read it. Then he dropped it to the ground.

"Why were you so upset?" I asked as we walked away.

He either didn't hear me or didn't choose to answer. "I still don't see Cecilia," he said, his eyes scanning the crowd.

Vaguely puzzled by the message I hadn't understood, and still having no idea why it had sparked Ricardo to such unexpected anger, I looked back at the *mestizo*. Before I turned away, I saw him stoop over and retrieve the paper Ricardo had dropped. Then he walked to the back of the cage and returned it to the container with the others. He undoubtedly had to pay a literate man to write the fortunes, and was not inclined to waste them. I doubted if he was even aware of what they said. The matter of the owl slipped from my mind.

"We'd better go into the church now if we want a seat," I suggested. "Here comes the procession." I motioned to the statue of *Nuestra Señora de Carmen,* which was visible over the heads of the crowds as it was borne on a platform slowly up the Street of the Bells toward the church entrance.

"But Cecilia?" Ricardo, obviously worried, paused to look once more around the crowded area.

I put my hand through his arm. "She's probably with her friends. No doubt she's already inside. Come, we can look for her after mass."

All during the service, Ricardo kept turning his head this way and that, restlessly scanning the crowd that filled the aisles as well as the pews of the church. I didn't look, for I knew, as he did not, that we would not find Cecilia there.

As we stepped into the aisle after mass was over and genuflected toward the altar, he said, "I don't think she's here. I've looked all around. It's not like her to miss mass."

We turned to follow the crowd out the back of the church, and I knew it was time to tell him what I knew. An empty church would be as private a place as any. "Let's go into one of these vacant pews," I suggested. "I know where Cecilia is. I'll tell you as soon as the crowd leaves. Meanwhile, we can both say a prayer for her. She will need our prayers, Ricardo. All that we can say."

He shot me a puzzled glance as we slipped into one of the back pews, but he did not dare question me until there was no danger of being overheard. We knelt there, our heads bowed, until the church had cleared of everyone but four or five women who were kneeling before the image of Our Lady at the altar rail.

Then I told him about Cecilia and Manuel.

"You let her go?" he asked in astonishment.

"How could I stop her?" I countered.

"You should have told me! I would never have let her run away with him. That *mestizo* is an unbearable egotist, utterly selfish and self-centered! He can never make her happy."

Suddenly irritated, I snapped, "How can you presume to decide that for her? She was right in making me promise not to tell you until after they'd left!" I was not really angry with him, because he was powerless to stop them now. My rage was directed at life, for what it was about to do to Cecilia.

Before I could apologize for speaking to him so sharply, he said contritely, "You're right, of course, and I wish them luck. If anyone were to tell you not to run away with me, I hope you wouldn't listen to them." He smiled at me.

I tried to return his smile. "You know I never would, any more than Cecilia would have listened." I was suddenly very tired, wearied by the pretense at gaiety to which I had forced myself earlier, by the strain of keeping Cecilia's secret, and, most of all, by the terrible knowledge of what was yet to happen to her eating at my heart. "Ricardo, can we go to a quiet place? We can't go home till dark, though that shouldn't be too long now since it's such a dismal day. I don't know where we can go, but can't you think of somewhere? I'm really not in a very festive mood."

"Why can't we go home before dark?" he asked, and I told him of the plan to slip in late and hope that no one would notice only two of us returned. I told him, too, about my intention of pretending Cecilia was sick in bed, and insisting the servants stay away from her.

He nodded his approval. "We should be able to stretch that ruse at least through tomorrow night. That would give them a day and a half. Surely we can keep her departure secret until then."

"I'll tell Teresa in the morning. We can trust her, and we'll need her help to keep the maids from suspecting anything is amiss." As I talked, I thought, *None of this will do any good. All this, all Cecilia's carefully laid plans are for nothing. Tomás will pursue her and catch her and bring her back in shame and defeat to the unhappy house she had thought to have left forever.* At the memory of the depressing vision, I could not keep the tears from rolling down my cheeks.

"You're crying," Ricardo said softly. Then I felt his hand on my arm. "Come, my love. Let's get out of here and go some place where I can hold you in my arms while you tell me what is making you so sad."

As we stepped out of the church, I was surprised to see that it had rained lightly while we were inside, and the

259

weather had cleared. All day, the sky had continued as dark and threatening and dreary as it had started. Now, as always happens when the normal light of day appears belatedly just before dusk after storm clouds have passed, the brightness seemed dazzling.

Momentarily, the clear sky raised my spirits. That morning, it had been just after I had looked at the ominous black clouds overhead that I had seen the equally dark tableau in the archway, and the gloomy scene had seemed a part of the dark foreboding of the weather. Could this unexpected brightness into which we had just emerged be a denial of the horrible portent which the black clouds had seemed to spawn? Could the sudden change in the weather presage the possibility that the forces which would destroy the hopes and dreams of Cecilia and Manuel might abate as well?

Ricardo's voice broke into my thoughts. "Look, over there to the south. There's quite a storm breaking."

My eyes followed the direction he indicated, and I saw jagged streaks of lightning etch bizarre patterns against the dark clouds from which they had come. This was to the south, the direction taken by the runaway lovers.

As I watched, gigantic bolts of lightning continued to slash and rip across the horizon, as though to mock my momentary hopes for the happiness of Cecilia and her Manuel, a happiness I knew was never to be.

Santiago—July 18, 1773

CHAPTER XV

We were able to delay the time when Tomás found out about Cecilia, but we were powerless to prevent it. He arrived at the house late Sunday night, the day on which I had guessed he would be apt to appear. Cecilia had been gone a little over two days.

He stamped through the house in a dark and vengeful fury, pausing only long enough to grab a hasty meal while Simón saddled a fresh horse. So intent was he on the chase that it didn't even occur to him to question the propriety of leaving Ricardo and me alone in the house now that Cecilia was gone. He tried to coerce Ricardo to join in the pursuit, but he let the matter drop when Ricardo quietly told him that he hoped Cecilia and Manuel did get away, hoped that they would never be found. Tomás grumbled something about Ricardo not getting any notions about running away with María Elena, and then dropped the subject.

During the short time he was home, I was surprised at the detachment with which I could study Tomás. As the man to whom I had been married—a petty despot, as stubbornly unreasoning and frequently equally as petulant as a small child—I no longer had any fear or awe of him. As my husband, he had lost the power to bully me, to make me feel anything for him but a contemptuous pity.

But I had been speaking truthfully that night when I had cried and told Ricardo I was afraid of him, for there dwelt in him that incarnate wickedness, an evil bereft of all reason. It seemed to me almost as though the emotion existed by itself and resided within him, much as a devil might dwell inside a soul. But Tomás was not an unwilling host, and did not

261

choose to exorcise his devil. Instead, he used it, turned it to his own purposes, let it take over the man who was Tomás Ricardo de Alvarado y Paz in order to strike out at whoever and whatever had incurred his wrath. It was this very embodiment of evil within him, this giving of life to a force which by itself could not have harmed anyone, that could make me catch my breath and start trembling with fear.

When he left in pursuit of Cecilia and Manuel, I felt compelled to watch him ride away, as though my eyes must confirm the fact that this evil was, for now, moving away from me, out of my life. Only then could I believe I was safe. Ricardo and Simón also seemed to be moved by the same compulsion to watch him leave, and the three of us stood in the street and watched Tomás quickly disappear into the heavy shadows of the unlit street.

But my relief at having him go away, at least for a time, was counterbalanced by the fearful knowledge that the evil he embodied would soon be striking out at Cecilia.

Poor Cecilia! I remembered her bubbling laughter the day she had left. How confident and happy she had been then! I brushed a tear from my cheek and said flatly, "He will bring her back."

"Perhaps not, *Señora*. The girth on his saddle may break before he gets too far."

Ricardo looked at Simón sharply, then threw his arm around the small *indio's* shoulder and gave him an affectionate hug. "You're a good man, Simón," he said as we all turned around and walked back into the house. But Ricardo's voice was tinged with sadness, for his heart was as heavy as mine since I had shared with him the knowledge of what was to come.

Simón knew nothing of this, and did not know his efforts to stop Tomás had been useless. There was a certain pride in his voice as he said, "It is little enough to do for the sad *Señorita* Cecilia. It made my heart glad to see her smile again those last few days before she went away. I knew she had a special happiness inside her." Before he headed toward the stables, he turned to us and asked, "When will you be leaving, *Señor* Ricardo, you and the *Señora*?"

It did not surprise me to learn that Ricardo had already confided in Simón. He frowned now when Ricardo told him it would be eight days before we could leave. "Couldn't you make it sooner, before your father returns? It would make my heart easier."

"And ours," Ricardo agreed. "But I can't collect my legacy until the twenty-sixth. We'll hope Father doesn't return before then." He shrugged helplessly. "If he does, then we'll just have to manage somehow."

"You know, *Señor* Ricardo, that I will do for you everything I can." Simón's simple words were spoken with such sincere devotion that they sounded more like a sacred vow than a mere offering of help. I knew he would not hesitate to give his life for Ricardo, if the need ever arose.

"I know you will," Ricardo acknowledged. His strong voice quivered slightly, and I could tell that he had been as touched by the depths of Simón's sincerity as I.

Another eight days of waiting! They seemed to stretch endlessly before us. Would they never pass?

Looking back from later years on the strange days that followed, the memory that comes through the strongest is that of my confused state of mind. There were so many things happening at once, so many currents and cross-currents of thought that swirled through my brain that it seemed scarcely possible to concentrate on anything at all.

Foremost in my mind was always my love for Ricardo, and the desire to get away quickly with him, before Tomás returned. And still, there were the pointless motions to go through, maintaining propriety, pretending that I was no more to him than the *dueña* of his father's house, that each of our lives continued as before, with my main concern that of household duties and his that of his studies.

I thought often of Cecilia during those days, worried about her, was deeply concerned over her ability to endure the terrible ordeal I knew she must face. I knew that she would probably have desperate need of some love and understanding when Tomás brought her back. But, if all our plans went as we hoped for our own sakes, Ricardo and I would not be likely to be in Santiago to help her. There was a feeling of guilt in the knowledge that, if we could, we would leave her to return to a deserted house, where she must bear, alone and friendless, the brunt of her father's unreasoning fury.

Also during this time, there was the growing dread of earthquake in the Valley of Panchoy, for the insignificant tremors, though unimportant in themselves, nurtured the growing apprehension. Perhaps the food situation itself, which had become alarmingly serious, was both cause and effect of that fear as well; fright feeds on empty stomachs, and of those there were plenty, especially among the poorer *mestizos* and *indios*. Beggars came to our door more often than ever before, no longer asking for alms, but for food, at which they snatched as savagely as wild dogs.

Within our own house, no one was hungry, but several of the maids were round-eyed with terror. They cleaned inside

263

the rooms with a frantic haste, as though they could not soon enough move away from the walls and ceilings which might tumble about their heads at any moment. They invented endless excuses to tarry near the doors or in the open patios, ready at a moment's notice to jump out of danger's way.

And I, who knew for certain what they only feared, curbed my impatience with them. Perhaps if I had not had so many other thoughts racing through my brain, I might have been more fearful myself. Maybe I was more frightened than I admitted. If not, why had I withheld my foreknowledge of a quake from Ricardo that night I had told him of some of my other visions? Had the omission been purely accidental, or subconsciously planned?

On the morning after Tomás left, Teresa came into the small patio to tell me that one of the maids had been called back to her village because her mother was dying, and she asked my permission to let her go.

"Do you think her mother is really ill?" I asked. "Or is the girl just frightened?"

Teresa shrugged. "Who can be certain, *Señora?* But I do know the house would be better off without her, for she forever speaks of her fears and keeps the other maids upset with her foolishness. Besides, if she goes, it will be one less person to feed."

I smiled. Teresa's reasoning was always delightfully simple and direct. "Then let her go."

"Yes, *Señora.*"

Another of the maids left the next day, the second one without asking permission. "One less mouth to feed," I shrugged, adopting Teresa's practical philosophy. Besides, what cared I if the rooms were cleaned less thoroughly or less frequently? I would soon be gone forever from the house and any concerns connected with it.

But the food problem was pressing, and could not be so easily shrugged aside. On the morning after Tomás had come through Santiago, I sent Alberto to the farm to bring back a wagon-load of supplies. He returned Tuesday night with the foodstuffs hidden, at Ricardo's suggestion, under a topping of hay. I watched the things being carried into the kitchen: a treasure of fresh and dried meat, fresh vegetables and fruits, flour, dried corn and beans. The feeding of our household would no longer be a problem. That worry, at least, was lifted from my mind.

There was more than enough food for our own use, so I sent some to Marta and Carlos. I knew that Carlos owned no farmland from which he could fetch supplies.

On Wednesday afternoon, Marta came to thank me. "My

264

dear," she said as she embraced me when I came into the main patio to greet her, "that was so thoughtful of you. We have been existing on very peculiar fare for the past few weeks. The fresh meat, and the fruits and vegetables! I can't thank you enough."

"I was glad to have some to send," I answered sincerely. Marta was one true friend I had made among Tomás's acquaintances, and it was with regret that I realized our lives would soon move on divergent paths, never to cross again. I slipped my arm through hers. "Alberto also brought a little chocolate from the farm. Come and we'll have a cup together."

"You must tell me about Cecilia," she said in her usual straightforward manner as we walked to one of the settees that faced the main patio. "Have you had any word? I know you must be worried about her."

I appreciated the fact that Marta was too honest to avoid the subject pointedly, as though it were something too terrible to be discussed, or to offer meaningless platitudes. Cecilia had foolishly confided in Luisa, and all of Santiago knew she had run off with Manuel.

"There is no word," I answered dejectedly. Nor, I knew, would any encouraging news ever come. "Oh, Marta, I do think Manuel would have made her happy!"

"Would have?" she asked perceptively. "You talk as though Tomás has already found them."

"If he hasn't yet, he will. He is a very determined man."

She made a sound of disapproval deep in her throat. "Tomás is a fool." She stopped talking abruptly when the maid answered my summons and I told her to bring us a pot of hot chocolate and some fresh baked bread and butter. When the maid had left, Marta continued, "As soon as Cecilia reached her fifteenth birthday, Tomás was beseiged by suitors for her. But no one was ever quite good enough for his daughter. I can't tell you how many good offers he turned down, marriages which could have made her happy. Only when that empty-headed Rafael asked for her hand did he feel that at last he had found a man with blood noble enough to match his own. And then, after Cecilia's illness, Rafael turned from her, just because of a few marks on her lovely face! Oh, he let it be known that she was the one who jilted him, he was gentleman enough for that, but everyone knew. And now, because Tomás was so obsessed with the importance of fine blood, she has run away with a *mestizo*! It serves him right! I hope they go some place where he can never find them!"

265

"I only wish it were possible," I agreed, knowing it was not.

I was glad when we turned to less hurtful topics, for my heart was particularly heavy that day with worry about Cecilia, and our conversation had deepened my concern. She had been gone five days. Was she still free, still with her Manuel? Or had Tomás already found them? Even now, was he so senselessly dragging her back to Santiago? And why? To what purpose? But an unreasoning man needs no purpose, no justification for his vengeance. Cecilia had defied him, run away, earned his displeasure; she must suffer for it.

At length, after we had finished our chocolate, Marta stood up to leave. "Thank you, my dear, for such a lovely treat, and for the food you sent." I walked with her to the door, and just before she left, she said, "Oh, I almost forgot, I want you and Tomás to come to my name's day celebration on the twenty-ninth. Every year on the day of Santa Marta, we have a big fiesta at the house. This year, it will be a much smaller affair. Goodness knows where I'll find enough to feed even half the usual number! With the food shortage, I suppose I should be glad so many of our friends have run from Santiago and won't be able to attend! I do think all this earthquake talk is morbid, though, don't you?"

"Morbid, perhaps, but—it is certainly a possibility."

She sighed exasperatedly. "So they've got you believing it, too! Really, you mustn't listen to all that foolishness. Just idle chatter, mostly. It started among the *indios*, and now so many others have taken it up, you would think everyone will be disappointed when we don't have a good shaking!"

"But the small temblors have continued off and on for so long now," I argued. "And a hard quake could come at any time." I felt compelled to make her take the possibility seriously.

"I suppose it could," she agreed, furrowing her forehead. Then she shrugged and laughed. "There, now! You'll be having me frightened if I stay here a minute longer! Don't forget the twenty-ninth. We'll be receiving friends all day long. Any time after two o'clock. Come early and stay late. I may not find enough food, but there will be no shortage of wine. And I'll have the best fireworks display I've ever had." With a good-natured smile, she again embraced me and was gone.

I had not promised to attend her saint's day celebration. By that time, Ricardo and I would be three days gone from Santiago.

Our talk reminded me of the earthquake to come, and as I crossed the patio, I glanced toward the door of the *sala,* toward the roof over the room which I knew would be demolished, the wall that would be virtually destroyed.

It had been over four months since my ride to the Valley of Almolonga, when I had first become aware of the tremendous power trapped within the earth, a power which, once escaped, must spend itself in destroying everything it could reach. I had since felt an awareness of that power in other directions, too, as though the ground all around the Valley of Panchoy was seething with destruction. And that destruction would be here, in this very house. When? How much time remained before that violence would be unleashed, would crumble houses like this to the ground, like so many castles built of sand?

My thoughts were borne of a heavy sadness, a feeling of desolation with which I had awakened that morning. Perhaps part of my dejection had sprung from my loneliness, for Ricardo and I had agreed that we could no longer chance spending any portion of our nights together, since Tomás could return on any day, at any hour. And so, for the first time in over a month, I had not lain in Ricardo's arms for any portion of the previous night, and I sorely missed the comforting reassurance the hours spent with him gave me. This was especially true since I had admitted to myself my jealousy of his avid interest in the studies he would soon be leaving. The realization of what I was asking him to give up for my sake lay heavily upon me, and I needed the constant reassurance of his touch, his special smile, his nearness to remind myself that he had no regrets about loving me, no matter what the cost of that love might be.

Ricardo himself was unknowingly adding to the weight of the burden I bore. It was part of the strangeness of those days following Cecilia's departure that a portion of him continued to exist independently of thoughts of me, or of Cecilia. It was not that he was in any way callous about the sister he dearly loved, nor did he in any manner love me less. It was just that he was able to detach himself from thoughts of us at times, so thoroughly engrossed was he with the guest lecturer from Lima, whose tremendous store of knowledge he respected and admired to the point of worship.

"He is so brilliant, Carlota, and has so much to say," he told me enthusiastically that Thursday as we ate our midday mean. "It's a rare privilege to be allowed to listen to him. Today, after he had finished his lecture, I went up to talk with him, as I have several times before, and he asked me to come back early this afternoon when he will be free, so that we might talk more. Can you imagine, a man like that wanting to talk to me!" His eyes were alight with pride.

I smiled and said, "You'll enjoy that, won't you?" He didn't know that his words, his enthusiasm were like knives twisting in my heart. If he could not be swayed from this passionate interest of his during such a time of crisis and turmoil in his life, could he ever be expected to give it up entirely? I could not help but wonder if he would ever show a like enthusiasm for farming.

That evening at the supper table, after his talk with Doctor de la Cueva, whom I had come to think of merely as the Great Man, Ricardo's conversation was virtually a soliloquy, and was all centered around the man's statements and ideas. Ricardo's excitement was contagious, but my sharing of his pleasure was quickly dampened by my jealousy. That mistress was still there, I reminded myself, tugging at his sleeve. How willingly I would have shared him with her had I not known it was impossible for him to have us both! I shifted uneasily in my chair, remembering that it was still four more days before we would be gone from her.

"Doctor de la Cueva is a *chapeton*," he told me, "like you, my love. He's only been over here five years, and yet I've never met any *creole* with more perception, more understanding of our problems. He puts across his ideas with such force and clarity that even a child could understand them. He studied for years with the greatest minds of Spain at Toledo, so his brain is a storehouse of knowledge as well as ideas. I'm so glad I haven't missed hearing him. How badly we need more men with his understanding over here!"

He talked on, pausing only long enough for me to make little meaningless comments. Finally, he smiled at me, that wonderful smile of his that always made my heart beat faster, and, seeking my hand under the table, he gave it a squeeze. "I'm boring you. I'm sorry, but I've never met a man whose ideas so exactly matched my own. He wants me to come talk with him again tomorrow afternoon."

"That will be nice," I said, trying to inject a little enthusiasm into my voice for his sake. Then, anxious to bring his thoughts back to me, to us, I asked, "Ricardo, when will we carry our clothing and the other things we will need to the hiding place you mentioned?"

I had the feeling that it was an effort for him to force his mind to change its course, to think of our plans and our future. "That's right," he said. "It's only four more days till we leave isn't it?" He paused to think a minute. "On Sunday, of course. There will be nothing unusual about us leaving on a picnic if we're seen. But this time our hamper will hold very little food."

"Oh, Ricardo," I whispered urgently, "I'm so afraid!"

"Afraid?" He looked surprised. "Of what?"

I shook my head, knowing I could not tell him that my biggest fear had to do with getting him out of Santiago before he became irreversibly committed to the mistress whose power over him I so feared. But would even physical separation serve to break him loose? Could he ever really be free of her?

He was looking at me, his eyebrows raised quizzically, still waiting for my answer.

"I'm just afraid something will go wrong, something will keep us from going." I smiled at him, suddenly ashamed of my fears, embarrassed at the vagueness of them. "I suppose I'm just jittery. I only wish we were gone from here, on our way to Mexico!"

"Soon, my love." His voice caressed me, his eyes brimmed with love as he looked at me. How could I doubt that he loved me more than anything else? "Only four more days."

"That seems an eternity," I sighed. Never had time seemed to drag so interminably.

The next evening, it was almost dark when he returned from his second talk with the man from Lima. As usual, he came directly from the stables into the small patio, where he knew I would be waiting for him. I sat on the stone bench I usually occupied, a volume of poetry in my lap, wondering what had kept him so long. At last, I heard the sounds of his arrival in the stables, and he came into the small patio and dropped his large frame into a chair near mine. Even in the waning light, I could see that his face was shining with excitement.

He smiled at me and said breathlessly, "I just can't believe it!"

I felt a strange prickly sensation at the back of my neck. "You can't believe what?" I asked, certain that I would not like hearing what he was about to tell me.

"Well, you know I've had several talks with Doctor Ignacio de la Cueva lately? I may not have told you, but he lectured for several months at the University in Mexico City before he came here."

He paused, and as I waited for him to continue, my mouth went dry. "Go on," I urged, yet fearing his next words.

"Today, just now, when we finished talking, he did me the greatest honor I could ever imagine. Carlota, can you believe it? He asked me to come to Lima with him next month, and study with him personally for two years! Of all the students he met in Mexico and here, he chose me!"

"Only you?"

"Only me." He could not keep the pride from his voice.

I forced my lips to form the question I did not want to ask. "What did you tell him?"

"Why, that I was flattered, that never in my life had I been so deeply honored as I was by his interest in me—"

Impatiently, I interrupted, "But did you say you would accept his offer?"

"Accept?" He looked at me in surprise. "Of course not. How could I?"

I did not feel the relief I had expected to feel at his answer. "Then you told him you must refuse?" I ran my tongue across my lips in an attempt to moisten them.

"Well, no, not exactly—"

"But you must do one or the other!" *Which one? Which will you choose, my Ricardo? For now you must choose between us. Your mistress or me?* I was aware of the thudding of my heart as I leaned forward and waited for his answer.

His voice was edged with impatience. "Of course I can't accept! But I couldn't tell him why, could I?" His impatience faded, but as he continued, I detected a wistfulness in his words. Or did I only imagine it? "I thanked him and said it would be the greatest privilege I could imagine to study under him."

"Is that all? Is that all you told him?" I prodded.

"What else was there? That's about all I could say, except that I'd let him know."

"Let him know?" I asked, more sharply than I intended.

He shrugged. "When I suddenly disappear from Santiago with my father's wife in a few days, he'll know then what my answer must be, won't he?"

"Yes, of course," I said. His words should have satisfied me, but I could not rid myself of the feeling that somewhere our conversation had gone amiss.

As far as Ricardo was concerned, that ended the discussion, but his words continued to trouble me the rest of the evening and his answers kept repeating themselves in my brain. I tried to occupy myself with some needlework after supper, but I pricked my fingers repeatedly and at last gave up and excused myself to go to bed early, feeling the need to be alone, away from Ricardo's distracting presence. I had to do some serious thinking, and that I could not do with any attempt at cool rationality when I was in the same room with him, for every time I looked over at him as he pored over his notes, my feelings for him banished all rationality. I loved him without reason, beyond reason.

As I rose to leave, he looked up anxiously. "You're not sick, are you? You've been so quiet tonight, except when you cry out every time you prick your finger. I've counted at least ten cries so far. I fear, my love, we had better always hire a seamstress to do your stitching."

I smiled at his teasing and made my way to the door. "I'm fine," I said, pausing to look back at him, wanting, needing one more moment with him before I left. "There's just so much to think about."

He grinned. "Me?"

I blew him a kiss. "Always you." How I yearned to run and fling myself into his arms, forget the doubts and fears that were busily gnawing at me! I longed to feel secure in his arms, in the knowledge that he loved me above all else.

Above all else. But did he?

"Good-night, my love," he whispered as I turned to leave. "Sleep well."

I did not sleep well at all, but lay awake most of the night, restless, tossing and turning, trying not to listen as that now familiar voice of wisdom spoke again. But it kept on relentlessly, deep inside my brain where I could not shut it off, demanding with an unshakable persistence that I listen, finding fault with any excuses I could find to keep from doing what it told me I must do.

But for you, the voice insisted, *he could have accepted Doctor de la Cueva, would have accepted eagerly.... But he didn't. He chose me,* I answered indignantly.... *But you heard that touch of wistfulness in his voice when he spoke of it, didn't you? You can't deny you heard it! ... I may only have imagined it,* I protested uneasily.... *You didn't. It was there.... He chose me,* I repeated.... *It wasn't a choice at all. He had committed himself to you.... He would still have chosen me.... Would he? ... He loves me! ... As much as he loves his lifelong dream? Try him! Turn him loose! Set him free! ... How could I do that? ... Leave him! Go away, somewhere he'll never find you.... That's unthinkable! I love him too much! And he loves me! ... But he will grow to hate you, if you let him turn down this opportunity for love of you.... Never! ... It will happen, unless you do as you know you must. Leave him. Set him free.... I won't! I can't! ... You must. Set him free. Set him free! SET HIM FREE!*

"No!" I burst into tears, knowing I had lost. Ricardo's mistress had won, after all, for her claim on him was far more valid than mine. He would never be able to release himself fully from his devotion to her; he would try, but the bondage would remain. Paradoxically, only by releasing him from his promise to me could I hope to hold his love, hold it always as it was at that moment, untarnished with regret, which would grow to resentment and finally to bitterness and hatred for what I had caused him to give up for my sake. I must set him free.

Life could have demanded of me no more painful task.

I stayed in my room on Saturday morning until Ricardo had left, for I knew that the very sight of him, the mere touch of his hand on mine would have easily swayed me from the course on which I knew I must so unwillingly embark. At mid-morning, when I could no longer find an excuse to avoid it, I went to the stables in search of Simón. I could not help hoping I wouldn't find him there, or that one of the other stable hands would be nearby and we wouldn't be able to talk. Once I found him, once I told him what I was going to do, asked him for his help, there would be no turning back.

Simón was in one of the empty stalls, and he was alone, the stables empty except for him. He smiled when he saw me, as he always did, but his smile soon faded. "You are troubled, *Señora*," he said. "It pains me to see you so sad. Have you had word, then, about *Señorita* Cecilia?"

I shook my head. "None yet." I took a deep breath, then forced my words out in a rush, before I changed my mind. "Simón, I must leave Santiago for a time—at least two or three months, longer if possible, even forever. I need your help." Once Ricardo had gone to Lima, what did it matter what became of me? Once he gave up expecting to find me, expecting me to return, then it mattered little what happened to me. If Tomás should find me, bring me back, the news would not be likely to reach Ricardo in far-away Lima.

Simón answered, "Certainly, *Señora*. I have already told you and *Señor* Ricardo I will help you all I can. But two or three months would certainly not be long enough."

My eyes misted and I swallowed hard to try to rid myself of the lump that had risen in my throat. Then I said the words that bound me to the commitment I dreaded to make. "I'm—I'm going away. Without Ricardo." The lump was still there, and the flood of tears I could not stem rolled down my cheeks.

"Without *Señor* Ricardo?" Simón's eyes opened wide in shocked disbelief. Then he added half-accusingly, "But I thought you loved him, as he loves you!"

I brushed away my tears, but it did no good, for as fast as I wiped them from my cheeks, others came to take their place. "Oh, I do, I do! It is because I love him so very much that I must go away alone, some place he can't find me. You must help me."

Simón shook his head vehemently. "I could never help you do that, *Señora*, for it would break his heart."

272

"I know it will, but only for a time. He'll get over it. If we went away together, he would be leaving too much, ruining his life for love of me. From that, he could never recover." In answer to Simón's uncomprehending look, I continued, "You know how hard *Señor* Ricardo studies, how much he loves his studies, don't you?"

Simón nodded, seemed relieved that at last I was talking of something he understood. "Yes, *Señora*. He will be a very fine lawyer one day. He has promised me that I may come and watch him ride through the streets of Santiago in his beautiful robes."

"If we go away together, he will never wear those beautiful robes. He will never be a lawyer."

He backed away, looked at me as though he had not heard right. "But that cannot be! He has been telling me since he was that high," his hand shot out to measure the height of a very small boy, "that when he grew up, he would see the laws of Guatemala were changed, so that we *indios* had more rights. That he promised."

"But how can he do as he promised you," I asked, "if he leaves Santiago with me forever?"

His eyes were wide with surprise, then he shook his head. "I did not think of that, *Señora*. Do you really think he would never come back?"

"We couldn't, not as long as Tomás lives." I forced myself to keep talking, to forget how many long years of fearful hiding lay ahead of me, if I could remain hidden from Tomás, or the worst alternative if I could not, forget about the significance of what I was saying in my determination to make Simón understand. I could not leave without his help. I told him about the famous man, how much it would mean to Ricardo to study under him. "It would be unfair of me to let him give that up," I said. "But it's out of the question for me to go to Lima with him, and he would never leave without me, unless he knew I was gone and absolutely would not return. If he knows there is no hope of finding me, he will go. When he returns, he will become famous himself some day, maybe even be as great a man as this other. Once Ricardo has gone to Lima, it wouldn't matter so much if Tomás should find me and bring me back. It is Ricardo we must think of." Gradually, as I talked, I saw the light of understanding on Simón's face, and I finished, "But where can I go? Can you find some place for me to hide, stay hidden for at least as long as it takes to convince Ricardo I am not coming back?"

"A convent, *Señora*. Perhaps that would be best—"

I shook my head at his suggestion. It was to avoid just that

273

that I had married Tomás. "No," I said emphatically. "There must be other places I can go."

Simón frowned. "But the places I know are also known to *Señor* Ricardo, and they are too close by. You need someone to take you farther away from Santiago." He thought a minute. "There is one such man. When I tell him you are running from *don* Tomás, I think he will gladly help you. For that he would risk coming to Santiago, for he has a strong hatred of the master."

"He knows Tomás?" I questioned.

Simón nodded grimly. "Too well. The man I am thinking of disappeared almost twenty years ago, as you want to do now. He was from my village, and though he has not returned, his sister lives there still, and I am certain she could get a message to him quickly, in a few hours."

"He has stayed hidden for twenty years?"

"He escaped, *Señora*. He escaped from the mines. It was *don* Tomás who sent him there."

Our eyes locked, and I caught my breath sharply. "The man Tomás sent to the mines! Oh, I'm so glad he escaped! I didn't know." I was touched by Simón's trust of me. He had just told me the man lived close to his village.

"The *Señor* doesn't know, of course. He thinks Gonzalvo died, but he didn't. He stayed in the highlands without seeing anyone for four years before he even let his family know he still lived. He knows the mountains like no other man. He can guide you, and hide you."

"And you think he would do this?"

"I think so, *Señora*."

"How soon could he get here? I should leave tomorrow or the next day."

"But that would be impossible! It will take four days for a messenger to reach my village, another three at least for Gonzalvo to return."

"Seven days!" I gasped. "Ricardo and I were planning to leave day after tomorrow." *Were planning to leave.* I stifled a sob. How it pained me to say that, consign our plans to the past!

"Six days at the very least," he said hesitantly. "And this, I cannot promise. If the rains are very heavy, it could be longer." He shrugged helplessly.

"You will send the messenger today, this morning?"

"Right now. I know just the man to send. I will find him at once." Simón turned and hurried away on his errand.

Six days. I considered the possibility of leaving the next day, hiding somewhere nearby until Simón's guide came for me. But where would I go? I would have to depend on Simón to find a place for me to hide, take me there. And, as he had pointed out, any place known to him would also be a place familiar to Ricardo. Then Ricardo would come and find me, and convince me I must forget all my foolish notions, run away with him as we had planned. And I would be so readily persuaded to do just that! Even now, I longed to call after Simón, tell him I had changed my mind.

But if I did, if Ricardo and I did go away together, what would happen? We would be idyllically happy for a time—maybe for six months, a year, even two or three years. But some day, sooner or later, Ricardo would begin to reckon the cost of his love for me and find it too high. He would begin to think again of all the wonderful ambitions he had given up, of the opportunity of studying with the Great Man he had refused, all for me. Gradually, resentment would seep into his mind, slowly, insidiously, and it would build up and inevitably focus itself on me, the cause of his lost opportunities and broken dreams and shattered hopes.

As I turned to go back into the house, a deep melancholy enveloped me. It was done. I was set upon the course that would take all the joy and happiness from my own life. The only thing I would have left was the satisfaction of knowing I had given back Ricardo's dream.

But what could I tell him now? What plausible excuse could I possibly have for not wanting to leave on the twenty-sixth, I who had been so eager to leave sooner?

Cecilia. The guilt I felt at having planned to leave two days later, whether or not Tomás had brought her back by then, was real, and surely Ricardo would not think it odd if I told him that I hesitated to leave before they returned, that my concern for Cecilia was even stronger than my dread of encountering the husband I detested again. Then, if they should return before the man from Simón's village came for me, I would have to find an additional excuse to postpone our departure.

Tomás. I shuddered at the possibility of seeing him again, but it could not be helped.

That evening at supper, when Ricardo mentioned riding out on our planned picnic the next day, I tried to sound calm as I said, "I'm looking forward to that. Let's go and leave our things as we had planned, but—I've been thinking, we really shouldn't leave until Cecilia comes home."

He looked at me as though he thought he had not heard right. "Not leave as soon as I collect my legacy? But I don't understand! You've been so anxious."

I lowered my eyes so he couldn't see the pain it cost me to say the words that would change our lives. "But Cecilia will need us! She'll be so alone!" I stared at the bright pattern of threads in the tablecloth. "We just can't leave till she gets back, even if it does mean facing Tomás again. Don't you see, she is going to need us desperately to stand between her and Tomás, shield her from him? There's no telling what he may demand of her. He may force her into marriage immediately, more than likely to someone she abhors." I raised my eyes to him at last, for my concern for Cecilia was very real. "Oh, Ricardo, she told me she thought she was going to have Manuel's baby!"

"No!" Ricardo dropped his cup to his saucer with a clatter. "Why, that dirty bastard! Excuse me, Carlota, but Cecilia was so innocent, so—"

"It's no use blaming Manuel now," I reminded him. "It doesn't matter any more. What does matter is that she will need us here when Tomás brings her back. She will be so alone."

Ricardo agreed with me at once, and I knew he had been more troubled at the thought of deserting his sister than I had realized. "I didn't want you to know how worried I was about her. You were so anxious to leave, I didn't want to suggest we wait. But I'm glad you suggested it. We'll talk to her, see if we can persuade her to leave with us, come to Mexico with us."

"She will have no reason to want to stay in Santiago," I answered. *But Ricardo, my love,* my heart cried out in agony, *you and I will not be leaving together, not be going to Mexico together!* Perhaps Ricardo could take her to Lima with him.

We set out early next morning for what seemed, on the surface, to be another of our Sunday picnic rides. I had no need to explain to Simón that it was necessary for Ricardo to continue to think I was going with him, so once we were in the stables, he helped us empty much of the picnic fare and hide it under a pile of hay. We refilled the hamper with the things we had left with him earlier, things we would need for our journey to Mexico, a journey we would never make.

As we rode out of the city, I tried to cast off the heavy sadness I felt in the knowledge that this would be our last such day together, ever. It must be a day to remember, I thought determinedly, a carefree and happy day. But my mood was solemn, and my attempts at gaiety were so forced and unnatural that they did not ring true.

By early afternoon, we had hidden our travel packs in a dry sheltered place Ricardo had chosen and gone on to a quiet spot higher up in the mountains. The air was noticeably cooler, and after the prolonged and unaccustomed heaviness of the air in Santiago, it was soothing and refreshing.

The heaviness of my spirit was not so easily thrown off. We were leaning against the broad trunk of a towering tree after we had eaten our light lunch, and I had to keep reminding myself that I must not let Ricardo suspect the gloom that hung over me. Yet it was impossible to act happy when I knew this was the last time we would ever be together without the constraint of having other people about. I tried to make gay little comments, tried to inject a lightness I did not feel into my voice and into my laughter. But I should have known Ricardo would not be so easily fooled. How could two people as close as we fail to sense what the other one felt?

Once, when I had tried particularly hard to make my laughter sound spontaneous and sparkling, he moved around to face me and gently tilted my face toward him, leaning down to brush my lips with a soft kiss. Then he put his arms around me.

"You are worrying far too much," he said, smiling reassuringly at me. "Everything will be all right. Trust me."

He assumed I was worried about Tomás's return, of course. He could not know that such fears had been pushed to the back of my mind by a far more serious concern. Still, I accepted the excuse he provided. I settled into his arms. "When I'm with you," I said, "I'm not afraid of anything." But it was a lie, for I was wretchedly afraid even at that very moment, appalled at the thought of leaving him. But I was even more afraid not to leave him, to watch in helpless horror as his love turned slowly to a hatred he would be powerless to hide from me. I was desperately frightened of a lifetime without him, endless years of the unfulfilled desire for his presence, his touch, the sound of his voice, just the knowledge that wherever he was, it was I to whom he would be returning.

"Ricardo," I said, looking up at him and trying to fix forever in my mind the way the flecks of sunlight filtering through the treetops glinted on his red-gold hair, making it shine like burnished copper, "remember that whatever happens, I love you more than life itself, and will go on loving you forever."

"Hush such foolish talk," he admonished gently. "You sound as though we were to be parted. Nothing will go wrong. You'll see. We will leave as soon after Father brings Cecilia home as we can. We'll just have to see how things go, but I'll work it out."

I didn't answer. Something was going to go wrong, for it was to be of my own doing, though it would be like picking

277

up a knife and cutting out my very heart. Would he understand why I had left, would he realize why I had to do it? Tears filled my eyes, tears he noticed at once and tenderly kissed away.

But my tears had affected him, too, and when he took my hand and pulled me to my feet, his seriousness matched mine. He led me to a smooth patch of ground and pulled me down beside him. "We must start back soon," he said as we lay down and he cradled my head on his arm. "But before we do, I would sample your gypsy charms. We've had far too many lonesome nights lately."

"Far too many," I agreed, my voice choking on a sob as I thought of the endless nights to come. I closed my arms around his neck and pulled him toward me with a desperation I could not hide, and long after our hunger for each other was satisfied, I continued to cling to him fiercely. How could I ever bear to leave him?

The next day was Ricardo's birthday, the day to which we had looked forward for so long. But now it was no longer the day on which we would leave Santiago and Tomás behind us forever, and the only thing that made it eventful was that Ricardo collected his legacy from Carlos. To me, that had become meaningless, for it had been important only as the means by which we could escape together to a new life. And now I knew that had been only a foolish dream.

Still, I stitched some of the coins into our clothing as we had planned. I would need some money when I left, and Ricardo must not suspect I was not going away with him. The biggest part of his legacy was in silver doubloons, much of it in gold *pesos,* some in *ocho escudo* pieces. Only a small fraction of it could be hidden in clothing. The bulk and weight of it amazed us both, and would certainly have been cumbersome to carry.

Would have been. I sighed heavily. There was no longer any need to worry about either its bulk or its weight.

After I had made my heartbreaking decision, the days seemed to speed by at an accelerated pace. I could scarcely take my eyes from Ricardo when we were together, and each time he smiled at me with his sweet and loving smile, I had to choke back the tears. How many years lay ahead of me, empty years without his smile to warm me, his touch to thrill me? How could I bear such emptiness?

And always at least once during each day, there would be a time when I would tell myself that certainly such a sacrifice would not be necessary, after all; that perhaps Ricardo's ambitions weren't as vital to him as I had thought; that in my doubt and self-guilt I had exaggerated in my own mind their

278

importance to him. But then he would come home from listening to the Great Man, or from a talk with him, and I would know that I had not overestimated their importance to him at all.

On the day after Ricardo's birthday, I awoke with a particularly heavy heart, for I couldn't help remembering that we should, according to our original plans, have spent the previous night well away from Santiago. And it would have been so easy, with Tomás still gone in pursuit of Cecilia! What better chance could we have had to escape from him? But instead of escaping from the man I despised, I was making plans to run from the one who made my heart leap just by entering a room, who gave meaning and purpose to my life.

I can't bear it, I thought as I dressed that morning. *I have said I would leave him, but how can I?*

It was very early, and I wandered aimlessly toward the stables. As I passed by the kitchen garden, I looked regretfully toward the empty rows that no longer held carrots for my favorites; now, anything edible was quickly taken for the stew-pot. I walked through the stables, pausing a moment or two at the various stalls to speak to one of the horses, stroke a silky nose. Which of them would take me away from Ricardo, away from my love? El Moro, the smaller of the two Arab horses, I supposed. Tomás had taken the other one. My guide could ride any of the other saddle horses. They would carry us away, away from Ricardo as well as Tomás. Away to what, I wondered? A lifetime of loneliness in a simple hut somewhere? It would certainly not be an easy task for a *chapetona* to remain invisible in Guatemala, even in the most remote places; villagers would talk, and the talk would spread, would in all likelihood eventually reach as far as Santiago. But, hopefully, the *indios* would talk mostly with each other, not with their masters and mistresses, so it was possible Tomás might never find out where I was, come after me and drag me back to a life of misery with him. But once Ricardo was gone, what did it matter? What difference would it make to me where I was, for everything that had any meaning would be gone, and I would be only an empty shell, a woman without hope, without life, without love.

"Good morning, *Señora*."

Startled out of my unhappy thoughts by Simón's voice, I turned and tried to smile at him, but the effort was weak, and I imagined my smile came out more as a grimace.

"Good morning, Simón," I answered dully, giving up the effort of trying to smile, too weary to pretend any more than was absolutely necessary to a peace of mind I did not feel. With Ricardo, I must continue to act as though nothing was

279

wrong. But Simón knew why a deep sorrow filled my heart; with him I need no longer pretend.

"It is three days since the messenger left," he said. "I think the weather has not been too wet anywhere in the mountains. With good luck, he could have talked with Gonzalvo's sister by now."

I made no answer. It was wrong to hope that any disaster might have overtaken Simón's messenger, but I could not help but grasp at that frail possibility. If Gonzalvo did not come, I would still have tried, wouldn't I? I couldn't possibly strike out alone, for I needed his knowledge of the mountains in order to have them swallow me as though I had been wiped from the face of the earth. If Gonzalvo was ill, or couldn't be found, or refused to come, what more could I do?

Ricardo would still grow to hate you. That unwelcome voice, that unwanted reminder! But there was no denying the truth of it. No, there was no other way. The truth remained no matter how I tried to push it from me. I must leave.

"It grieves me much to see you so sad, *Señora*," Simón said sympathetically. "I think perhaps *Señor Ricardo* would rather be with you than to wear his black robe and ride through the streets of Santiago behind the trumpets."

"Do you really think so?" Eagerly, I grasped again at the hope I had just discarded, no less desperately than a man dying of thirst snatches at a proffered drink of water.

"It may be so."

Maybe it is so, I thought with renewed hope, only too willing to believe it was. Simón had shown before that he possessed a great deal of insight. And he certainly knew Ricardo well. Could he be right?

But less than an hour later, as I sat across from Ricardo, watching him bolt his breakfast of precious eggs without even seeming to realize what he was eating in his eagerness to be gone to the University, I knew I had only been following a mirage. Talking with Simón, I had heard what I had wanted to hear, built my own illusion from the frail substance of his words. But now that illusion dissolved before me much as I have heard a non-existent oasis dissolves before the eyes of a parched and weary desert traveler. Only reality remained, the reality of Ricardo hurrying off to listen enthralled to the Great Man.

And so it continued, and my spirit was as buffeted and battered as though it stood in the winds of a shifting gale, alternately blown this way and that, between hope and despair. But always, I ended in despair, each time yet more desolate than I had been before.

That night, Ricardo and I sat in the family sitting room, he eagerly rewriting the notes he had taken that day, and I pretending to work on a piece of needlepoint. But I could not keep my mind on my labors, and at length I gave up the effort. Putting it aside, I sat silently, deep in the depression that held me. It was some time before Ricardo looked up and smiled at me.

"You're sad tonight, my Carlota," he said. It was late, and the servants never came to the front of the house after they had cleared away the supper dishes, so it was safe to talk. From what had by now become ingrained habit, we kept our voices low. "What is it? Are you worried about Cecilia? Or about us?"

I answered indirectly. "It has been eleven days since she left. I wonder if Tomás has caught her yet?"

"I suppose he must have. Since you're sure he's going to catch her, it's most likely to happen not too far from Santiago."

"They could return at any time," I agreed despondently. With their return, even these quiet evenings alone with Ricardo would be over. And they were all I had left. The thought deepened my depression.

"Well," Ricardo said in an attempt at cheerfulness, "the sooner they return, the sooner we can be gone, hopefully taking Cecilia with us."

"Yes." I forced the lie to my lips, forced myself to smile at him, knowing that I must cling to the myth that I still planned to go away with him.

I could not bear to take myself away from Ricardo that night. When the candles were sputtering their last, he stood up and stacked his papers. He had been copying his notes in a small fine hand, and when I asked him what he was doing, he replied that he was condensing them so that he could take them with us when we went to Mexico. How desperately he was clinging to the dream he thought he must relinquish! He did not know it was the dream we shared of being together always that was never to be.

I removed the cut lengths of yarn from my lap and stood up. After Ricardo blew out the candles he drew me into the darkest corner of the room, where he gathered me into his arms. "Good-night, my love," he whispered as he brought his lips down on mine.

"Good-night, my dearest Ricardo," I answered, clinging to him tightly in my desperate need of him, grateful that he had sensed that need and known it was stronger than the necessity for caution.

Unwillingly, we drew apart. I went to my room and closed the door behind me. The emptiness of the room closed in on

281

me, and I thought, *This is how it will be forever: an empty room, an empty heart.*

As I undressed, the emptiness became more oppressive, unbearably so. I sat on the edge of the bed in my nightgown and started to raise my feet onto the mattress, but I stopped. Soon, there would be nothing but this deep silence and the dreadful loneliness, and I must force myself to accept it, tolerate it. Then I must accept, too, the knowledge that I would never again be able to move into Ricardo's waiting embrace as I had a few minutes before. But now, he was here, in this very house, only a short distance away from me. Our embrace had only left me feeling more alone. I needed him desperately, hungered not for a sexual union, but a quiet comforting nearness, the reassurance of his body pressing intimately against mine. My yearning for his touch was so strong that I did not, could not consider consequences at that moment. Even if it meant Tomás coming upon us together, I could not stay away from Ricardo that night.

I opened the door and ran around the tiled porch to Ricardo's room.

"I had to come," I said simply as I closed the door behind me.

"I'm glad you did," he said, and held out his arms to welcome me to his bed. He helped me settle beside him, comfortably, in the crook of his arm, and I felt the strength his nearness gave me.

He kissed my forehead. "Now, relax and go to sleep. Rest well, my darling."

Content in the knowledge that he had sensed my precise needs, as I had known he would even though he could not know the reason for them, I was soon lulled by the rhythmic sound of his deep breathing as he slept beside me, and I drifted into a sound and trouble-free sleep for the first time in many nights.

I knew nothing more until he woke me gently and told me it would soon be dawn. I returned to my room, feeling renewed and strangely soothed and strengthened by my night of rest in Ricardo's arms.

Santiago—Wednesday, July 28, 1773

CHAPTER XVI

They stood there, Cecilia and Tomás, framed in the archway that led from the kitchen patio, their faces half obscured by the deep night shadows. I strained to see them, just as I had before.

And like an actress who has rehearsed a part and knows well what must be said, I took in the scene before me, moving my eyes from one to the other and asked, "Manuel?" This time I was certain I had said it aloud, for I heard my voice crack.

Ricardo and I had been in the family sitting room after supper Wednesday night when we heard the muffled sounds of activity coming from the stable yard. We had looked at each other and wordlessly moved together out of the room and into the main patio, knowing too well what we would see. But Ricardo had only heard my description of the scene that greeted us, and was not fully prepared for the poignancy of it. I heard him take in his breath sharply, and knew he was profoundly shaken by the impact of what he saw.

Again, as in a well-rehearsed scene, Cecilia looked at me as I knew she would, her eyes dry but filled with an overwhelming sorrow gone far beyond the shedding of tears. She made no attempt to answer me. Whatever had happened to Manuel, she was not able to talk about it just yet.

They emerged from the deep shadows of the archway into the relative brightness of the patio, Tomás propelling Cecilia along by means of the firm grasp he maintained on her arm. Cecilia, seemingly devoid of any volition of her own, moved wherever he pushed her.

As I watched them, I was reminded of Diablo the night

Tomás had tied him to the back of the wagon and taken him to the farm. There was in Cecilia's manner, in the way she let herself be shoved about, the same docility, the same apathy and surrender. I remembered how gay and full of zest and hope she had been the day she left, and I was suddenly enraged that Tomás could have done this to her. But hurling epithets at him would do no good now. It was Cecilia who needed our attention, and as soon as I recovered from the shock of seeing her so utterly defeated I ran to her.

"Oh, my dear, I am so sorry!" I put my arm around her shoulder.

She nodded, scarcely perceptibly, in acknowledgement of my useless words.

Ricardo also moved quickly toward her, ignoring Tomás as I had. "Poor, dear little sister," he said compassionately.

"I think," Tomás said pompously, "that I managed to get her into the house without being seen. I've sent Simón to fetch our horses down at the end of the street. We can say she has been in retreat at one of the convents to pray and purify herself for her coming marriage. Then, as soon as is seemly, she can be married. There is a man who has a farm near mine whose blood lines are pure. He is quite poor, and will welcome her dowry. There will be talk, of course, but it will soon die down after she is gone from the city."

I looked at him in utter disgust. Had he no consideration at all for her feelings? Did he think she was a puppet, to be maneuvered through motions as he pulled on first this string and then that one? Ricardo's thoughts obviously paralleled mine, for he glared at Tomás with open contempt.

"There will be no forced marriage, Father. All of Santiago knows she ran away with Manuel. The time for pretending is over." Returning his full attention to Cecilia, he leaned down and scooped her up into his arms. "Come, sweet sister, Carlota will see to having Teresa prepare a warm bath for you. You look about to drop from fatigue and strain."

Cecilia looked up at Ricardo gratefully before her head dropped against his chest, and she let him carry her to her room, where she submitted to Teresa's and my ministrations. After we had bathed her, I brought some of my salves and we put them on the many scratches and cuts and festered insect bites all over her. She let us do this, speaking only in toneless monosyllables when she talked at all. For a while, I was afraid she had lost her reason. But any mad people I had seen in the course of my life had eyes that were either blank and lifeless and dull, or wild with an unnatural frenzy, and Cecilia's were neither. They were filled with an unspeakable hurt, and bewilderment, but they were not mad.

She did not begin to talk for hours. With no explanation to Tomás, I had taken my things from our room and moved in with her. She appeared to be sleeping when I blew out the candle and climbed into the bed beside her, but as I lay quietly by her side, I realized from the irregularity of her breathing that she was still awake. From time to time, she emitted a long painful sigh. At last, her breathing became easier, unlabored and even, and I thought she finally slept.

Just as I relaxed and was about to give myself up to sleep as well, I heard the plaintive hoot of an owl close by. It cut eerily into the silence of the night with a strange unworldly sound, and I stirred uneasily.

"You're not asleep either, are you, Carlota?" Cecilia's voice was surprisingly wide awake. "Did you hear the owl? I wonder if he was calling over our roof?"

Her words brought back the memory of the little *cenzontle* and the fortune that had so angered Ricardo, something to do with an owl calling over our roof-top. "What is the significance of it?" I asked.

"The *indios* are very superstitious. They say if an owl calls over a house, someone in that house will die. Foolishness, but they really do believe it."

That, then, was why Ricardo was so upset with the fortune, afraid it might frighten me if I knew. "It does have a sad sound to it, doesn't it?" I said. "I can see why the *indios* would come to be superstitious about it." But it was the very eeriness of the call itself rather than any beliefs about its significance that made me feel vaguely apprehensive. Coming on top of the events of the evening, I found it unsettling and even alarming, but I did not tell Cecilia that.

As Cecilia started to talk, I soon forgot about the owl. I felt she was not so much talking to me as she was sorting out her thoughts for her own benefit. I was glad I was there to listen, which I did mostly in silence, saying only enough to let her know I was awake as she poured out her thoughts.

"He ran," she began as though she had already been telling me about the time when Tomás had found them. "Manuel ran when Father got close to us. He ran away and left me."

I remembered Ricardo's low opinion of Manuel. He had been right, then, and Cecilia had been blinded to Manuel's weakness by her love for him. Still, I wondered if they might not have been happy together if Tomás had not appeared and exposed that weakness. It was Tomás at whom I directed all my venomous thoughts; not Manuel.

Cecilia paused for such a long time that I thought she was going to say no more, but finally she continued, "It has been my misfortune to love weak men, Carlota. Why do you suppose that is? I once loved a boy named Luis, when we were both very young. We vowed we would marry only each other, but when his family told him they were bringing him a bride from Spain, one of his cousins, he accepted the news meekly because he was deathly afraid of his father's disapproval. And then there was Rafael, who promised to climb the highest mountains and swim the swiftest rivers for me. But that was before I caught the pox, and he was actually afraid of the sight of my face after it was marked, and cringed from me. Then, after I thought I could never love again, I met Manuel. I thought his love for me was strong, but it wasn't as strong as his fear of Father." She gave a short little laugh. "He did apologize, just before he fled. He said he was sorry to have to desert me that way. 'You are his daughter,' he said. 'He will not harm you. But I am a *mestizo,* and he will say I have abducted you, and you know what they will do to me.' So he asked my permission to go. What was I to say, Carlota? Was I to tell him, no, you cannot leave. You must be willing to die for me? I couldn't make him want to stay. That was the thing. He didn't want to stay with me, face up to Father. Even if I had refused him my permission to leave, begged him to stay, he would have gone. And that is what I couldn't forgive, not at first."

"Perhaps he really did want to stay with you," I suggested, feeling I must say something, "but he knew it would do no good in the end."

"That's always possible." She sounded amused, as though she must humor me by agreeing. "I've been lying here these past hours, thinking. Now that I'm here, resting in my own bed, and I no longer have to use my strength to keep moving, I've been able to lie here and think. You've no idea what a luxury that is, Carlota, to have time to think again. When you're moving through the mountains, not certain where you are or even which way it is you want to go, knowing pursuit is not far behind you, you have no time to worry about anything but how to keep going, away from that pursuit, hoping you can keep just a little way ahead of it. And then you come to a river swollen with recent rain, and you have to concentrate all your energies and thoughts on finding a place to cross that river. And all the while, you know the pursuit is gaining on you."

"We kept Tomás from finding out you had gone until late Sunday," I said. "It was the best we could do."

"I know you tried, and I appreciated it. But it doesn't matter any more what happened. It's all over." She paused. "Even the child, if there was one. That's over, too. It's best that way. What would I do with a child now?"

286

Cecilia spoke without bitterness, and that was, to me, the surprising thing. Even when she had been talking about the weaknesses of the men it had been her misfortune to love, there was an acceptance, a vigor in her voice that heartened me, made me hope that she was strong enough to take this most recent blow life had inflicted upon her, that what I had taken for docility and the breaking of her spirit when she had come in with Tomás had only been confusion and fatigue.

She continued. "Since I have had time for the luxury of thought tonight, I have done a lot of thinking about Manuel. I have forgiven him completely in my heart. I have even said a few prayers for his safety, and his happiness. He can never return to Santiago, of course, but I hope, wherever he goes, that he will find peace. And Father. I bear him no grudge, either."

"You have a generous heart," I said, brushing a tear from the corner of my eye. In her place, I could not have found it so easy to forgive either of them.

"God has given me the strength to set myself free from bitterness and resentment. I have felt His strength actually flow into me these last few hours as I was lying here. Can you believe that though I haven't slept for more days than I can count, I no longer feel even a little tired? God is my strength, Carlota. That I have learned.

"Do you remember before I left, I told you I felt that at last my life seemed to have fallen into a pattern? Well, now I truly believe that all of this—even Father bringing me home—is part of that pattern, that it was designed to test me, strengthen me, make me see what it was always meant for me to do. Now I am certain.

"In the morning, very early, I will leave for the Convent of the Clarisas. I am telling you this so that you can tell Ricardo, and you and he can both know that my heart has found peace at last. I will turn to God, and through Him, through my prayers, I will always be close to you both. Father will assume I have left to find Manuel. I doubt if he will even try to find me again. I think that long before he caught me, he became as weary of the chase as I."

"But, Cecilia, are you sure? Are you very sure that this is what you want?" Even though she had left no doubt in my mind that she would be unwavering in her decision, I felt compelled to question her.

"I am very very sure." She sighed deeply, but this time her sigh was one of release, of contentment. "Now, I think we should both get some sleep. I will remember you in my prayers always. You have become as dear as a sister to me."

287

"And you to me," I said, scarcely able to talk through the choking in my throat. "Good-night, dear Cecilia."

"Good-bye, Carlota."

I closed my eyes and slept, and when I opened them again as the first pale light of morning filtered through the cracks in the shutters, she was gone. It was not until then that I remembered that she had said not *good-night*, but *good-bye*.

Ricardo was not surprised when I told him about Cecilia as we breakfasted together, without Tomás, who was sleeping off his exhaustion.

He listened as I repeated what she had told me, then nodded. "I'm happy for her. I've always felt that Father had us figured backwards, that it was she who had the vocation for a religious life, not I. She'd have become a novice three years ago if Father would have permitted it. What a lot of pain she would have been spared! But now, I think she has found peace at last."

"I'm certain she has. Oh, Ricardo, if you only could have heard her last night when she was telling me what she decided! She was so positive, so unwavering, so—so contented." I sighed. "But we'll never see her again. There's something so final about her choosing the Clarisas. They're so strict, so cut off from the world, for all that they're right in the middle of Santiago!"

"That's true. But remember it was her own choice. Of all the orders, she chose them. She'll be happy there, I'm sure of it. Besides, we won't be here to visit with her anyway," he reminded me, finding my hand and giving it an affectionate squeeze.

You're right, I thought. *We won't be here. But it will not be as you think, for you will be in Lima and I will be— where?* "We must be happy for Cecilia," I agreed. "She is free of Tomás, and she has gone where she wants to be."

"And now we're free to leave. We've seen her safely home, safely out of Father's reach. He can never hurt her again. I'm so glad you suggested we wait for her." He released my hand.

I yearned to put my hand back in his, never withdraw it till we were far away from Santiago, together. If he had suggested we leave right then, at that very moment, I would not have had the strength to refuse. Never had I been more ready to forget my resolve. I would have thrown it aside at the slightest encouragement.

But now it was Ricardo who said we must wait a while longer. "We can't go while Father can follow us too closely," he said. "We must give ourselves as much head start as we can, at least twelve hours or so. We'll just have to see how things go, watch for our chance."

"Maybe he'll go to the farm again today." I said evasively.

He nodded. "He just might, to avoid any embarrassing questions about Cecilia. On the other hand, he's hard to predict. Since he's apparently already decided to put out the story that she is in retreat at one of the convents, he's quite likely to stay here and face it out, pretend nothing is wrong." He sighed and pushed himself away from the table. "Since it seems we can't go just yet, I will have to leave you once more. Find out what you can this morning about Father's plans. Then we'll be better able to decide what to do. We must leave as soon as we dare." He stood up, and with a final touch of our hands, he was gone.

Cecilia had guessed right about Tomás. He awakened late in the morning, and emerged from our room in his dressing gown, his eyes still heavy-lidded with sleep. When I told him she was gone again, he stamped into her room as though he didn't believe me. Finally convinced, he stormed and raged about the house a while longer, but in the end he took no action. Perhaps even the demon in him was weary. Certainly Tomás showed signs of the tremendous exertion the effort of catching Cecilia had cost him. That day, he looked easily ten years older than his age of forty-six.

After his angry tirade on being convinced she had left, he sat down heavily on one of the chairs near the door to our room. I had continued trimming some of the plants in the large pots nearby after I had broken the news to him.

"So she's left," he said tonelessly, "and on foot this time! Well, let her go to her lowly *mestizo*, then! I'll not fetch her back again. We will say she's still in retreat. No one knows she was here last night besides us and Simón and Teresa. And they know they had better not say one word about it to anyone, or I'll flog them within an inch of their lives!"

"They can be trusted," I said hastily, taking off my gardening gloves and putting them down on the tile floor of the porch. "They would never say anything to hurt Cecilia."

"Cecilia!" Tomás repeated her name angrily, scowling at me. "I never want to hear her name cross your lips again, except as it must be used to answer direct questions about her. She is in retreat at one of the convents. She doesn't want it known which one. That is what we will say."

I nodded my agreement, wondering if he had any suspicion how close to the truth he was.

"As far as I am concerned," he continued, his expression grim, "she died last night. And with her died the dynasty I hoped to establish," he paused to look at me disdainfully, "since you seem to be barren."

I looked at him in surprise, not because of his last remark

289

about me, but because of the other things he said. Was that really the way he envisioned himself, I wondered? The founder of a dynasty? But why must it have been through Cecilia, if not through me? Why not Ricardo? "There is Ricardo," I said, testing.

"Oh, yes." There was no missing the sarcasm in his voice. "There is Ricardo." He dismissed the subject with an impatient wave of his hand and stood up. "I hope there are eggs for my breakfast."

What utter callousness to concern himself so about what he would eat for breakfast when he had just discovered the loss of his daughter, the daughter he professed to love!

"Alberto brought some from the farm last week. I'll have the cook boil two if there are any left." I hurried toward the kitchen, glad of an excuse to break away from him. Every moment spent in his company was abhorrent to me.

After I gave instructions to the cook, I went out to the stables and found Simón anxiously waiting to talk to me. "Señora, he is here. Gonzalvo has come!"

With his words, all the hope drained from me. I had not known until Simón said that how much I had relied on the possibility that he wouldn't arrive.

"Already?" was all I could say, and it was a cry of dismay.

Simón understood my reaction at once. "You do not have to go away with him, Señora. He will not mind leaving again without you." He watched me with his soft compassionate eyes.

I saw him through the mist of the tears I was forcing myself to withhold. "I must go away. I must, for Ricardo's sake." I said the words more for my own benefit than for Simón's.

He shook his head and sighed deeply. "Then when would you go?"

"When?" He was waiting for me to name a time, not some vague time in the future, but soon, in the next few hours, today. My heart felt like a gigantic stone in my breast, and would, I knew, forevermore. I opened my mouth to speak, but I could not bring myself to name a time. How could I leave my love, my life? How could I?

When I did not answer, Simón spoke again. "If I may make a suggestion, Señora, this is the day of Santa Marta. Always, the Señora de Ortega Batres has a big fiesta on this day, and always the Señor goes."

"Oh, yes," I said, remembering Marta's invitation. "I had forgotten all about it."

"The fiesta is always a very long one," he continued, "and always the Señor stays late and drinks much wine. If you would perhaps make an excuse not to go to the fiesta, if you felt suddenly too ill to go, then you and Gonzalvo could leave this afternoon. I am certain *don* Tomás will not stay home because of you."

"This afternoon?" Leave so soon? My heart lurched. "Wouldn't it be better to wait until dark?" I grasped eagerly at the hope of any delay, however small.

Simón shook his head. "*Señor* Ricardo might stay at home tonight, and then how could you leave? Anyway, Gonzalvo and I have been talking, and we think it would be best if you could leave in the light. We have made a plan. About half an hour after the *Señor* leaves, we will bring the closed carriage around to the front of the house. Gonzalvo will be your coachman. He is much the size of Alberto, and dressed in Alberto's livery he can easily pass for him if he keeps his head turned away from the house of the ever-watchful *Señora* Ramirez. The carriage itself will block her view of you as you get inside, and she will assume you are dressed for the fiesta of *Señora* de Ortega Batres, and that you are going to join the *Señor* there. The carriage will start toward the Ortega Batres house, but it will turn the other way when it is out of sight, and take you to the edge of town. There, two horses will be waiting for you and Gonzalvo. Then you will have some hours of good daylight in which to travel fast, and the hours of darkness for cover. That is our plan, *Señora*." He sent me a searching look. "If you still think you should go. Did you hear the owl call last night?"

"The owl is only a bird, Simón," I admonished, yet chilled by his reminder, by the remembered sound of the owl's dismal call.

"But he knows, *Señora*, he knows."

Before I could answer, Tomás's voice rang out impatiently from the door to the stables, summoning Simón, who scurried away at once. I turned and began to stroke El Moro's nose, as though this were merely another of my casual visits to the stables.

Tomás walked in and found me there as soon as he had sent Simón to saddle a horse for him. "Really, Carlota," he said, eyeing me disapprovingly, "I would think you could find better things to do with your time than coming in here to pet the horses. Pilar never would have thought of entering the stables except when she was going riding. It's unladylike of you to spend so much of your time here."

"Perhaps it is," I agreed without thinking, too concerned with other thoughts to pick up the petty battle of wills between us. In the past six weeks, I had forgotten how his presence wearied me. That, at least, I would be leaving be-

291

hind. But, I thought with a fresh stab of pain, I would be leaving Ricardo as well.

Tomás looked at me in surprise for a minute, but he said nothing. A few moments later, Simón came in to tell him his horse was saddled. Before he turned to go, he asked me if Marta had said anything about her name's day party.

I nodded. "She mentioned it last week."

"Well, then, we'll be going, of course. I always go about three o'clock. See that you're ready. This time, I want you to wear your rubies."

He wouldn't be leaving today for the farm, then, but would stay and go to Marta's fiesta, as Simón had surmised.

"Yes, Tomás," I answered automatically. "I do hope I'll be able to go," I added, remembering Simón's suggested plan. "I don't feel too well this morning. A touch of fever, perhaps."

"Shall I stop in and tell Dr. Lopez to call?" There was no gentleness or concern in his voice, but only a frank annoyance at my complaint.

I shook my head. "That won't be necessary. I won't be bled, and that's all he knows to do. I'll try some of my herbs. They may help."

"You must certainly force yourself to go, if you possibly can," he said gruffly. "It is important that we face up to this business of the past few weeks and act as though everything is fine."

Always the pretense. "Yes, Tomás," I answered. "I'll see how I feel later."

He rode off. Ordinarily, I would have been amused at the thought that my sudden unexpected meekness must certainly have left him puzzled.

Ricardo came home at noon, and I was waiting for him in the small patio. I heard the sound of his arrival in the stable yard, heard him greet Simón. *The last time*, I thought. *This is the last time I will ever wait for him here, the last time my heart will jump at the sound of his voice. Never more will I feel his arms enclosing me. Never more will my lips know the pleasure of meeting his, or my body the boundless joy of becoming one with his.*

How could such sorrow be borne?

I was seated on the stone bench nearest the chairs under the roofed area, as usual. On my lap I held an open book, but I hadn't even looked at the title of it as I grabbed it off the shelf in the family sitting room a short while before. Nor had I looked at it since. As Ricardo came in the creaking gate, I jumped up to greet him, and my book skidded across the tiles.

"Ricardo!"

292

"Easy, my love," he whispered, picking up the book and smiling as he handed it back to me. "You'd better sit down again over there where you were, and I will sit here." He dropped into the chair nearest my bench. "Now, tell me quickly before Father comes in what you found out about his plans. Will he be going back to the farm today?"

When I was once more settled with the open book in my lap, I answered, "No. Today is the day of Santa Marta, and we're invited to Marta's name's day party."

He hit the arm of his chair with the flat of his hand. "What bad luck! I had forgotten all about that. Father always goes. You'll be going with him, of course." I didn't answer, and he continued, "Maybe that's not so bad, after all. Marta's fiesta is always an all-day affair, ending late at night with a fireworks display. Father holds his wine well enough, but after such a long day of drinking, I'll wager he sleeps deeply. And he's already thoroughly exhausted from chasing after Cecilia and Manuel, I'm sure."

I nodded, agreed, "I'm sure he'll sleep deeply."

Ricardo was too engrossed in his own thoughts to notice the lack of enthusiasm with which I answered him. "We must leave tonight," he said. "Otherwise, you'd have to share his bed, and that I don't think I could bear."

"Nor I," I answered truthfully.

He frowned. "But what about tonight? Are you certain you can keep him from—from touching you before he falls asleep? If I thought—"

I said carefully, "I can promise you he'll not put a hand on me tonight."

"You're sure? I know he'll be heavy with wine, but, if I thought there were any chance—"

"There's no chance at all," I said firmly, knowing that I would be far from Tomás's reach by nightfall.

As we talked, I watched Ricardo closely, trying to store in my memory his every gesture, every change of expression on his beloved face. There would be endless lonely days and lonelier nights in which I would have only these memories to draw upon.

"As soon as you're certain he's asleep tonight," Ricardo said, "come out to the stables. Earlier this evening, I'll take the horses out of sight just beyond the bridge. I'll be waiting for you there, for Simón to bring you just as soon as you can break away after you're sure Father is sound asleep. It will take you longer to get there on foot, but it will be better that way. Give Simón everything you have to bring except your clothing before you leave for Marta's." He smiled at me.

"Just think, my darling! Half a day and we'll be gone from here forever!"

If only it were going to be as he had just described it! It was not easy to return his smile when I remembered that in a matter of only a few short hours, I would be riding away from Santiago without him, never to see his beloved face again. It took all my effort to keep my voice even as I asked, "Will you go back to the University this afternoon?" I had to be certain he would not be home when I must leave. I waited for his answer, the tears I dared not release crowding behind my eyelids so tightly it made my eyes ache.

"I had better, hadn't I? Besides, I may get to have one more talk with Doctor de la Cueva. It's such a pleasure to discuss our problems with him, Carlota. He is as appalled at the strength and power of the church here in Santiago as I am, and he sees the time it takes to get word from Madrid as the biggest problem of our government, with no Viceroy here."

He talked on for a few minutes, telling me things that the Great Man had said, but I no longer paid any attention to his words. Even now, I thought bitterly, his mistress must intrude, clinging to him selfishly. Not even in these last few minutes we would ever have together would she let him be altogether mine!

I jumped up, unable to bear it a moment longer. "I had better see about dinner. Tomás will be home any minute, and he doesn't like to be kept waiting."

I ran from the small patio, knowing that if I had stayed there one second longer, I would have dissolved hopelessly into tears.

I had no need to remind myself to pick at my food that day in order to set the stage for my feigned illness a little later, for I was entirely without appetite. Tomás noticed it.

"Carlota, you must lie down for an hour or so before we go. I could use a nap as well, but I must go over the accounts." Then he added, "I trust you are wearing something fashionable? Even the Captain General and his wife always come to Marta's party."

I didn't bother to remind him that my clothes were probably the most fashionable in all of Santiago. It wasn't worth the effort. I said simply, "I have had my red silk dress pressed."

He nodded. "That will do, I suppose." He never would have admitted being pleased over my choice. "You will be certain to wear your rubies? All of them, the bracelet as well as the earrings and necklace, of course."

"Of course." I could not resist adding, "And my diamond

294

bracelet and sapphire ring as well." Had my heart not been so heavy, I would have found the situation laughable. I was promising to dress as gaudily as possible and wear twice as many jewels as the limits of good taste would dictate. It was just such an ostentatious display of wealth that Tomás liked, so he would have been hard-pressed to find fault with it. But though I was going through the motions of preparing for the party, I had never had any intention of getting dressed for it in the finery I had just described.

As soon as we had finished our meal and risen from the table, Ricardo said that he must go.

"So soon?" I tried to keep the alarm from my voice. "Isn't it unusually early for you to leave?" Painful though I knew it would be, I yearned for an opportunity to be alone with him just once more, if only for a minute. I did not want to take final leave of him like this, in Tomás's presence.

He moved toward the door. "If I hurry, I can talk to Doctor de la Cueva for a few minutes before he starts his lecture. He always gets there early."

"Oh." I felt a sharp pang of resentment. She was there again, persistent, unyielding, demanding.

Ricardo addressed us both. "I don't suppose I'll see you at supper today. You'll be at Marta's quite late, won't you?"

"You know I always stay the whole day," Tomás answered in the surly tone he always used with Ricardo. "She doesn't ever start the fireworks until almost midnight."

"I'll not see you any more today, then, so I'll bid you sleep well right now." As he turned away from Tomás, his eye caught mine briefly, long enough for him to half-lower one eyelid in a suggestion of a wink at our private joke.

As I watched him stride toward the kitchen patio, heard the gate slam behind him, it took all my self-control to stand still, keep from running after him, clinging to him, telling him I could never, never leave him. I am sure my pallor was convincing as I told Tomás there was something wrong with my throat and I would go lie down right that moment as he had suggested.

"Cecilia's room will be farther from the clatter in the kitchen," I said. "I'll go in there." It was also farther away from Tomás's office, and he would be less likely to hear the sobs I could scarcely hold in check till I reached Cecilia's door and I knew I could not muffle completely as I threw myself down on her bed and cried into her pillow.

By the time Tomás knocked imperiously on Cecilia's door an hour later, my general dishevelment was such that he could not possibly doubt I was ill.

"Come in," I called weakly, and when he opened the door

295

and announced that it was time to get dressed for Marta's party, I told him he would have to go alone.

"Please close the door," I said, knowing I did not want the close scrutiny of my face a well-lit room would afford him. "I've a terrible headache, and the light makes it worse."

He closed the door and walked over to the bed, looking down at me. "You don't look well at all," he agreed after studying me a minute. "Your eyes are all puffed up."

"They get that way when I'm ill," I lied. I, who had always been robustly healthy and could scarcely remember having been ill a day in my life!

Tomás laid his hand on my forehead, and even with concerted effort I was not able to keep from shuddering at his loathsome touch.

He misinterpreted my shudder. "You're fevered, too, and shivering. Most certainly you cannot go."

I pulled the covers high, as though I were suffering from a chill as he thought, turning my face away from him. "You must go without me, of course." I knew that in his inherent selfishness, it had never occurred to him to stay home with his ailing wife.

"Of course," he agreed readily, turning to leave. "Inconvenient, your getting sick right now when it's important to stop any scandalous talk about Cecilia."

I shifted deeper under the covers as he left the room, thinking that soon he would have to face far more scandalous talk than he could possibly stop.

Santiago—Thursday, July 29, 1773

CHAPTER XVII

It was about an hour later when I heard Tomás leave. He went on horseback, even though it was less than a ten-minute walk to Marta and Carlos' house. He would not have demeaned himself by arriving on foot if the party had been next door.

I lay there for a while after I heard Simón tell him his horse was out in front, heard his boots click on the tiles, then the slam of the front door. When it seemed unlikely that he would return, I threw off the covers and went quickly to my room. I dug into the bottom of my trunk for the riding skirt into which I had stitched a number of Ricardo's doubloons and *pesos,* the skirt I had intended to wear when we left together. I tried not to think of that as I slipped it on, chose a sturdy blouse to wear with it, and took another handful of doubloons to put in the bottom of my saddlebags. Ricardo would not begrudge them to me, I was certain. I took a cloak from the wardrobe and carried it to the *zaguan,* ready to slip around my shoulders before I left the house.

With a sigh that was more of a sob, I slipped out to the stables by way of the *patio de placer,* careful to stay out of sight of any of the servants. Perhaps, I thought hopefully, something had gone awry with Simón's carefully laid plans. I wanted something—anything—to stop me, something beyond my control to keep me from leaving without Ricardo. I had to try to leave him in order to absolve myself from the guilt I would feel at having destroyed his lifetime dream, but I could not give up the final desperate hope that, at the last minute, it would be impossible for me to go.

In the stables, I met Gonzalvo. Even in the darkness of the

empty stall to which Simón led me, I could see the man's eyes were direct and honest, like Simón's. They also had, deep within them, the same unquestioning kindness.

Perhaps that was why I was so shocked to hear the venom in the first words he spoke to me. It was not what he said so much as the manner in which he said it that surprised me. "It will be a pleasure to take you far away from *don* Tomás." He forced Tomás's name out between his teeth, as though he could scarcely stand to have it on his tongue. It should not have surprised me, since Simón had already told me that Tomás had sent him to the mines, but I still found the seething hatred in his voice at odds with the kindly eyes. But then, the hatred had festered within him for almost twenty years of enforced solitude, so perhaps it should not have surprised me so.

Nor should it have surprised me that Simón had told Gonzalvo only that I was running from Tomás, and had not mentioned Ricardo. "We must go where my husband cannot find us," I said. "Where no one can find us." *Not even, God give me strength, my dearest Ricardo.*

"You needn't fear, *Señora.* I will not let that terrible man murder you, too."

I gasped, felt my mouth go slack.

"Murder?" I repeated when I could find my voice, profoundly shaken at the implication that it had happened already, at some time in the past. Tomás a murderer? As evil as I knew him to be, my mind rebelled at the thought.

It was not Gonzalvo, but Simón who answered. "Gonzalvo has told me much this morning, *Señora. Don* Tomás caused the death of the other *Señora.* Before, I suspected something—but now, I know it to be true, and it is worse, far worse than I had thought. I have known always in my heart that the *Señor* is a very bad man. I did not know until this morning just how very wicked he is."

My mind was busy trying to absorb the things Simón said, as the ugly word Gonzalvo had spoken kept repeating itself in my brain.

Murder . . . Murder . . . Murder.

"Tomás—killed—Pilar?" I could scarcely hear my own voice at all. "Is that what you're saying?"

Gonzalvo nodded grimly. "Just as surely as though he had plunged a sword through her heart."

"But that's impossible!" I protested, unwilling to accept the horror of what he was saying. "She went riding—she was thrown from a horse." And yet, as I protested, I knew it must be true. Simón would not lie, and as I looked again into Gonzalvo's dark honest eyes, I knew that neither would he. And

298

Tomás, in one of his fits of dark fury, could be capable of anything. That was the thing I had sensed the first day of our marriage and had been shrinking from ever since.

"The horse was known to be a killer, *Señora*." Gonzalvo looked directly at me as he spoke. "She would never have ridden such a horse if the *Señor* had not forced her to do so."

I shook my head in disbelief. It was difficult to accept the frightening reality of Gonzalvo's words. How different was what he was telling me from the story I had pieced together from the questions I had asked! I had envisioned Tomás enraged with a groom's stupidity for letting Pilar take the dangerous horse, and in his grief and rage at the unnecessary death of his beloved wife, shooting the horse and sending the groom to the mines. But, according to Gonzalvo, this was not the way it had happened at all.

"But why?" I protested. "He loved her! He built a mausoleum for her out of the finest marble, commissioned the best sculptor to carve it. He praises her still! Why, only this morning . . ." I hesitated, remembering his comment about Pilar going to the stables only when she wanted to ride. My words died off to nothing, for some other words had sprung into my mind, something else Tomás had said that morning. It concerned not Pilar, but Cecilia. He had said it was important to face up to the matter of Cecilia, act as though everything was fine.

Pretense. With Pilar, too, he had only been pretending everything was fine. Ever since her death, he had been putting on a show, playing the part of the bereaved and grief-stricken husband for all of Santiago to see. Nor had he let down his guard so many years later with me. The pretense continued, had even been exaggerated in the privacy of our room. I wondered if, by now, the pretense had not become to him more real than the truth it was designed to hide.

So he had not loved her, after all. But many husbands and wives do not love each other. That is scarcely justification for even an obliquely indirect murder, such as Simón and Gonzalvo were suggesting.

I looked at both of them, my gaze coming to rest on Gonzalvo. "Why?" I repeated. "Even if he didn't love her, why would he have wanted her dead?"

It was Simón who spoke. "Believe me, *Señora*, we would have spared you the knowledge of this. But we talked it over this morning, and we decided you must know. The other day you said to me it would not matter if *don* Tomás found you and you had to return to him after *Señor* Ricardo has gone away. That is not true. You must not let him find you, ever. For your own safety, you must let Gonzalvo take you where

299

you are sure to be safe from him. You must live in less comfort, in loneliness. But once you leave the *Señor*, you must never let yourself be returned to him. Never!"

"I see." I nodded my understanding and acceptance of what he was saying. "But why?" I persisted. "Why did he do it?" Tomás was on trial in my mind, and I must give him every chance to be proven innocent of the hideous accusations, must know the facts before I judged him guilty. He was narrow, petty, tyrannical, grasping—all these things and more. But, murder? What could have prompted even such a man as he to the devious murder of Pilar at which these two were hinting so boldly?

Gonzalvo fixed me with his open and honest gaze. It was impossible to doubt the truth of his words. "I heard them quarrel in the stables, *Señora*. It was late afternoon, and *don* Tomás—" he spat on the ground after saying the hated name, "he did not know I was there and I had heard, until afterwards. The *Señora* told him something that sent him into such a fury as I have never seen before or since. He was like a madman. I heard it, I heard it all, and later when he knew I did, he sent me to the mines, where he knew no one would listen to what I said." He shook his head sadly from side to side and smiled a wry little smile. "He did not know he would not have had to do that to keep me silent. Because the *Señora* was good, because I knew she would have wanted me to keep what I heard locked within my heart, that is why I would not have told, why I have not told anyone what I heard. It would have hurt someone the *Señora* loved very much, someone innocent who would have suffered, who would have been looked down upon by you Spaniards. Not even now, not even to you will I tell what it was I heard her tell him."

My mind absorbed what he was saying, added to it the many things that had puzzled me since my arrival in Santiago. I turned away from Simón and Gonzalvo for a minute, feeling the need to stop and think. There was something here that I must understand, a door which must be unlocked. I could not rid myself of the feeling that although Gonzalvo's words concerned Pilar and Tomás, they also deeply concerned me. Simón must have felt that this was true, too, or he would not have asked Gonzalvo to reveal this information to me.

What could Pilar have told Tomás that had fired him to such a flaming fury? What would it be that, after all these years, still had the power to hurt someone Pilar had loved, someone innocent, so that even now Gonzalvo would not tell me what it was? What was it that made Spaniards look down on one of their fellows?

It was so simple, once the answer had occurred to me. The information Gonzalvo had just given me unlocked the door to so many puzzling facts, and now I was puzzled by them no longer.

Tomás had not loved Pilar. She had not been the dutiful wife, the paragon of virtue he would have had me believe; that was all part of the fantasy he had woven to hide his wounded vanity. It was easy to assume that Pilar could have been pushed beyond her endurance by him, as I had, and that she could easily have sought and found affection elsewhere, the affection which Tomás was incapable of giving. What was more of a source of pride to a Spaniard than pure blood, legitimately endowed? What stigma was it that could never be fully overcome in our blood-conscious society, the stigma from which *Papá* had gone to such lengths to protect me?

Bastardy.

Ricardo was not Tomás's child.

A less spiteful man than Tomás would not, having rid himself of a faithless wife, have taken his wrath out on a helpless child. But Tomás had done just that. I thought of his constant hostility toward Ricardo, which he had never troubled to disguise. And the bickering, the belittling, the constant barbs, even—yes, that would explain it—his desire to force Ricardo into a monastic life, keep him from marrying, keep him from propagating the name to which Tomás knew he had no right. But he could not openly deny Ricardo the use of that name, for to do so would have been to admit openly that he had been cuckolded. And that Tomás would never bring himself to do.

If I still had had any remaining doubts about Ricardo not being Tomás's son, they would have been resolved by the words I remembered Tomás had uttered at the height of his frustration that morning when he had found out Cecilia had gone again, that with her departure had died the dynasty he had hoped to establish. I remembered the sarcasm in his voice when I had mentioned Ricardo's name. *Oh, yes. There is Ricardo.*

Ricardo was a constant thorn in his side, his very existence an ever-present reminder that he had been played for a fool by his wife.

I turned around to face the two silent *indios* again. I was surprised at the relief I felt in knowing that Ricardo was not Tomás's son. I was also grateful to the man who, by his

301

silence, had kept the stigma of bastardy from the man I loved.

"You don't have to tell me the secret you've kept so well all these years, Gonzalvo. I know. And thank you." I looked at him, saw that he understood I was thanking him not for what he had just told Simón and me that day, but for what he had never revealed to anyone else.

He nodded and then continued, as though, once started, he felt compelled to finish the story. "The *Señor* had me saddle up the horse, *Señora*, the horse that would hardly allow me near him so bad was he, and he would permit no weight heavier than the saddle on his back, and scarcely permitted that. I managed to get the saddle on him, but I could not finish making the cinch tight.

"The *Señor* saw that it was not tight enough, but still he pushed me away impatiently and slipped the bit into the horse's mouth.

" 'You say you will leave me,' he said angrily to his wife after she had finished taunting him and stood weeping against the wall of the stables. 'Well, then, here is your horse, all saddled and waiting.'

"When I protested that the horse was dangerous, and also that the saddle was not firmly on him, the *Señor* knocked me into a corner with a strength I did not know he possessed. And still he held fast to the horse, telling the *Señora* to come and mount him.

"And the *Señora*, she who was so impulsive, said she might as well be dead as married to him, and she grabbed the reins from him and jumped onto the horse no one could control. The horse bolted as soon as he felt her weight, as *don* Tomás knew he must do." He shook his head. "I will never know how she managed to stay on that wild stallion as far as *Cerro del Manchen*, *Señora* but she did. There, a little way up, we found her, but not until the next morning.

"The *Señor*, once he knew I had heard their quarrel, he would not let me out of his sight except while he ran to the house and got a pistol. Then he took me with him to search for her. All night we looked, but it was too dark to tell which way she had gone. Next morning early, we found her on *Cerro del Manchen*. Her neck was broken. The horse was not far away, the saddle hanging to one side. The *Señor* took out his pistol and killed him.

"I know with a certainty in my heart that if he had not found his wife dead, he would have used the pistol on her."

"And that is why he sent you to the mines," I said in full comprehension, "and why you have had to remain hidden. He would never have been convicted of her murder, but with

302

you gone, he could keep pretending to the world that his marriage had been proper to the very end."

"*Señora*," Gonzalvo said with a deep frown furrowing his already lined forehead, "since I have said too much and you say you know now the secret the first *Señora* revealed, the secret I promised myself I would never tell a living soul, nor have I, I would ask you to lock it inside your heart and keep it there as it has been kept inside mine."

"I love Ricardo," I said in answer. Then I looked at Simón. "You guessed, too, didn't you?"

Simón smiled and nodded. "Yes, *Señora*. That is the other reason I wanted Gonzalvo to tell you what he told me this morning. And I am glad he is not the son of *don* Tomás, as I am certain you are." He turned to Gonzalvo. "I swear to you by the skirts of the Blessed Mother of the Holy Infant and by the gods that dwell in Fuego, that this secret is as safe with the *Señora* and with me as it has been with you."

Gonzalvo seemed satisfied with Simón's vow, at his casual mixture of two conflicting religions. I turned again to Gonzalvo. "I would ask one more question of you, if you can and will tell me. Who is Ricardo's father?"

He smiled softly, and I knew he had lost any fears that Simón or I might betray his trust as he answered, "A Norwegian architect with red-gold hair. He died not long after the *Señora*. This morning, I had a glimpse of *Señor* Ricardo from where I was hidden, and his hair is the same color. The *Señora* loved his father very much. I had often helped her meet him, carried notes between them. Then he left Santiago suddenly and was gone for almost two years. But he could not stay away from her, and he had just returned from Peru. That afternoon, she had gone to him, but the *Señor* returned to Santiago unexpectedly that night, so he was in the stables when she came in, and he caught her."

The three of us stood there, unmoving, transported back to an evening long past, seeing not each other but the reckless and impulsive girl still in her teens, the girl who had found love, and who, in her despair and passionate hatred of her husband, had taunted him with the knowledge that her lover had fathered the son he thought was his own. We saw a younger Tomás receiving this information, his face contorted, his breathing raspy, so enraged by what his wife had told him that he wanted her dead.

It was Simón who broke the spell, returned us all to the present. He shifted his feet, said urgently, "Come, Gonzalvo. Now that our good *Señora* knows why she must never return to *don* Tomás, we must get her away from him. *Señora*, if you will go into the *zaguan*, I will come for you there as soon as we bring the carriage around to the front."

Gonzalvo left to harness the impressive pair of matched bays Tomás kept only for the carriage, and I turned to Simón and took his hand in mine.

"You will tell Ricardo why I had to go, won't you? I don't dare leave him a note. It might fall into Tomás's hands. I am depending on you, Simón. You must explain to him, make him understand why I had to do this. You must convince him it is hopeless to look for me, that he will never be able to find me." The moment was almost upon me, the moment when I would walk out of Ricardo's life forever. I had decided what I must do, and now it could be avoided no longer.

Simón's eyes were moist. "I will, *Señora*. You can trust me."

"I know I can."

"I wish you did not have to go, *Señora*."

I nodded, unable to say any more, and let go of his hand.

My knees felt weak as I turned and made my way through the small patio. As I walked through the archway that separated it from the main patio, I stopped, looking again at the *sala*, remembering the way I had seen it that day in Tatiana's crystal—its roof gone, its walls collapsed, with only the door and part of the wall around it standing, the door so incongruously closed against intruders. I remembered, too, the disquietude I had felt as the scene had unfolded before my eyes, the feeling that something was wrong.

Ricardo! What if the earthquake I knew was most certainly coming were to strike while he was still in Santiago, still living in this house? How would he know he must avoid the *sala*? I cursed myself for a fool for not having warned him of the danger.

I turned and ran back to the stables.

Simón, who had been bringing one of the horses around to the front of the carriage, stopped what he was doing and walked over to me. "You have forgotten something, *Señora*?"

I nodded. "One thing more I want to ask of you, Simón. There isn't time for me to explain, but I—" I hesitated, wondering how to tell him that I knew what was coming. But there was only time to be direct. "In my mind, I sometimes see things that haven't happened yet." I paused, waiting to see the effect of my words.

I needn't have worried about his acceptance of my strange gift. He nodded as casually as though I had just told him to saddle El Moro. "I once heard of a woman in a village not far from mine whose mind traveled ahead."

I continued, "Sometime, I don't know when but it may be

soon, there will be an earthquake here, in the Valley of Panchoy. It will be a bad one. I—I have seen it."

Still unperturbed, he nodded.

"If Ricardo is here, in the house, watch after him for me, will you? The *sala*—it isn't safe. The roof will fall in. I don't know about the other parts of the house, but this I have seen."

"If I can, *Señora*, I will keep him from there."

"Thank you, Simón. And thank you for—for understanding." I leaned over and kissed his weathered cheek, which was wet with tears.

"You're a good man, Simón."

I turned and again made my way through the smaller patio, then diagonally across the main patio to the *zaguan*. I dropped heavily onto the bench built into the tiled side wall, and, leaning back against the wall, closed my eyes and prayed for the strength to go through with what I had decided I must do.

The first thing I noticed was the howling of the dogs. It was as if they must all yowl at once, and I wondered vaguely what had set them off, for I could hear no other sound out of the ordinary.

But I did not have to wonder long, for I soon heard it, the deep rumbling noise which their sensitive ears must have picked up long before mine. It sounded, at first, like the roll of distant thunder. A rainstorm, not too close, I assumed, wondering idly if it were somewhere in the same direction I was going.

I didn't even know which direction that was, I realized. But what did it really matter? One way was the same as another. Every direction led away from Ricardo.

Away from Ricardo. I opened my eyes, looked at the door, the door through which I must walk in a few minutes. Could I? Did I have the strength, the final courage it would take to go through with this? It was not too late. I could still change my mind, challenge Ricardo's elusive mistress, fight her for him, try to keep him.

Church bells. Through the broken thread of my tumultuous thoughts, I heard them, faintly, tentatively, as though whoever was ringing them was not quite certain they were doing the right thing. Nor was it the light clear bells of *Santa Clara* that I heard, and that puzzled me, for the bells of Santiago had their own special sequence, as though they must ring in that specific order, no matter how many times a day they were to sound. But why were they being rung now? Surely, it was not yet time for matins.

My mind reviewed the time that had passed since Tomás

had left. He said he would leave at three, and he was very punctual always. After he had left, I had stayed in bed about ten minutes longer, in case he returned for any reason. Then it had taken another five or ten minutes for me to dress, and I had spent maybe ten or fifteen minutes with Gonzalvo and Simón in the stables. That would have been three-thirty, a little after. And then I had run back to talk to Simón again. Possibly another five minutes. Now I had been sitting in the *zaguan* for only a short while, so it could hardly even be four o'clock yet. Somewhere between three-thirty and four. The bells were still ringing, more of them now, as my mind busied itself with the mental arithmetic, and they were getting louder. They should not be ringing in the middle of the afternoon.

The faint rumble I had noticed seemed to be getting louder, too. The storm must be moving in this direction, I thought. Odd that a storm should move so fast. It had sounded so much farther away only seconds before. Two separate storms, perhaps.

I strained my ears, listening carefully. It was an odd noise, not the sudden clap of an afternoon thundershower, but a constant grumbling that had a strange vibration to it.

And the bells. Now they all seemed to be ringing at once, as though they must make themselves heard above the baying of the dogs and the rumbling noise, and must fight each other for precedence over one another.

Somewhere nearby, a horse neighed.

It was then that I noticed the bougainvillea branch swaying, even though not the faintest hint of a breeze came over the roof-top into the patio.

When the wall against which I had been leaning and the bench on which I had been sitting lurched and a large crack appeared alongside me as I watched, I jumped up in alarm.

Earthquake! This was no easy, gentle swaying motion such as we had experienced occasionally these past months, but a heavy jarring tremor quickly building in intensity.

I ran to the door. As though by magic, it opened as soon as I slid back the bolt, swinging of its own volition. Just coming down the street was our carriage, with Gonzalvo seated on the coachman's box and Simón holding tightly to one of the horses, who was flicking his head about in alarm. As I watched, both of the animals began straining at the traces and pawing the air with their hoofs. Simón, close to me now, shouted, "It is your earthquake, *Señora*. It has come."

All up and down the street, doors were bursting open and people were dashing onto the cobbles, where they milled about in confusion and uncertainty, bumping into one another and not even seeming to notice. From the house directly opposite ours, *Señora* Ramirez rushed unsteadily out to the center of the street and flung herself onto her knees near me. She rolled her eyes heavenward as she folded her hands and began shouting fervent commants to all the saints to stop the quivering of the earth. Several of the old woman's servants catapulted from the house behind her and dropped to their knees, adding their supplications to the heavens to those of their mistress.

I looked back at our house, saw Teresa and several of the maids rush out. As I watched them come, a gigantic crack appeared on the front of the house, just to one side of the large double-doored entrance.

Beneath my feet, the ground continued to shudder as though it would rid itself of all of us, and the cobblestone next to one of those on which I stood popped from its place and flew high in the air. As I dodged, it clattered back to earth on the spot where I had just been standing an instant before. A dog, wild with frenzy, brushed the back of my knees and almost knocked me off my shaky feet. Individual sounds blended together, one into the other, and drowned out the noise of the cracking of walls and the shattering of windows so that they seemed to be breaking in silence.

It was all over, as suddenly as it had begun. I had no idea when the rumbling stopped, but suddenly I realized it was there no longer. The bells, easily audible again, sounded a few final clangs and were silent.

Gradually, the dogs stopped yelping and the horses, though continuing to stamp and snort nervously, became more calm. The voice of *Señora* Ramirez, strong and clear, could be heard above all the others as she continued to shout prayers and promises to heaven.

In the quiet that followed, people continued to dash out of the houses. Some, obviously caught during the middle of their siestas, did not even seem to realize they were not fully clothed. The air was filled with the sound of people sobbing, and many other outcries to heaven joined those of *Señora* Ramirez. I looked around in confusion, amazed at the number of people who filled the street. Did all these people really live on our street? I wondered in surprise. I would never have guessed it to be so many.

Relieved that it was over, I silently prayed that Ricardo was safe, wherever he had been. I moved further along the street, as dazed and confused as everyone around me seemed to be, and my eyes absently scanned the front of our house. The *sala* stood, virtually untouched except for some bits of adobe that had fallen, and the shattered windows.

For a moment, I stared at its outer walls, still solid and firm, and its roof, completely intact except for a scattering of loose tiles that had fallen to the cobbles.

A prickle of alarm made its way up my spine as I realized the danger was not yet over.

As I stood there, benumbed, riders began to race by, their bodies straining, their faces taut, each bent on some urgent private mission. It was a wonder they did not ride down any of the people in the street, who miraculously managed to scatter before them, barely getting themselves out of the way in time.

Teresa started to go back into the house. I grabbed at her dress. "No! Not yet! It's not over!"

She looked at me questioningly, but she did not go inside. "I have heard it said that the center of the street is the safest place. I will tell the others to stay away from the walls."

Talking to Teresa seemed to release me from the stupor in which I had been helplessly suspended, and I ran over to Simón to help him calm the horses. In spite of his efforts and those of Gonzalvo, up on the coachman's box, the animals were still extremely nervous, and kept dragging the coach slowly forward.

It was then that I noted a small boy, two or three years old, standing all alone by the wall of our *sala*, his mouth opened wide as he screamed out his fear and his indignation that a callous world was paying no attention to him. I left Simón and Gonzalvo to cope with the high-strung carriage horses and ran to scoop up the child, carrying him away from the walls I knew would soon be destroyed. As I lifted him, and started back toward the center of the street, he wound his arms tightly around my neck.

At that moment, Tomás rode up, frantically jumping from a horse I did not recognize. His eyes lit momentarily on me, and they registered nothing beyond recognition. In one motion, he flipped the reins out of his hand and flew into the house. I shouted at him to stay outside, but if he heard me, he paid no attention.

Just behind him rode Ricardo, and at the sight of him, all thoughts of Tomás flew from my mind.

"Ricardo! You're safe!" I shouted over the screams of the child.

"And you! Thank God!" He jumped down beside me. "I rode first to Marta's, looking for you there. Father was just coming out, and when I asked him about you, he shouted at me that you were at home." He paused, looked about him. "Where is he? He was just ahead of me."

I nodded toward the house, and then I remembered something my eyes had seen but my brain had not registered a moment before. When Tomás had run into the house, he had had the *sala* key he always carried already extended in his hand, its golden chain dangling toward the ground. "He's gone into—" I gasped. "Into the *sala!*"

"He's mad! What if there's another tremor? It's not safe! I've got to get him out of there!" He turned and ran toward the house.

"No!" I lunged, grabbed ineffectively at his sleeve, felt it slide from my grasp and watched in helpless horror as he darted through the door and disappeared into the house.

"You mustn't go in there!" I screamed uselessly after him, unable to follow because the child, thrown into fits of hysteria by my own sudden panic, was clinging to my neck with the deathgrip of terror and all but choking off my wind.

I leaned over, tried to set the boy down on the cobbles, but he held fast. My attempts to free myself only made him shriek louder and cling to me still more desperately.

Frustrated, I picked him up again. Why, why hadn't I told Ricardo about the earthquake, the destruction of the *sala?* Why hadn't I warned him? I tried to run forward, follow him, but the shrieking, wriggling mass in my arms made movement virtually impossible. It was all I could do to keep the child from strangling me in his terror.

I looked around wildly for Simón, saw him just past our house, still fighting the panicky horses.

"Simón!" I shouted at the top of my lungs. "Ricardo! He went into the *sala* after Tomás! Stop him!" My own cries mingled with those of the child as I tried to make myself heard over his screams.

Miraculously, Simón seemed to hear me, for he dropped the reins and disappeared at a fast run into the opened doorway. I saw Teresa nearby, motioned with my eyes for her to come, and began stumbling toward her.

"Quickly! Take this child! I must go in after them!" I said, chokingly. I grabbed impatiently at one of the boy's arms as I twisted and turned, trying to break myself free of the viselike grip he had clamped around my neck. Finally, with Teresa's help, I was able to duck and wrench myself away as she lifted him from me.

But it was too late. By the time I was free, the rumbling had begun once more, and the earth swayed crazily and gave such a violent shudder that I was knocked onto my knees. Instinctively, I put my hands out in front of me as the cobbles seemed to heave themselves up to meet me.

At first, I heard the bells again, surely every bell in Santiago, and they were all clanging crazily. Then I could no longer hear them in the tumultuous noise all around me, as my head filled with sounds so deafening it seemed it would surely burst.

For what seemed an eternity, my world consisted of the small section of the cobbled street on which I knelt, and on which I tried repeatedly to stand. But it was no use. The whole world was undulating dizzily. I would raise up on one foot and start to place the other foot next to it, only to have the first one jarred out from under me.

I looked up to see a runaway team bearing down on me, and somehow managed to throw myself forward out of its way, so that a back wheel just grazed me. It might have been our own carriage and team. I couldn't tell, but it didn't really matter.

And surrounding that small portion of the street that continued to hold me helpless captive, the sounds were thunderous as all around me walls and roofs came crashing down. Nearby, a dog chased itself around in circles, snapping madly at its own tail. Another dog sat beneath the windows of our *sala*, nose pointed straight up in the air. I suppose it was yowling, but that sound, like all the others, lost itself in the tumult. It was impossible to identify individual noises any more in the cacophony of sound that in itself seemed to be causing walls and roofs to tumble to the ground. Through the choking dusty haze that filled the air, I saw the second story of the house next to ours disappear from one moment to the next. I dodged a riderless horse that fell to the ground in a heap as soon as it roared past me. When I looked again at the spot where the yowling dog had sat in front of our *sala*, I realized he was no longer there. Neither, I noticed with a sudden intensification of my terror as I remembered Ricardo's last words, was the roof or most of the wall over the windows.

"Ricardo!" I wailed, continuing to try to push myself to my feet. But my cry was lost in the tumult and my efforts were as futile as they had been before.

Only when there seemed to be no more walls remaining to be toppled did it stop. As the dust began to settle, the earth seemed enveloped in a deep silence, as one by one, those people who had been shouting, pleading to the very heavens themselves to stop the terror and still the quaking earth, realized they no longer had to shout to be heard, and gradually lowered their voices, until a stunned hush fell over everything and everyone. It lasted only a moment, and then as people surveyed the chaos and ruin all about them, there was the sound of soft weeping, or the hysterical cry of the name of a

310

loved one, and the coughing as the freshly raised dust filled everyone's lungs.

I had but one thought, and as soon as I could stand, I pushed myself to my feet onto legs that trembled still, as much as though the rolling and shaking of the earth had not stopped.

"Ricardo!" I said his name in a desperate whisper, afraid to say it aloud, fearful of what I would find when I went through the gaping door into the house, and into the *sala*.

I made my way to the entrance of the house. The doorframe itself and the two large doors that filled it were still intact, but the smaller door inside one of the larger ones, which had been swinging wildly a few minutes before, hung now at a crazy tilt by a portion of its one remaining hinge.

"Ricardo!" I called again, louder this time, as I clawed and scrambled over what had a few moments before been part of the walls and roof of the *zaguan*.

"Ricardo!" I repeated again. "Where are you?" I cried desperately, my heart thundering in my chest. My legs felt as though they were made of cotton, and I fought to keep them from folding weakly beneath me as I clambered on all fours over the piles of rubble which continually gave way beneath my feet.

Once, when my foot slipped and wedged itself deep within the debris, I jerked it free impatiently and felt a flash of pain. I ignored it, pushing my way forward over an endless mound of crumbled adobe bricks and broken beams and shattered tiles.

As I half-stumbled and half-fell into the patio itself, I looked all around me, aghast at the devastation. Not only the *sala*, but most of the other rooms opening onto the patio were also roofless. As I started anxiously toward the *sala*, I saw Ricardo, lying face down in the patio, his legs buried under a pile of roof tiles and some of the porch beams.

I stopped, frozen with fear at the sight of him. He was lying motionless, face down, his hands extended limply over his head. Why wasn't he moving?

"Ricardo!" I called on a choking sob. I was half the width of the patio away from him when I saw him, but in my desperation and fear, I covered the obstacle-filled distance in a matter of seconds and threw myself onto my knees beside his quiet form.

I leaned over and touched a bruised place on his forehead, and he groaned. Never had a sound been so welcome. He was alive!

"Thank God!" I said as tears of relief flooded from my eyes unchecked. But he was trapped. I had to get him out of there! I moved toward his feet, frantically began to pick up pieces of rubble and throw them from him.

"Carlota?" He stirred, raising his head. He was blinking, looking all around, and I realized he did not know I was there. He was only calling me, as I had begun to call his name a few minutes earlier.

"I'm here, Ricardo," I said, moving where he could see me. "Are you all right?" I asked anxiously.

He pushed himself up onto his hands as high as he could, nodded, then dropped back weakly as the effort proved too much.

I gasped, but he muttered, "All right, I think." His voice was hazy as he added. "Dizzy—got hit on the head."

"How about your legs?" I asked, moving back to start again throwing off the endless bits and pieces of rubble that had fallen on him. "I'll try to get you out," I said, knowing that the beams which had fallen on top of some of the rubble were too heavy for me to lift alone.

Ricardo raised his head again, then shook it as though to clear it. "Father! And Simón!" he said, suddenly remembering them as he began to emerge from the haziness that followed his momentary unconsciousness. "Have you seen them?"

"No! I forgot about them! I was worried about you. I must get you out."

"I'll be all right! You mustn't bother with me now!" As full consciousness flooded back, his voice became crisp with authority. "Can you get into the *sala?* That's where they went. I saw Father unlock the door and go in. I would have run in after him and dragged him back into the patio, but Simón shouted at me not to go in there, then he tackled me from behind. He must have run in after Father himself. I was stunned for a minute after I fell, and before I could get myself up, the quake started." He tried to turn his head around to look toward the *sala,* but the position in which he was trapped made it impossible for him to see in that direction, for it lay directly behind him. "You'd better hurry! They may need help! Oh, where is everybody?"

I had wondered the same thing, but such had been the pandemonium in the street that it would be a long time before most of the people reacted with any sense at all. Only my terrified concern for Ricardo's safety had caused me to act with such speed and determined purpose.

"But your legs—" I objected, still grabbing rubble with both hands and thrusting it away from him as fast as I could.

"Don't worry about me!" he said exasperatedly. "One leg

312

hurts, but I can move my toes. How is the *sala*? Is it—are they all right, do you think?"

I stood up, then, and for the first time I looked toward the *sala*. But I knew before I looked what the answer to his question would be. "The roof has fallen in," I said. "I'll see if I can help them." I looked at the ends of the gigantic beams that supported the roof, and I knew that anyone in there would certainly be beyond my help.

"Hurry!" Ricardo urged. "But be careful."

But I could not hurry, for I stood as if rooted to the spot, unable to move, unable to look away from the door, puzzled by it. Why? It was not just the fact that it stood there, so ridiculously shut tight against any intruder, who could now so easily climb over the wall to enter. There was something else, and I could not quite grasp what it was.

Habit is strong, and in times of shock when our minds do not function as they should, we often revert to habitual motions. That is what happened to me. I moved toward the room, my eyes and my thoughts still riveted onto the door. I made my way over the debris that littered the porch in front of the *sala*, was piled high along its wall, and unthinkingly tried to open the door and walk in. It would certainly have been blocked by rubble on the inside and would never have opened, but I did not reason clearly at that moment. I tried to open the door. To my surprise, I found it was locked.

"Are you sure they went in the *sala*?" I threw the question back over my shoulder at Ricardo.

"I told you I saw Father unlock the door. He was just going in when Simón shouted at me. Then he knocked me down and yelled, 'Let me go after him!'" Then he questioned impatiently, "Why do you ask?"

"The door's—" I do not know what made the lie jump to my lips, "—stuck." The door was not stuck. It was locked. But why should it have been, if Tomás had just unlocked it? It would still be unlocked, with the key—that's what was wrong! The key should be out here, still in the keyhole, its golden chain dangling. Tomás had unlocked it and entered, and in his rush to save his treasures, he surely would have left the key in the lock. The door could have slammed shut when the quake started, but it would not have locked itself.

"Naturally, the door would be stuck." Again, impatience. "What's taking you so long? Can't you get in any other way?"

"I'll climb over the walls."

"You'll need help to free them if they're trapped."

A moment later, standing on the pile of crumbled adobe

313

banked along what remained of the inner wall of the *sala*, I looked into the room and called out, "Simón? Tomás?"

But there was no stirring, no answering. Within what remained of Tomás's storehouse of treasures, there was only a deathly hush.

My eyes scanned the room, and near the door, not far from where I stood, I saw Simón's hand sticking up from the rubble that buried most of the rest of him. He had fallen on his back, and in his lifeless hand, raised as though in triumph, was Tomás's key to the *sala*.

Just beyond the body of Simón, barely visible beneath the mighty beam that had crushed both the servant and the master he had trapped inside the room with him, lay Tomás.

"Are they all right?" Ricardo called anxiously from the patio. "Oh, curse this trash all over me! I'm stuck tight. If only I could get out of here!"

"Just a minute," I called to him. I made my way over to Simón's body and took the key from his hand. Then I climbed back over the wall and returned to the door, slipping the key into the keyhole. Ricardo's grumbling at the ill luck that held him trapped covered the small clicking sounds as I unlocked the *sala* door. A moment later, I knelt by his side and told him, as gently as I could, that there was nothing to be done for either Tomás or Simón.

"I'll get someone to help me free you," I said as I leaned down and kissed his cheek, which was moist with tears for the man he considered his father, who hadn't loved him, and the *indio* who had loved him even more than his own life.

The aftermath of the earthquake of Santa Marta was a prolonged nightmare for all of us in the Valley of Panchoy. It took Teresa and me several hours to find someone who would help us free Ricardo, yet more hours to remove the mound of rubble that held him captive. His leg was broken in two places, and it was the next day before a doctor could be found to set it. Everything was made more difficult still in the days and weeks that followed by the torrential rains that followed the quake.

The devastation in the city was tremendous. Few of the houses and buildings remained standing, but because of the warnings of that first less severe shock and the ten minutes intervening between it and the violent damaging tremor that followed it, the loss of life from the quake itself was relatively light, considering the destruction. But many more lives were lost afterward, in the epidemics and disruption that followed.

The shock was one from which the city was never to recover. As soon as people had brushed the dust from their

314

shoulders, a bitter battle began between the secular and ecclesiastical factions in Santiago. The church, jealous of the power and wealth it had amassed in the city, insisted that the capital could be reconstructed, that the devastation was far less than that wrought by the earthquake of San Miguel in 1717, after which Santiago had been rebuilt more beautifully and more solidly than it had been before. But the civil authorities, under Captain General Don Marin de Mayorga, saw the quake as a providential chance to move the capital away from the site of the churche's entrenchment. Ricardo said in disgust they were like two dogs fighting over a bone, neither faction caring about the people themselves. Not for several years was the matter resolved, but eventually the King's power prevailed, and the capital was officially moved to the Valley of La Ermita, where it remained There, the church never regained the tremendous power and strength it had known in the Valley of Panchoy before the Earthquake of Santa Marta.

But in spite of the many edicts forbidding any to remain in Santiago, there were some who refused to leave. They stayed, to try to rebuild their lives and their homes, not knowing or caring about the politics of the matter, but only knowing that they had loved their beautiful valley and chose to continue to live in it.

It was several months before Ricardo was able to travel, and we slipped quietly out of Santiago in the confusion that remained long after the trembling of the earth had stopped, and we were married by a village priest on our way to Lima. Ricardo spent two years studying with Doctor Ignacio de la Cueva, from whom he learned the wisdom of patience as well as the particulars of his chosen field.

Ricardo could never get over his surprise at the unexpected devotion Simón had shown to Tomás by risking—and losing—his own life for him.

"I guess he was more devoted to Father than I had thought," Ricardo said after he had begun to recover from the shock of their simultaneous deaths. "You never know what the *indios* are thinking."

"You never know," I agreed.

A few days before we were to leave for Lima, he told me he had ordered a tombstone for Simón's grave.

"Simón was a very special servant, Carlota I hated to think of him in an unmarked grave. The tombstone will be placed this afternoon, if you'd like to go see it."

Later that day, we went to the small churchyard where he was buried, and in the slanting rays of the afternoon sun, I read the special epitaph Ricardo had ordered engraved on the headstone under Simón's name:

A Loyal and Devoted Servant

I nodded my approval. "He would like that, I know."

Ricardo did not know how true were the words he had chosen. Nor did he suspect that Simón's devotion was not to Tomás, but to Ricardo and me. He had given his own life to take from ours the man who stood in the way of our happiness.

Nothing of what I learned that day of Santa Marta in 1773 did I reveal to Ricardo, nor did I ever tell him how close I had been to leaving him. I let the past lay buried in the rubble of Santiago de los Caballeros. I often wondered if I really would have had the strength to go through with my plans to go away with Gonzalvo.

In later years, I had to stifle many a secret smile whenever someone remarked on the purity of our children's Spanish blood. Somewhere, in a place from which no one returns, I could imagine a tawny-skinned gypsy and an unknown Norwegian with red-gold hair also sharing a secret smile.

are you missing out on some great Pyramid books?

You can have any title in print at Pyramid delivered right to your door! To receive your Pyramid Paperback Catalog, fill in the label below (use a ball point pen please) and mail to Pyramid . . .

PYRAMID PUBLICATIONS
Mail Order Department
9 Garden Street
Moonachie, New Jersey 07074

NAME_____

ADDRESS_____

CITY_____STATE_____

P-5   ZIP_____